THE LEGEND OF SKARA BRAE

LUCIE MAXWELL

For all those who believed in me when I did not

Prologue

There was once a time when magic was used freely by all who needed it. Sorceresses created incantations, dragons hoarded glittering gold, and throughout the Five Kingdoms people lived in peace. Then, one day, a tyrannical king, corrupted by power and greed, banished all magic, claiming it to be evil and treacherous.

'Cast them out,' he said. 'Cast them all out. The land must be purged of their pestilence.'

For thirteen years fierce battles raged and many lives were lost. Magic Folk were hunted mercilessly. The king's wrath poisoned the land. Famine and drought followed fire, flood and fury. Thousands starved while the king persecuted Magic Folk for their imagined crimes. The realm was left desolate.

By the time the war was over there was no power left to fix what had been broken. Magic seeped beneath the shadows until such a time as it might be revived. It disappeared for a hundred years until the day a princess was given a key on her sixteenth birthday.

An extract from *The History of Ancient Magic*

1
The old boot

Standing under a thick canopy of trees, Mera and I were shaded from the low light of the setting sun. Dusk was settling and soon the night-time creatures would be roaming here. The forest was strangely quiet.

In the distance I could see the lights of the Castle twinkling like a thousand stars. Its twisting turrets reached high into the sky, towering over the city of Drammear, which spread out like a pitching sea before it.

A cool breeze ruffled my cloak and I turned my gaze upon Mera who stood close by me. Her auburn hair fell to her waist in soft curls. Arched brows framed her deep blue eyes. While her skin was pale her high cheekbones always glowed a healthy rose. She was wearing a simple peasant dress that she had borrowed from her lady's maid, though it was hard to mistake her for anything other than a princess. At sixteen she was less than a year older than me but she had the command and poise of someone twice that age. I thought of myself in comparison. My hair was unkempt and the colour of dry earth. My skin was sun-kissed and my hands were calloused. I wore a shirt that had once belonged to my father and an old belt held up trousers that were too big for me. We must have looked an odd pair.

'It's a shoe,' I muttered.

'It isn't just a shoe, Lex,' she insisted. 'Look again and tell me what you see.'

I turned back to the object that sat innocently on the dusty path before us. You wouldn't believe what I saw.

That's right, just a shoe.

Mera had dragged me impatiently the whole way from the village of Lilyworth, where I lived with my mum and eleven-year-old sister, to the outskirts of The Great Forest that reached across the land from the Castle to the far, uncharted corners of the kingdom. I'd had trouble keeping up, almost tripping over my undone laces more than once, but eventually she'd brought me to a halt and pulled an old, dirty boot out of her bag and put it on the ground.

'I'm sorry, I don't see anything. Listen, I have to go home. My mum will notice I'm missing. Look at the sun.'

I pointed across the path to the tall, westerly trees where a bright glimmer of orange light was streaming through the leafy branches, casting a pool of golden sunshine at our feet. It encircled us, protecting us from whatever lurked in the dark shadows of The Great Forest.

It was late.

'You should go too,' I said. 'You wouldn't want to get caught again.'

'Oh you don't need to worry about that. I made a deal with my lady's maid. I promised I'd be back by sundown and she wouldn't tell the Royal Guard I had left the Castle. The city is only a half an hour walk from here and I can run that distance in no time. They'll never even know I was gone.'

'But what if she panics and tells them before sundown? You'll get into trouble if you get caught out here. They'll just tell me to run along but it's different for you.'

She smiled. 'She won't. Besides, Caron is hardly the strictest lady's maid I've ever had. "Princess Mera" she'd say, "By the gods, what if something had happened to you?" And I would reply, "But dearest Caron, shouldn't I be allowed to roam freely in my own kingdom?" at which point she'd mutter something about me always having an answer for everything and our all too brief conversation would be over.'

I felt worry gnawing at my stomach but I ignored it. Mera was one of my only friends and I scarcely saw her as it was. We lived in separate worlds.

Mera's voice cut through my thoughts. 'Will you please look.'

'All I can see is a shoe. What's so special about it?'

'Please, trust me on this. Just look.'

Seeing how earnest she was I turned and looked hard at the boot. There was mud splattered up one side and there was a hole at the front that looked as though a mouse had nibbled through it. The heel was worn nearly all the way down and the sides were scuffed. I noticed the laces were done up wrongly, loosely strung horizontally across the metal clips instead of crisscrossing, like the rungs of a ladder.

Wait, it was a ladder.

I watched, hypnotized, as the boot transformed before my eyes. The hole became a minute door with elegant carvings around the edge. The mud splatters shimmered and turned into windows, chinks of light shining through miniature curtains. A ladder was propped against the front where the laces had previously been.

It was a house. I could see an old woman bustling about with pots and pans. She hummed a ditty as she worked. Delicious smells wafted towards me. I felt more astonished than I had ever been in my whole life.

I stepped back, stunned, and felt Mera grab my arm. Her clear blue eyes stared into mine.

'You see it don't you?' she whispered. 'Like that nursery rhyme; there was an old woman who lived in a shoe...'

I could still do nothing but stare.

'There's more magic out there, just waiting for us.'

The sun had almost set by now. Only a few rays lingered. The moon hung low and bright in the cloudless sky. It cast a strange ashen glow, like corn on an overcast day. It illuminated Mera's pale face. There was nothing but the sound of the crickets and rustling leaves and our breath.

I raised a shaky hand to rub my forehead. 'What was that?'

'The beginning,' her voice rang with fiery determination. 'Tomorrow meet me in the abandoned hut by the river at dawn. Tomorrow I will tell you about the fire giants and ice elves. Tomorrow everything changes.'

2
The hut

I arrived at the hut early the next morning and sat impatiently as I waited for Mera to arrive. We'd been using the hut as a meeting place for nearly three years now. We'd first met in the city on a market day in Drammear but after my dad died protecting me in a hunting accident a year later, leaving me only with the pendant he used to wear, I didn't have a reason to be there anymore so we moved our meeting place here.

My dad had been a carpenter. He had taken me to the city for the first time on my twelfth birthday to show me how he sold the figurines he made. After a while he sent me off to play with the other boys who had come to market with their fathers.

'Off you go then, lad. You have fun.'

A group of us had been running down the main parade when I saw her. A cart had come unhinged and was rolling away down the street, picking up speed as it went. People were jumping out of the way but one girl didn't seem to have noticed. Finally she heard someone yell and she flattened herself to the wall but the cart was still going to hit her. I sprinted across the street and managed to pull her into a recess in the wall just in time.

'Are you all right?' I asked, turning to check that she was unhurt.

She looked quite flustered. She had a hand on her chest to calm her rapid breaths. She managed to nod and say, 'Thank you. You saved my life.'

I had been about to reply when I noticed that dangling from a silver chain around her neck was the royal emblem and I knew at once she was the princess. I was about to run but the panic in her face made me pause.

'Don't tell anyone,' she pleaded.

'I won't,' I promised.

'I slipped away from my lady's maid and borrowed a servant's uniform. I wanted to explore the city. You see, I've never been outside the castle walls by myself before.'

Something about her statement made me feel sad and I found myself asking, 'Would you like some company?'

'I would love it,' she beamed. She tucked the silver chain out of sight and followed me back onto the street.

For a reason I didn't fully understand at the time she seemed to want my company. I realise now that she was lonely, and perhaps too a little curious about me. We spent the rest of the afternoon together until the Royal Guard found her and took her away, but before she left she made me promise to return on the next market day. So I did. Every week on market day for the next year found us, a peasant boy and a princess, playing happily in the streets.

Our hut was nothing more than old wooden slats held together by a web of vines. It was nestled against a rocky ledge at the bottom of a small ravine through which ran a river. During summer the trees swayed in the warm breeze and the soft earth was bathed in dappled light. Even now in winter it felt like a dreamlike place. All around the hut you could hear the snuffling of squirrels, the wind whipping against the side of the ravine, and the susurrus of the stream along its rocky bed.

Just as light from the rising sun was beginning to creep through the cracks in the walls the door banged open and Mera swept in. She smiled at me conspiratorially. She whipped off her cloak and bulging bag and sat down beside me.

'Are you ready?' she asked.

I nodded back, feeling strangely nervous.

She opened her bag and began pulling things out. There were a number of books bound in cracked leather that she placed gently on the floor. The title of one of them caught my eye. It was called *The History of Ancient Magic*. The books had strange symbols inscribed on the bindings. Before I could take a closer look Mera placed the old boot down in front of me along with a cup and saucer no larger than a thumbnail, and a large, iridescent talon.

'What is all this?' I asked.

'They're magical relics,' she grinned, pulling off her gloves. 'You'll never guess where I found them. Do you remember that rusty, old key my father gave me for my birthday a few weeks ago? The one he said was a family heirloom? Well I finally found out what it opens. I dropped a candle in the library and it rolled into a storeroom. When I bent down to pick it up I noticed that there was air coming through the wall. I investigated a bit and found a small dip. I ripped the wallpaper back and found a keyhole. The key fit perfectly. I pushed and the whole wall moved. Behind it was this great, dusty room. It had shelves upon shelves of books and these strange objects. Like that boot, and this cup and saucer. Go on, touch it.'

I reached out to pick up the tiny porcelain cup. The moment my finger connected with the cup it expanded rapidly in size. I drew my hand back in shock and the cup returned to its original size.

'Oh gods,' I whispered. 'What is this?'

'I already told you, they're magical relics, from before magic was banished from the kingdom. Do you know what this could mean, Lex?'

'No,' I replied.

'It means that we have a way to bring magic back,' she beamed.

I stared at her, nonplussed. 'Bring magic back? I don't understand. Why would you want to do that?'

'Magic isn't truly evil. I've always known that. And look,' she reached for one of the books and flipped through its ancient pages until she found what she was looking for. 'I've been researching. It's all in here.'

I took the book from her with tentative hands. I looked down at the page before me to see the depiction of a ring of grey standing stones encircling a heather strewn hill. The words above it read, *The Ancient Temple of Skara Brae*.

Mera twisted a strand of hair around her finger as she spoke. 'Skara Brae was the first village to use magic. Of course it had been around for centuries before but that was only individuals, witches, sorcerers, magical objects and beings, you know. Skara Brae was the first community to refine magic and use it to better their village. Surrounding settlements came to them in times of need. Unfortunately they liked to experiment with spells and they became arrogant, thinking themselves impervious to damage.'

She flipped again to one of the last pages and I found myself recoiling in horror at the picture there. Bodies littered the ground, blood pouring from gaping wounds, mouths open in agony.

'Lovely,' I muttered.

'Indeed. They were all wiped out. When they were gone all their magic disappeared too. Their monuments crumbled, hidden by sand and lost in time.'

'Well, as interesting and honestly disturbing as that story was, what's the point of it?'

She flipped back to the picture of the standing stones so that I could read what was written underneath.

Many believe this to be the original temple of the people of Skara Brae where cultural and religious events would have taken place. Unfortunately invaders have largely destroyed it and now a ring of standing stones and an underground vault is all that remains of the once great temple.

'This is where it started,' Mera's voice lowered. 'This is where it ended. These broken stones still contain power. The books tell of a spell that, when used correctly, could revive that power and vanquish all those who oppose magic. There was once a group of powerful sorceresses called the Sisterhood. They had been around for hundreds of years, probably thousands. They began to withdraw from the world as the power of magic grew, disliking the idea of luminary. They'd slipped out of existence, unknown even to Magic Folk, by the time of the Thirteen Year War. Seeing what would happen to the world if magic were to be eradicated, they created a plan. They would bind themselves within the stones of Skara Brae, almost like moving onto another plane of existence. This was so they could let their powers grow over the years until the time came for them to be called upon to help their people. I have found the spell that will awaken them. We must perform it and set them free so that they can return the magical kingdom to all its former glory. When it is done I will confront my father. He is a good man, he will see. And even if he doesn't listen to me, he will have to listen to them. They will make the world see how blind they have been. This is where we need to go.'

'You want to go there?'

'Of course! Listen to me. Magic Folk don't deserve the persecution they have suffered. It's my duty to help everyone in my kingdom and this is how I must do it, but I'll need help. I want you to come with me.'

I took hold of my father's pendant and rolled it nervously between my fingers. I didn't know what to say. Mera's words had left me stunned. Magic wasn't evil? I had always been told otherwise. Could she be right?

'Mera this is dangerous. Even talking about it is illegal.'

She took my hand. 'I know. This is a lot to take in but you've always had faith in me before. Have faith in me now. We can do this together. You're the only person I would trust to come with me.'

I gazed into her face for a moment. I knew Mera was beautiful. I suppose that if I met her now I would have easily fallen in love with her. I'd known her for nearly four years. She was my best friend. I knew her so well it felt, in a way, that I had known her my whole life. I loved the way she spoke and the way she might suddenly grab hold of my hand for a few moments when she had something really important to tell me and the way she got so excited by things.

But I remembered an agreement we'd made a month or so ago in this very hut.

She'd said, 'Lex, I'm going to be sixteen in a few weeks and I think I need to say this now. You know I like you a lot. You're my best friend. Coming to see you is one of the nicest things I do, but we're getting older now and I need to say that I don't want you falling in love with me. It would spoil everything. We're much better as we are.'

Until that point I'd often secretly wished that Mera would fall in love with me. I hadn't been expecting her to say what she'd just said, and it felt like a sharp shock.

I looked at her now. She was just as beautiful as ever, staring me at with her imploring blue eyes and suddenly I realised that I would follow her anywhere. I knew at that moment just how precious she really was to me. I also realised that if I tried to persuade her to change her mind about us just being friends, it *would* spoil everything.

'All right,' I replied, my voice trembling slightly. 'I'll go with you to Skara Brae.'

'And we're only going to be friends?'

I gave a nod. 'Yes, if that's what you want.'

3

Lilyworth

The first thing I noticed when I opened my eyes that morning was the sound of retching. I pushed myself out of bed and was concerned to see my sister sitting in bed holding a bucket. Much like every room in the cottage, our bedroom was small. There were only a few feet between our two beds with a tiny window above them. The dark wooden walls had a number of shelves that housed our meagre possessions. Two small hope chests sat at the end of our beds covered in burn marks and wax from the candles that were kept there.

'Are you sick, Elvie?' I asked.

She nodded. She was awfully pale. Her matted hair stuck to her sweaty face.

I kneeled down next to her. 'Do you need anything?'

She shook her head.

'How long have you been awake? You should have woken me.'

'You wouldn't have been able to do anything,' she muttered.

I put my hand on her shoulder and frowned at how warm she was. 'Are you sure you don't need anything? Water?'

She shook her head again. 'It just makes me feel worse. Don't you have to get ready for work?'

'Not for a little while.'

Our conversation was interrupted by a loud crash.

Elvie groaned. 'That'll be Mum. I was meant to help her today but I don't think I'll be able to.'

'Don't worry about it. I'll go and see what I can do. You stay here and get better.'

I stood and kissed her forehead before exiting the room. The dining room looked as though a wardrobe had exploded in it. Clothes were draped over every free surface, the backs of chairs, a line of string from the kitchen to the front door, dangling from the mantelpiece dangerously close to the fire. One of the chairs was lying on the floor and Mum was next to it picking up clothes.

'Morning Alex, dear,' she called, sounding harrowed.

I eyed her fatigued appearance with concern as I righted the chair. Great purple rings sat under eyes. Her hair was shot with grey though she was just shy of forty. You would never know she and Elvie were mother and daughter to look at them. The only clear resemblance was their small stature. Where I had my dad's height and curls, Elvie had taken after our father with her paler skin, dark blonde hair and round, chubby cheeks. She even had his dimples.

Mum on the other hand had olive skin, darkened by long periods in the sun. Her hair was brown and always smelled like peppermint. She had unassuming, soft green eyes. I found her eyes steady and calming. They were the exact shade of green that I called home.

'Can I help?' I asked.

'No, no it's fine. I just need to find Mrs Cole's blouse and...' she trailed off, looking frantically around the room.

'Mum,' I pulled the clothes out of her hands and put them on the table. 'Sit down. Take a break.'

She looked like she was about to object but at the last second she nodded.

'Just for a bit,' she insisted.

I went into the kitchen to pour her a glass of water. I set it down in front of her and reached for the clothes still on the floor.

'You should take the day off,' I suggested as I began to fold. 'You work too hard.'

'Chance would be a fine thing. No I've got to get Mrs Cole's washing back by this afternoon and Elvie's too sick to do it.'

'I'll do it.'

Mum shook her head. 'I can't ask you to do that. You've got to get to work.'

'You're not asking, I'm offering. I have some time before I need to be there. You stay here with Elvie.'

'Well, if you're sure.'

'Of course I am.'

Mum smiled gratefully. She held out her arms for a hug and I happily obliged.

'What would I do without you, Alex?' she asked, squeezing me tightly.

I made my way into the village, a parcel of clothes tucked under my arm. Ignoring the light rain, I pulled my cloak around me and walked on through the mist that had settled along the open roads.

Lilyworth wasn't a large village. It was hardly more than a handful of shops surrounded by a smattering of small houses. The mill sat right in the middle of the village next to the stream that ran through its centre. Past the mill was the old temple. No one had used it for many years, not since people stopped worshiping the Faith, but nobody seemed to want to claim the building either so it had become derelict. People had once believed in the gods and their power to create and destroy, but not anymore. If the gods had ever existed they were long gone now, as lost as those whose ashes we scattered to the wind, so I was surprised to see a group of people gathered in a loose ring outside the temple's moss-stained walls. Some people were pointing and laughing. I moved closer and noticed Rab

21

in the crowd. Pushing the parcel further under my cloak, I approached.

Rab was one of the only people in the village I trusted completely. He was also the only person who knew about my secret meetings with Mera. He had been married to my aunt Charlotte before she had died in childbirth. A huge man in his mid-thirties, covered in tough, flaxen hair, he might appear quite fearsome from a distance, but once you got to know him, a kinder man you never would meet. He hadn't remarried after my aunt had passed away and these days he spent most of his time spoiling Elvie and me. When I got to where he was standing I tapped him on the shoulder and asked, 'What's going on?'

Rab looked down and smiled his warm smile.

'Hey kid,' he ruffled my damp hair. 'What are you doing in town so early?'

'I'm taking some clothes back for Mum. What's everyone looking at?' I asked again, peering into the middle of the circle where I saw a man in a ragged brown robe kneeling over a bowl of water, plumes of smoke creeping around him from clay pots. His grey beard was so long it scraped along the ground when he moved.

'He's a Man of Faith,' Rab explained. 'He's here to talk to us about the old gods.'

I looked closer at the man. His robe was stained and the bottom was covered in mud. His skin was grey and pockmarked. He wasn't the first Man of Faith to come to the village. I didn't know why but I had always felt wary of them. I found myself wondering if we had magic then would we have these unnerving men wandering around? I watched as he dipped his hands into the water, making strange circling motions. Every now and then he would flick his hands backwards so his face received a fine sprinkling of water. I didn't understand why anyone would want to do this, particularly as it was already raining. The man was chanting something but I couldn't make out the words over the buzzing of the crowd.

'What's he saying?'

'It's a prayer,' Rab answered. 'Back when people believed in gods this is how they communicated with them.'

'By flicking water at themselves?'

'I never said it made sense,' he smiled.

'What does the smoke do?'

'I'm not sure. I think it's got something to do with warding away bad spirits.'

'It's going to ward me away too,' I companied, wrinkling my nose as the odious scented smoke reached my nose.

The man had stopped his chanting now and was standing with his hands folded in front of him, the smoke circling around his ankles. He spoke in a reedy voice. 'And now that I have shown you the cleansing ritual any sinners who wish to be cleansed may-'

'You should probably get those clothes delivered,' Rab suggested as an angry murmur ran through the group of onlookers. 'You'll want to get them back before the rain gets them wet.'

'All right,' I nodded, watching as the people around us started throwing dark looks in the strange man's direction.

'Go on then,' Rab encouraged, nudging me slightly out of the circle.

I said goodbye and walked away from the crowd now calling out angrily at the man.

Once I had delivered Mrs Cole's clothes I hurried to work. I worked as the apprentice of a carpenter named Eric. He had been a journeyman to my father, who had worked as a carpenter in Lilyworth since he was a child. After my father's death Eric had taken over the shop. It was a few years before the carpentry guild had granted him the title of master craftsman and by the time he was appointed I was old enough to become his apprentice. It was hard, but there was no other work for me in Lilyworth. By the time I was finished I was bone tired. Eric let me go just as the sun was beginning to set and I walked home in the fading light.

My cottage was full of people when I reached it. Mum, Rab and Mrs Aceldama, one of our neighbours with a large waist and even larger opinion of herself, were sitting around the table nursing cups of tea. I greeted them as I walked in.

Mum patted the empty seat next to her. 'Hello dear, how was work?'

'It was fine. How's Elvie?'

'A little better I think. The healer is with her now.'

At that moment the bedroom door opened and Healer Lawrence walked out.

'How is she faring?' Rab asked before anyone else could.

'She's not in any danger,' he replied. 'Her fever has broken and she seems to have her appetite back. If she carries on like that she'll be back to normal in no time. Let me know if anything changes but I should imagine she'll be fine.'

'Thank goodness,' Mum sighed.

'There Kate, I told you it would all be fine,' said Mrs Aceldama.

Healer Laurence nodded. 'Well I must be off.'

Mrs Aceldama stood. 'I'll walk you out. Wyman will be expecting me home. Goodbye Kate, Rab, Lex. Give Elvie my best.'

When they had gone Mum went to check on Elvie, leaving Rab and I alone at the table.

He turned to me and asked, 'You all right?'

It struck me that I hadn't had an opportunity to talk to Rab about my last meeting with Mera. I was on the verge on telling him when something stopped me. It probably wasn't the right time anyway, with Mum and Elvie in the next room. I decided this was something I should keep to myself, at least for a while.

4

The Brethren of Peace

It was the first time in nearly two weeks that Mera and I had been able to meet in our hut. Until a few days ago she was being punished for disobeying her mother, the queen. Though to hear Mera tell it, her mother was the one in the wrong.

She'd managed to smuggle me a note during her confinement saying, *It's not as though what I did was terribly wrong. I'd found my lady's maid crying and of course I'd wanted to know what was wrong. She told me that her father was very ill and was unlikely to last more than a day or two. I wouldn't hear of her staying in the castle a moment longer. Of course that meant that I had to dress myself. I thought I had done a quite a fine job but apparently my mother didn't agree. The way she yelled you would have though I'd have come done to meet the Meyromese noble family naked. I suppose my dress was a bit mussed and I wasn't wearing any of the jewellery she'd put out for me, but she was being completely unreasonable. She's far too worried about making me presentable. When I am queen I shall wear what I like and do as I wish and no one will stick pins in my hair. People will dress as they please, I shan't be fussed. They may walk around in their bedclothes if they want.*

I smiled when I thought of everyone in the castle, usually so neat and well dressed, ambling around in nightgowns.

She is so angry with me that it's possible she won't ever forgive me and I'll be left here until the day I die. If that happens make sure to avenge me by never dressing presentably and always acting inappropriately in serious situations.

I had laughed so loudly when I read that part that I woke my sister.

Now, however, she was free to prowl around the castle again. Not three days after her release she could be found lying in a patch of weak winter sunlight by the river recounting the events of the joust that had occurred the previous day.

'It was brilliant, I wish you could have been there,' she enthused.

She had rolled over into a brighter patch of sun and was lying flat on her stomach, smiling at me with her chin resting on her hands. The way the light fell formed a rose-gold crown atop her head.

'So do I, but I couldn't get away from work,' I replied.

'You work too hard. And your mother. I could help if-'

'We get along just fine.'

I knew Mera wanted to help, especially after my dad's passing, but I never felt right accepting anything from her. Not that it stopped her from bringing me things and all but forcing them into my hands when I tried to say no. On three separate occasions I had come home to find pouches of money tucked inside my bag. She'd have us all living up at the castle if she could.

'How is your mother? And Elvie,' Mera asked.

'They're well. Mum's as busy as ever, but you know how she is, wouldn't stop working for a minute even if the house were on fire.'

Mera nodded. She and Mum had met a few times when we had to go to market in the city. I was sure Mum had guessed who she was but she had never said anything.

'And Elvie's fine,' I continued. 'She had a cold a couple of weeks ago but she's back to normal now.'

'I wish you'd let me-'

'No,' I cut across her again. 'You've done enough already.'

Mera looked like she was going to argue so I changed the subject quickly. 'The joust was good, then?'

'Oh it was wonderful. The hand-to-hand combat was pretty good too. Someone used a Morningstar.'

'What's a Morningstar?'

'It's a spiked, metal ball on the end of a large stick. I've never seen one fought with before. They nearly bludgeoned poor Sir Ulric to death. I thought Lady Eleanor was going to faint. And then, of course, there was Sir Frederick with the sword. Do you remember when he found us hiding behind the old temple?'

'How could I forget?' I grumbled. Sir Frederick was a member of the king's personal guard. I wasn't particularly fond of the Royal Guard at the best of times but I was fond of Sir Frederick least of all. 'He called me a wretched street urchin and said if I didn't run along he'd have me hanged for befouling the streets of Drammear.'

'Well his appalling manners aside, he's very good with a sword. Although he does toy with his opponents sometimes. There was a green knight, Sir Gavin I think his name was. Anyway, Sir Frederick could have knocked him out with a few swift blows, but he danced around him for a while. I don't know if that was kind or cruel, but there you are.'

'It all sounds very bloodthirsty to me.'

'Well they don't have magic, what else are they supposed to do with their time?' She looked a little wistful for a moment. 'I'd have loved to have had a go.'

'Your mother still won't let you train, then?'

Mera's face darkened.

'Oh no, that wouldn't be a *civilised* activity for a young princess. Honestly, the way she treats me you'd think I were a glass doll. If I were a boy I would have been learning for years already. But alas, instead of swords and armour I get jewels and dresses. Well that's perfectly fine for some people, but not for me.'

'You could always ask your father,' I suggested.

'I've tried, believe me, but he won't consent either. I bet Mother has persuaded him I shouldn't be allowed to train. He always agrees with her, even if he doesn't actually agree with her.'

'Why don't you go directly to your master at arms? He could train you and your parents wouldn't have to know.'

Mera's face took on a pensive expression. 'Actually that might just work. Sir Rowan wouldn't be happy about defying the king and queen but as they've never officially told him no… I could at least persuade him to teach me the theory and that's better than nothing. You know what, Lex? I'm quite fond of you and your good ideas,' she grinned.

Her bright smile caused warmth to spread through my chest. Ever since Mera had begun telling me about magic the strange moments of affection I had when I thought of us together had been increasing. They normally passed after a moment but for some reason I couldn't shake this one. I shifted uncomfortably. They were not feelings I should be having.

She sat up and dusted off her dress. 'Anyway, enough chit chat. I wanted to tell you more about magic, specifically about the dangers we might face on our journey. You see, when the Thirteen Year War was being fought to remove magic from the kingdom a number of secret societies were formed. One of these was the Fellowship of the Mark, so named for the society's distinctive symbol.'

She reached into her bag and brought out a piece of parchment. When she handed it to me I saw the drawing of a butterfly resting on a bulrush.

'There were a number of letters I found in that hidden room from Fellowship members. Apparently they would leave this drawing on buildings that were safe to meet in and then once the meeting was over the image would be burned or scraped off, leaving only a rough mark so that the symbol couldn't be copied by the enemy.'

'Clever,' I mused.

'Indeed. The members were mainly Magic Folk to begin with but as Non-Magic Folk joined their numbers swelled and they became a force to be reckoned with. For a time it seemed that they would win the war. That was when the Brethren of Peace appeared. From what I've read they were not just willing but eager to slaughter to achieve their goal. Their specialty was infiltration and eventually they managed to get inside the Fellowship. The appearance of the Brethren squashed the resistance and turned the tides of the war. Magic Folk vanished nearly over night. The Brethren was meant to have disbanded after the war but I found an account of a raid on a village that was supposed to have been organised by them only twenty years ago. I have a feeling that they're still around today, and if they are then we need to be extra vigilant. If they catch wind of what we're doing they won't hesitate to kill us. You haven't told anyone about this have you?'

I shook my head, feeling slight panic at her words.

'We need to get moving on this. I think we should set the date for our departure at three months. That will give us enough time to plan the journey while learning some magic. That will have us leaving on the twenty-first day of April. What do you think?'

'Sounds fine,' I muttered. I wasn't really listening. I was thinking about what Mera had said about this Brethren of Peace. It brought a whole new element of danger to our plan.

'Are you sure this is really worth the risk?' I asked.

'Of course it is, Lex. Don't you understand how important this is? Magic Folk have been persecuted for decades. We've got to help them. You see that, right?'

I nodded. She was right, of course. She always was.

'Good. I ought to be getting back. Next time we meet we'll start practicing magic.'

Excitement flared in me at her words. 'Really? Oh brilliant.'

Mera smiled at my enthusiasm. She took back the parchment and slipped it into her bag. She hopped up and said, 'Oh before I forget, I was searching the secret room when I found a passageway at the back. I followed it and it took me to one of the guest rooms. I explored a bit more and found that there's a whole network of passageways behind the walls of the Castle. There's even one that leads to the dungeons.'

'That's incredible. You are being careful, aren't you?'

'I always am. I'll see you soon.'

'Bye,' I waved as she left.

I stood too and watched her walk away from under a juniper tree before turning and beginning the walk home.

My cottage was on the road that leads into the Lilyworth. The cottage itself was small but it was surrounded by an abundance of land. At the back were two diagonal lines of fruit trees, one apple and one plum. The two adjacent lines were joined at the top by a Dogwood tree like the tip of an arrow, pointing northward. In between the trees was a vegetable garden, which fed us throughout the year. Above the garden was a small hill, from on top of which you could see the entire village.

Reaching the front door, I pushed it open and was surprised to see Mum asleep in a chair. Elvie must still be at the village hall. A few days a week the younger children attended school in town. On Elvie's next birthday she would turn twelve and would be too old to attend and would have to join Mum as a washerwoman or else find some other work.

31

I went to Mum's room and grabbed the blanket from her bed. Back in the dining room I draped it over her. I knew she'd be angry with me later for not waking her but I hadn't seen her look so at peace for months.

I cast an eye around the room. It hadn't changed in years. The table was covered in piles of laundry. A number of cloaks hung on pegs by the door. Elvie's toys were scattered in front of the fireplace. I bent down to pick them up. As I carried them into the room we shared I noticed a ragdoll with a patch stitched across its shoulder. I remembered Elvie being very upset when the arm had torn. She only cheered up when Mum had sewn it back together with the little patch, telling her that the doll had been to the healer and was all better. I felt myself smiling as nostalgia filled my chest. It left me wondering how I was ever going to leave this place.

5

The princess and the sorcerer

'This is actually very exciting. I mean, I've enjoyed listening to you read from books and everything, but real magic? That's exciting,' I was practically jumping up and down as Mera took out candles and placed them gently on the grass. We had spent every spare moment we had in the past two weeks learning about magic and now we were going to try our hand at it.

The bare trees around us swayed in the breeze. My grandmother used to say this wind was lazy because it went right through you. Mera looked up at me from where she was sitting on the cold, scratchy grass, rearranging her supple leather gloves.

'Indeed, lighting candles is an enthralling business,' she drawled, but I could see a hint of a smile behind her sarcasm.

'Admit you're excited. This is the first time we're actually using magic. Have you ever lit a candle without a match before?' I asked, grinning stupidly.

'Yes actually, I did it yesterday,' she replied, pulling out three small leather pouches and laying them on the ground in front of her.

My smile faded. 'You did it yesterday? Inside the castle? Mera, that's so dangerous.'

'Don't worry, I was perfectly sensible about it. Besides, I had to practise. How am I supposed to teach you something I can't do myself? This is a lesson, remember.'

She began taking objects out of the pouches. In the first was a small purple flower that I recognised as wolfsbane, the second had star anise and in the third was a tiny phial filled with a viscous amber liquid.

'What's that?' I asked pointing at the phial.

'The sap from a maple tree. All these ingredients will help us cast the spell. Remember how the spell book says different herbs and plants have certain properties that can help you perform certain spells. Well wolfsbane has connections with heat and fire, the star anise is for protection and the sap is for creation. Once we get the hang of it we'll be able to perform the spell without them, just the incantation *ligbryne lícian* to call up the fire.'

Mera had laid out the candles in a circle. She took out a serrated blade and started cutting the wolfsbane into tiny pieces. She used the blunt side of the knife to crush the star anise and then sprinkled them both into a little bowl. She uncorked the phial and dripped the sap on top. She finished it off by mixing the ingredients together with the tip of the knife.

'All right,' she breathed, sitting cross-legged in front of the candles. 'It's ready.'

I sat opposite her and watched in anticipation as she began chanting under her breath.

'*Ligbryne lícian, ligbryne lícian, ligbryne lícian.*'

Nothing happened.

Mera opened her eyes, looking hopeful, but her face fell when she saw the unlit candles. I cast an eye around the field we were in. Until recently a farmer had been keeping his cows here, but some of them had become ill. He'd moved them out and hadn't used it since so it had become overgrown. The grass was coarse and rough. The trees around the edge had been pushed over by rough winds, their branches reaching out to us like many gnarled fingers. The grey sky loomed overhead, threatening rain.

Mera cleared her throat, raised her hands and began her chanting again. '*Ligbryne lícian, lígbryne lícian, lígbryne lícian.*' But still nothing happened.

She tried this four more times but the candles remained stubbornly unlit.

'Ugh! It's more difficult that it looks. And this wind isn't helping,' she complained as she pushed the auburn hair that was whipping around her face behind her ears.

'Maybe we should go somewhere else,' I muttered, glancing around the field again. For one daunting moment I thought I saw someone standing under a sagging willow tree at the far end of the field but when I looked back there was no one there.

'No. I'll get it. I will,' she insisted. She closed her eyes and gently folded her hands in her lap, breathing in deeply. Still with her eyes closed she raised her hands slowly over the candles, chanting, '*Lígbryne lícian, lígbryne lícian, lígbryne lícian.*'

The wind died down so fast I though for a moment we'd been frozen where we sat. The air around us was still and quiet. It was as though time had slowed down. The circle of candles between us shimmered. Through the silence I felt a quiet hum, like a small vibration in the earth beneath me. As I watched the candles began to spark and crackle. Mera continued chanting, her eyes firmly closed. I leaned forward, entranced, and to my utter amazement a flame unfurled out of the candle directly in front of her.

'Mera!' her eyes snapped open at my cry. 'You did it!'

Mera smiled broadly. 'Oh I did. Wow, that… that's really… very tiring,' she slumped slightly as the wind picked up again and snuffed out the flame. 'That's disappointing.'

'But you did it! You actually lit one!'

'No really,' Mera said leaning forward, holding her head in her hands, 'I don't feel…'

I scrambled to my feet and rushed towards her but was too late to catch her from falling sideways, landing on the grass with a soft thump.

'Mera! Mera what's wrong?' I knelt beside her and lifted her head. She blinked open her eyes.

'What happened?' she asked.

'You fainted,' I said, helping her stand. 'Are you all right? Do you feel ill? Did you hit your head?'

'No,' she said, standing up straight and brushing her dress clean. 'I'm fine now.'

'What happened?' I asked

'Magic needs power,' she explained. 'Usually it draws energy from the earth but when magic was banished its connection to the earth was severed. Without that magic has nowhere to draw power from so it takes it from the person who's casting the spell. It can drain you if you don't concentrate properly. I thought small spells like this wouldn't have much of an effect but maybe I was wrong.'

'Does it hurt?' I asked.

'No,' she replied. 'You just feel sort of tired and hazy, like you're falling asleep.'

'So the spell you found to bring back the Sisterhood, would it do this too?' I asked.

'I imagine it would happen with any spell you're not concentrating on, but maybe it will be different with that one because of the nature of it. I'm not sure we can know until it happens.'

'How will it work?'

'Let me show you,' Mera sat back down on her side of the circle and I mirrored her. She pulled out a small book from her bag that looked so old it was falling apart. She opened it gently and took out a piece of parchment. She unfolded it and pointed to a list of ingredients. 'These are the things we'll need.

Sap of the dogwood tree, crushed carnation root and peony extract. Then the spell is in two parts.'

She handed me the parchment and I could see two lines of script in the language I had come recognise as that of magic. It read *gesamnian thrymlic magen* and then áhreddan thrymlic magen.

'The first part is to draw in magic,' Mera continued. 'And the second is to release it.'

'You really think we can do this?' I asked.

'Of course I do. We just need to learn how to use magic. That's why we're starting with the simple things and we'll move up from there.'

I glanced at the candles, which sat on the ground next to us and said, 'Can I try?'

'Of course, but be careful.'

I looked down at the candles and closed my eyes, trying to do as the book said and *collect my energy and connect with the power from all around me.* I breathed in slowly and raised my hands above the candles as Mera had done. It was so quiet that I could hear her breathing across the circle and the rustling trees that surrounded us. I could smell the fresh grass in the field and the rain that had fallen the night before. I felt the air around me begin to swirl and twist itself into invisible, intangible shapes.

'*Ligbryne lícian*,' I began, so quietly it was almost a whisper. '*Ligbryne lícian, ligbryne lícian.*'

But, just like Mera's first try, nothing happened. Disappointment flooded through me.

'Don't worry,' Mera said. 'Try again, you'll get it.'

I began again, this time really trying to feel the connection between the candles and myself. I wiggled my feet in my worn shoes, pressing them into the earth to feel the vibrations that had tingled up and down my back when Mera had done the spell. I readied myself, muttering the incantation under my breath, but still nothing happened.

'You're trying too hard,' Mera's voice cut across my concentration.

'Yes, thank you,' I muttered.

I tried once more, breathing in deeply, focusing on the candles. I closed my eyes and pictured them igniting in my mind. I could feel their heat warming my body. It spread from my fingers to the top of my arms, prickling all the way down my spine.

'*Ligbryne lícian, lígbryne lícian, lígbryne lícian.*'

I opened my eyes.

At first all I saw was Mera's shocked face but then I looked down and was astonished to see six glowing candles. I glanced back up at Mera, amazed at the sight before me.

'That's amazing, Lex,' she breathed, her face alight in the glow of the candles.

Everything was sharpened. The grass that had been dulled by the overcast sky shone bright and green. I could feel the cool wood of my father's pendant against my chest. The trees around the field began to swish and sway so loudly that it was deafening. The sweet smell of the morning dew intermingling with the scents drifting over from the village was overpowering. I didn't feel drained at all.

Mera was smiling at me. 'Well done. Clearly I'm going to need to practise to keep up with you.'

I looked at Mera as though I was seeing her for the first time. Strands of red hair that had fallen out of her braid were brushing against the side of her face. Her pale skin was flushed and her eyes shone brightly. How could I not have appreciated how beautiful she was before? I reached across the candles and caressed her cheek. Her skin was so soft. Her hand reached up and stroked my arm gently.

Suddenly her smile faded and she slowly moved my hand away from her face. 'Lex...' she muttered.

I felt the connection break. The candles were snuffed out instantly and I felt as though the wind had been knocked out of me. I took a deep, steadying breath.

'This can't happen,' Mera continued.

I felt my face flush. 'I know.'

'That was our agreement. Nothing can distract us from the quest. It's more important than... Well than anything that might happen between us.'

'I understand.'

Mera frowned. 'Do you? Because you know how important this is to me. Feelings and yearning and wanting don't matter. Romance can't be felt here.'

'Is that something that you feel?'

'It doesn't matter how I feel. This is how it is. Either you respect that or you don't. But I do hope you respect me.'

I suddenly felt terrible shame. 'Of course I respect you. I would never want to do anything to ruin our friendship.'

Mera's face softened.

'I know you wouldn't. Let's not talk about this any more. Do you want to try again?' she asked, pointing to the candles.

'Definitely,' I nodded.

I would put these reckless ideas out of my mind.

6
The tale of King Manuvendra

It was my sixteenth birthday, and three weeks since Mera had first shown me that old boot. Our time together had been filled with magic. Learning about magic, studying magic, practising magic. We were finding it more and more difficult to cast spells. Often, when we were so frozen from the icy wind and desperate for a fire would it grant us warmth, or when I was feeling particularly angry or elated. It seemed to only come to us when it wanted to. Mera grew frustrated by it, deciding to spend more time learning the theory, but I felt that if I tried hard enough I might learn its ways.

The two of us were sitting on Herron Hill, which overlooked Lilyworth, deciding what to do with the day. I saw my cottage on the fringe between the village and The Great Forest. A long way off to the left was the castle, its huge towers looming over the rest of Drammear, clustered within the city's vast walls.

'Do you really want to sit up here all day doing nothing?' Mera asked me.

'We're not doing nothing. We're talking.'

I didn't really mind what we did. As long I was with Mera I was happy.

'All right, it's your birthday,' Mera said, pushing her hair back behind her ear. 'Speaking of which, I know you said you didn't want a gift, but I ignored you. It's not much anyway. I don't think it really counts.'

She reached into her bag and pulled out a book, which she handed to me. I saw that it was the book of spells from which we had been learning all we could about how to cast magic.

Mera had tied a purple ribbon around it in lieu of paper. I untied it and flipped open the cover. On the inside she had written, *Dear Lex, you've been the best of friends all these years. I hope you deem this a token of the trust between us. Your loving friend, Mera.*

She continued. 'I know you've seen it a thousand times before but I thought you should have it. Officially, you know. You're better than me, anyway.'

Happiness swelled in my chest. 'This is a wonderful. I love it.'

'I thought your sister might like the ribbon. You mentioned she needed a new one.'

'Yes, she does. Thank you,' I set the book down beside me and pulled Mera into a hug.

'Oh,' she huffed. 'You're welcome.'

I held onto her tightly. I wasn't sure if she liked me hugging her but she didn't seem to resist. A few moments later when we parted she was smiling too. I thought of our agreement that nothing was to happen between us and wondered just how firm her resolve was. Knowing Mera, very.

'So,' Mera said. 'If you don't want to do anything exciting for your birthday, what do you want to do?'

'You could tell me a story. You're good at that. Perhaps how the Thirteen Year War began.'

'That's not exactly a happy story.'

'Tell me anyway,' I entreated.

'Well if that's what you want,' she shrugged. She curled her legs under herself and placed her hands by her knees so that she was leaning forwards slightly. 'Magic was common until King Manuvendra came into power a hundred years ago. He was a greedy man. The first thing he did was increase taxes to an extortionate amount. People couldn't pay them. They couldn't afford to buy food or clothing. The kingdom was prosperous before he took power but soon enough people were struggling to live. The outlying villages were the first to feel it. Poverty spread inwards towards the city like a poison leaching towards the heart. He made examples of people who couldn't pay. He strung them up to wooden posts in the street and let them hang there for days until they died exhausted, ridiculed and begging for it to end. That's tame compared to some of the other things he did.

'But people fought back. It became more common for people to use magic to grow their own crops and conjure up other things they couldn't afford. That angered the king. That's when his campaign against magic really began. He created laws that prohibited the use of magic under certain conditions. He began to segregate Magic and Non-Magic Folk, creating a rift between them. One day he started capturing creatures of magic.

'They were kept in the dungeons for weeks. All the while he had been seizing magic texts. He ordered the books to be thrown into a pile in the courtyard. It was then that he began to bring out the Magic Folk that he had been keeping imprisoned. The first person brought out was an old dwarf. The books were set on fire and the dwarf, though injured and malnourished, tried to run but the guards caught him. People watched as the man was thrown onto the pyre. No one dared to save him, even as he screamed in pain.

'They were all burned. Every single one of them roped to a stake and set alight. Can you imagine it? With screams of terror, noble and innocent races were brought to their deaths.'

I winced. 'That's awful.'

'He burned the books and he burned the people. After that it was war. Sorceresses banded together and hurled spells at the Castle. The dwarfs and the centaurs built up armies to attack the city. The elves and the fairies destroyed crops and livestock that brought wealth to the king. In return he sent out legions of men to destroy the forests and kill all the magical creatures that lived there. Everywhere you went was teeming with betrayals and lies and murder,' Mera shuddered.

'Sounds like one of your adventure stories,' I said distractedly, staring off towards the castle.

'Well it was a terrible time to live in,' she trailed off.

The wind rushed past us. I felt the need to change the subject. I had heard people in the village talking of royal visitors in Drammear. The discussion was mainly about the eligible prince, which had my stomach in knots. I had been hoping that she would bring it up but I couldn't wait any longer.

'I hear you've got company at the castle. Prince Aric of Foraise?'

Mera's face changed instantly from contemplation to complete and utter loathing.

'Oh yes,' she drawled. 'Prince Aric. He has made quite the impression. Everybody simply loves him. The prince, with all his grand clothes, and his fine airs and graces. Oh he has everybody in raptures. Even my father seems pleased with him, which is just unheard of.'

'It looks like he's made quite an impression on you too,' I smiled, secretly delighted that she seemed to dislike the prince so much.

Mera leap up and began pacing back and forth. 'He's so rude. Strutting around the castle as if he owns it, showing off about his extensive lands and extreme wealth. He's so arrogant. I can't stand him. Did I tell you that he was complaining about how uncomfortable the pillows were? Honestly, his head is so swollen I'm surprised his crown still fits. And poor Caron had to traipse all over the Castle looking for the softest, plumpest, silkiest pillow for his royal head. I tell you, he really is something. God forbid your pillows lack sufficient fluffiness. I mean, what a calamity!'

43

I laughed. 'Maybe he's not that bad once you get to know him.'

Mera stopped her pacing and turned to me. 'No, he's worse. He's always asking to be accompanied outside for a pleasant leisurely walk. It's as though he thinks I don't have more important things to be doing with my time. Honestly.'

That caught my attention. 'He wants to walk with you?'

'Oh yes,' Mera's voice was venomous. 'I know exactly what he is doing. He wants to marry me, inherit this kingdom and add my family's wealth to his own hoard of gold. He seems to think that he is the most important person in the world. But I can assure you he is nothing special. I know people far below his station worth ten times his value. I'm too young to be even thinking about marriage. I'm barely sixteen for goodness' sake. I just know my father is planning for us to marry. But I won't. I simply won't be forced into a marriage just because it is expected of me. My father will say it's for the good of the kingdom but I very highly doubt it would be. What use is a queen who doesn't even begin to respect her king? How will having two people who do not get along ruling the kingdom be good for it? It's not as though Aric wants what's best for anyone but himself. Just keep feeding him more power and riches and he'll be content. Well he can have them all he wants, but he can't have me.'

I tried to fight the stab of jealousy I felt at the mention of their betrothal but it overwhelmed me. 'You can't marry him!' The words were out of my mouth before I could stop them.

'I don't plan on it,' Mera insisted, sitting down beside me. 'My father would never force me into a marriage if I really insisted on it. Don't worry, this won't interfere with our plans.'

For one stupid moment I thought she meant the two of us, together, but then I realised she meant our plans to leave. There

44

was a tight ball in my throat as I swallowed. I knew I had to get these ideas out of my head but they had been growing stronger.

I couldn't love her. I just couldn't. Mera and I had been friends for so long, it would be too strange. She wouldn't want such advances. I thought back to the way her hand had lingered on mine when I stroked her cheek across the candles. The way I caught her looking at me sometimes was not the way friends should look at one another. It gave me a strange sort of hope. My mind suddenly raced with thoughts of her hand in mine, my arm tight around her waist, our lips about to meet.

I shook myself out of the daydream. This was stupid. This could not be love. Mera had made a firm resolution and she had made me promise to honour it. Whatever I dreamed of couldn't be, no matter what we felt. A princess could not love a peasant any more than a swan could love a fly.

I turned to her and said, 'You never told me the end of the story.'

'What? Which story?' her brow was furrowed in confusion.

'The one about King Manuvendra and the Thirteen Year War. How did it end?'

'Oh, well, after all those years of slaughter it was just too much. Most magical beings were in hiding or dead already thanks to the Brethren of Peace. They gave up. The king was overjoyed. For the next thirty years he ruled over a kingdom of people who abhorred him but were too oppressed to do anything about it. When he died his eldest son took the throne. Thankfully he was a much better king to his people, but he had inherited his father's fear and disgust for magic. He didn't send out hunts to slaughter them as his father had done but if anything even remotely related to magic appeared he would have it immediately destroyed.'

'That's terrible.'

'That's why we're doing this.'

I turned towards Lilyworth and found my cottage again. Elvie was outside playing with a friend. Mum must have been cooking because smoke was rising from the chimney. She was making something special for dinner tonight and had invited Rab to join us. I knew I'd have to leave soon if I wanted to be on time but for the moment I couldn't pull myself away from where I sat with Mera in companionable silence.

7

The sorcerer's quickening

Wind whooshed around the clearing causing great spirals of snow to be thrown upwards. It cascaded down from grey clouds, buffeted by the wind on its decent. Bronze leaves rustled in the breeze as they fell to the ground leaving tree branches bare. A small porcelain doll with a delicate dress patterned with golden sprigs hung in the air. All of a sudden the doll dropped like a stone, causing a small hole to appear in the soft blanket of snow as it disappeared from sight.

'Ugh!' Mera yelled. 'I can't do it! Why can't I do it?'

She stomped towards the doll and snatched it up, leaving a fresh track of footprints behind her. 'This is completely useless, it's never going to work.'

'Calm down. You'll get it.'

I felt bad for her. We'd been practicing this spell for hours and she still hadn't been able to perform it properly. My own doll, a pretty thing in a deep green dress, was dancing elegantly through the snowy air, leaping from one leaf to another, as graceful as a ballerina in the moonlight.

'Why can't I do it?' She thrust her arm out sharply, holding the doll tightly in her palm with a look of intense concentration on her face. I watched her as she muttered the incantation under her breath.

'Maybe we should take a break. You're tiring yourself out,' I sighed, knowing what the answer would be before I'd even finished my sentence.

'No. I'm not stopping until I get this right.'

I sighed again. Mera's stubbornness wasn't going to get us anywhere so I walked towards her, my feet crunching through the snow. I felt the connection break and I had to pause for a moment to catch my breath. My doll returned to its previously inanimate state, falling to the ground with a dull thud and I continued. Mera's head snapped up as I came to stand in front of her.

I prized the doll from her clenched fingers. 'You need to relax. You're forcing it but it's subtler than that. You really have to feel the magic, let it flow through you.' I turned her palm up to the sky and placed the golden doll in her hand.

'You seem to be an expert at this all of a sudden,' she grumbled.

'I learned from the best.'

She took a deep breath and I could hear her muttering the incantation. *Lific alif.*

The doll rose slightly off Mera's palm, hovering for a second before flopping back down again. Mera let out a groan of frustration.

'You're almost there. Just calm down, all right.'

Mera closed her eyes and breathed in deeply. *Lific alif, lific alif.*

This time the doll lifted itself completely off Mera's hand and rose into the air. The tiny figure stood for a moment hovering above us, raising its dainty arms as though it was about to dance, but before it could start it drooped and fell back into Mera's palm. Her face fell.

'I'm never going to get it am I?' she asked, dejected.

'Maybe we should leave it for today.' I suggested. 'We've been practicing for hours and it's freezing out here.'

Mera nodded and pocketed her doll.

I scooped up my own doll and handed it to Mera who slipped it into the pocket of her thick coat. I pulled my cloak tightly around me as we trudged through the snow back towards our hut. We had left a fire going while we practised. I sat in front of it to warm my frozen hands. I looked at Mera as she sat down next to me.

'You did well to get it to move at all, you know,' I said.

She pursed her lips. 'You didn't seem to have trouble with it. The books say that some people have a natural talent for magic while others may struggle. I supposed I'm not gifted.'

'But without magic in the land you know it's much harder,' I insisted. 'Of course you're gifted.'

Mera chuckled then looked sad. 'Thank you for your vote of confidence but in this instance I'm afraid you're wrong.'

I felt suddenly a desire to comfort her, to hold her and let know how much she mattered. Just as I was about to reach out for her she moved. I ran my hand through my hair to excuse the movement.

'Lex, I've been thinking. What if we left earlier than we planned?'

I was taken aback by her proposal.

'Earlier? Why?'

'Well I just think we're as prepared as we're going to be. The route is planned and we can keep learning as we travel. I know we said three months but it just feels like we're waiting around for no reason. Besides, my father's been hinting recently about changes. I have a feeling he's going to begin my succession lessons soon. He's been putting them off but a prince or princess has to have started learning by their seventeenth year.'

'I don't know. I mean there's still a lot we can do in the time we have left.'

'Like what?'

I shifted uncomfortably. 'You know... stuff.'

I hesitated. I was unwilling to say it but I had been thinking recently about this quest. Mera seemed so determined but I

49

had concerns. Despite how much I tried I could not push these changing feelings for her out of my mind. I knew that to at least some extend she felt the same way for me but she wouldn't admit it. Was it really a good idea for us to be going away together with these unresolved feelings? It made me feel uneasy.

'Stuff? What does that mean?'

'Well,' I hesitated, 'I still don't know what I'm going to say to my family. And I wanted to stay until after the Festival of Tomorrow.'

Mera raised her eyebrows. 'A festival? This is more important than a festival.'

I felt a jolt of frustration. She had never taken my village seriously and I was beginning to wonder if she took me seriously either. 'Think about what you're asking of me. How am I supposed to just leave my family?'

She looked taken aback. 'Where is this coming from? You already agreed that this is more important than all of that. We have a duty.'

'Well what about you? In less than a year you will be eligible to take the throne. If anything were to happen to your father you would be queen. You have duties and responsibilities to your people here too. Are you really going to neglect them? We can't just cut all our ties and scamper off on an adventure!' I shouted.

'I don't want to take the throne!' she yelled back, her face contorting with disgust. 'I don't want to strut around in fine clothes and jewels, dictating laws to my willing subjects when there are people out there who need my help. Magic Folk are a part of this kingdom too. I'm obligated to defend them, especially when it was my ancestors who did this to them. I would rather abdicate than sit around, tending to my so-called duties, than…'

But Mera never got to finish her sentence because at that moment the fire blazed so violently it pushed us both to the ground and just as suddenly it was snuffed out. I looked around to see if Mera was hurt. She had flung her arms out to stop herself from falling. She looked shocked and a little ruffled but unharmed. She seemed to come to her senses and stood abruptly. Her eyes were cold as she looked at me through the darkness.

'I can see how you feel about this. If you aren't completely committed then there's no point in you coming. I'll go alone.'

She snatched up her bag and hurried out of the door.

I shook myself and called out to her. 'Mera wait!'

I scrambled up and raced outside but she was gone, the only trace of her was the footprints she left in the snow.

8

The confession

I tried to run after her but it was as though she had vanished into the night. I followed her footprints as far as they went into the forest but when they disappeared I had no way to track her.

I made my way home slowly. Mera's words still echoed through my mind. *I don't want to take the throne!* I always knew Mera had struggled with the day to day of court life but to actually wish to abdicate was another thing entirely. If Mera refused to take the throne what would happen? I doubted the king and queen would take kindly to their only heir renouncing her birthright.

I often forgot how far apart Mera and I really were. Mera was rich and powerful, the crown princess to the throne of Culrain. Her family had ruled for hundreds of years. My mother barely had the money to feed herself, let alone Elvie and me. I abruptly felt very angry with Mera. What right did she have to give up all she had when there were people starving in the streets?

Although, an annoyingly reasonable voice in my head said, *she would gladly sacrifice herself if it would save her people.*

I recalled a time a little after the festivities to celebrate Mera's thirteenth birthday when there had been a fire in the lower town. Sixteen families had lost their homes, as well as the lives of three young children. Mera had wanted to help them but her mother had told her that they couldn't cry themselves to sleep every time one of the Common Folk died. During the revelries she had been gifted a priceless jewelled necklace from the royal family of Seion. It was a truly extravagant thing of which I have never seen the like. It glittered like sunlight on rippling water, dripping with fire opals in a golden chain. It could have fed my entire village for years. Mera immediately had the necklace melted down and sold so that she could give the money to the victims of the fire. When her mother had found out she had been furious. She'd had all of Mera's books and toys removed from her rooms and had confined her to the castle for weeks. Mera hadn't regretted it for one minute. She said it was no punishment at all for the relief it gave those families and that she would have done it a thousand times over if it could have given those children back their lives.

My feet crunched on dry, dead leaves. I followed the direction of the white stones that lined the path showing me the way home. The moon was hardly visible. The dirty grey clouds caught any light it would have provided.

When I reached my cottage I could see a candle flickering on the old broken table in the dining room. Through the window I saw the shadow of a woman cast against the wall. It jumped erratically as the small flame danced in the slight draft that always managed to creep in through the crooked door. Mum sat at the table with a half angry, half worried look that only meant trouble for me.

The moon was visible from behind the clouds now and its light guided me towards the door. I turned the handle and pushed. The door creaked open. I closed it quickly behind me to keep out the cold, sliding the bolt into place.

Mum didn't speak. She simply sat there, unmoving, her face half in shadow. She stared down at her hands rested on the cracked wood, her shawl drawn tightly around her slim shoulders.

'Mum-'

'Where have you been?' she cut across me.

'I couldn't sleep, I went for a walk.'

'On your own?'

'Yes.'

'You can't go running around with her anymore. It's not safe,' she looked up at me.

I was shocked. I'd had no idea she knew about Mera and me.

Her eyes were full of sadness. 'Things are changing, Alexander. You're growing up, both of you. You have to remember that your actions have consequences. What if you get caught?'

I couldn't answer. I knew what she was saying was founded in truth, not just a mother's worry. I rubbed my cold hands over my face.

'There's been talk, sweetheart, about a visitor to the castle. He's said to be a perfect suitor. She's sixteen, isn't she? An age to be married,' she paused and suddenly I understood her concern.

'Oh, no, Mum. It's not... that's not what this is,' I could feel my face heating up. I slid into a chair.

'You mean,' she began hesitantly. 'That after all these years... you've never realised that she's a... young woman.'

My face burned. 'I know what she is. I also understand that she is the princess and that one day she will be queen with a king by her side. But I do trust that whoever that king may be she will be the one to choose him. It won't be her family and it won't be to this so-called perfect suitor. That's her worst nightmare.'

'That's a lot of insight you seem to have.'

'Mum, you have to trust that I know what I'm doing.'

'I'm just worried about you. I don't want to see you end up with a broken heart,' her voice was full of concern.

'You can't worry about me every time I step out the door. Besides, I swear to you we aren't doing anything wrong,' I lied.

'I always worry about you. It's called being a mother. One day you'll understand how hard it is for a parent to see their child growing up. You've been my baby boy for sixteen years.'

'Sixteen is hardly a baby. We're all getting older. I'll be the one taking care of you soon,' I joked.

But instead of smiling like I thought she would she blushed and looked down at the table. Her hands began nervously tracing the split there.

'Actually, there is something else I wanted to talk to you about.'

'What is it?'

'Well... you know Samson Tubal-Cain?'

I nodded. 'Of course. The blacksmith.'

'Yes. He's asked me to marry him.'

I didn't know what to say. Mum said nothing.

'Samson Tubal-Cain has asked you to marry him?' I asked.

'Yes.'

'The blacksmith? The one who told me that if I didn't stop making noise near his forge the mountain trolls were going to take me away?'

'Yes.'

'The one with the... hair?'

'Yes Alex, that Samson Tubal-Cain. And while I will admit that his hair can be a bit unruly at times, I ask you to please refrain from insulting my betrothed.'

'Your betrothed? So you said yes then?'

'I did.'

I had a sudden desire to be anywhere else but here.

'I'm going to bed,' I muttered.

'Alex-'

'Goodnight.'

I pushed back the chair and stomped off towards my room. She didn't call me back.

Quietly, so as not to wake Elvie who was sleeping peacefully in her bed opposite mine, I slipped under the covers. She looked so peaceful, lying there in the darkness, not knowing or understanding the confusion I felt.

How could Mum be getting married again? How could I have missed it? My hand jumped to my father's pendant. I really must have been completely wrapped up in my own world of Mera and magic. I knew Samson Tubal-Cain by sight, but not personally. A tall man on the wrong side of forty, he was barrel chested with a mess of tangled black hair that was often knotted on top of his head when he worked in his forge. I wondered if all that sweaty work meant he smelled. Like Mum, he had olive skin, but his eyes were as grey as storm clouds. Likely all he would want to talk about was the quality of his hammers. I sighed. I would have to try and get on with him for Mum's sake.

I lay in my bed thinking about everything that had happened that day. Mum's questions about Mera had my mind whirring. In truth I felt more confused about Mera every day. I knew I loved her as a friend, that she was beautiful and extraordinary, but I didn't have a name for what I felt for her now. Nothing was going to happen when she kept insisting that we must remain friends. A part of me, a part I was not so proud of, wondered if going on the quest with her would break her resolve. Perhaps I could finally prove to her that I wasn't just some simple peasant from a boring village, that I could be extraordinary too…

I felt anxious, as though I'd been broken into tiny pieces and stuck back together with a few essential parts missing. My mind was shutting down and I couldn't concentrate. Every time I had a clear thought it slipped away from me. Instead of fighting sleep, I gave in. As I heard Mum shuffling into her room I drifted off into an uneasy sleep, full of dreams of far off lands and ancient sorceresses, of a beautiful princess and an endless journey.

9

The Festival of Tomorrow

Mum and Samson were married in a small ceremony at the top of our garden four days later. Mum looked radiant. She wore flowers in her hair, a dress of woven lace that had once belonged to her grandmother, and a smile of pure joy. Elvie, who at first had shared my reservations, was now ecstatic at the though of having Samson in our lives. I, on the other hand, was not convinced.

Samson did not seem to be a bad man. Even through my blatant dislike of him I could see that. I should have been kinder to him, he was a part of my family now, but the fact remained that he wasn't my father. Every time I saw him I was left with the bitter thought that it should have been my dad who took my mother's cloak for her, who tucked Elvie into bed at night, who sat in the large, straight-backed chair at the head of the table when we ate dinner.

But I had bigger things to worry about than Samson. My fight with Mera still rang in my ears. When I left the hut I had been angry and didn't really think Mera would go without me but with every day that passed without seeing her the more I worried that was exactly what she would do. Each morning I woke with dread, worried I would leave my room to hear news that the princess had vanished. Every moment I was at work I itched to be away so that I could go to our hut, just to wait and see if she would return. Every night I would spend fitful hours in bed, unable to sleep for the dreams of my dear friend losing her way in the wilderness.

After nearly a week of yearning to see her face she appeared. I was sitting in our hut flicking through the spell book when I heard footsteps and the door opened. Mera stood in the doorway, snow covering her hood.

'Mera,' I sprung to my feet. 'You're here.'

'I am,' she replied, not looking me in the eye.

'I wasn't sure you would come back.'

'I wasn't really going to leave without you.'

'Are you sure? You seemed pretty determined.'

'Look I was angry, all right. I shouldn't have yelled at you. I'm sorry. Let's just move on, shall we?'

I was taken aback but I didn't want to pick a fight when Mera seemed so eager to put it behind us.

'Sure,' I nodded. 'Let's move on.'

'Good,' Mera moved into the room, letting the door swing shut behind her.

She seemed apparently determined to act as if nothing had happened, but something felt off about our conversation. Our fight wasn't mentioned again. There was no discussion of us leaving earlier. I pushed the whole thing to the back of my mind where I could pretend that it had been a rather nasty dream but sometimes I found myself concerned that Mera's patience would run out. It was during the Festival of Tomorrow, three days after her sudden reappearance, that it became impossible to ignore the nagging worry in my mind about what Mera might be planning.

The Festival of Tomorrow was an important celebration in Culrain to honour the end of the year and the start of the new one. It was an eight-day long event, beginning a week before the new year officially began. The first day started with a large family dinner, and then in the evening people would make their way to the village centre to watch the parade that marked the start of the celebrations. The rest of the week was full of festivities in town. On the final day people would write a wish for the new year on a piece of paper, fold it into the shape of a bird, and sail it away down the river in the hope that the bird would carry your wish away to be granted. There were always games for the children, plenty of food, and stalls selling charms and pendants that were meant to give luck in the coming year.

For the first time in years my family were celebrating the start of the festival properly with friends from the village coming for lunch. We had even decorated the house for the occasion. The last time we celebrated like this was the year before my dad had died. I was looking forward to the food more than the company. There were two families with children, but both were closer to Elvie's age than to mine, and none with common interests. It was likely to be more taxing than entertaining.

'Mum,' called Elvie from where she was sitting by the fireplace making decorations to hang on it. 'Can you help me? I can't get it right.'

'I think we've done all we can for today. I'll leave the boar in the cooker for the morning and everything else can be done tomorrow,' Mum said looking over the kitchen at the pots and pans scattered over the work surface. 'Oh and can you put the bread sauce in a dish and cover it please?'

I nodded and grabbed a bowl from the nearest cupboard. I scooped the sauce into it, covering it with a cloth, which I secured with a piece of string, and placed it with the other pots ready for tomorrow. I followed Mum into the living room.

Elvie was sitting on the floor in a circle of cut out and crumpled paper. She had tried to make little figurines out of scraps of fabric to represent the dancers in The Setting and The Rising of The Sun, a traditional ballad told at this time of year, but it hadn't gone very well. After about the hundredth time of her accidentally stabbing herself in the finger with one of the sharp needles, Mum had taken her sewing kit away from her.

Elvie had been stuck with cutting out paper after that, but she hadn't minded. She was happy to be given an excuse to use the small paint set I'd given to her as an early Festival of Tomorrow gift, which I'd managed to get with a little bit of help from Mera. There was a long piece of string in her hair, which she didn't seem to have noticed, and she was holding a paper cut-out of a lady in a long gown that she had painted a rather splotchy green. There was a tiny hole at the top of the lady's head through which she was attempting to thread the string.

Mum knelt down next to her and taking the string out of her hand, said, 'Now, what are you trying to do here?'

'I can't get the string to go through that hole,' Elvie explained.

'All right, let me see. It's only frayed a bit here, look,' she smiled, pointing to the tattered end of the string. 'Easy to fix.'

Mum pulled a small kitchen knife out of the pocket of her apron and quickly cut off the end of the string. She took the paper lady and pushed the thread through the hole, made a small loop and tied it in a knot. She gave it back to Elvie saying, 'There you are, all done. Now you can hang it on the mantelpiece.'

'Thanks, Mum,' Elvie pushed herself off the floor and walked over to me. 'Can you hang it for me, I can't reach.'

'Of course I can,' I said, taking the paper lady from her and placing it over the fireplace.

'It all looks so pretty!' exclaimed Elvie, watching the row of flickering candles over the crackling fire.

'It really does look wonderful. You've done excellently with all the decorations, Elle,' replied Mum.

'No I mean the light,' Elvie insisted.

'You'll have to remember to thank Sam for all the extra candles, then,' Mum smiled.

My smile slipped slightly as I stood back to survey all of Elvie's fine work. The wall above the fireplace that usually stood bare was covered in a wide assortment of decorations. Along the mantelpiece were the dancers from the ballad tied to a piece of string so that they hung over the edge, illuminated by the light of the fire. Higher up on a freshly hammered nail was a large, wobbly sun rising out of some clouds.

I turned back to my sister and said, 'There you go Elvie, all done.'

She grinned and darted over to give me a hug.

'It all looks wonderful Elle, well done,' smiled Mum, gazing around the room. 'I think everyone's going to be very impressed with all your hard work.'

My mind wandered to Mera and what she was doing at this moment. Surely not decorating the dining room with paper cut-outs while her parents smiled down at her handiwork. She was probably preparing for the banquet the royal family held every year for the festival. Mera hated it. Just another unnecessary excuse for her mother to dress her up like a doll, she said. Once the idea of Mera refusing to wear court approved clothes to a royal banquet would have amused me, but now it just made me feel slightly sick.

I glanced out of the window and watched the snow falling. I thought about getting the shovel to clear a path when the door swung open and Samson walked in.

'Hello everyone,' he called, striding across the room, getting snowy footprints all over the floor, and kissing my mum on the cheek.

'Hello dear. How was your day? You didn't get too cold walking home did you?' she asked concerned.

'Oh yes, I had a great day. Rab says hello, by the way. He can't wait for tomorrow. And you, my love, worry too much. I had my trusty cloak to keep me warm,' he replied, shaking out his trusty cloak and getting even more snow on the floor. 'Wow, look at all of this. Those decorations look great.'

Elvie smiled brightly and ran over to hug him. He picked her up. 'You're looking very excited. If you don't calm down you won't be able to sleep tonight and then you'll be so tired you'll sleep through lunch tomorrow.'

Elvie stopped smiling immediately, looking crestfallen. 'Can I go to bed now?'

Mum laughed. 'Not until we've had dinner and you've cleaned up that mess from the floor.'

'All right,' Elvie nodded.

Samson plucked the string from her hair and let her down so she could scamper off to clear the debris from the hearth.

He turned to me and said, 'So Lex, had a good day?'

'Fine,' I muttered. 'I think I'm going to clear a path outside. I doubt Mrs Babick will be able get through all that snow.'

'I'll come and help,' he offered.

'I can do it,' I huffed, turning toward the door and pushing it open.

I grabbed the shovel that was leaning against the wall of the cottage and started furiously shovelling the snow off the path. I tried to shake off my anger but there didn't seem to be a whole lot to be happy about. My mind again wondered to Mera. My confusion had only grown since she had returned. She certainly didn't seem like she was about to run off, but I wouldn't put anything past her. All I could do was hope that she would wait for me.

The table was set, the guests had arrived and taken their seats and the food was served. The noise in our overcrowded house had reached a monumental level from its added occupants and was beginning to grate on my nerves.

There were fourteen of us gathered for lunch. Mum and Samson were sitting at the head of a rounded table, talking with Rab who sat on Samson's left, and Linden and Marigold

Barberry on Rab's left. On their right were Elfreda Babick, Clotilda Aceldama and Wyman Aceldama. The children sat on a square table with Horace Aceldama and me at the end, Reid and Oleander Barberry on our right, and Hyacinth Barberry and Elvie on our left.

Wyman and Clotilda Aceldama were butchers. Mrs Aceldama, or Tilly to her friends, was a large, talkative woman with a round, ruddy face. Mr Aceldama was an average looking, balding man. His pinched face gave him the impression of being unimpressed with everything around him. He had been a friend of my father's from childhood. Their son, Horace, took after his mother in appearance, but didn't appear to have any personality at all.

Linden Barberry looked like a tree stump. He had a tuft of brown hair sprouting from the top of his square head and a scruffy beard. He was a sensible man, though quite blunt at times, which gave an accidental impression of rudeness. Mrs Barberry was the opposite of her husband. Where he was short and wide, she was tall and slim. It looked as though she could be blown over by a light wind at any moment. She was extremely shy, to the extent that sometimes she couldn't bring herself to speak even when asked a direct question.

As for their children, I got on with them as well as I did with Horace. At thirteen Hyacinth was the eldest. I didn't know much about her as I had hardly ever heard her speak. Reid and Oleander, the twins, were a year younger than their sister. They both had their mother's willowy features, though Oleander was much shorter.

Mrs Babick was as senile as she was old. Her skin was so wrinkled she looked more like raisin than a person. She walked with a cane and her hands shook but she wasn't frail. I wouldn't be surprised if she outlived us all.

I heard the sound of Mrs Aceldama's loud voice booming across the room. 'And last week, we had our prize bull stolen, didn't we Wyman? Just ready for the slaughter, he was too. Would have been prize meat for the shop. It must be those uncouth children running wild in our village, no other explanation for it. And as for the parents, there are none. No parents to speak of. They've left their children to terrorise the rest of us. Shocking, it really is.'

I shook my head and suppressed an indulgent smile at their discussion of the recent string of vanishing food and livestock in the village. Most people put it down to foxes or wolves, but the Aceldamas always had their own ideas.

'I shouldn't worry, Tilly,' replied Mr Barberry, who seemed as unimpressed with the Aceldama's outlandish ideas as I was. 'I'm sure that your business won't be in any danger because of one cow.'

'I remember,' croaked Mrs Babick, causing everyone to pause their conversations and look up at the old widow. 'When theft was the least of our worries. We had to travel through ten feet of snow at the break of day with all our goods if we wanted to get to market. And if we didn't trade at market, we didn't earn a living, and if we didn't earn a living we didn't eat! One winter my parents barely had enough money to feed themselves, let alone the seven of us children. That was the year we lost Betsy, and all my toenails dropped off on the same day. What are you staring at Rab? Pass me that butternut squash, would you, my old arms can't be hauling plates across the table.'

I watched as everyone went back to their conversations and Rab passed a bowl to Mrs Babick. He looked up and winked at me, and I lowered my head, snickering at Mrs Babick's inane babble.

The moment passed and I sighed. I suddenly didn't want to be sitting here with all these people. I got up and walked into the kitchen on the pretence of refilling my cup from the water jug. As I turned I noticed a figure standing in the doorway and realised that Rab had followed me.

He closed the kitchen door, drowning out the noise from the dinning room, and studied my face. 'What's going on with you, kid? Is this about your mother and Samson? Even you must see how happy they are and I know you wouldn't want to deny your mother happiness.'

I shook my head, 'Of course not, it isn't that.'

'Well what then? Come on, you know you can trust me with anything.'

I wanted to tell him everything but part of me felt I should keep my mouth shut. I decided on a compromise.

'Let's say you were given the opportunity to do something good, not just good, great. But it was dangerous and you would have to leave everything you know behind. Would you do it?'

Rab furrowed his eyebrows in thought. 'Well that sounds like a tricky situation. All right, since you've been so vague here's what I'll say. Lilyworth is a small village, filled with small people, in a small kingdom. I've watched you grow from a boy into a young man and I think you could do so much more than all of this. You have nothing to prove but if you wanted to I know you could do anything you put your mind to. You just need to have faith in yourself the way I do, the way your mother and sister do. They way your father did. I know he would be proud of who you are now, so whatever decision you make I know it will be the right one.'

I felt touched by his words. Confidence flooded through me. 'Thank you Rab.'

'No problem, kid. Hope it helped. Now come on, there's still a whole lot of food to be eaten in there.'

Rab turned and walked back into the dining room. I was left alone in the kitchen with a plan already forming in my mind.

10
Drammear

Finding the courage to make my decision had taken such a long time that I was anxious for there to be no delay in telling Mera so as not to give me the opportunity to change my mind again. The next morning I rose early, donning my cloak and making the journey to Drammear. By the time I reached the city my shoes were muddied and my legs tired, but I didn't stop.

I knew exactly where she would be. In the days leading up to the new year she could be found on the streets outside the castle gates with her lady's maids giving food to the poor.

The city was usually empty at this time of the morning. In a few hours the streets would be bustling with people selling their wares at market, but for most of the year this hour was reserved for sleep. On this day, however, those who were able would gather in the street to get the best of the food. The street was dotted with people, half asleep and wrapped tightly in their cloaks to keep them protected from the bitter wind.

Mera was on the main parade when I found her. She wore the plain brown dress that all women in service to the royal family wore, the royal crest stitched just below the left shoulder. I made my way along the street towards the carts lined with food.

I slipped into an empty stall next to the uncharacteristically quiet tavern. It had windblown coverings hanging from the beams above it through which I watched Mera approaching. She walked close to my hiding place with one of her maids. In her arms she carried baskets full of bread and meat. She wasn't close enough that I could hear what she was saying but I saw her lips moving as she handed food to an old woman who sat alone in a doorway.

I pushed apart the curtain so that if she were to look my way she would see me. When her maid turned back to the cart I whistled, staying just long enough for her to turn and catch my eye, before ducking back behind the curtain. A few seconds later her surprised face appeared in front of me.

'What are you doing here?' she whispered, placing her baskets on the floor.

'It's good to see you too,' I smiled, leaning forward to hug her.

'Well, yes, of course,' she said, hugging me tightly before pulling back. 'I'm just a little confused. Are you here to help?'

'No,' I shook my head. 'I'm here to tell you; I'm ready.'

She looked confused a moment longer, the crease on her forehead forming a slight 'v' shape between her eyebrows, but then she beamed.

'Really? Are you sure?'

'I am. I had a talk with an old friend. He reminded me that opportunities like this only come along once in a lifetime. Besides, you always said it, if you have the chance to help someone you should take it.'

'I'm so glad. I'm just so glad. You're really coming?'

I almost laughed. 'Yes, I'm coming. But before we leave I need to know something. What exactly happens when we find Skara Brae?'

'Actually that would be down to you,' she admitted.

'Down to me? What do you mean?'

'You remember I told you about the spell that will release the Sisterhood? You have to be the one to perform it. Your magic is stronger than mine. You can do it. I know you can.'

Mera's words hit me like a gale force wind.

'You clearly have a lot of faith in me to believe me capable of that,' I muttered, suddenly unsure.

'Of course I do, Lex. You're extraordinary. You have to stop thinking of yourself as second rate. Don't give me that look, I know you do and it simply isn't true,' she took my hands in hers. 'You are important. And you can do this, you'll see.'

I felt a strange sense of pride at Mera's words. I smiled slightly awkwardly. 'If you believe in me Mera, it must be true.'

Mera beamed. 'Excellent. Then we must leave right away. There are some preparations I have to make. Pack as much food as you can. I've putting money away so I'll bring that. And the ingredients for the spell, of course, it wouldn't do much good to leave without those. Will you be ready by nightfall?'

I nodded, not trusting my voice enough in that moment to speak.

'Good,' she nodded to herself. 'I have to get back before they notice I'm missing. I'll see you at midnight, then. By the hut, as usual.'

I nodded again and she hugged me quickly before picking up her basket and walking back through the rippling curtain. I stood for a moment, slightly dazed and missing her arms around me. I shook myself and I too made my way out of the empty stall. I drew my cloak around myself and hurried home.

11

The last sunrise

I made my way back home as quickly as possible. Mud and other muck from the city streets covered my boots. The sun was rising rapidly now. It illuminated the cotton clouds in an array of reds, pinks and oranges. It struck me that this would be my last sunrise here. I let the light soak into my skin, trying to memorise the feeling.

The dawn chorus had reached its peak as I got to the outskirts of the village. I quickened my pace, anxious to return home before Mum noticed I was missing. I snuck inside, sliding the lock into place. I heard movement from Mum and Samson's room so I hurried to mine, whipping off my cloak, toeing off my muddy shoes and shoving them under the bed. I slid under the covers, pulling the scratchy blanket up to my chin so that no one could see I was fully dressed.

I lay as still as possible trying to quiet my breathing. Elvie rose as the sun began to fill the room. I feigned sleep while she rustled about getting ready for the day. As soon as she left the room I rolled over and sighed.

Eventually I dragged myself out of bed and traipsed towards the door. I opened it quietly and leant against the frame. Elvie sat at the dining room table sleepily munching on a bowl of steaming porridge. Mum sat next to her with some clothes she was folding into neat piles. Samson must have left for the forge earlier that morning. I was reminded of a day not long after my dad's death when Mum still bore the signs of the nightly tears she cried for him. She held Elvie tightly to her with one hand while the other rested on the table. Mrs Barberry sat beside her holding her free hand while Mrs Babick peered at them from across the table.

Mrs Barberry spoke in her soft voice. 'You must find work, Kate. It's no good for you to sit here with nothing but memories to comfort you. Please, consider it.'

'She's right, you know,' Mrs Babick added, smacking her lips. 'Why, even an old crone like myself must keep busy. I often say occupation is the best remedy for any ill. Why do you think I've lived this long? I'm simply too busy to die. Hah!'

'But how am I to care for two young children all by myself,' Mum sighed.

'I'm not denying that times will be hard, but you have to keep going for when they're good again. Come and work in the shop, at least until you find your feet,' Mrs Barberry insisted.

'She's right again, Katherine,' Mrs Babick fixed Mum with her strangely pale eyes. 'You have the courage of a woman and a mother. Suffer you may, but in the end you will always return having bettered your misfortunes.'

Mum sighed again. It was then that she noticed me.

'Alex, sweetheart,' she tried to smile. 'I didn't know you were awake.'

'Don't hover there, boy,' chastised Mrs Babick. 'People who stand in doorways are neither coming nor going.'

I scurried over to Mum. She lifted me onto her lap and pulled me into a hug. I clutched her tightly and whispered, 'Are you sick?'

'No, my darling,' she replied. 'I'm fine, I'm just fine.'

She had not been fine, of course, but over time she had pulled herself out of the darkness into which she had fallen. It had been difficult at first but her courage was unwavering and in the end she landed on her feet.

'Alex,' Mum's voice pulled me out of my reverie. 'You're awake. Would you like some breakfast?'

I nodded, not trusting myself to speak for the lump that had formed in my throat. I stepped forward, ruffling Elvie's hair as I sat in the seat next to her. She glared at me, munching grumpily on her oats.

'Morning,' I grinned.

She grunted in response.

'I was thinking that today we could go up to Herron Hill and build snow forts,' I suggested. She had been begging me for weeks to take her up there so I knew she would jump at the chance.

Her head shot up immediately. 'Really?'

'Yes, really,' I smiled as Mum placed a bowl of porridge in front of me.

'That's a lovely idea, Alex,' Mum smiled gently at me. 'What's brought this on?'

'Oh, nothing really,' I lied. 'I just thought we should make good use of the snow.'

'Well don't forget to wrap up warm,' Mum reminded us. 'I don't want either of you getting sick.'

Elvie was now scoffing down her food so fast it was almost flying off her spoon.

'Slow down Elle, you'll choke,' Mum said in a reproving voice.

Elvie began speaking, but found her mouth was too full to form coherent words. She swallowed, and began again. 'But I want to play with Lex.'

'Well we can't go just yet. We promised Mum we'd go to the market for her and get a new part for the loom, didn't we? And you said you wanted to get something for Samson to thank him for all the candles,' I reminded her.

'Oh. Yeah,' Elvie muttered, deflating slightly.

I picked up a cloth and wiped porridge from her chin. 'We'll go afterwards, I promise.'

'All right,' she nodded enthusiastically.

Elvie and I made our way into the village through the thick snow that covered the path. Elvie was so wrapped up in winter clothes to protect her from the biting cold that she looked nothing more than a bundle of fabric. She grinned at me from behind three layers of scarves, her un-brushed hair poking out from behind an old woolly hat that had once belonged to me. I took a moment to memorise the look of joy on her face.

At market I quickly found the new piece for the loom. In order to get out of the cold I chivvied Elvie along, hoping she would find something for Samson as fast as possible. In the end she picked out an old wood pipe with a magpie carved into the one side and an ambling hedgehog on the other.

'Do you think that he'll like it?' she asked, tracing the image of the hedgehog.

'I'm sure he'll love it, Elvie,' I said, my hand gripping firmly on her shoulder to keep from losing her in the crowd.

After Elvie chose her gift I looked for a new bag. The one I currently had was much too small and riddled with holes. Eventually I found one that was large enough to carry a good number of supplies and looked much less likely to give out at any moment. The man I bought it from showed me how a sleeping mat could be rolled up and tied to the bag using the straps at the bottom. I thanked him and Elvie and I made our way back home.

I was beginning to feel a mounting sense of dread. I knew I would have to talk to Mum soon. In a few short hours I would be saying goodbye to my family with no idea when or if I'd ever been seeing them again. I did my best to ignore the nagging ball of fear that had settled in my stomach as Elvie and I made our way to Herron Hill.

In the fading light we sat in our snow fort huddled together for warmth. We'd spent the last few hours laughing and playing together in the snow. I began to sing a local song about a boy who left home and Elvie joined in when she recognised it,

'Oh the young man said to his mother one day,
"Mother I've got to go."
She said, "But son, how will we go on?"
He said, "Mother I've got to go."
'Oh the young man said to his father one day,
"Father I'm leaving for good."
He said, "Who then will bring summer harvest in?"
He said, "Father I'm leaving for good."
'Oh the young man said to his brother one day,
"Brother I'm saying goodbye.'
He said, "How will we know when we'll see you again?"
He said, 'Brother I'm saying goodbye."
So the young man packed up his things and went
To find his own way then,
But the world wasn't kind and so he returned
And he never left home again.'

It was now that I had planned to say goodbye to her, to ask for her forgiveness for abandoning her, but I found that words failed me. Instead I put my arms around her and pulled her tiny body against mine so that my chin rested on her head.

'Are you all right?' her voice echoed slightly in our icy cave.

'Of course I am,' I replied. 'I'm fine. I'm just fine.'

It was after dinner that I found my chance to talk to Mum. I knew Samson would be going to the tavern with Rab so he would be out for the evening. Elvie was tired from our day in the snow so she went to bed early. I cleared the table while Mum pulled out her sewing. I pressed my shaking palms together in an attempt to calm myself.

'Mum,' I began, taking the seat opposite her.

'Yes dear?' she replied without looking up from the shirt she was stitching.

'There's something I need to talk to you about. Something important,' I said, trying to ignore the shake in my voice.

Mum looked up at me. 'Of course, dear. You can tell me anything,' She placed her work down on the table and levelled me with a look of motherly concern.

'W-well…' I stuttered, wishing I had planned ahead what I was going to say. 'I'm leaving, Mum.'

Her mouth fell open in shock.

'What do you mean you're leaving?' she demanded, her eyes wide in surprise.

'I mean that I'm leaving here. I'm leaving Lilyworth. I have to leave, it's… it's important,' I replied.

'Is this about Sam?' she prompted, her confusion growing.

'No, Mum, I promise that it's got nothing to do with Samson. Please understand, if it wasn't so important I wouldn't be leaving,' I reached out to grab her hand.

'What then?' she murmured, a mixture of confusion and sadness evident on her face.

'It's… Mum, I…' I hesitated, unsure of how much I should tell her.

The truth, I thought. *I owe her the whole truth.*

And so I began from the moment I met Mera, to her asking me to go with her to Skara Brae, to our first feeble attempts at magic. At some point she had drawn her hand back and now it fluttered around her mouth. She looked utterly crestfallen.

'Oh gods,' she breathed. 'How could I not have seen? I should have seen.'

'Mum, please don't be upset. You understand, don't you, why I have to go, why it's so important. It's what Dad would have wanted,' I knew that it was callous to bring my father into this, but I wanted to prove to her how serious I was.

Apparently, however, I had miscalculated the impact it would have. She was shaking her head now, her hands both flat on the table and a glint of anger in her eye. I noticed my mistake too late.

'No,' she muttered, then again more fiercely. 'No. That is not what he would have wanted. He sacrificed himself so that you could be safe, so that you could live a full and happy life, not so you could run off and get yourself killed.'

'But I'm never as alive as when I'm practicing magic,' I insisted. 'It's a part of who I am now and I can't turn my back on it.'

'How can you be so selfish?' she stood suddenly, looking down on me with a bitterness I had never seen before. 'How can you have such disregard for me, for your sister?' she cried.

My voice rose to meet hers. 'I don't want to leave you. But I've made a promise now and I can't go back on it.'

'It's that girl, isn't it?' she hissed. 'She's the one who has you abandoning us for magic.'

I took a deep breath to steady the rush of emotions that crashed into me at her words.

'Mum,' I pleaded, eyes closed, hands pressed together. 'You cannot blame Mera for this. It was my decision. I have the power to help people, I should use it.'

For a moment I thought she was going to shout at me again, but then her face crumpled. She seemed to fold in on herself as though she were deflating. Her hands flew to her face and I heard the sound of muffled sobs.

I rose quickly and went to her.

'Please don't cry,' I pleaded as I put my arms around her.

'I just- I just,' she stammered.

'I know,' I nodded, stroking her hair soothingly. 'I'm sorry Mum, but it's going to be all right.'

But I could feel her shaking her head against my shoulder.

'I can't lose you too, Alex. Not you too.'

She moved and I released her. She ducked her head low to wipe away the tears on her face.

'We'll talk about it tomorrow,' she muttered, moving away towards her bedroom. 'No more tonight.'

I felt my heart sink.

'Mum,' I called out, desperate that the last thing she heard from me was wasn't said in anger. 'I love you.'

Mum's smile was tight but she replied, 'I love you too,' before walking into her room and closing the door behind her.

I sat at the dining room table for a while after Mum had gone to bed, saying goodbye to the place that had been my home all these years. Eventually I dragged myself into my room and sunk into my bed. I had to wait until Samson got home before I could leave. He often checked on Elvie before heading to bed himself. Now that I thought about it he was probably checking on me as well.

After a while I heard the front door open and close. A minute later the bedroom door opened a fraction. There was a short pause as he made sure we were both safely tucked up in bed before the door closed again. I hopped up and grabbed my new pack from under my bed. I had tied a sleeping mat to the bottom and in it I had packed all the food I could, a change of clothes, a spare cloak and a handful of silver coins, all the money I had saved. I tiptoed over to where Elvie was sleeping peacefully and kissed her on the forehead.

'Goodbye, Elvie. I'll see you again,' I promised, before making my way over to the door.

I listened closely to make sure Samson had gone to bed before pushing the door open. The room was deserted. I had planned on leaving a note for Mum, but there was nothing else I could say to her. Instead I lifted my dad's pendant over my head and put it on the table. I took one last look around the room before slinging my pack over my shoulder and heading out the door.

I reached the hut just before midnight. A fire was already glowing inside. I found Mera sitting on the floor studying a map. She looked up as I came through the door.

'You're here, brilliant,' she grinned. She rolled up the map. 'Are you ready?'

I nodded. 'You?'

'I think so.' she stuffed the map into her bag and came to stand in front of me, looking serious. 'Last chance to turn back.'

I shook my head. 'No way.'

Mera grinned again. 'Let's go then.'

She extinguished the fire and I followed her out of the hut.

12

The Hooded Hermit

Mera and I were walking through the dark along an open, muddy path. The light had faded some hours ago. We'd walked through the night and all day to get as far from the city as possible. We had made good progress, stopping only occasionally for food or a short rest. I could already feel my boots rubbing uncomfortably and my hands were going numb from the cold. We were heading for an inn that Mera had passed on a journey she took to Seion, the kingdom on Culrain's northern border.

'We should stop soon,' I suggested, rubbing my tired eyes. 'And eat. I don't think we're going to find that inn.'

'It's got to be on this road. I remember it wasn't far past the last crossing. Two, maybe three miles at most,' Mera insisted.

'But you were in a carriage then. It might've been further than you thought and we don't want to be walking all night,' I reasoned. 'I say we give it ten minutes more and then we find somewhere to camp.'

'All right, ten minutes.'

We fell back into silence as we walked on. I looked ahead, straining to see any light that would suggest life but there was nothing. Somewhere in the distance a fox called to its mate and another screamed back. An owl hooted at us indignantly. I felt uneasy walking in the dark, as though unseen eyes were watching me. Presently I heard something other than the noise of The Great Forest that stood to our right. I looked ahead and saw a small path leading off to the left.

'I can hear people,' said Mera before I could say anything. 'And those are lights at the end of that path. See, I told you we were close.'

'Finally,' I muttered, thinking only of soft beds and feathery pillows. The pack I was carrying had been getting heavier and heavier the further we walked.

We turned onto the path and sure enough a few minutes later the bright lights of an inn were leading us to its doorstep. I could hear loud cheering and laughter from inside. *The Hooded Hermit* was painted in bright red lettering on a dark sign that swung creakily in the slight wind. The building's unusual brick spire towered over us as we dashed through the door and into the warmth inside.

The inn was loud and brightly lit. Candles glowed on heavy wooden tables and in thick metal holders on the walls. People sat dotted around the room, chatting and drinking. In the corner was a large table where a group of rowdy men were playing a game of cards.

'Hood,' I muttered.

'What?' Mera replied, startled.

'Put your hood up, someone might see you,' I explained.

'Oh yes,' she tugged up her hood and we moved over to the bar.

The barman looked up as we approached. He was fairly tall, with a wide face and ruddy cheeks, wild, mousy brown hair and a brilliant moustache.

'What can I do for you?' he asked in a slow, warm voice.

'We were hoping that you would have a room free?' asked Mera, keeping her head bowed.

The barman cast a slightly suspicious eye over her and replied, 'I do as a matter a fact. That'll be eight crowns for the night then, Miss…'

'Kirkton. Thank you, we'll take it,' she said, bringing out her leather pouch from the pocket of her cloak.

Trying not to yawn while Mera paid for the room, I looked around the inn. I noticed a poster nailed to the wall behind the bar. Mera's face stared out at me from the page and the caption underneath read, *10 000 crowns for any information pertaining to the whereabouts of HRH Princess Mera of Culrain.* My heart lurched in my chest. I turned, quickly scanning the room, half expecting to see the Royal Guard advancing, but no one was taking any notice of us.

'You all right there, son?' the barman asked, handing the key over to Mera, who looked at me questioningly.

'Yes, fine,' I muttered, clearing my throat. 'What's all this then?' I nodded to the poster.

'Oh that. Well, would you know, the castle's gone and lost the princess. The Royal Guard came storming in here, not above an hour ago, demanding that we put up these posters. Caused quite a ruckus, they did. As if it'll help. And I asked them, what's the princess supposed be doing in my inn?' he chuckled, his moustache shaking. 'They didn't find that very amusing though. Just told me to put up the posters and report any information back to the castle immediately. Anyway, where did you say you were from?'

'Dunlow,' I answered, naming a town in the south of Culrain. 'My cousin and I are heading to the village of Corracullen to visit our family.'

'Ah, I see,' he nodded. 'Long journey.'

'It certainly is and we've been travelling all day, so if you'll excuse us we'd like to take our things to our room,' said Mera.

'Of course, didn't mean you keep now, Miss Kirkton,' he replied, smiling. He turned and called through the doorway behind him. 'Ned! My son'll show you to your room.'

A boy no older than eight or nine came racing through the door, smiling widely. He had the same round face as his father.

'Room eighteen,' said the barman, and Ned scampered off towards the stairs, beckoning for us to follow.

'Thank you,' I said, picking up my pack and following Mera to the stairs, eager to get as far away from the poster as possible.

The boy took us up two very crooked flights of stairs and along a winding corridor before stopping outside room eighteen. He bade us goodnight even though it was barely six o'clock and hurried back downstairs.

The room was small but cosy. There was an identical bed on both sides and a dresser below a small, murky window that looked out across a courtyard and into the fields beyond it. I slung my pack onto one of the beds and turned to look at Mera who had taken off her cloak and was folding it over the back of the chair, looking worried.

'It's going well, isn't it?' I muttered darkly.

'We've been gone a day. One day. How could they possibly get out here that fast? They're normally much more incompetent than this. Maybe...' she trailed off, sinking onto the bed and looking thoughtful.

'We'll just have to be more careful. Keep your hood up anywhere public, and we should really stay off the main roads. I know it'll be more difficult, and a lot slower, but we didn't get into this for comfort. It's better to be safe than sorry. Mera?'

Mera was still staring off into the distance. She jumped when I said her name.

'Sorry, Lex. Yes you're right. We should stay off the paths,' she nodded in agreement.

'Are you all right? Not thinking of turning back are you?' I asked, only half joking.

'What? No, of course not,' she looked surprised. 'I was just lost in my thoughts. Let's unpack.'

A few minutes later, after she had unpacked nothing but a few maps, Mera spoke. 'We should get something to eat and go to bed. We need the rest and the earlier we head off, the better. I think I've found a route we can take that will keep us off the main roads.'

'Can we just rest for a moment first?' I asked, lying back on my bed and sighing. It was neither as soft nor the pillow as feathery as I had imagined, but it was a relief nonetheless. 'I have to take these boots off.'

'If you want,' said Mera, not looking up from her maps.

Still lying down, I pulled up my foot and wrenched off my shoe.

'Ah,' I sighed in relief, slipping off the other one too.

'Those shoes are falling to bits,' she commented.

'Shoes are expensive,' I muttered.

'Maybe we should ask the innkeeper if he has any old ones he can give you. He might, you never know,' she suggested.

'All right, I'll ask when we go down for dinner.'

'I'll go now if you want,' she offered. 'I want to look around, anyway. You can stay here and rest.'

'Is that a good idea?' I asked, sitting up. 'What if someone sees you?'

'I'll be careful, don't worry. Stay here. I'll be back in a bit.'

Mera left the room. I lay back down, listening to the muffled sound of merriment downstairs. It struck me then that this would be the first time Mera and I would spend the night together. Unbidden, a feeling of anticipation rose in me. Again the feeble hope that the two of us being together on this quest would break her resolve entered my mind. What did she think of us sharing a room? Perhaps she too wondered at the possibility. Perhaps she would change her mind.

But Mera would never change her mind, not once it was so firmly set. I turned onto my side feeling stupid and absurd when the door sprung open and Mera came crashing back in.

'What's wrong?' I asked, noting her dishevelled hair and panic-stricken face.

'We have to leave,' she panted, throwing a pair of mouldy shoes my way before running over to her bed and picking up the maps spread out across it.

'What are you talking about? What happened?' I jumped up and watched her hurriedly stuffing the maps into her pack.

'Well I had just collected the shoes from the innkeeper and I was coming upstairs when I knocked into someone who was passing the other way. My hood fell back,' she explained.

'Did they recognise you?' I asked, panicked.

'I'm not sure,' she admitted. 'They didn't say anything, but they looked right at me. It would only take them walking over to the bar and seeing that poster for them to put two and two together. We have to leave, now. Quickly, pack you things.'

I didn't need any more prompting. I stuffed my old shoes on as fast as possible, throwing the ones Mera had found into my bag to try later. We scurried out of the room, Mera hoisting her hood as far over her head as possible. At the bottom of the stairs we paused, peering into the busy room beyond. There was no way we could get through there without being noticed.

'Maybe we should find another way out,' I suggested.

'Good idea. There must be a back way,' Mera agreed.

Mera turned and led me down another corridor. It took us out into the deserted courtyard we'd been looking down on from our room. There were no torches here. We had only the light of the moon to guide us. At the back was a small gate, which led into the fields behind the inn. Without a moment to lose we hoisted our packs over our shoulders and ran out through the gate into the darkness beyond.

13

The manor house

We had left *The Hooded Hermit* two days ago and hadn't been to another inn since. Not daring to enter places where Mera might be recognised, we followed the fields northeast along the edge of The Great Forest. Our route, while not the quickest way to Skara Brae, had the advantage of being uninhabited. With all the stories of dangerous creatures living there people tended to avoid it. With a little bit of luck we would be able to sidestep any unwelcome encounters.

It was bitterly cold. We were walking across an open field, pulling our cloaks tighter around us, trying to retain the smallest bit of warmth. The earth was frozen solid, the crisp grass crunching underfoot where Jack Frost had sprung through the air casting a glimmering sheen over the ground. The frigid wind nipped at my fingers through the small holes in my gloves.

Sudden movement by the line of trees caught my attention. Despite the harsh winter they were full and green with a fine dusting of silver frost. Someone was standing by them, cutting off branches and examining each one before placing it into the little wicker basket at their feet. As we got closer I could see that it was a young woman with dark, silky hair braided neatly into a long plait that fell to her waist and swayed slightly as she moved. She was small and slight and looked almost frozen in the icy winter air. White clouds billowing around her as she breathed, glimmering slightly in the low sunlight.

'Look at that, Lex,' Mera's voice caught me by surprise and I turned quickly. She stood pointing with a pink finger towards the trees in front of us. I saw a high chimney poking over the top with smoke pouring out of it.

'There must be a house there. Maybe they'll let us warm ourselves by the fire for a while,' she spoke with excitement and started forward eagerly, but I grabbed her arm to stop her.

'Wait. Maybe we should ask her first,' I nodded towards the girl still standing by the trees.

Mera glanced over at her and narrowed her eyes with suspicion. 'What is she doing?'

'I'm not sure,' I replied. 'But she probably works at that house.'

'I don't know. She might not. She could be anyone. We should go straight to the house,' she said.

'Come on Mera, she doesn't look dangerous. Besides, we don't know who lives in that house. Maybe we shouldn't go there. Remember what happened the last time we went somewhere full of strangers,' I pointed out.

'I suppose,' she muttered. 'But I doubt this house will be full of drunken men looking for any extra cash they can get their grubby hands on.'

'I wouldn't call ten thousand-'

'Fine,' Mera cut me off. 'We'll do it your way.'

She pushed past me and made her way over to the girl. I trailed after her. Mera lifted the hood of her clock to cover her face.

The girl turned as we approached and looked at us with curiosity. She had a sweet, round face and large, dark brown eyes. She looked like she might be the same age as me. Her skin was a warm brown. She moved a slender hand to push her long braid over her shoulder.

'Can I help you?' she asked in a soft, bright voice. She blinked her dark eyes at me and for a moment I didn't know what to say.

'Hello,' Mera began. 'Do you belong to the house over there? We've been travelling for a long time and need a place to stay.'

'I do,' she replied. 'My master is away from home at the moment but I'm sure the housekeeper will be able to tend to you.'

'That's great. I'm Mia and this is my cousin, Lex,' she unconsciously shifted the hood of her cloak, making sure her face was half in shadow. 'Are you able to take us to the housekeeper?'

'Of course. My name's Ilyssa. It's nice to meet you,' Ilyssa smiled.

Before I could stop myself I blurted out, 'What are you doing with that tree?'

She turned to me. 'I'm taking pine branches to spread around the house. My master particularly enjoys the smell of the outdoors despite not actually wanting to spend any time there. Mrs Granite wants it to be fresh for his return.'

'Oh. Right.'

Ilyssa picked up the basket. 'It's this way. Follow me.'

Before I even knew what I was doing my feet were moving and I was trailing behind her. I felt Mera's eyes on my back as we walked after her but didn't turn around.

We walked on in silence. As we rounded the line of trees I saw a huge house ahead of us. It looked more like a warring fort than a place where people actually lived. It had castle-like turrets and hundreds of tiny slits in the walls where archers could shoot their arrows into the enemy below. There was a high, wrought iron gate that ran around the grounds, sealing it in. Despite its unwelcoming presence I was eager to get inside. My hands were beginning to go numb from the cold.

Ilyssa took out a key from the pocket of her dress and unlocked the black gates. They creaked ominously when she pushed them open. 'Welcome to Deathgrove,' Ilyssa said as we passed through.

'Deathgrove,' Mera repeated. 'Cheerful.'

'I know,' Ilyssa replied. 'The house is said to be haunted. It's built on the site of an old cemetery, that's where it gets its name. I don't believe it of course but sometimes when I'm working late at night I'll hear something or see something out of the corner of my eye. There's never anything there though.'

I sincerely hoped she was joking but didn't have time to ask because we had reached the heavy oak front door. As we stepped inside a feeling of warmth enveloped me. My fingers prickled unpleasantly as they began to regain feeling. I saw a fire crackling in a room off the hall and a pack of large, black dogs warming themselves by the hearth. They looked up as we walked in and growled.

'There you are girl. Finally! What took you so long?' a harsh voice called from the top of the stairs. A large woman in an ugly brown dress was hurrying towards us. 'I thought you weren't coming back. And when I couldn't find that inept brother of yours I thought the two of you had run off. But of course even you aren't that stupid, are you? Saying that, I still haven't found the boy. I suppose he's down at the tavern again, squandering my master's money. He deserves a whipping for that, he does. More trouble than he's worth. I don't know why the master keeps you. Useless, insolent and expensive, that's all you are, the pair of you. Now I hope you're done with that pine because you've got to place it sharpish. But mind it's not visible, girl. The master don't want to see bits of tree poking out from under the mantelpiece. And once you've done that you need to light the fire in the master's room. Your brother was supposed to do it but once again he's neglected his work so you'll have to pick up his slack. Oh and you need to finish mending those clothes.

Goodness knows how long I've been asking you to do that! Who are you?'

I wanted to step back from under the woman's imposing glare. She had a red face and bloodshot eyes. She had scraped her greying hair into a tight bun that was pulling her wrinkling skin taut. I imaged how her face would sag when she took it out.

Ilyssa stepped forward and said, 'Alaric said he wasn't feeling well this morning. He'll be in bed. I'll check for you Mrs Granite.' Mrs Granite didn't look too impressed by this explanation, but Ilyssa carried on regardless. 'And this is Mia and Lex. They're travellers looking for a place to stay for the night.'

Mrs Granite swelled with indignation. 'A place to stay for the night! Are you really as stupid as you look, girl? Bringing strangers who cover their faces into your master's house! Well I'll have none of it. Out! Out this instant! They're probably thieves and murders. I don't want the likes of you disgracing this respectable place,' she looked almost on the point of physically pushing us out when Mera stepped forward.

She pushed her hood back and looked directly at Mrs Granite who, luckily, showed no signs that she recognised her. 'Please ma'am, we don't mean any harm or disrespect to you or your master. We have been travelling for days and wish to entreat upon your kindness for food and rest. Of course, as I am sure a woman of your intelligence can tell, we don't expect anything for free. We will work our part. Perhaps I can help Ilyssa mending those clothes and my cousin can take over her brother's work. He's stronger than he looks.'

Mrs Granite cast a critical eye over me. She seemed, however, to have been calmed enough by Mera's sycophantic speech to be reasonable.

'All right, I suppose we may need the extra help what with the master coming home so soon and Alaric shirking his responsibilities. But I can't have you taking up unnecessary space. You'll have to sleep in their room. It's that or the stables. Ilyssa, don't just stand there, girl, take them up to your room and prepare their beds. Then you two girls can get to work on those clothes. You'd better be finished before the master returns or there'll be trouble. And you, boy, have Alaric show you his duties, and make sure he does them too. Sick or not he has to work for the master's kindness just like the rest of us, the lazy toad. And somebody needs to light the fire in the master's room. Well get on with it,' and with that she strode across the hall and disappeared into another room.

'Well, she's a delight,' commented Mera.

'She's not that bad really. It's the master you want to watch out for. He's got eyes in the back of his head and a thirst for punishment,' explained Ilyssa, leading the way through a small door concealed behind the main staircase and up a set of rickety stairs. 'Mrs Granite's caprice is nothing compared with the master's sudden rages. The number of times Alaric has come back with bruises all over him. He never learns either. He's got a smart mouth but not a smart enough head to keep him out of trouble.'

'That's horrible,' I muttered. 'Why don't you leave?'

Ilyssa smiled. 'You sound like Alaric. Where would we go? How would we fend for ourselves? We haven't got any family left and nobody's going to accept two extra mouths to feed into their home. Besides, our parents died with a debt still owed to this household. The master would be after us in a second if we ran away.'

'You could find a way,' I persisted.

'But this is our home. It's all we've ever known. We're clothed and fed, which is a lot better than some can say. Besides, we have no experience with travelling. We would be lost within five minutes. That's enough about us. Where are you travelling? You never said.'

'We're going to visit some family in Corracullen. It's not far from here,' I repeated our established lie as we walked along a narrow corridor, passing doors with different names on them. We must have been at the top of the house now. We arrived at a door at the end of the hallway. The wood was old and cracked with the words 'Ilyssa and Alaric' on it in peeling white paint.

'This is the servants' quarters,' Ilyssa explained. 'Alaric and I share a room because the others are all full. We used to be in separate rooms but then the new footman arrived so Alaric had to move in with me.'

She unlatched the handle and pushed. The door opened with a groan revealing a small table and two beds on opposite sides of the room. It was going to be a bit of a squish with Mera and me here too. In the bed under the window someone lay sleeping, a tuft of thick, black hair stuck up from under the blanket, soft snores filling the room.

Ilyssa walked over to the bed and shook the person lying there, ignoring their groan of protest. 'Alaric, wake up. There are people here and Mrs Granite is looking for you.'

'Mrs Granite is a mean old hag to be nagging somebody with a blinding headache. Well, she's a mean old hag either way but this just proves it,' grumbled a muffled voice.

'Well if you hadn't been up all night drinking you wouldn't have a headache and Mrs Granite wouldn't need to be nagging you. Now get out of bed, lazy, we have company,' Ilyssa reached for the covers and threw them back exposing a copper skinned boy who looked about two years older than me and very muscular.

He turned over and blinked sleepily. 'Company?' he yawned and stretched. 'Who's this then?'

'This is Lex and Mia,' Ilyssa introduced us. 'They're travellers. Mrs Granite has said that they can stay here tonight. They're going to help us with our work today so please get up.'

I smiled weakly at him and Mera nodded. His eyes flicked between us for a moment before his face broke into a brilliant smile.

'Great,' he beamed, climbing out of bed and grabbing a shirt from the table. 'You can help me outside, Lex, is it?'

I nodded awkwardly. 'Yeah.'

'And Mia?' he added, scraping his hair back into a small bun.

'That's right,' Mera replied.

'Gotcha,' he grinned. 'All right then Lex, let's leave the girls to it.'

And with a surprising amount of energy he was striding off down the corridor with Ilyssa calling out after him, 'Don't forget to light the master's fire!'

'Yeah, yeah,' he called back.

I muttered a quick goodbye to Mera who waved me off and I followed after him.

Alaric took me out through the kitchens into the immaculate gardens, talking animatedly all the way. The lawns extended a long way back. I could just about see the edge of the forest through a misty haze.

'Wow,' I muttered. 'It's very... tidy.'

'The gods strike me down if there's a single blade of grass out of place. The master likes his order. Once when I broke something in his chambers, accidentally of course, he made me scrub the entire thing, top to bottom. I wasn't allowed to stop until the damn place was gleaming. Took me ages.'

'He sounds like a kind-hearted man,' I replied dryly.

'He's a piece of work is what he is. If it wasn't for Ilyssa I'd be as far away from this place as possible,' he said, kicking a pile of leaves so they scattered across the path. 'But she insists that we're better off here, so here we are.'

I wondered momentarily if we could take Ilyssa and Alaric with us but instantly realised it would be impossible. The way Alaric spoke about Ilyssa made me think of my own sister. She would know that I had gone by now. I wondered if Mum would tell her the truth.

I looked out across the grounds again and saw some of the hulking black dogs that had been sitting next to the fire earlier that morning. They skulked along the edge of the forest. My gaze seemed to draw their attention. As I watched they turned to look at us, their milky white eyes staring, their hackles raised. I shivered involuntarily. Alaric noticed where I was looking.

'Watch out for them,' he advised. 'I'm not scared of a lot, but those dogs… there's something not quite right there. He uses them sometimes, the master, as punishment. I've never done anything bad enough to warrant it, but I've seen it done.'

Alaric looked vaguely sick as a memory washed over him. The sound of snarling barks and tearing flesh entered my mind. I wanted to say something but felt like I was intruding on his business. Fortunately I was saved the necessity of speaking as we had arrived at the edge of the forest where an axe was laying against a block, a pile of wood just behind it.

'So, as I'm sure you can tell, we're chopping wood today. You've done it before, I assume.'

'I have,' I nodded.

'Great. I'll start. If you want to the put the wood on the block for me we can swap when I get tired.'

'No problem.'

It was hard work. I was soon sweating with exertion. The sun had risen over the tops of the trees and burned through the clouds so that by the time we had finished its heat was beating down on us. I couldn't help thinking that we would have done this much faster if we'd had magic to aid us.

While we were working Alaric had been telling me stories about life at Deathgrove. 'One time I was supposed to be helping Jack with the horses but instead I'd snuck into the kitchen to get something to eat. I hadn't had lunch because I'd been cleaning the candle wax I'd spilled all over Mrs Granite's carpet. Anyway, I was halfway through this delicious apple pie, right, when the cook comes in and catches me. She hit me over the head with a frying pan. I swear I saw stars. I've still got the scars from when she hit me with a glass bottle that time I knocked all the milk over.'

Alaric didn't appear to be fazed by any of the punishment he got for disobeying orders. I think the joy of annoying Mrs Granite outweighed any of the effects it might've had.

When we finished with the wood we had to muck out the stables and feed the horses. Weary from the work, I stood for a moment and stroked a beautiful bay with a tired hand. Alaric brought over a bucket of oaks and placed it on the floor for the horse.

'She's a real beauty, isn't she?' he asked, ruffling the horse's mane as it stretched down to eat the oats. 'If I could spend all day with these beasts I don't think I'd mind living here.'

'You really can't convince Ilyssa to leave?'

Alaric shook his head. 'No. She's scared that they'd come after us.'

'She said your parents died with a debt owed. What did she mean?' I asked.

Alaric hesitated.

'I'm sorry,' I backtracked. 'You don't have to tell me. That was rude.'

'No it's not that. I don't mind talking about it. It's just that I don't really know. All that the master ever said was that they owed him money and they died before they could pay him back. I was only a year or so old when they died so I don't remember.'

'I'm sorry,' I replied, secretly grateful for all the years I'd been able to spend with my dad before he passed away.

Alaric shrugged. 'Not your fault. Anyway, I don't know about you but I'm starving. Want to go in for lunch?'

I nodded and we made our way out of the stables and back towards the main house. When we arrived we found Mera and Ilyssa already in the kitchen laughing at a table on the far side.

'What are you ladies giggling about? Talking about me and my good looks, are you?' Alaric grinned, pushing past the cook, who scowled at him menacingly, to get to their table.

'No, you and your considerable ego,' replied Ilyssa.

'You wound me,' he joked. He pulled out a chair beside his sister and grabbed all the food within reach, wolfing it down hungrily.

I sat in a chair next to Mera. She smiled and passed me some bread and a plate of cold meats.

'So Lex,' Ilyssa said. 'How was working with Alaric?'

'Oh you know, slave driver that he is,' I joked.

Ilyssa laughed softly. 'Of course. Very hard working, my brother.'

'Oi,' Alaric cut in. 'I'm an exemplary worker I'll have you know.'

'Ha, I've never heard such a lie,' Ilyssa replied.

'To be fair we did a lot of work this morning,' I said, defending him.

'Thank you. See, Lex is on my side,' Alaric raised his eyebrows at his sister.

'Lex, how could you betray me like this?' Ilyssa joked.

'Calm down,' Mera muttered.

'Mera,' I chastised her.

But neither Ilyssa nor Alaric had heard her comment as they were now arguing about who did more work.

I turned to Mera and asked. 'So how was clothes-mending? Finally putting those sewing skills of yours to good use.'

Mera laughed. 'I was never really one for needlework, was I?'

'Oh well, I'm sure Ilyssa was more than up for the task,'

Mera bristled at my words. 'I can stitch, Lex. I'm not completely incompetent.'

'I know that,' I replied, taken aback. 'I didn't mean to upset you.'

'I'm not upset,' she sniffed.

'I know when you're upset, Mera. I just meant that Ilyssa probably does it all the time.'

'Oh well if Ilyssa-'

'You haven't done it yet? Oh Alaric, Mrs Granite will do her nut, and Gods know what the master will do,' Ilyssa's exasperated voice cut across Mera's angry one.

'What's wrong?' I asked.

'He still hasn't lit the fire in the master's room,' she explained. 'When Mrs Granite finds out-'

'Oh, who cares? Let him come home to a cold room for once, see how he likes it,' Alaric retorted.

'You'll care when he takes your dinner away from you again. Oh Alaric, just go and do it now. It won't take a minute,' she implored.

'No, I won't,' he retorted adamantly. 'If you want that fire lit so badly you'll have to do it yourself.'

'Well I'm not doing your work for you, that's for sure,' she said, going back to her sandwich. 'And when Mrs Granite's yelling herself hoarse at you, don't blame me.'

'Not to worry sweet sister, I think I'll be all right,' he smiled warmly.

Before Ilyssa could reply Mrs Granite came bursting into the kitchen with a face as red as beetroot shouting, 'He's here, he's here! Don't just sit there you useless children. Alaric, go and help Jack take the master's luggage. Cook, he'll be wanting food. He's had a long journey and after he's rested a while he'll be hungry. You two, just sit there and don't get in anybody's way,' she clicked her fingers. 'Come on, now!'

A flurry of movement and noise followed her words. Alaric leapt up, calling, 'See you later,' over his shoulder, Mrs Granite chivvying him out the door. The cook started firing off instructions and the scullery maid began running around, grabbing pans and dashing off again.

I saw Ilyssa darting towards the door and Mera called after her, 'Where are you going?'

'I have to light that fire!' she shouted back.

We didn't see either Alaric or Ilyssa for the rest of the day. The house was alive with activity. People were running back and forth and Mrs Granite was barking out orders like a ship's captain. Most of the time she made us keep to the room, claiming that she didn't want us flailing about under her feet. I had a growing curiosity to see the man who created all this commotion. When we crept down to the kitchens for supper we heard him talking to Mrs Granite in the room by the front entrance. I couldn't see his face. His chair was facing the fire and its high back masked any view of him. When the dog that lay next to him lifted its huge head and snarled in our direction again we scuttled off, afraid to be caught listening to their conversation.

We were in kitchen tucking into a bowl of chicken broth when Mera spoke.

'So you and Ilyssa seem to get along quite well.'

I hesitated with the spoon halfway to my mouth. 'Um, well yeah. I mean, don't you? You spent all morning with her.'

'Oh yes she's lovely,' Mera replied, tearing a piece of bread in two. 'She'd enchant anyone she meets.'

'I suppose,' I muttered, uncomfortable with where this conversation was heading. In truth Ilyssa's face had been filing my mind all day, and for some reason I didn't want Mera to know how much I liked our new friend.

She continued. 'I wouldn't blame anyone for falling in love with her.'

I sighed. 'What are you getting at?'

'Nothing. I'm just saying she's very pretty and bright. Someone would have to be mad not to take a shine to her.'

I put my spoon down. 'Well I suppose if that someone, having made no promises to anyone else, happened to find Ilyssa both pretty and bright, they would be well within their rights to fall for her.'

'Well… I suppose you would be correct.'

'I suppose I would.'

We both went back to our meals in silence.

By the time Alaric stumbled into the room that night and flopped onto his bed it was dark outside, and most of the lights in the house had been extinguished. He was asleep within minutes, snoring softly. Mera and I lay down on sleeping mats that had been squished into the tiny room. I must have fallen asleep because it was well past midnight when I was awoken by the sound of Ilyssa returning.

'Did I wake you?' she whispered. 'I'm sorry.'

'That's okay,' I replied.

'It's so late. What kept you so long?' I heard Mera's voice in the darkness and realised she must have woken up too.

'Oh the master needed this and then he needed that. Alaric often doesn't come back until the sun is beginning to rise. I mean, you'd think he'd want to sleep after travelling for so long but…' she trailed off with a yawn.

'Sounds like hard work,' I muttered.

'Well I can't exactly complain. Oh I'm so tired I can't even be bothered to change,' and with that she lay down and said no more.

I stretched out on my thin sleeping mat and sighed. I'd never had a job working for a master so I didn't know if it was normal to keep your servants deprived of sleep, but it didn't seem right to me.

'Are you awake?' Mera's voice cut across my thoughts a few minutes later.

'Yes,' I murmured.

'Do you think they're asleep?' she whispered.

I listened to Alaric's snores and Ilyssa's rhythmic breathing. 'Yes.'

Mera sat up. The moonlight that streamed through the window hit her face. She seemed to be mulling something over. Finally she muttered, 'Do you think there's anything we can do, Lex? For Ilyssa and Alaric, I mean. We can't just leave them here with these horrible people.'

'That's exactly what I was thinking. But if they don't want to leave I don't see what we can do. If they were to come with us-'

'They can't come with us,' she cut across me.

'No, I know, I was just saying that if they were to open to magic-'

'There's no point thinking about it because they can't.'

'Well all right but where else would they go? And think about it, they could actually help if-'

'Shh!' she cut across me.

'Don't shush me,' I said indignantly. 'I'm serious Mera, if they were open to-'

'No Lex, be quiet. I think I heard something outside.'

I turned towards the door, straining my ears to hear the sound of footsteps but there was nothing.

'I definitely heard something,' muttered Mera, getting up and stealing over to the door.

'Maybe it was a ghost,' I suggested half-heartedly.

'Don't be silly, Lex, there's no such thing as ghosts,' she said, although she didn't sound half as confidant as she had a minute ago. 'Come on then, let's see what's going on.'

'Are you serious? It's an old house. It probably creaks all the time. Really,' I implored. 'It's late, let's just go to sleep.'

'No, I'm going to see what it was. You can stay here if you want, but just think about how you left a poor, defenceless girl wander off in a strange house all on her own.'

I shook my head, thinking that *poor* and *defenceless* were the last words I'd choose to describe Mera, but I got up and edged over to her.

She twisted the handle of the door slowly and let it swing open with an ominous creak. We peered around the door into the darkness, my heart beating restlessly in my chest.

'Do you see anything?' Mera asked.

'No.'

We crept out into the hallway but there was nothing there. Only the sound of the wind blowing through the cracks around the windows and the occasional screech of an owl outside pierced the silence.

'You and your over-active imagination,' I muttered, treading carefully back inside and sitting down on the mats.

Mera slid back into the room too.

'Go to sleep,' I yawned. 'It's late. It's been a long day and I'm sure tomorrow will be even longer.'

'Fine, I will forfeit to your defeatist attitude,' she conceded, lying down in her bed. 'But I still say I heard something.'

'Goodnight, Mera.'

'Goodnight, Lex.'

14

The master's return

That morning I woke with the sun. The grey light of dawn was streaming through the tiny window. I rose and saw that Ilyssa and Alaric were both gone. Mera was sleeping soundly beside me.

It was so strange. Just yesterday I would have been overjoyed to wake so close to her. Now, however, I didn't feel the same urge to reach out and touch her the way I had before.

I watched as she shifted slightly in her sleep. I considered waking her, we should be leaving soon, but decided that one more hour asleep wouldn't hurt her. I had an urge to explore a bit before we left. I wasn't quite ready to leave our new friends behind.

I stood and left the room. I wandered down the stairs, not meeting anyone on my journey. It was very quiet. Something drew me up the main staircase and eventually I found myself in a corridor with a large window at each end and number of heavy oak doors. The overcast sky outside made the blue painted walls look grey. I was walking past a mahogany chest with a vase of ugly flowers on top when I noticed one of the doors was ajar. I recognised the voices of Ilyssa and Alaric coming from inside the room. I was about to go in and greet them when I heard my name.

'-and Lex are in danger if he finds out who they are,' I heard Ilyssa's panicked voice say.

'We need to get them out of here,' Alaric replied.

I was confused. Could they have figured out who Mera was? But how would that put us in danger? I decided not to hide in the shadows. I opened the door and stepped into the room.

They both turned to look at me with panicked expressions. Ilyssa hastily shoved a piece of parchment behind her back.

'Lex,' her face was pale. 'How much did you hear?'

'Why are we in danger?' I asked.

Ilyssa and Alaric shared a look.

'We have to tell him,' he shrugged.

She nodded and turned to me. 'All right Lex, listen to me. We know who Mia is, or Mera I should say. But not just that, we know why you're here. We know that you're going to Skara Brae to bring back magic to Culrain.'

I felt panic pulse through me. 'How could you know that?'

'Well I wasn't really sure,' she admitted. 'But I knew I recognised Mera from somewhere. That's when I remembered seeing something in my master's papers.'

She held out the parchment for me and I took it from her. It was a sketch of Mera. Underneath was written, *HRH the crown princess of Culrain.*

Tearing my eyes away from the parchment I said, 'That doesn't explain how you know what we're doing.'

Alaric answered me. 'We overheard it from our master. He is a member of the Brethren of Peace. The Brethren have been watching the princess for years. They have spies everywhere. We have to get you out of here.'

A sense of dread was unfurling in my chest. We had walked right into a trap. How could we be so foolish?

'I need to get Mera,' and I would have raced back to the room right then if I hadn't heard the sound of approaching footsteps in the corridor.

'Oh gods he's back,' Ilyssa whispered.

101

'Quick, in here,' said Alaric grabbing Ilyssa and me and shoving us both into a wardrobe, closing the doors behind him.

It was very cramped inside. I was stuck between Ilyssa and Alaric and a number of heavy coats. I tried not to feel uncomfortable pressed up against Ilyssa. I turned my attention to the slight gap in the doors through which I could see two people enter the room.

I recognised Mrs Granite and her ugly brown dress standing in front of a large desk. The man who sat behind it must have been the master of the house. He was a giant of a man. His huge arms rested on the arms of a high-backed chair. He was completely bald but he could be no more than forty. In the dull morning light his face looked mangled and I noticed that he had a number of scars running across his cheek and down his neck. His sunken eyes were fixed on Mrs Granite. In his thick hands he held a silver goblet.

'Are you sure about this Mrs Granite? Are you absolutely positive it's her? Here?' his voice was eager.

'I couldn't be more certain, my Lord. I knew from the moment I laid my eyes on them that they was good for nothing liars and runaways. Then last night I overheard them talking, my Lord, about magic of all things. In this house! That's when I knew, my Lord, it was her. That one you've been looking for. So this morning I woke before them other servants and came straight here to tell you,' Mrs Granite finished with a conceited smile.

'You have done well, Agnes. I am very pleased with you,' he set the goblet down slowly and pressed his hands together as though in prayer. 'And what about this boy whom she is with? Who is he?'

'Oh he's nobody, Lord Listoros,' Mrs Granite waved off the question. 'He's just a boy. She probably put some spell on him. She'd need protection if she planned on making her way through that forest unscathed. Only the gods know what matter of beasts are just waiting for some tasty treat to walk into their nests. Although she could've found somebody a bit better, I'm sure.'

'Well the girl has always been known for making strange decisions. The boy was probably in the wrong place at the wrong time and now he's going to pay for her foolishness,' Lord Listoros looked down at his hands absentmindedly. He began to twist a signet ring on his index finger. 'This is exactly what we need right now. We must treat this situation with great delicacy. Here is what I want you to do. Continue on with your day as normal and when they have awoken alert me immediately. You will then tell them that I wish to speak with my young guests. When they arrive at my chambers they will be offered a drink, anything their little hearts' desire. Go to that cupboard over by the window, Agnes. Yes that's the one. Now bring me the bottle you see inside. No not that one, the small one to the left. Yes, that's it. In this bottle is a poison so deadly it can strike the life from a man's heart within minutes. I doubt two children could put up much of a fight, even with their petty magic. One sip and that will be the end of our little princess. I thank you again, Agnes. The Brethren will not forget this. I will make sure of that. Now come, I have preparations to make and you must tell the kitchens to prepare a feast. I must write to Lord Malaigle directly. We will have much to celebrate this night.'

They walked together out of the room. When we heard the doors close behind them we tumbled out of the wardrobe.

'Oh gods,' I muttered.

Ilyssa grabbed my wrist. 'We have to get to Mera now. If we're quick we can get out of here before they even know we're awake.'

'We?' I asked.

'We're coming with you,' Ilyssa insisted.

'I thought you didn't want to leave,' I reminded her.

'We've been looking at a way to get back at our master for years.' Alaric told me. 'We don't agree with his war on magic. You've given us the perfect way to get back at him for all the years we've had to put up with his torment.'

'We can come with you, can't we?' Ilyssa implored, stilling holding onto my arm.

I hesitated for a moment, thinking of the conversation I'd had with Mera the night before. She clearly didn't want them to come with us. But surely she would change her mind when she heard what they had to say. We couldn't leave them here after that.

I nodded. 'Of course you can.'

'Brilliant,' Ilyssa grinned.

'Come on then, let's go before they come back,' Alaric prompted.

As quick as we could without rousing suspicion we left the room and sped back to the servants quarters. Mera was awake when we got there. She had packed our things away and was perusing a book. She looked up as we entered the room, clearly confused as to why we were all out of breath.

'What's going on?' she asked.

'Quick, get your things,' I answered. 'We need to get out of here. Lord Listoros, the master here, he's a member of the Brethren.'

She breathed in sharply. 'Oh gods. Oh gods! How do you know?'

Ilyssa stepped forward. 'We told him. We overheard him talking to Mrs Granite. He's planning on killing you. We're all getting out of here.'

'Wait, all?' Mera blinked. 'You can't come with us. We'll get you out of here of course but you can't go where we're going.'

'And why not?' Alaric replied. 'We've as much right to fight against the Brethren as you do.'

'It makes sense,' I added as I went to pick up my pack.

Mera stared at me. 'Lex you can't be serious.'

'There's no time to argue. We need to go now,' I pointed out.

Mera fumbled for an argument but clearly she couldn't think of anything because she sighed and said, 'All right, fine, you've won me over.'

'Great,' Alaric grinned.

'Quickly Alaric,' Ilyssa urged her brother as she packed her sparse belongings into a bag. 'Get your things. We don't have long.'

'Don't worry little sister, I'm always prepared,' he reached under his bed and pulled out a lumpy bundle and a bow with a quiver of arrows. 'You know, just in case.'

'Of course,' murmured Ilyssa. 'All right, everybody ready? I think we should try and sneak out the back. We don't want Mrs Granite catching us and through the kitchen is probably our safest bet. It's misty again today so we'll have cover once we're outside. What do you think?'

'Sounds good,' I agreed.

'Right, well if you lot are done chatting,' Alaric cut in. 'Let's go. I don't plan on sticking around to see the master's reaction to this little escape party.'

We crept downstairs as fast as possible and stopped outside the kitchen while Alaric peeked inside.

'There's too many people in there. We'll never get through without being seen,' he told us.

'We'll have to go out the front way then and hope no one's there,' said Mera.

We tiptoed along the empty corridors. There was a clatter of noise as we passed the dining room where the servants were laying the table for Listoros' breakfast. We scuttled past and

105

managed to reach the entrance hall undetected. Ilyssa had her hand on the door when we heard Mrs Granite calling out behind us, 'And where, exactly, do you think you're going?'

'Oh, fantastic,' Mera muttered.

'Run,' called Alaric.

Ilyssa and I pushed the doors and they swung open. We scrambled down the stone steps into the freezing air leaving Mrs Granite screaming behind us.

'Come back here this instant! My Lord! My Lord, come quick! They're escaping! The brats are getting away, you must stop them!'

I didn't look back for fear of tripping but I heard Alaric curse and guessed that somebody was chasing us. Sure enough, a few seconds later I could hear a thunderous footfall just behind us.

Breath tore from me in gasps and I felt my heart thudding in my chest. Distantly I heard Ilyssa exclaim, 'Gods, he's set the dogs on us.'

Someone shouted, 'Run!'

I turned back for a moment and fear caught me in its tight grasp. What must have been nearly twenty dogs were running towards us at an incredible speed, snapping their viciously sharp teeth. They were huge. On their hind legs they would have towered over me. Their powerful muscles rippled as they tore through the grass towards us. We'd have barely a minute before they were upon us.

Blood pounding in my ears, I tried to overlook the panic that was clawing its way up my throat at the thought of what would happen when they pounced and cleared my mind. Dropping my pack, I stopped running and turned towards the dogs, ignoring Mera's cry of, 'Lex what are you doing?' and raised my hand towards them.

'*Farblad!*' I yelled.

The dogs were sent flying backwards through the air, landing with a sickening thud by the steps of the house. I closed my eyes and bent over, clutching my constricted throat, trying to breathe normally and stop my heart from beating out of my chest. I felt somebody's warm hand on my shoulder. I turned my face up to see Ilyssa standing next to me.

'Are you all right?' she asked me in a breathless voice. I noticed she too had dropped her pack.

I stood up straight, nodding.

'Good gods Lex,' muttered Alaric.

'That was incredible,' Ilyssa added. 'I've never seen anything like that before.'

Trying not to be too pleased by the clear awe on her face, I looked back at where the dogs had landed and saw that we had run through the open gates and were standing by the giant pine trees that lined the grounds of Deathgrove. A dense mist was swirling through the forest, around our ankles and up towards the house. For a moment I thought I saw a figure moving towards us, but a second later I realised it was just the fog being pushed about by the wind. A crow cawed in the distance.

'We should leave before they send something else after us,' I murmured.

Alaric whistled and shrugged his pack further onto his shoulder, still panting heavily but grinning nonetheless. I picked up Ilyssa's pack and passed it to her. As I passed it over she caught my hand and whispered, 'Thank you.'

'You're welcome,' I replied, swallowing noisily.

She released me and I walked over to where Mera was standing, watching us with her hand on her chest to calm her breathing. As I approached she smiled at me.

'Are you all right?' she asked.

'Couldn't be better,' I answered.

'I bet. Come on then,' she called to the others. 'We've got a long journey ahead of us and we should get away from here as soon as possible. They'll be after us any minute.'

She reached out and put her arm around me as we began to walk away from the house. It was only then that it really hit me what had just happened. I started laughing breathlessly. Mera chuckled too as she leant against me. We all walked on together into the thickening forest, the rising sun cutting out a pathway through the darkness ahead of us.

15

Thistlethorn Wood

We didn't stop until well after nightfall. When we thought we had gone far enough that it was safe to stop we set up camp in a small glen. We sat around the fire eating rye bread and the last of the cheese. Mera pulled out the map.

'Do you know where we are?' I asked.

She shook her head. 'No. I don't really know what direction we went in after leaving Deathgrove.'

'Well we're not in the Great Forest,' said Alaric. 'This is Thistlethorn Wood, which means we've been heading northwest.'

'I see it,' Mera replied, pointing to a clump of trees on the map. 'It's quite big, there's no way to tell what part of it we're in. I need a better map than this. Let's all get some rest and we can try to work it out tomorrow.'

I saw Alaric move as though to speak but then he stilled. I was sure he been about to ask about magic, but there would be time for that. For now we needed to get as far away from Deathgrove and the Brethren as possible.

We took turns keeping watch while the others slept. Everything looked more sinister by night. There was something about the way the trees bent in the wind, creaking and howling and screeching that made me feel tense. The scurrying of animals across the forest floor reminded me that we were never alone. The slightest movement in the twilight made me twitchy, always wondering whether it was just another harmless animal or something more ominous.

We left early that morning and headed north in the hope that we would reach the end of the forest or that a path would appear and lead us out, but none showed itself. When night fell we were tired and worried and sank straight into our makeshift beds. It did not look brighter by morning.

We hadn't had time to restock our supplies, so we were soon running low. We were able to find some food in the forest but it would not last forever. Mera and I could catch small animals, squirrels, pigeons, woodcock and the like, plus there were some edible wild plants that I was familiar with, though not many. What I didn't know Ilyssa made up for. She seemed to know exactly what we could eat and what would kill by just a glance. Alaric put his bow and arrow to good use. His aim was true and just a bit frightening. He could hit a bird in flight straight through the eye.

The only thing we couldn't replenish was water. We only had two water skins between the four of us and we were running out. On the third day after our escape we found a small pond and drank thirstily but this wouldn't sustain us either. We needed to find somewhere to get more skins quickly or we would be in trouble. At one point we considered turning back to the village that was close to Deathgrove but fear of the Brethren followed us like a whip at our heels, so we carried on our journey as far away from Lord Listoros as possible.

On that third evening we set up camp, exhausted from the day's walk with parched lips yearning for a drink. Ilyssa shared out the water while Mera set about starting a fire. Alaric had taken off his shoes and was inspecting a rather nasty blister there. Ilyssa smacked him on the arm and said, 'Put that away, will you, no one wants to see or smell your horrible feet.'

'Sorry, but look at this thing,' he replied, waving his foot in his sister's direction, who looked disgusted and moved to sit next to me. The heat from her body next to mine was hotter that the fire in front of me. I saw Mera eyeing our closeness. I thought of our conversation in the kitchen at Deathgrove and felt a little guilty, though not enough to move. Alaric's voice brought me back to the conversation. 'It's painful too. I don't suppose you have any magic remedy that'll cure me, do you?'

I didn't want to say no to his hopeful face but I had to shake my head. 'Sorry, no.'

'Ah well, I'll solider on,' he slipped his sock back on though I could still see the blister through a large hole. 'So is it likely that we'll meet other princesses on their way to Skara Brae or it just you?'

Mera sighed and said, 'I would find that unlikely. Remind me, how is it that you two even know about Skara Brae?'

'We told you, Lord Listoros is a member of the Brethren of Peace,' Ilyssa answered. 'They have meetings at the house sometimes. They all sit in the dining room and discuss their business. A few months ago they mentioned how you had discovered the secret of Skara Brae. They weren't happy. They said it would end everything they worked for if you got there.'

'Well that's good I suppose,' Mera said.

I stared at Mera. 'How is that good? Now we know that the Brethren still exists it's going to make things a lot harder. They'll be following us the whole way.'

'I meant about what she said about it ending everything they worked for,' she replied. 'It means we're on the right track. Besides, we've been avoiding the Royal Guard well enough, we can avoid the Brethren too.'

'If you say so,' I muttered.

'I know so. Anyway,' she turned her attention back to Ilyssa and Alaric. 'What do you know about the Brethren?'

I noticed that every time Mera looked Ilyssa's way her eyes dropped for a second to where our knees touched. I shifted uncomfortably.

'Not much more than you already know, I imagine,' admitted Ilyssa. 'I don't know names or anything, but I remember Lord Listoros being honoured by a visit from someone very important from the castle. That night a huge chest appeared in his room. I couldn't help myself, I had to look inside. That's when I first saw a picture of you, Mera. Oh, it feels funny calling you that. Shouldn't I be saying your Majesty?'

'Yeah and aren't you supposed to curtsy or something?' Alaric added with a smile.

'Don't call me that,' grumbled Mera. 'And if I see anyone curtsying I'll box your ears.'

We all laughed.

Alaric spoke up. 'Forget about royalty for a second. I want to talk about magic. So it's really real then? I mean, I knew about it from all Listoros had said, but I never really believed it until I saw you blast those dogs back.'

'Yeah well,' I muttered, only slightly enjoying the look of wonderment in Alaric's eyes. 'We were lucky it worked. Since magic was banished it's nearly impossible to practise it. It usually only works when it wants to, or if you're in great need of it. And we definitely were.'

'You say that as if magic has a mind of its own,' Ilyssa said.

I nodded. 'In a way it does. You have to respect it like you would any power.'

'That's fascinating,' Ilyssa smiled, her warm brown eyes staring into mine.

'I think so,' I muttered.

'So,' Mera's voice was louder than usual. 'Neither of you regret coming with us?'

'No way,' replied Alaric emphatically. 'Besides, we can't go back now. Those dogs will get us this time. And if they don't Mrs Granite certainly will. I bet she'd love to see us all killed.'

'Yes, well, you used to ruffle her feathers quite a lot. Who can really blame her?' commented Ilyssa.

'Oh that old hag deserved everything she got. Bet she's celebrating right about now. Finally got rid of us. Been trying to do that for years. And as for Listoros, he was a great, ugly beast and he only knew spite. We should've left years ago. I'm glad you two came along. I'm glad you're here to put a stop to these rotten, good-for-nothing lordlings who think they're better than everyone else. I'm coming with you to Skara Brae.'

'Me too,' added Ilyssa. 'Where my brother goes, I go. We'll help you put an end to all this hatred that's ripping the world apart.'

'It'll be dangerous,' Mera warned them. 'And long. I can't say that you'll ever find your way home.'

'We don't have a home,' Ilyssa stated. 'From now on we'll make our own home.'

'And as far as danger goes, none of it can be as dangerous as goading Cook back at Deathgrove,' Alaric joked. 'Now she is a dangerous woman. Seriously though, we'll be prepared. We know how to defend ourselves.'

'Well,' sighed Mera, rubbing the back of her neck, 'I can't deny you wouldn't be helpful. I guess that settles it. Today Thistlethorn Wood, Tomorrow Skara Brae.'

The next morning we found the end of the woods. We came across a path and decided to follow it. Mercifully it led to the small town of Notgrove. We drank heartily from the well in the town centre and then set about restocking our supplies. Ilyssa found some decent cooking utensils and water canisters that looked that they would last for a good long while. Alaric, drunk on freedom, went straight to the local tavern with a very stern word from Ilyssa that he was to behave himself and that

113

if he spent all the money in his share she'll leave him behind to fend for himself.

The three of us found an inn that had a room available for the four of us and decided to leave our new supplies there while we walked about the town. It was small and there was not much to see, but it was nice to be out of the woods.

Mera, attempting to be shrewd, began asking around for maps of the area, but failed in both. At some point she found an old merchant who had what he said was a detailed map of Seion, but refused to show it to her before she produced some money, asking a hefty price. Mera wasn't fooled. She managed to get a hold of the so called map, which ended up being a startlingly detailed list of every place in Culrain that you could buy picked eggs. Mera, infuriated, almost scared the man into an early grave by shouting about disloyalty and dishonour until I was able to drag her away but the scruff of her neck muttering, 'Subtle.'

When it came time for dinner and Alaric had still not returned, Ilyssa led us straight to the tavern and lo and behold there he was, a man and woman both sitting on his lap, singing along loudly to a bawdy song about a king and his consorts. Ilyssa, with a face that suggested this was not the first time she'd found her brother like this, moved over to him.

'Alaric,' she sighed, but she didn't get to finish because the man on Alaric's right crowed, 'Ooh, someone's in trouble. Who's this, your wife? She can join us if she likes.'

Alaric laughed until he saw Ilyssa's face and stopped promptly. 'Sorry ladies and gentleman, but I think my sister wants me home.'

The man and woman groaned, but leapt up to allow Alaric to stand. He turned back to them and took the woman's hand.

'Bronwyn, it has been a true pleasure,' he smiled, kissing her hand. Turning to the man he said. 'Gethin, you are quite the gentleman,' and without hesitation kissed him full on the mouth. Grinning like a cat that's got the cream he turned and grabbed Ilyssa's wrist, pulling her towards the exit.

The woman, Bronwyn, called, 'You're always welcome here Allie, any time!'

Stifling laughter at seeing Alaric blowing the couple kisses as Ilyssa dragged him from the tavern, we followed them through the doors and onto the street.

'Must you do this every time?' sighed Ilyssa. 'We don't have money to waste, Alaric.'

'No, no, Lyss, you mishundersand-stand,' slurred Alaric, swaying back and forth slightly. 'I only bought two drinks myshelft. Self. No, that lovely, sweet couple down there you just met remember, they were lovely weren't they. They own the place! So they were more than happy to let me drink *on the house!* Look!' He started pulling coins from random pockets and dropping them into Ilyssa's hands. 'Two drinks I paid for is all. Oh! And I got this.' From the inside of his jacket he pulled a slightly wrinkled bit of parchment and shoved it, not at Ilyssa, but at Mera, who took it from him.

She opened it and gasped. 'Oh Alaric, well done! Look, he's found us a map. Fantastic!'

'How did you manage that?' asked Ilyssa

'Well you see, little sister, the tavern has its advantages. Always interesting people in the tavern. I asked around and as luck would have it good old Gethin had one that he didn't need. Only had to sweet talk him a little and he handed it right over,' he stood there, grinning widely.

'Well Alaric,' sighed Ilyssa. 'You've proven yourself useful. I suppose I won't be leaving you behind after all.'

'We might want to sober him up before we have dinner,' I suggested.

'Yes, let's find a bucket of water to stick his head in,' Ilyssa agreed.

After Alaric had sobered enough and I'd eaten so much chicken pie I felt my stomach would burst, we headed up to our room. Ilyssa put Alaric to bed, still humming merrily to himself, and we sat on Mera's bed to discuss our next leg of the journey. We found the town we were in on the map and discovered we'd been heading too far west, away from the edge of The Great Forest. We plotted a new course that would take us straight into Seion and out of The Brethren's clutches as quickly as possible. Then we'd head northeast until we got back onto the original course into Meyrom and straight on to Skara Brae.

'And then what?' asked Ilyssa. 'When we get to Skara Brae, what do we do?'

'In essence,' said Mera. 'Bring back magic.'

'It's a little more complicated than it sounds,' I cut in.

'Well, of course. I mean, you can't just say a few funny words and hope to recover what is essentially a lost world,' Mera began to explain about Skara Brae and its origins, about the Sisterhood and her plans to confront her father.

Ilyssa sat in concentrated silence. When Mera finished she took a deep breath. 'Wow. How sure are you that it's going to work?'

'No plan is ever completely perfect, but we've got to try, right?' Mera said.

'I suppose so,' muttered Ilyssa. She looked down thoughtfully. The light from the candles danced across her face, making her brown eyes look momentarily golden. I wondered what she was thinking. She was probably regretting agreeing to come with us and desperately thinking up excuses to leave.

'You think we're crazy,' I muttered.

She looked up, surprised. 'No. I think you're brave.'

My cheeks turned red. 'Oh.'

'I mean, you've put everything you had aside to help people you don't even know. I mean, how many Magic Folk have you known?'

'None,' I admitted. 'But as my good friend over here always says, if you have the power to help someone you're obligated to use it.'

'Good to know you've been listening to me, Lex,' Mera's smile was tight. 'But now, I think, we should go to bed. It's getting late and I don't want to stick around here for too long. I know it seems safe, but you can never be too careful.'

'You're right. Maybe by the time we get into Seion Alaric will have had his fill of drinking his freedom away,' Ilyssa sighed.

Mera looked over to Alaric's sleeping form. 'Is he always like that?'

'You've no idea the amount of times I've had to chase people out of the house before Mrs Granite found out,' she smiled, shaking her head slightly and rising. 'Anyway, you're right. We should get some rest. Goodnight.'

'Night,' Mera and I replied in unison.

We all got into bed. Mera snuffed out the last candle and I drifted off to sleep trying not to think about the two women sleeping a few feet from me.

The next day we set off early, with much grumbling from Alaric about the brightness of the sun, making sure to stock up on food before we left the village. As per Mera's plan we headed north towards the boarder, stopping every now and then to rest.

In the distance I could see the beginnings of a mountain range, at the foot of which The Great Forest skirted. We were still making our way through fields but the path Mera had marked out would lead us through the rocky terrain between

Seion's mountains and The Great Forest and then we'd be moving into Meyrom and at the very top of the land we'd find Skara Brae.

'We should stop here,' called Mera from the front of the group. 'I'm not sure if we're quite in Seion yet but we could be going for hours and still not be sure. I'd like to set up camp before we run out of daylight.'

We started unpacking our things, Mera delegating the jobs. 'Alaric, will you get some kindling, please? Lex you can set up the sleeping mats and Ilyssa you can put everything out for dinner.

While positioning my last mat I noticed Ilyssa take out six of the makeshift plates and then hurriedly put the extra two back. She caught my eye and blushed. 'I normally put out two more settings for my parents. It probably sounds silly but it makes me feel like they're still here.'

I moved over to sit next to her. 'I understand. I like to think that my father is still here with me. Sometimes I think I can hear him laughing. He was always laughing.'

'I'm sorry. I didn't know you'd lost your father. Were you very young?'

'Thirteen. It was a hunting accident. He was protecting me from a wild boar. He pushed me out of the way but got caught on the boar's horns himself. There was nothing that could have saved him. Well I suppose magic could have, now that I think about it.'

'Oh Lex,' Ilyssa put her hand on my shoulder. It was steady and comforting, as though her empathy was rippling through me. I felt at once as though some invisible thread had sprung up between us.

'It was a long time ago,' I muttered

'But it still hurts,' she said.

I turned to look at her. The sadness on her face made my heart ache. I reached out to take her hand but changed my mind at the last minute and ended up patting her awkwardly on the arm that was still resting on my shoulder.

She gave me a kind smile before facing away from me and watching Mera attempting to teach Alaric how to build a fire.

'Just place it down gently, gently,' Mera insisted, but Alaric kept accidentally knocking the whole pile over.

'We should probably do something before she kills him,' Ilyssa suggested.

'Probably,' I nodded.

She got up and went to help, taking the branch that Mera was about to swing in Alaric's direction out of her hand and putting it down on the pile. As she moved away I felt the invisible thread tug at me, calling me after her.

16
The town with no name

The days were becoming steadily warmer as we made our way into Seion. I'd always heard it was hotter there, not anywhere near as hot as Beagbach to the west next to the Endless Desert, but certainly warmer than Culrain.

However the increasing sunlight wasn't constant. There were days when the sun refused to be roused from its cloudy bed, leaving us to the harsh winds that whipped across the relatively flat landscape between here and the Windgerest Mountains. Some days the wind was so fierce it could rip up our camp if it wasn't properly secured. We lost a set of spoons that way. I was taking them out of my pack when the wind swooped down and tore them from my unsuspecting fingers. Before any of us knew what was happening they were clattering away across the plane.

It was on one of these violently windy days that we found ourselves walking past rows of old, crumbling houses. What remained of their skeletal structure was blackened as though a great fire had swept through the streets. No house had been left untouched. Here and there were relics from families long gone. I spied some charred pots engulfed by bushes. An old stone wall had been pushed over by the roots of trees, cascades of weeds tumbled over the remains.

We walked on in silence, observing the ruined town. We came across what must have been the town square. Most of these buildings were relatively undamaged having been made of stone, though some had toppled over after years of dereliction. These buildings too bore signs of a fire though it was clear that it happened many decades ago. The building that had taken the worst damage appeared to be a temple. I recognised the seal of the gods on one of the bricks. The tendril-like sun had a crack running through it. There were large, misshapen stones piled against what had once been a doorway as though somebody had tried to barricade themself in, or perhaps attempted to trap someone inside.

'What happened here?' Mera's voice, though soft and full of sadness was oddly loud in the eerie silence of the abandoned town.

'War,' came a voice from behind us.

As a group we whirled around to see an old, wizened woman hobbling towards us. She carried a dirty, frayed sack that gave a heavy clunk every time she took a step. She was by far the ugliest woman I had ever seen. She was almost bald save for a smattering of thin, ratty strands. Her skin was covered in dark liver spots and was grey with dirt. A slick tongue was dragged back and forth across her shrivelled lips revealing cracked, yellowing teeth. Her breath rattled in her bony chest as she advanced. She smelt of rotting meat and stale urine. She stopped a few feet short of us, staring with drooping, mismatched eyes.

'War touched some places worse than others, that's for sure,' she spoke in a voice as cracked as the walls of the temple. 'This was one of the worst ones, I'll bargain.'

'Do you live here?' Alaric asked.

The woman gave a shriek of laughter.

'Live here? Dear child no one lives here no more, not in a long while. No one wants to live in a place like this. It don't exactly get visitors, neither. What's your business here?'

'Just passing through,' I answered, eager to end this strange conversation. There was something about this woman that made my skin itch. It reminded me of when my aunt Charlotte had passed away and we'd been ushered in to say goodbye. Her body had been laid in the bed in which she'd died, the stillborn child tucked into her motionless arms. I had been scratching that memory out of me for days.

'Aye, I reckon that's true,' the woman grinned, showing every one of her remaining teeth. 'Not much to pass through though, is there? Not much but ruins and ghosts.'

She began to cough, great hacking things that shook her whole body and made it sound as though she were trying to cough up her own lungs. She pulled out an old handkerchief and dabbed at her mouth. When she pulled it away I saw blood staining the cloth.

'What did you mean about war?' asked Alaric.

'What war do you think I'm talking about, boy? Are you thick? Before my time, of course, I'm not that old,' she let out another shriek of laughter. 'But my parents, they knew, they were there. Lived here when this town was a town, back when Magic Folk weren't hunted like vermin.'

'You mean you knew Magic Folk,' Mera asked, her interest peaked.

'Aye, that's right. The people here didn't agree with that mad king, you see. They didn't like the things he said, so they helped them Magic Folk escape. Hid them and the like. This used to be one of the last stops before Seion, you understand, back before the boarders changed and Culrain let this part of the kingdom go. At the time they hadn't gone as far as pursuing Magic Folk in other kingdoms. Well, the king must have found out because one day, with no warning at all, troops came storming into the town. They grabbed people and they beat them. Blood was spilt that day, make no mistake. These were innocents, mind.'

'If they were innocent why did they kill them?' asked Ilyssa.

'They did it just to get at these poor desperate souls who don't want to die. Well, the people wouldn't give them up, so the guard decided that they all had to go. Burnt the whole place to the ground. People ran. Some got away. Them Magic Folk didn't, though. Got trapped in the temple. It were supposed to be a place of refuge, you see, sight of the gods and all that. Fat lot of good it did them. Cursed the king to the high heavens that evidence of his wickedness would always remain. The town weren't a home no more. Those that survived couldn't come back, not when it reminded them of what had happened.'

'That's awful,' Mera muttered.

'I'll say, girl. Well, I've dallied enough for one day, got to be off. Don't want to get caught in that storm that's coming. You lot'll want to find shelter until it passes. Might find something here, who knows. Mind out for them poor souls that died here, though. I doubt they take kindly to strangers anymore,' and with a final high pitched cackle she limped away.

'Well that was terrifying,' Alaric said, breaking the stunned silence that had settled after the woman's abrupt departure.

'Do you think that was all true?' asked Ilyssa.

'Probably,' replied Mera. 'The Royal Guard committed all manner of atrocities during the Thirteen Year War. All following orders, I'm sure. But there will be places that have suffered worse even than this.'

'Well one thing's certain, she was right about the storm,' Alaric said as a clap of thunder rolled across the sky.

'Let's find somewhere dry before it hits,' Mera suggested. 'Hopefully it won't last long. I don't know about you but I don't want to stay here any longer than I have to.'

After a quick search of the remaining buildings we found a room that was mainly intact. Save for a small crack in the ceiling it was safe enough to stay in without fear of flooding or collapse. It must have been a kitchen once. There was a stove that had rusted and fallen in on itself and the collection of pots and pans was covered in enough debris to suggest some creature had been living there recently. The size of the room indicated that whoever had lived here had been wealthy, for all the good it had done them. No amount of money could have saved them from the King's wrath.

We got inside just in time, escaping the onslaught of rain that began the moment we heaved our packs into the room. We settled in and waited for the storm to pass. When the howl of the wind did nothing but increase and rain began to leak in through the cracked ceiling it was clear that we would have to stay the night or risk getting drenched. There was no wood for a fire, so we huddled together, eating the cold leftover rabbit for dinner.

Alaric tried to raise our rain-dampened sprits by telling jokes and bawdy tales, but surrounded by the ravaged town they fell flat. After a while we slipped into silence.

I tried not to think about the people who had lived and died here all those years ago. What manner of monster could do that to hundreds of innocent lives, people who had only been trying to help. No matter how many times I heard about it I was always astounded by the violence that had been inflicted during the war. Manuvendra must have had poison boiling in his veins to have allowed these horrors to occur.

I wondered briefly if Manuvendra had ever regretted his actions, if he had ever felt remorse for all the suffering he had caused. I knew that I could never take a life, not even in vengeance. What would killing someone do to a person? Was there a way back once your soul had been so marred?

I was shaken from my thoughts by Mera's sleepy voice. 'We ought to turn in, I think.'

'Great idea,' replied Alaric, eagerly shaking out his rolled up sleeping mat. 'I for one am ready for this day to be over. I had enough of creepy places living at Deathgrove. I'll be happy to leave this place behind too.'

'I'll take the first watch, shall I?' Mera offered, barely managing to stifle a yawn.

'You're exhausted,' Ilyssa said. 'I'll go first.'

'If you're sure,' Mera replied sleepily.

'I'm sure,' Ilyssa nodded, setting up her makeshift bed against the wall so that she could lean against it while she watched.

After a chorus of mumbled goodnights we settled down. I fell asleep to the sound of soft snores and the violent *tang-tang-tang* of the dripping water hitting metal.

Some hours later I was shaken awake by Alaric who blearily mumbled something that could have been, 'Your turn,' before shuffling back over to his mat and falling into it. Rubbing my eyes, I pulled myself into a sitting position and looked around.

I noticed right away that the storm had passed. The ceiling had stopped leaking and outside I heard nothing but a faint whisper of wind through the trees. People always spoke about the calm before the storm, but I found the silence directly after one to be equally eerie. Something with enough force to silence a forest must have a great power.

Taking watch was boring, even for those who liked the quiet. I had no idea what time it was. There was no light, nor any way to count the passing minutes save my own imagination. I sat with my back pressed against the cold wall, squished between Mera and Ilyssa's sleeping forms. I hadn't thought much about the two of them recently. I knew my feelings for Mera had changed and I knew she could tell and wasn't happy about it. Part of me was angry for it. She had no right to be upset that I didn't feel for her that way when she had always insisted that nothing ever could happen between us. It wasn't my fault that I had changed. The way I felt about Ilyssa was different to the way I had ever felt about Mera. It felt light, almost kinder. There was no confusion the way there always had been with Mera. The connection I had felt spring up between us had not loosened. I sighed. I did feel guilty about what was happening to Mera and me. If I wanted to save our friendship I would have to talk to her about it all.

The hours trickled by. At one point Mera woke with a gasp, glancing around the room in confusion. When she saw me she calmed.

'Bad dream,' I asked.

She nodded.

'Try and get back to sleep,' I suggested.

Mera shifted in her pallet, then paused and turned back to me. 'Lex...' she started.

'What's wrong?' I asked.

'There's something I've been meaning to talk to you about something. It's... it's about Ilyssa.'

I felt an odd flurry of guilt and joy when she said Ilyssa's name. I shifted uncomfortably.

'I don't think now's a good time,' I indicated the others sleeping next to us.

'They're asleep. Please, this is important.'

'All right.'

Mera sat up properly and faced my head on. I waited for her words with trepidation.

'Things are different now,' she began. 'When it was just the two of us we could pretend, but now with the others here... Look the thing is, despite all I've said about nothing ever happening between us, I can't deny I didn't want it to.'

It took me a minute to process what she had said. By the time I understood her meaning she was speaking again.

'It was right, what I said. Nothing should ever have happened, it would have got in the way, but I think this is getting in the way now so I have to say it. I'm jealous. I never thought it would happen and that's my fault. I was being selfish. Part of me was flattered that you liked me that way and I don't think

I wanted to lose it. I'm sorry for that, I really am, because your friendship is so important to me and I don't want to be the one to hurt you. So whatever happens please know that you're my best friend and I will always love you.'

Her words filled me with relief.

'You have nothing to apologise for,' I told her. 'You told me time and again what you wanted from me and I ignored you because it wasn't what I wanted. That was selfish and I'm sorry. I should have respected your wishes.'

Mera shook her head. 'You can't ignore your feelings. We're here now and there's nothing that can be done about it. I just hope that we can be friends the way we were before.'

'Of course we can,' I smiled. 'Look, you should get back to sleep and in the morning it'll be a new day.'

'All right,' Mera nodded. I could only just make out her face in the darkness but I could see she was smiling. 'You know, Ilyssa's a really nice girl.'

I shook my head. 'Goodnight Mera.'

'Goodnight Lex.'

I stretched out my arm, taking her hand in mine and squeezing it gently. The friendly gesture made Mera smile. She released my hand to tug her cloak around her more firmly and settled back down to sleep.

Eventually morning came. The quiet outside had been lessening as the sound of the forest returned. The dawn chorus twittered loudly as light began to enter the room. Ilyssa woke with the sun. She stretched her slim arms above her. Her skin glowed golden in the low light. I thought about the conversation Mera and I'd had the night before and smiled.

'Morning,' she yawned as she sat up.

'Morning,' I replied, suddenly energized. 'How did you sleep?'

'Good. The storm was stopping when I woke Mera up for her watch, so at least it was quiet. Although I've always slept well through storms. I don't know what it is but there's something about the sound of rain that's oddly comforting,' she mused.

'I know what you mean. When I was younger my dad used to tell me that storms were the sound of lightning and thunder spirits celebrating. I always liked the idea of spirits having a celebration in the sky. I told my sister that once when she was scared by all the noise and she told me that I was an idiot. Said there was no such thing as lightening and thunder spirits and what would be the point of them anyway?'

'She sounds like she has spirit herself, your little sister.'

I grinned. 'Oh that she does. I hope she's all right. I left in such a hurry I didn't have time to say a proper goodbye.'

'I'm sure she's fine,' Ilyssa gave me a reassuring smile. 'And think of the stories you'll be able to tell her when you get back. Her big brother will be a hero.'

'I wouldn't go that far. Well I'm going to go and see if there's anything we can use for a fire. I've got to say, I don't mind cold rabbit when I have to, but it's much better hot.'

It felt good to stretch my legs after sitting down for so long. I walked through the abandoned house and stepped outside. I immediately regretted leaving my cloak behind. The storm may have passed but there was still a slight breeze and standing in the shade gave me goosebumps. I walked on, rubbing my arms to keep warm. The streets all seemed to lead to the town square where the collapsed temple was, so after a few minutes I found myself standing by the broken fountain and surveyed the damage from the storm.

Here and there were a few branches strewn across the cobbled streets and I found myself having to navigate puddles on the uneven ground. I was surprised that the charring on the buildings hadn't been washed away after all this time. Perhaps the curse the Magic Folk had placed had stuck. Or perhaps there were some stains that just didn't wash out.

I reached down for the branch that lay at my feet and then noticed it was soaked through and would be useless for a fire. I grunted with frustration and dropped it back on the ground. So much for a hot breakfast.

The sound of footsteps had me turning. I saw Ilyssa walking through the windswept square towards me. She stopped beside me with a smile.

'The others are awake,' she said. 'And Mera wanted me to tell you that "all the wood is going to be wet, you dolt." That's a direct quote.'

I grimaced and nodded. 'Yes I'd just worked that out, actually.'

Ilyssa looked around, taking in the charred stones and ruined temple and sighed, 'This is so horrible. All those lives cut down. And it'll always be here, like a reminder, some sick memorial to the atrocities of war.'

She sat down on a large piece of rock that might once have been the wall of a house. I sat down next to her, not so close that we were touching, but close enough that I could hear her breathing softy. It was as though I could feel the distance between us.

I looked again at the collapsed temple. The fire must have cleared half the forest away, but over the years it had returned. Huge, century-old oaks had crept up on the derelict buildings, finding their new homes amongst the rubble and dust. Roots had spread out through the cracks and set their foundations there. Ivy spiralled along the fallen spires, its green leaves fluttering gently in the wind. When spring came little yellow daisies and daffodils would pop up along the side of the wall. I could already see bird nests perched between broken fragments of rock. Soon this temple would be full of birdsong.

'There'll be life here again,' I said.

'How could you desecrate a place like this?' Ilyssa muttered.

Her question caught me off guard and I turned to face her. 'You believe in the Faith?'

She blushed. 'Well, no, not really. That is, I don't believe all those stories about how the gods created the earth and all that, but there's something comforting about sacred places. They give me a sense of serenity. They're the only place I've really felt safe.'

'A Man of Faith came to our village once,' I remembered the day with sudden clarity. 'He was trying to convert people. He probably would have done better if he hadn't told us that we were all sinners.'

'No that tends of offend folk,' Ilyssa smiled.

'So do you pray and all that?' I asked, recalling the odd rituals the man had been practicing full of chanting and noxious smoke and an obsession with washing his hands.

'No, nothing like that. You don't need structure to believe in something,' Ilyssa replied.

'That's the problem you have with the Faith? Structure?' I queried.

'Well not the only thing,' she admitted. 'Like I said, I don't take the stories literally but I think the messages they send are mostly good. Everything they say about kindness and love and respect, that's what I take from them. And there's something about a temple that I really like. No one's too loud or too busy. It lets me feel at peace. I remember once we were travelling to Foraise with the master. We passed through a village that still practised the Faith. Their temple was so beautiful. It had a river running through it and this wonderful waterfall where they left offerings. I could have sat there for days listening to that water gurgle. Then again, maybe I just like the quiet.'

I watched Ilyssa as she spoke. There's something wonderful about the way people speak of the things they're passionate about. Ilyssa's lips had curled into a warm smile. Her eyes were alive and bright as she spoke. I could have listened to her all day.

'Listoros was so angry when he found out where I'd been,' she continued. 'He hates the Faith. He says it steals power from those who should have it by right. Ever the royalist, that one. Not that there's anything wrong with that, of course. The monarchy does much better by the common folk than they did during the days of the Thirteen Year War, that's for sure. And Mera… well she's not what I expected.'

'She'd be glad to hear you say that, I'm sure. She never likes to do what's expected,' I said.

'You would've thought someone who'd been raised in a castle wouldn't be quite so eager to live like this but I don't think I've heard her complain once,' Ilyssa contemplated.

'I don't think she was too sad to leave that life behind. Mera's one of the only truly good people I know. But her penchant for saving people is also one of her biggest flaws. Sometimes I worry about that. She'd be such a good queen if she put her mind to it, but she's so adamant she wants to abdicate. And once she puts her mind to something…' I trailed off, feeling a little uneasy talking about Mera to Ilyssa.

I didn't know why I was so eager to tell her all this, but there was something about her that captivated me. I thought again about the fierce tug I had felt towards her. I had a feeling that if she'd asked me to I would have spilled all my secrets.

A particularly strong gust of wind had me wishing for my cloak again.

'You're cold,' Ilyssa noticed, reaching out and touching my arm. The warmth of her hand sent a tingling sensation through me.

'A little,' I conceded, not wanting her to let go.

'We should probably go back,' Ilyssa suggested. 'Mera and Alaric will be wondering where we are.'

Ilyssa drew her arm back and I had to hide the disappointment the absence of her touch made me feel.

As we walked back to the building in which we'd made camp I took one last look at the crumbled temple. I have never been even remotely interested in the Faith, but looking at the broken ruin behind me it was especially difficult to believe that anyone with any kind of power was watching over us.

17

The traveller

The easy rolling hills of Culrain had given way to the craggy rocks and steep knolls of Seion. As we hiked on the ground began to curve upwards until every day was an uphill climb. As the days grew hotter we found, much to Mera's chagrin, that we were stopping more often to rest from the heat. On one particularly warm day we came across a river and spent a happy afternoon splashing about in the shallow water. Ilyssa, Alaric and I sent small waves down the river for each other to jump over. Mera spent most of the time sitting on the grassy bank pouring over the maps until a particularly large splash from Alaric sent cool water all over her.

'Oops,' he whispered, looking abashed as Mera pushed her soaked hair out of her eyes with a murderous look on her face.

'Which one of you idiots,' she started, barely concealing the anger in her voice. 'Splashed water all over the only map we have?'

Ilyssa and I stood snickering as Alaric sank into the water, trying to hide.

She glared at him. 'You are in so much trouble.'

She kicked off her already wet boots and jumped into the water, chasing him across the pebbly riverbed until she caught him around the neck.

'Help!' he yelled. 'She's going to drown me!'

Ilyssa and I laughed. 'You're on your own.'

The maps lay forgotten on the bank, drying in the hot sun.

We had just left the cottage of an old farmer and his kind-hearted wife who'd given us food and shelter for the night when Alaric had pushed through a thick bush at the edge of the field to find a road on the other side.

Surprised, we piled out onto the dusty path. We hadn't seen a well-made road in a while. Despite our trepidation of travelling on the main roads we followed it for a short while until we came across a sign that told us that if we carried on northwest for twenty miles we would reach the village of Raufen and that a little before that was a tavern called The Dancing Sun. Alaric breathed a sigh of relief.

'Brilliant, we could stop off there. Maybe they'll have a map of the area,' he grinned.

Mera harrumphed. 'Yeah one that hasn't been soaked through with water.'

'Also a larder full of ale,' muttered Ilyssa.

'Well, that too. Come on, it's not that far. We could reach it before sundown,' and he set off with renewed strength.

'Wait,' called Mera as we hurried after him. 'I'm not sure if that's a good idea. We shouldn't stay on this path for long. You never know who you're going to meet on a road like this. I know we've been feeling safer now that we've put some distance between us and Culrain but–'

'Come on, Mera,' Alaric interrupted her. 'This road is taking us in the right direction. If we see anyone who suspects us we can give the same explanation we've given everybody else, visiting family. And you've got your little hood. No one will even notice you. You never know, you might even have fun.'

We waited for Mera's response, expecting her to disagree and command us all to stay on the path marked out on the water-damaged map. After a moment of consideration she sighed and muttered, 'All right. One day can't hurt, I suppose.'

'Great!' cried Alaric.

I laughed at his enthusiasm and Ilyssa shock her head. We walked on, the conversation mainly carried by Alaric who was talking animatedly about his dream to one day own a tavern himself.

'And I would build up this reputation and I'd hire people to talk about how great it is and everyone would want to come to Alaric's Inn because it would be the best around,' he enthused.

His passion for taverns carried on for a most of the morning, stopping briefly when we paused for lunch and his attention turned solely to food. It took us a little longer than we thought to reach our destination. By the time we got there the sun was low in the sky. We shrugged off our heavy packs and stuffed them behind the barrels of hay that had been left out for the horses where no one would see them.

Alaric pushed open the door and we stepped inside. *The Dancing Sun* was noisy and crowded. We pushed our way through the groups of people who were wobbling back and forth between the bar and their tables, frothy ale spilling over the side of the enormous flagons. As we passed one table I heard a man fervently insisting that he'd seen a pumpkin walking around his garden.

'No really Ethan, it just got up and walked on outta my pumpkin patch. I donno where it thought it were goin'. I called it back an' everything. "Oi, pumpkin!" I says, "Where'd you think you're goin'?" But it didn't answer see, on account of the fact that pumpkins can't talk, like. So I ran after it, but it weren't nowhere in sight. Mad world we live in, ain't it? Mad.'

'Albie,' his companion muttered, trying to pry the oddly green drink away from his friend. 'You're drunk.'

We made it over to the bar where a large woman with dark, curly hair that had a green ribbon running through it was serving a group of rowdy men. Once they'd staggered off she turned to us and asked in the nasal accent of Seion, 'All right there my dears. What can I get you?'

Alaric gave a huge grin, leading across the bar to yell, 'Four of your finest tankards of mead, my good lady.'

'Coming right up, lad,' replied the woman, who bustled away to get the drinks.

'Well this was an excellent idea,' beamed Alaric.

I smiled at Alaric's propensity to enjoy himself in any situation, especially if drink were involved.

'Don't get too comfortable,' Mera warned. 'We can't spend too long here. We should probably get moving quite soon actually, I'm sure that–'

Alaric cut across her. 'Mera, do you ever relax?'

Mera looked affronted for a moment. 'Well, I mean, that's not really the point, Alaric. We're here to… you know what, never mind.'

Ilyssa and I smiled as the barmaid returned with our drinks. Alaric paid her and picked up his flagon eagerly.

Ilyssa struggled to pick up her flagon, which was almost as big as her head. 'This must be the longest you've ever gone without drinking, Alaric. I'm impressed.'

'Well you see little sister, I'm very impressive,' he grinned.

Ilyssa raised her eyebrows. 'I always thought, big brother, that you were more annoying than impressive, but to each their own I suppose.'

As Alaric pretended to be insulted, I picked up my drink and looked around the room. I could see the man who had thought his pumpkin had walked off staggering towards the door, his friend calling after him, 'Albie, you forgot your shoes!' At a table in the far corner of the room was a very lost looking couple who were sitting together nibbling on a bowl of something grey and soggy and throwing dirty looks at the table next to them where a swarthy man with shoulder length, black hair appeared to be entertaining a group of angry looking men. A particularly large one, who had a head so shiny that he looked like an egg, was taking up two chairs. The man with the black hair was gesticulating wildly and he kept almost banging into the people behind him. On the other side of the room a group of women were sitting, laughing raucously at one another.

'...And what's more,' I heard Ilyssa say. 'If I hadn't gone and found him right then he'd have ending up in the pond, soaking wet and cursing the poor dog nine ways to Sunday.'

Mera laughed. 'My goodness, I think you're almost as clumsy as Lex.'

'Hey,' I interjected.

'Oh you've joined us, have you?' said Mera, sipping her drink.

I was about to reply when I heard a loud thump and looked round. The man with black hair had stopped throwing his hands about and was staring up into the face of the bald man who was now standing. His fists were clenched tightly, clearly having just pounded then on the table. The tavern had gone quiet. The woman behind the bar was nervously wiping glasses. I suddenly wished we hadn't come here. Another of the men from the table stood up. He was tiny compared to the bald man, with a fat face and fingers that glittered with jewelled rings. When he spoke it was with an oily, voice.

'See, the thing is, Ezra,' he drawled. 'We don't believe that sack full of lies, do we boys?' The other men at that table growled menacingly and one of them cracked his knuckles.

'Right,' the man called Ezra replied in a heavy Seioni accent. 'No I didn't think you would. Well I guess that doesn't leave us with many options then.' In a flash he spun around and grabbed the bowl from the couple's table. He threw it at the small man who cried out in shock as it struck his face, giving him time to run for the door. I didn't see if he got there, however, because at that moment everyone in the tavern began to panic. People were dashing to and fro trying to find a way out. The door became blocked as everyone tried to cram through it.

'Come on, Lex, don't just stand there!' yelled Mera. 'Move!'

'Move where?' I asked. 'There's nowhere to go.'

'Out the back,' pressed Ilyssa.

We ran behind the bar and through the little door that led to the storeroom, looking for a way out. Behind a shelf filled with crates and barrels I could see the outline of a door that had to lead to freedom, but there was no way to get to it with all the heavy boxes blocking it.

'Now what?' Ilyssa moaned.

'Well we can't stay in here. Maybe it's calmed down out there,' I said.

We peered around the edge of the door and saw the man called Ezra being pinned up against the wall by the huge, bald man. He had one hand wrapped around his throat and Ezra was turning slowly purple.

'We should help him,' said Alaric, stepping through the doorway and back into the tavern, but Ilyssa grabbed the scruff of his shirt before he got too far and dragged him back.

'Are you trying to get yourself killed?' she hissed. 'That man would crush you without a moment's thought. Use your head!'

'All right, all right, calm down,' he placated her. 'Lex, can you do something? We can't just leave him to be killed.'

I looked carefully around the room. Most people had run straight for the exit, but some were still looking for a way out. 'Not in here, not without being seen. Besides there's no guarantee it would definitely work.'

'Well, we have to do something,' he dropped down and scooped up an empty bottle that had rolled towards us on the floor. He lobbed it towards the place where Ezra was being slowly choked to death. We all dropped down under the bar.

I heard the smash of the bottle hitting something solid and then the thump of someone falling to the floor followed by even more screams and yells. Mera ducked her head around the corner.

'Good shot, Alaric. You got him right in the head. Looks like that idiot gets to live to see another day. Right, I suggest just making a mad dash.'

Nobody could think of a better idea, so we stood up and sprinted towards the door. Mera went first, then Alaric, then Ilyssa and finally me. We were about halfway across the room when something collided with the side of my head. It sent me spinning to the ground, losing focus for a moment. Everything was buzzing and blurred. I lifted a hand to where my head was throbbing and felt a small bump but no blood. Sighing thankfully I blinked my eyes rapidly until the table I was lying under came into focus and I could lift myself off the floor. Dizzily getting to my feet, I looked around and saw that Alaric and Ilyssa had made it to the door, but instead of running through it they were staring with panic-stricken faces at Mera who was being slowly backed into a corner by a nasty looking man holding a knife.

Before I could react Ezra ran up to them and brought a bottle down on the man's greasy head. Shards of glass scattered across the floor and Mera flung her arms up to protect her face. The man slumped to the floor and didn't get back up. Looking slightly dazed, Mera lowered her arms and muttered a weak, 'Thank you.'

'Not a problem, your Highness,' Ezra grinned in response.

Mera's look of mild bewilderment turned into one of utter horror.

Ezra ignored her astonishment, simply saying, 'Grab your friends and let's get out of here,' and then he turned his back on her and high-tailed it out of the door.

Mera stood frozen for a movement before she shook herself and ran after him, Ilyssa, Alaric and I following right behind. We spilled outside, where the last of the patrons were running up the path towards the village.

'Hey! Wait!' Mera called out.

Ezra turned back, his eyes flicking between us. Now that I could see him clearly he looked no older than seventeen. Finally he settled on Mera with a cheeky grin. 'Yes, your Highness? Did you need something else?'

'Why are you calling me that? Who are you?' Mera asked, a note of panic in her voice.

'Isn't that how we speak to royalty anymore?' he smirked.

'What makes you think I'm royalty?' Mera queried.

'Well other than the fact that you have the air of being spoon fed all your life, I happen to know what the Princess of Culrain looks like. And you, my dear, are she.'

'Why on earth would a money-grubbing trickster like you know what the royal family of a kingdom you don't even live in looks like?' Mera snapped.

'Well everyone has to have a hobby,' he joked. 'And besides, what makes you think that I'm a money-grubbing trickster? That hurts you know, we've only just met. I could be a nobleman.'

'Well you do have *the air* of a lowlife,' Mera spat back.

'Fair enough,' he conceded. 'But I'm clearly a lowlife with a conscience, or did you not catch my act of heroism back there? You're welcome, by the way.'

'The entire problem was caused by your stupidity!' Mera huffed. 'I don't know who those people were but only an idiot would get involved with them. And now look what you've gone and done. The whole tavern is ruined.'

'Simply a business deal gone a little askew. Anyway, the tavern's not ruined. Now they've got a story to tell. Business will be booming again by this time tomorrow,' he grinned.

'Do you really think,' Mera began, her voice dangerously low, 'that it's perfectly acceptable to just-'

'All right, all right, let's all just calm down,' I interjected before Mera started spitting fire. While she seethed, Ezra simply looked on amused. I could still feel my head pounding.

'What do we do now?' Ilyssa asked.

'Well we'd better get going. I'm sure our knight in shining armour here will be straight off to the castle. How much is the reward now?' Mera spat.

'What makes you think I'm going to turn you in? You clearly don't want to be found. I happen to know a little bit about that myself,' he said calmly.

'How very gallant of you,' Mera replied dryly. 'I'm sure your experience hiding from the law and the lawless alike serves you well.'

'Maybe we should take him with us. He won't be able to give us away if we can keep an eye on him,' Alaric spoke up.

'Are you insane?' Mera hissed. 'That's a terrible idea.'

'You never know Mera, it might be a good one,' Ilyssa reasoned. 'That way we know he's not giving away our position and maybe he could show us a little about defending ourselves. I don't know if you've noticed but he's quick in a tight spot and we may be encountering more and more of those.'

'They do have a point,' I said cautiously.

'We don't need any protection he can give us, we've got mag-'

'Umm, Mera,' I said loudly, cutting her off.

'Sorry, Lex. See, even talking would be difficult with him around,' Mera jabbed a finger in Ezra's direction.

'But we do need someone who knows this kingdom,' pointed out Alaric. 'I vote that he stays.'

'We're not keeping him! He's not a stray dog!' yelled Mera

'Well we can't let him go, he knows who you are,' Alaric replied

141

'If I could just interject here…'

We turned to where Ezra was standing, watching us argue with an amused look on his face.

'First of all, I'm not planning on telling anyone where you are, as I have already said. Secondly, I have no idea what you're up to, nor do I care to find out, but if you hope to get through this region unscathed you're probably going to need some help from someone who knows it. See those mountains over there? They keep the nobility on the other side safe from the riff-raff on this side. There are some pretty nasty people around and, no offence, but you're not looking too well protected. Thirdly, I am currently in need of a little help myself. You see, those lovely men in there, who are probably coming 'round about now, are slightly peeved with me.' Mera huffed, but Ezra carried on as if she hadn't made a noise. 'It's likely that I wouldn't get far on my own. So you see, it's a win-win situation.'

We all turned to Mera who looked thoroughly unimpressed. 'Fine, fine. You know what, it's fine. Come along, it'll be fun. It's not like we're doing something serious or dangerous or entirely secret,' she reached down behind the hay bales and roughly pulled up her things from where we had left all our packs. 'Why not all sit down and wait around for the Brethren to find us. We can all laugh about it later. Oh no, wait, my mistake, we'll all be dead.'

She stalked off up the path in a huff. We hurriedly picked up our packs and followed her.

Ezra caught up to me and muttered, 'Is she always this angry?'

'You think this is angry?' I replied. 'Wait until you make her really mad, you'll be wishing for this.'

'Well that I'm looking forward to. Actually if you could persuade her to stop for a minute I can get my horse. Might make the journey a little easier.'

'You have a horse?' I asked, hoping that, that meant the end of hauling our heavy packs all over the place. I raised a hand to my head as it gave a particularly painful throb.

'I do indeed. His name is Valiant,' he grinned. 'And I've got some other things that might help if your spirited friend will let me get them.'

In the time it took to coax Mera back Ezra had saddled his horse, a beautiful bay stallion with a white star right in the middle of his forehead. He attached his few possessions to the saddle and then offered to do the same for us. Ilyssa, Alaric and I accepted gladly, but Mera stubbornly insisted on carrying her own. There wasn't time to argue. We heard movement from inside the tavern, so we headed off quickly. Mera insisted that we stay off the main road, at least until we had put some distance between us and the group Ezra had infuriated. Not wanting to make her angry again, we agreed.

After a while the pounding in my head got too much to bear and I had to stop. Ezra had me sit down on a grass mound while he looked at my head. I felt his calloused fingers pressing against a sore spot along my hairline and I hissed in pain.

'Sorry,' he apologised.

'Will I live?' I asked.

'You'll be fine,' he grinned. 'Drink lots water and get some rest. You shouldn't sleep for too long at one time, though. Someone will have to wake you up every few hours to check on you.'

Mera, whose annoyance with Ezra seemed to have subsided some, looked at me with concern.

'We should stop here,' she said. 'No one's going to be looking for us in a field. It's dark anyway. We can get up early and move on. I'll take your watch Lex.'

'I can take his watch if you like,' offered Ezra. 'Given that it's somewhat my fault.'

'No thank you, that won't be necessary,' she snapped.

Ilyssa and Alaric started unpacking our things. I heard Alaric mumble, 'I guess we're not eating tonight.'

'No really,' Ezra insisted. 'I can do it. You don't have to worry about me falling asleep, I've done it before.'

'That really isn't this issue here,' Mera's eyes were narrowed. 'You see, I don't know about you, but I am not accustomed to letting strangers watch over me as I sleep. We may wake up tomorrow to find you've murdered us all.'

I scoffed, remembering how we'd happily walked into Deathgrove and stayed in Ilyssa and Alaric's room having only met them that day. Luckily Mera didn't hear me.

'Hmm, can't really wake up once you're dead, can you, your Highness?' pointed out Ezra

'Don't call me your Highness,' Mera hissed.

'All right,' intervened Ilyssa, as Alaric ushered me into bed. 'It's been a long, eventful day and I'm sure you're both tired, but your yelling isn't helping us stay hidden. Now let's just say for arguments sake that Mera, Alaric and I do the watch for tonight. You can argue about it to your hearts' content tomorrow, but for now let's just get some sleep.'

'Fine,' muttered Mera and stalked off to grab the mat next to me. Ezra went over to tether his horse and Ilyssa went to help Alaric with the last of the packs.

After a while the pounding began to subside and I started to drift off, the sound of Mera's angry grumbling fading away into the darkness.

18

Sword fights and warnings

The more I got to know Ezra the more I liked him. He had an infectious charm and a cheeky smile. Even when he wasn't laughing there was a constant air of joy about him. We were all grateful for his company. All except Mera that is, whose distain she didn't try to hide. The morning after the incident at *The Dancing Sun* she had wolfed down breakfast and been extra sharp with everyone while we were packing. She had snapped at me to sit down and let the others do it, even though I'd insisted that I felt much better. She calmed down a little as the day drew on and we moved away from Raufen. Enough that she stopped yelling at Ezra every five minutes anyway.

'I often travel through the east of Seion,' he told us as made our way closer to the mountains. 'I know the area very well.'

'Where's home for you?' Ilyssa asked.

He gestured around him. 'The whole of Seion is my home. Though I spend most of my time in the east. Like I said, the noble families like their space and we like ours.'

Mera scoffed again and muttered something that sounded suspiciously like *homeless good-for-nothing*.

The path he planned to take us was nearly the same as the one Mera had suggested. It would have us passing along the bottom of the mountain range of Windgerest Mountains and back towards the Great Forest. We had almost reached the foot of the mountains when a stench reached our noses.

'Ugh, what's that smell,' complained Alaric, covering his nose and mouth with his shirt.

'It's the marshland,' answered Ezra. 'Don't worry, you'll get used to it.'

'What marshland?' came Mera's voice from behind us. 'There's no marsh marked on the map. Are you trying to lead us into a trap.'

'Of course not,' Ezra chuckled. 'I'm not surprised it's not on your map, many don't have it. You're lucky you found me. Not many know the way through. You could get yourself into an awful mess in there if you're not careful.'

Mera didn't look impressed but she kept quiet.

'How long will it take to cross it?' I asked.

'Not more than a day,' he replied. 'We aren't too far from it now. We should make camp before we start and cross in the morning.'

We camped at the foot of the mountain with the marshland stretched out in front of us. In an attempt to distract us from the smell Ezra taught us a Seioni song about a girl who was left up the mountain to die by parents that didn't want her.

His voice was sweet and strong and even without an instrument to accompany him he had us captivated as he sang,

'When she was a babe she was left there to die,
Fly, oh mountain girl, fly,
But the mountain it saved her when it heard her cry,
Fly, oh mountain girl, fly.

'The eagles they found her and fed her with flowers,
Fly, oh mountain girl, fly,
And sheltered on the mountain, oh it gave her powers,
Fly, oh mountain girl, fly.

'Every day she watched the eagles go flying,
Fly, oh mountain girl, fly,

She longed to join them and said so in sighing,
Fly, oh mountain girl, fly

'One day she ran to the edge of the cliff,
Fly, oh mountain girl, fly,
And feeling the wind take her she jumped into it,
Fly, oh mountain girl, fly.

'Along with the eagles she soars through the sky,
Fly, oh mountain girl, fly,
And now with her powers she never will die
Watch that mountain girl fly.'

We went to bed in high spirits that night. The next day we began our trek across the marsh. Ezra took us step by step along the safest path, guiding his horse over the soggy ground. Even so it wasn't an easy journey. I almost slipped over a number of times. At one point Ezra had to fling out an arm to catch Alaric when he slid off the path and almost landed face-first in the mud.

'Thanks,' he muttered.

'Not a problem,' Ezra smiled. 'Guess we're even for that bottle you threw back at the tavern.'

'You never told us who those people were,' said Ilyssa, who had rushed forward to help Alaric back onto the path. 'You know, the ones who almost killed you.'

'Oh, them. Just your every day businessmen,' Ezra replied. 'The kind who'll rip your guts out if you're late on a payment or two.'

'And how many payments were you late on?' asked Mera snidely.

'Maybe more than one or two,' he grinned back. 'I would've paid them eventually. I suppose it's too late now. I'll just have to avoid this area for a while. You picked a bad place to travel through without a guide. It's full of thieves and bandits. Not to mention the marshland. You see why the nobles stay on the other side of the mountains. Nicer land, fewer criminals. And that's where the castle is. Wouldn't want to stray too far from the royals. They might miss their arses being kissed. No offence, Mera.'

Perhaps luckily Mera was too busy attempting to drag her foot out of particularly sticky bit of mud to hear him. I went over to help.

'Have you calmed down?' I asked, pulling her leg, which came out with a horrible squelch.

'What? Oh, *him* you mean,' she muttered. 'Well, no one's listening to me anyway. I may as well save my breath.'

'I really think you're being silly about this. He seems like a good guy. He's brought us this far. What reason would he have to suddenly change his mind now?'

'We have no idea who he is,' she insisted. 'We don't know his motives. We don't know why he wanders aimlessly about the countryside. Why does he want to avoid the nobles so badly? What does he have against them?'

'Some would say that was a perfectly normal reaction to have to nobles,' I commented.

Mera carried on as though I hadn't spoken. 'And honestly, I just don't like his attitude. He's smarmy. He thinks too highly of himself. Look at him strutting ahead there. I've met plenty of people just like him and they're always looking for something to gain.'

'He isn't smarmy,' I sighed. 'He's jolly. And he isn't strutting. He's very kindly showing us the safest route through the marshes. Besides, even you can't deny that the horse is helpful.'

'I've got nothing against his horse,' she muttered. 'Apart from its ridiculous name.'

'I think you're just upset because he keeps calling you *your Highness* and he talks back when you're being pushy.'

Mera's head whipped around to face me. 'What? I'm not pushy. Lex, I am not pushy.'

'If you say so,' I smiled.

Leaving Mera muttering in irritation I hurried to catch up with Ilyssa, Alaric and Ezra who were walking ahead talking about the two expertly forged swords that Ezra had been given by a blacksmith for helping him with some local thieves.

'Must have been very troublesome thieves,' Mera had murmured when he'd pulled the swords out for the first time, looking at them with interest.

'What do you have to defend yourselves?' Ezra asked as I came to stand beside Ilyssa.

Eyeing me cautiously, Alaric said, 'Well my bow and arrow have come in quite handy.'

Ezra looked at him as though he'd grown another head.

'That's it?' he asked incredulously. 'Gods, you're lucky you haven't all been killed in your sleep. I could teach you if you'd like. To fight with swords, I mean.'

'But we don't have any swords to fight with,' Ilyssa pointed out.

'Well I've got the spare you can practise with. It might be an idea to get another one from a blacksmith,' he suggested. 'And some armour too. A sword's not going to do you much good if your opponent has cut your arm off.'

'And where, exactly, do you propose we get the money to buy all this?' Mera cut in. 'Or are you perhaps suggesting we steal it?'

'We might have enough for a sword. Not for armour though, that's very expensive,' Ilyssa said. 'We could have a competition to see who gets it.'

'Great!' Alaric clapped his hands together, startling Valiant. 'Ezra you can judge.'

'Well I'll have to teach you first,' he pointed out. 'Let's concentrate on getting through the marsh before we start competing over swords. It shouldn't be much farther.'

As the sun was dipping low in the sky Ezra pulled back a particularly large and spiky bush and to my great relief I saw that we had reached the end of the marshes. A rocky path led away from the muddy grassland and into a much more solid looking field. The land in Seion was generally drier and less plentiful than the land in Culrain. The earth that stretched out before us looked like yellow mud that'd had all the moisture drawn from it. It was patterned with a number of cracks through which sprouted tufts of grass. The grass here was coarser than I was used to and much sparser. Taupe rocks thrust randomly out of the ground so that we had to watch our feet more often so as not to trip over.

We carried on northwest while we still had daylight and finally found our way back to the Great Forest. We settled down at its edge, using the water from our canisters to clean off the worst of the mud that was caked onto our clothes. After Ilyssa and I had made dinner, Alaric began recounting stories he'd picked up from his years of frequenting his local tavern. Ezra joined in when he started singing a song about a man as small as a thumb who wanted to play with Giants.

'There was once a small man, as small as a thumb,
He didn't like his height but he did like him rum,
It gave him the courage to cross over the bridge,
To go and see the Giants who basked in the sun.

'Over the other side he found the Giants playing,
He crept a little closer to hear what they were saying,

But they caught the little man and they thwarted his plan,
And they took to the court to be judged by the king.

'Before the king said a word the man cried out in alarm,
"Please don't kill me Sire, I mean you no harm,
I only wished to see what I was told could not be,
Being as great and as tall as a barn."

'The king considered his words, he pondered them greatly,
He said, "I've been thinking of the small folk quite lately,
How they hunt us like animals and treat us like criminals,
But you seem so different my choice isn't made hastily.

"'We Giants understand what it is to be thought strange,
And you too, little man, your size cannot change,
So you must stay here with us, live your days with no fuss."
And so he did and was happy as life could arrange.'

Over the next few nights we moved farther into the forest. We didn't wander too far though, not wanting to got lost or come across one of the dangerous magical creatures that were said to lurk in its depths. As the ancient trees grew closer together, the canopy became so thick that only a few rays of sunlight were able to trickle through to the forest floor below. I was certain that they had never felt the sting of the woodcutter's axe. The animals that lived in this part of the forest made unfamiliar sounds. Where I was used to the high twittering of birdsong and soft scurrying of squirrels, here we were followed by strange squawks and guttural grunts. There was a curious power in the forest. I felt an odd humming in the trees, thudding through the ground, whispering in the wind. It pushed at me, urging me onwards.

Mera, who was becoming more and more sleep deprived by the day, finally caved in and let Ezra take watch at night. Although I have a feeling that for the first few nights she stayed awake too, just to make sure he didn't steal all of our possessions and run off into the night with them.

Not being allowed to talk about magic combined with the distraction of Ezra beginning to teach us sword fighting meant that it was easy to forget why we were travelling. It turned out that I was very bad with swords. I didn't have the coordination that it required and despite all the years I'd spent sawing and hammering as a carpenter's apprentice it hurt my arm to keep holding the sword at the right level to the point where I wasn't finding learning enjoyable at all. I always ended up letting the tip drop to the ground.

Ezra had clearly been learning for a long time. He kept talking about footwork and stance and different types of swords. He and Alaric talked at length about the design that was etched into the hilts of his swords. Ezra mentioned that it was based on the house of a nobleman he had known. Even Mera seemed impressed by the swords' perfect balance. She herself had spent a lot of time poring over weapons in the castle's armoury.

Ilyssa was in her element. She took to fighting like a duck to water. She was always happy to stop and practise, even if it was just with a stick as she got used to the weight of a real sword. She beamed with pride when Ezra told her he had never seen someone pick up footwork so quickly. Alaric was pretty good too, though not as good as his sister, and Mera was almost as bad as me.

We were making good progress with our journey, getting closer to Meyrom every day. I began to wonder what was going to happen when we reached the border, whether Ezra was going to continue on with us or if he would stay in Seion. I didn't want to lose his company but it would be impossible to shield him from our goal the closer we got to Skara Brae. I had no idea how he would react if he found out. Seion's royalty had never been as passionate as Culrain's had in removing magic from the kingdom. I suppose that we'll have to deal with that if and when we come to it.

'You're holding it wrong,' gasped Ezra. 'Turn your palm so that you're gripping the handle at the side.'

'I'm trying,' Mera muttered angrily. 'Don't push me.'

Ezra sighed as Mera clutched at the heavy sword, which wobbled precariously in her hand.

'Here, let me show you,' he placed his own sword back in its scabbard and moved over to her side where he gripped her arm and turned it to the correct position. 'You have to hold this stance or you leave yourself open for your opponent to strike.'

Mera twisted her arm, a look of pained concentration on her face very similar to the one that appeared when she'd first tried to learn magic, before letting the sword tip fall to the ground.

'It's too heavy,' she sighed, disappointed.

Ezra gave her a comforting smile. 'Maybe we moved onto the sword a bit fast. We could go back to the stick for a while.'

Her face went red with what I could only assume was indignation before she snapped, 'It's fine, I've got it. Go back over there.'

'I'm only trying to help you,' Ezra muttered.

'Well you're doing a very bad job of it, aren't you?' Mera hissed.

The two of them continued to bicker as Ilyssa, Alaric and I watched on in amusement.

Walking through the forest we had come across a small clearing just a short way from where a babbling brook led into a pond. Ezra remarked that this would be as good a place as any for him to continue to teach us how to fight, so we had spent the last few hours doing just that. I had opted out, deciding that swords and I simply didn't mix. Alaric and Ilyssa had sparred for a while but it was soon clear that Ilyssa was superior. Now that she could hold the sword's weight, only Ezra was able to beat her in a fight.

When Mera's turn came she had risen, determined to master this skill. Honestly, I think she just wanted to prove she was as good as Ezra. It clearly didn't matter to her that she could barely hold the sword.

All of a sudden I heard a sharp crack behind us. I whipped around but couldn't see anything through the trees.

'Be quiet a minute, would you,' I called to Mera and Ezra, who were still arguing.

Mera turned and asked, 'What is it?'

'I'm not sure,' I replied. 'I thought I heard a branch snap.'

'Maybe it's just a deer,' suggested Alaric.

For a moment none of us could see anything in the thick trees and then, appearing suddenly out of the gloom and making Valiant whinny and toss his head back, a hulking creature stepped towards us. Its huge, razor sharp talons gleamed in the fading sunlight as it prowled into the clearing. I recognised the creature immediately. With the head and wings of an enormous eagle and the body and tail of a lion it could only be a griffin. Its beak tipped down into a sharp point. Its icy blue eyes, vivid and wild, focused intently on us as it advanced. Its golden feathers shook slightly as it flexed its massive wings. The iridescent claws on its back legs flexed as it padded along, its tail swishing back and forth as it came to a stop just inside the clearing.

Ilyssa, Alaric and I stumbled back to stand with the others. Ezra, who had frozen when the griffin first appeared, now gripped the handle of his sword and drew it, ready to fight.

Mera noticed his movement and whispered angrily, 'Put that down before you insult him.'

'Insult it?' he sounded incredulous. 'What is it?'

'A griffin you fool, now put your sword away unless you want to get us all killed,' and before anyone could stop her she stepped forwards.

Once in front of the griffin she bowed low and said, 'I'm sorry if we have disturbed you.' I noticed her hands trembling slightly.

The griffin regarded her coolly and replied in a deep, slow voice, 'The only disturbing thing here, Princess Mera, is your appalling skill with a sword.'

Mera looked affronted for a moment but then collected herself. 'You know who I am? Then you must know where we're going.'

'I do indeed. I know precisely what you are doing,' the griffin, who had been regarding Mera with his piercing gaze, turned suddenly to me. I felt as though I had been plunged into an icy bucket of water. His eyes flicked back to Mera and he continued. 'And I must tell you now, that your ridiculous quest for magic must stop. Turn back while you still can.'

I saw Ezra start at his words.

'What do you mean? We want to revive magic. We know what to do. That's why we're going to Skara Brae. With the help of the Sisterhood we can return magic to the land. The Brethren won't stand a chance at resistance.'

'Ah yes,' murmured the griffin. 'Those men who call themselves a brotherhood have been quite troublesome for us Magic Folk. I remember a time when we were free, before we were forced to hide like common rats, cowering in the shadows. But the Sisterhood cannot help you with that.'

'So does that mean you'll help us?' Mera's voice was filled with excitement

'Help you?' the griffin looked almost amused. 'No, child. I will not help you defeat this so called Brethren of Peace.'

'I don't understand,' Mera's smile faded. 'They are the enemy here. Why won't you help?'

The griffin raised its great head and stared down at her. 'Do not mistake what you are doing as a fight against evil. History will remember this as a difference of opinion. You won't be seen as the light fighting away the dark. You will be one side of a battle and it shall be the loosing side. Let me be perfectly clear when I say that you have no chance of winning this war. You are unprepared for their power. Whatever dreams you possess will be no match for the reality they will bring down upon you. You may hope all you wish for a better world, but you should save the precious time you have left before they find you too.'

'You're a coward!' Mera shouted, suddenly angry. 'You're running and hiding. Why aren't you fighting? This is your life we're talking about.'

'Call me a coward all you wish little princess, but we shall see in the end. When your bravery has forsaken you, when the enemy has you vanquished, when you have no hope left and you weep for the life you could have had, I will still be alive and safe. Then call me a fool. Winning a battle does not guarantee you the war and they will continue to battle you. Fight after fight, lives cut down endlessly. Their bloodlust will not falter. They will never stop hunting us. We cannot win.'

'Then go. Leave! Run away! Save your precious skin,' yelled Mera.

The griffin gave her a final piercing look with his cold blue eyes and, turning slowly, walked back into the forest as quietly as he had appeared.

Mera, brimming with rage, screamed and flung the sword she was still holding to the ground. She grabbed the maps that were scattered on the ground from where she had been perusing them earlier and threw them after the griffin, but he was long gone.

'Mera, stop,' I called, as Ilyssa went to pick up the maps before they were damaged.

'Oh you want me to stop too, do you? Shall I sit down quietly and let the adults sort it out? A difference of opinion! He is a coward and when this is all over he's going to regret saying that. Ugh,' she shivered, as if disgusted at her own words. 'What am I thinking? We're children, we don't know what we're doing? There was only supposed to be two of us anyway. You two weren't meant to be here! And you!' She rounded on Ezra. 'You certainly aren't meant to be here. You weren't meant to know any of this and now we can't let you go.'

'What? I can do what I want, thank you. I'm here by choice and if I want to leave I will,' replied Ezra.

'No you will not. We can't risk that. Now you're a burden!'

'Hey! I'm not a burden.'

'Yes you are! You're a threat! And you eat all our food.'

'Oh well, I'm so sorry,' Ezra drawled. 'My humblest apologies, your Highness, for saving your life. I cannot express my sorrow, your Grace, for leading you safely through what is a very dangerous and almost entirely unmapped part of the kingdom. How can I begin to ask you to accept my apology, your Royal Rudeness, for trying to give you the skills that none of you possess and that may well save your life while asking for absolutely nothing in return?'

'Oh please, as if it's unreasonable to be suspicious of someone who, as you so eloquently put it, gives so much while asking for nothing,' Mera spat. 'You make a very good point. Why haven't you asked us for anything? You're away from those thugs you were doing *business* with so they're no longer a threat to you. We don't even know who you are. How did you come by these maps? They have a house seal on them, which means they belong to a noble family and those swords have a house sigil on the hilts. I bet you killed a nobleman and stole his maps and swords.'

'All right, that's a little har-' I tried to interrupt but Ezra cut across me.

'Good gods I have never met someone who is so ungrateful. Is that how you treat everyone who tries to help you? I'm glad I didn't work for you in your royal homestead. Your servants must think you're unbearable!'

'All right, you two,' insisted Ilyssa. 'I really think-'

'Unbearable? How dare you!' screeched Mera. 'I have sacrificed everything for the good of my people. I have left everything safe behind to help those in need. What were you doing before we met you? Drinking your way through every tavern in Seion? Have you ever worked an honest day in your life?'

'Oh you privileged little-'

'All of you, stop shouting, now!' yelled Alaric. 'This is not a safe place to be yelling yourselves hoarse about things that are meant to be kept secret. You're acting like children and you're upsetting the horse.'

He was right. Valiant was pawing at the ground nervously, pulling at the rope that tethered him to the tree. Mera and Ezra bowed their heads and muttered apologies under their breath. Ezra went over to sooth Valiant.

'Great,' Alaric clapped his hands together. 'Now that's sorted, who's hungry? I think that Ezra and Mera should do dinner as punishment for nearly ripping one another's heads off.'

Mera, who was still breathing heavily, stalked over to the packs. She began roughly dragging things out and chucking them on the ground. Ilyssa went over to calm her down and probably also to make sure she didn't break anything in her anger. I looked towards Ezra, who had moved away from

Valiant and was now sitting at the base of a tree stump with a dazed expression on his face. He sat with his hands in his lap, squinting slightly, looking strangely like a dog that had lost its stick. I caught Alaric's eye and tilted my head towards Ezra. We moved over and crouched down in front of him.

'How're you doing?' I asked.

'Well, it's not every day a griffin walks into your camp and starts talking about magic,' he replied, surprisingly calm.

'Yeah that can be a little strange,' I said, not really sure what I was meant to do. I figured that Mera would want us to tie him up, but I doubted he was going to run off. He looked a little too shaken to get very far and the thought that the griffin was out there somewhere in the forest was probably keeping him rooted to the spot.

'I mean, I'd heard about magic, but I though it was all gone. Didn't that mad king kill all the magic people a hundred years ago?' he rubbed his hand across his face. 'It's a bit alarming to have it sprung on you like that.'

'You think that's bad, try seeing him doing magic for the first time while you're being chased by fifty man-eating dogs,' Alaric jerked his thumb at me.

'I don't think it was fifty. And maybe we shouldn't -'

'You can do magic?' Ezra asked

'Yeah,' I nodded. 'Mera too.'

'And you've been letting me light the fire by hand all this time,' he asked indignantly.

I let out a nervous laugh. 'Sorry. It doesn't really work like that anyway. Besides we had to be careful, you know. We weren't sure how you'd react.'

'I understand,' he nodded, running a hand through his shaggy hair. 'How did you four end up here?'

'Well...' I sat down next to Ezra and told him the whole story.

Ezra listened in silence. When I finished he stayed seated for a moment, letting everything sink in.

'Wow,' he muttered.

'Are you all right?' I asked.

'Yeah, yeah. I guess that my swords have been pretty useless,' he said, still looking slightly dazed.

'No, not at all,' I insisted. 'You were right. We should know how to defend ourselves without magic, especially when we can't use it most of the time.'

'Plus I think Ilyssa's having the time of her life,' added Alaric. 'And it's always great entertainment watching Mera with a sword.'

Ezra smiled for the first time since the griffin had appeared. 'She really hates me, doesn't she?'

'She doesn't hate you,' I said. 'She just doesn't trust you yet. Give her time. She'll come around. And maybe stop calling her your Highness.'

'That seems like sound advice,' he nodded.

Ilyssa called us over to help with dinner then, so we all got up. I went to sit next to Mera who was angrily folding the maps back up and stuffing them into her pack. I put my hand on her arm and she paused. Then she closed her eyes and laid her head on my shoulder.

'What are we doing, Lex?' she asked.

I put my arm around her. 'Who knows? But we're here now. That griffin didn't know what he was talking about. He was just scared. He didn't want to risk his own life. We've come this far, we can get the rest of the way too. Or are you telling me you want to go home?'

'Home,' she muttered. 'I don't even know what home is anymore.'

'Well you can always come and live with me,' I joked.

She snorted and moved to face me. 'Yes I'm sure your mother would be quite pleased with that. She must hate me.'

'No, I'm serious. It might be a bit of a squish with all five of us, though. You may have to sleep on the floor, or outside. But you're used to that by now,' I smiled.

Mera smiled too. 'Or I could go off and live in the wilderness. Become a cave person.'

'Or you could go with Ezra. I'm sure he'd love to have you with him. I can picture it now. They'd hear you coming from a mile off, yelling at each other.'

Mera let out a snort of laughter at my suggestion.

She quieted and said, 'I've been a little unkind to him, haven't I?'

'You do call him an untrustworthy, homeless prat a little more often than necessarily,' I replied.

'Oh, he just... I don't know what it is. He gets under my skin. And those swords-'

'Mera, you're scary enough without a sword in your hand. Maybe you can just let this one go,' I suggested.

She sighed. 'Maybe you're right.'

'I'm always right,' I said, standing up and offering her my hand. 'Now come on, let's go get some food before Alaric eats it all.'

19

The woman in the glade

We decided to stay in the clearing for another night. No one felt up to walking the next day. The griffin's words still rang in our ears and my feet were thankful for the break. Mera put her head in my lap and slept some more while I perused the spell book. It felt good to be able to practise magic again. I hadn't properly tried my hand as magic since we had left Deathgrove and I was a little rusty. I tried twisting the smoke from the fire into shapes. I almost had the outline of a ship but then the wind picked up and blew the smoke away.

At the edge of the clearing Ilyssa was deep in conversation with Ezra while he groomed Valiant. Alaric was on the other side, practicing with his bow on the trees at the clearing's edge and making the leaves quiver with every blow. The tree had a number of arrows buried deep in its bark.

Mera stirred, blinking in the bright sunlight.

'Morning,' I said, still focused on the book in front of me.

She yawned widely and stretched, almost hitting me in the face with her arm. Muttering an apology, she sat up and looked around. 'Is Alaric planning on making that tree into kindling?'

'I think he's working on his aim. Not that he needs to. He knocked a wasp out of the air earlier.'

'Blimey,' she mumbled, pulling her long hair back into a tidy knot. 'Is there any food? I'm starving.'

'Sure, we left you some. It's over by the pot,' I jerked my head to where Alaric had set aside a plate for her.

Mera grabbed it and took a seat beside me. Over by Valiant Ezra turned to us and said, 'Anybody fancy a duel?'

'Not me,' Alaric replied. 'I think I'll stick to my bow and arrow.'

'Lex?' Ezra asked.

'No, I don't think swords and me agree with one another,' I smiled.

He turned to Mera. 'Dare I ask?'

Mera simply shook her head.

'Looks like it's just us then,' Ezra told Ilyssa.

'Brilliant,' she grinned.

Mera and I watched as Ilyssa and Ezra sparred. They didn't use real swords when they were properly fighting. As we didn't have any armour, and nobody wanted to slice the other person's hand off, we thought it best to use small branches that we chopped down from a tree and fashioned into a rudimentary sword. Ilyssa wasn't as strong as Ezra, nor did she have the experience that he did, but she was quick and light on her feet. She used her agility to tire Ezra out. She let him lunge at her, overextending, then she danced around him and struck him with her stick. I winced as she landed a particularly brutal blow on his leg that made his knee buckle. He rolled quickly to avoid being struck again. Even without real swords they were managing to injure each other. Ezra had some nasty bruises across his body and Ilyssa had cuts all down her arms from when she'd miscalculated her balance and fallen into some brambles.

'One day,' commented Mera, 'they are going to really hurt one another. What are they going to do when they break an arm or twist an ankle?'

'Hobble, I expect,' I replied.

We'd been lucky so far not to encounter any serious injuries but it was just a matter of time. I knew Mera and I could handle sprains, having had to stagger home on days when we'd injured ourselves in the forest, and Ilyssa would know what plants could be used for medicine, but anything worse and we'd be out of luck.

I looked back to where Ilyssa and Ezra were fighting. Ilyssa was now standing over Ezra, her mock-sword at his throat, breathing heavily.

'Yield,' he panted. 'I yield.'

Ilyssa smiled triumphantly, leaping out of the way to let Ezra get up. He stood and held out his hand, saying, 'Well fought, Ilyssa. I'm seriously impressed.'

'Watch out, Lex. You've got competition,' Mera poked me in the ribs.

'Shut up,' I elbowed her back, feeling my face go red.

'Did you see that?' called Ilyssa breathily, coming over to sit with us and looking flushed but pleased.

'You were amazing,' I grinned.

'You know sis,' mused Alaric as he walked over to us. 'I think you've proven that you deserve the sword. Next town we get to, we should try and find a blacksmith.'

'Oh really?' her eyes danced with excitement. 'But what about you?'

'I've got my bow,' he held it up in case we had missed it. 'And besides, I saw what you just did to Ezra and I don't really fancy competing against that.'

'Believe me,' Ezra winced, rubbing his shoulder where Ilyssa had hit him. 'You don't. I think I'm going to go wash the mud off. There was a pond in that glade we passed on the way here.'

'I'll go with you,' I said, closing my book. 'We need some more water.'

Ezra and I set off towards the glade. We had just reached it when I flung out my arm to stop Ezra from going any farther.

'What is it?' he asked. 'Not more griffins.'

'No. Over there,' I nodded towards the pond where a woman was standing, her long dress flowing as though caught in a breeze, though the day was still. A bronze circlet garlanded her head, set with brilliant blue jewels that sparkled in the dappled sunlight. She turned towards us and smiled. She had a swarthy complexion like Ezra and many of the people in Seion but there was something different about her. Something in the way her skin almost glowed with an ethereal light, something in the way she held herself. On the surface her smile was bright and welcoming but beneath it felt dangerous.

'Hello,' Ezra called out to her. 'Are you lost?'

'No child,' she replied, her voice filling my mind with the memory of hot, sweet honey and spices. 'I am not lost, but you are.'

Ezra baulked at her words and fell silent. She turned her bright, amber eyes on me.

'Alexander Eriksson,' she hummed my name. I felt a trickling of warmth spread through my body as she spoke. 'You have come far, young one, but your journey is not yet over.'

'Who are you?' I whispered.

Her smile brightened and I blinked. 'My name is Aisling. I am one of the seven of whom you seek.'

'You're one of the Sisterhood?' I gasped. 'But how can you be here? I thought we had to reach Skara Brae to find you.'

'You must reach Skara Brae. As for how I am here, well, I am not here, not really,' she turned to the pond. Reeds whistled and swayed in the breeze. Insects buzzed and flew around the small flowers that lined the edge of the pond. A mother duck was quacking at her ducklings, which were swimming in circles around a ribbiting frog. 'You might call me a vision. When my sisters and I retained our power this glade was my home. Your passing through here has awoken me, as my sisters have also begun to waken. You are stirring the magical world. You must continue your journey to Skara Brae. Once you have reached it you will find what you need.'

165

'You know that we make it there then?' I asked 'Can you see that?'

'Be careful, child. Knowing isn't always an advantage. Seeing what is to come can be a burden. But if you really want to know…' she turned back to us and tipped her head to the side, considering me. 'Yes, I suppose it is time. Listen well for I shall not be repeating myself.'

Aisling took a deep breath. She appeared to swell slightly, a non-existent wind whipping through her hair as she spoke,

'At a time when magic has dwindled to naught,
And the powers that oppose seem unable to be fought,
There is one who can prevail to return what was taken,
And restore the people and the land that was shaken.

'Though small and unimportant at first he may seem,
With the aid and the guidance of the future queen,
His power will grow and his bravery swell,
Until his opponents with ease shall he fell.

'But be warned and take heed, he alone is not enough,
Only pain and betrayal will come of the queen's bluff,
If this comes to pass, he and more will be lost,
Beware of you foes, for this is the cost.'

'This is a prophecy that was foretold many centuries ago. When my sisters and I retreated into the earth we knew that we would be waiting a long time before we awoke. Now it seems that time has come. I wish you luck, child. You too, Jezrahiah Adalitz. May you find your way home. I must leave you now, but we will see each other again.'

'Wait, what does that mean?' I called but Aisling was already beginning to fade.

'Make sure you know who your enemies are,' she called, before disappearing completely.

Ezra and I stood there for a moment, stunned. Eventually Ezra found his voice. 'We should go back. Lex, come on.'

He put his hand on my shoulder.

'Yeah,' I muttered. 'Yeah, I'm coming.'

We turned and headed back towards camp. Something Aisling had said dawned on me. 'Ezra, did she call you Jezrahiah?'

Ezra looked pained for a moment. 'It's a family name. Please don't tell the others.'

'Sure,' I replied, concealing a smile.

When we got back to camp I saw that Mera had picked up the book I had dropped and was trying her own smoke shapes. I saw with pride that she had manifested a galloping grey horse that rode in circles around Valiant's head. Ilyssa and Alaric were sitting next to Mera, laughing as Valliant tried to catch the smoke horses in his mouth. Every time he got near one it would vanish and he would look around, confused as to where it had gone. He nickered softly when he saw us approaching. Mera, Ilyssa and Alaric looked around.

'Oh good,' called Mera, closing the book with a snap. 'You're back. Did you get the water?'

'No,' I said. 'We ran into someone.'

'All the way out here?' she asked.

I told them what had happened. When I mentioned the prophecy Mera piped up, 'A prophecy? What?'

Ezra recited it. I felt a slight rush of panic at the line, *he and more will be lost.*

When Mera heard it she went pale. 'The queen's bluff,' she muttered.

'Yeah, I was confused about that bit as well,' I admitted. 'It's strange that you haven't come across it before in all those books you've read.'

'Oh. Yes,' she mumbled. Her face turned red and she looked down.

I noticed her blush and frowned. 'What was that?'

'What was what?' she asked.

'You blushed.'

'I didn't blush.'

'Yes you did. Do you know something?'

She looked uncomfortable. 'Nothing you don't know.'

'Mera,' I pressed.

I looked at her intently and saw her hands twisted together uncomfortably.

'I have seen it,' she said so quietly I almost didn't hear her.

'You've seen it?' I asked, completely nonplussed. 'Why didn't you show me? This could have been a huge help.'

'Because she told me not to,' Mera mumbled.

We all stared at her.

'Who?' I asked. 'Who told you?'

'Fallyn. She's the leader of the Sisterhood. I found the prophecy and she came to me. She said it was important. She told me what I had to do but she said I couldn't tell you about the prophecy. Not yet.'

I was stunned. 'You should have told me anyway, Mera. You're supposed to tell me everything.'

'I wasn't meant to tell you,' she looked around, as though hoping for support but the others stayed silent.

I felt anger unfurling in my chest. 'So you lied to me? All this time you've been lying. Well, I guess we know what the queen's bluff is.'

'Please, you have to understand,' Mera begged. She held out her hands towards me, entreating me to listen, but all I felt was betrayal. 'She said I couldn't tell you, that I had to wait. You couldn't know at the beginning. She said it was important.'

'What makes you think she was right?' I shouted. 'What makes you think anything would have been different? You were my best friend, Mera! My only friend. What makes you think I wouldn't have followed you to the ends of the earth if you'd asked me? If you'd just told me why.'

'I'm sorry, Lex,' she whispered, tears filling her eyes. 'I'm so sorry.'

'I can't...' my voice broke. I could feel red-hot fury boiling through me. 'I can't look at you right now,' I turned and stormed off into the forest.

20
The vast ravine

I didn't know where my feet were taking me but after a while I found myself back at the pond. All trace of Aisling was gone. I still held the canisters that Ezra and I had been meaning to fill. I threw them down violently and heard one crack but I couldn't bring myself to care. I sat down heavily, my hands shaking in tight balls. I threw myself backwards, lying on the ground with my hands over my face.

What was Mera playing at? Did she really think that keeping things from me was helping anything? All this time I'd trusted her to be the person I could rely on and it turned out to be just one big lie. I heard footsteps approaching behind me.

'Whoever it is, I really don't want to talk,' I muttered into my hands.

'Well that's all right,' I heard Ilyssa reply. 'We'll just sit.'

And sit we did. We remained there in silence for a long time. The sun moved behind a cloud and cast a dull, grey light through the trees. After a while I sat up and propped my elbows on my knees. I stared out at the little pond. The animals that had been there when Aisling appeared had vanished too. Perhaps they had scarpered when I'd thrown down the canisters, or perhaps they didn't like the look of the storm clouds that were gathering overhead.

'How are you doing?' Ilyssa asked in quiet voice.

'I don't think I have ever been so angry before,' I replied.

'She was just doing what she thought was best for you,' Ilyssa replied reasonably. 'She's really sorry.'

I scoffed. 'She doesn't want my forgiveness. She wants my help. I'm only here because she thinks I'm useful.'

'Lex,' she chided. 'You know that isn't true. She was your friend long before she even knew about the prophecy. You said she was your best friend. Well you were her best friend too. It can't have been easy for her, finding out about the prophecy, not knowing what it meant, not being allowed to tell you. No, don't look at me like that. You know she couldn't tell you. Do you think you could have gone against the direct word of a very powerful sorceress? Especially when doing so could have had terrible consequences. She didn't know what was going to happen. She was scared. She was trying to do the right thing. You don't have to forgive her right away but at least admit that she did what she did with the very best intentions.'

Before I could answer there was a crack of thunder.

'Storm's coming,' Ilyssa muttered. 'But it'll pass. They always pass. Come on, let's fill these canisters and get back to the others.'

Ilyssa picked up the broken canister and gave me a quizzical look.

'I was angry,' I mumbled.

'We'll get a new one the next town we come to.'

'Let me try something,' I held out my hand.

She passed it to me. I took the canister. There was a crack running down the side. I breathed in deeply and said, '*Remian.*'

The crack sealed itself. I smiled, pleased at my work. I gave the canister back to her good as new. Her fingers brushed mine as she took it from my grasp.

'Well that's certainly a useful trick,' she smiled, walking back to the pond and filling it up.

Just then there was another thunderclap and rain started falling down heavily. Ilyssa pulled her hood up quickly. Dark spots appeared on the brown material as rain slashed onto it.

I lifted up my head and let the rain wash over me. It soaked into my hair. Cool water cascading over my face and down my neck. As the rain soaked my skin I felt my anger begin to fade.

I looked down and sighed, 'We should go back.'

We ran back to camp, treading carefully so as not to slip in the mud. I saw that Ezra and Alaric had erected a makeshift tent between the trees at the edge of the clearing. They were both sitting under it next to a fire, sheltering from the worst of the rain. Mera on the other hand was in the centre of the clearing, walking back and forth, wringing her hands. She looked up when she heard us coming. We stared at each other from across the clearing. She made as though to speak but I looked away quickly and followed Ilyssa into the tent.

A bitter wind whipped through the clearing and made us all shiver. I moved over to the fire to warm my frozen fingers. I regretted letting myself get soaked through. Hopefully none of us would catch a cold.

'What do you think we should do?' Alaric was asking. 'Should we stay here until the rain passes or should we try to find shelter somewhere else?'

'We don't know that there's anything close by,' replied Ilyssa. 'What do you think Ezra? You know the area best.'

'I'm not sure,' he admitted. 'There are no villages close enough, that's for sure. There may be somewhere that's better sheltered, though. Perhaps a couple of us should go and scout.'

'I don't know how keen I am to go out in this,' commented Alaric, squinting up at the black sky.

'I'll go,' offered Ezra.

At that moment Mera walked into the tent looking bedraggled. Her mouth was pressed into a hard line and she swallowed before she spoke. 'I'll go with you.'

There was a pregnant pause before Ezra replied, 'All right then. Let's get going.'

Mera and Ezra set off. They took Valiant with them. He was too big to fit under the makeshift tent anyway. Ilyssa, Alaric and I sat as close as we could get to the fire without getting burnt, huddled together for warmth. After a while the rain began to ease but Mera and Ezra still hadn't returned.

'I hope they're all right,' worried Ilyssa, peering out at the direction Mera and Ezra had gone. 'I wonder what they're doing.'

'Fighting probably,' replied Alaric, trying to sound jovial, though concern coloured his voice. 'I'm sure they're fine. They'll be back soon.'

But a few hours later and they still had not returned. The clouds had rolled away, the tent was packed up and the sun was low in the sky by the time we heard the sound of people approaching. We looked up to see a very disgruntled looking Mera and Ezra with Valiant in tow. All three of them were absolutely caked in mud.

'Mera hasn't killed you then,' joked Alaric. Then noticing their muddy appearance, he added, 'What happened to you?'

'We ran into some trouble,' Ezra grumbled. 'We hadn't found anywhere so we were coming back when Valiant got his leg stuck in the mud. The rain turned the ground into a quagmire.' He threw down his pack, which was sodden and almost as muddy as he was.

'We tried to help him through it, but he kept flicking mud into our faces whenever he lifted his hooves,' added Mera, whose trousers, shirt and cloak were similarly muddied. 'It took us almost an hour to calm him down.'

'We managed to get some leaves under him to make the ground more solid but he didn't seem to want to go after that. Took us ages to get him to walk on. And we had to keep putting leaves down so he didn't sink back into the ground. Absolute nightmare,' Ezra huffed.

'I'm going to wash,' muttered Mera, who stalked off towards the pond.

'I should probably get all of this mud off Valiant,' added Ezra, making to walk after her. He stopped and asked, 'Is everything all right here?' His eyes darted to me and then away again quickly.

'Everything's fine,' I assured him. 'It's too late to travel now. We should stay here another night.'

'Good plan,' Ezra nodded before following after Mera, the blue of his cloak nearly obscured by dark brown muck.

'Well,' sighed Ilyssa after Ezra had disappeared into the trees. 'That's all they needed to get along. A bit of mud and a stubborn horse.'

'If only it had rained earlier,' smiled Alaric.

'Shall we do dinner then?' Ilyssa suggested.

Ilyssa and Alaric began preparing the food. By the time Mera and Ezra came back a vegetable stew was simmering away. Hungry after their muddy adventure, Mera and Ezra wolfed down their food. We stayed huddled around the fire for a while, but no one was especially talkative that evening. Ezra took first watch as the rest of us hunkered down to sleep. I was woken some hours later by a hand on my shoulder.

'Lex,' a voice whispered. 'It's your turn to watch.'

I yawned widely and sat up. Mera was crouched down next to me. I nodded at her, standing up and stretching. When I looked back down she was still sitting there, looked at me with sad eyes.

'Lex,' she started. 'Lex, I-'

'I get it, Mera,' I cut her off. 'I get why you did it. But this is going to take time, all right?'

'All right,' she nodded, going back to her mat.

I watched her for a minute and then, unable to stop myself, I blurted out, 'What does it means? The last two lines of the prophecy. *If this comes to pass, he and more will be lost, beware of you foes, for this is the cost.* I'll be lost? Who's losing me?'

'I don't know. I wish I did,' she admitted.

'Doesn't sound too pleasant, does it?' I muttered.

Mera paused. 'I really am sorry, Lex.'

I sighed. 'Go to sleep, Mera.'

We walked in silence for some time the next day. The forest looked refreshed after the storm that had torn through it. The air smelled clean and fresh, and bright green, dewy leaves flashed in the morning sun.

Mera stayed away from me that day and the next. She stayed quiet too, spending her time either walking with Ezra and Valiant at the front or hanging back and letting us all walk ahead of her. She didn't even yell at Alaric when he tripped on her pack, ripping it along the seam. She sat in reserved silence during the evening while the rest of us clustered around the fire. When night fell she slept restlessly, tossing and turning. I was willing to admit by this point that I was missing my best friend but I still didn't feel ready to talk to her. My anger had ebbed away for the most part but I was still left with a strange, hollow feeling at the sight of her.

I found myself spending most of my time with Ilyssa. Her smile made my insides feel both warm and full of live worms. She reminded me of home, of the warm summer breeze that drifts through my hair on lazy days when I lay in the grass under the sun. Her dark, wide eyes were deep and safe. I recognised the scent of honeysuckle when she brushed against me. Her laugh was like birdsong. The invisible string I felt connecting us pulled me closer. I was being drawn to her more and more each day.

Three days after Aisling had visited us we came across a narrow, rickety bridge over a deep ravine. A river gushed along its rocky bed far below. I didn't like the look of it. I wasn't sure what it was, but I felt certain that we should try to find a way around it, but Ezra disagreed.

'If we don't cross here we'll have to travel nearly fifty miles west before there's a safe place to cross,' he told me.

I sighed. I had to admit that would be a long diversion.

'Come on, Lex,' Alaric implored. 'It'll be fine.'

'What do you think?' I asked Ilyssa.

'Well I can't say it looks like the safest bridge I've ever crossed, but I think it's better than going all the way around,' she replied.

I nodded. 'All right then, let's get going before I change my mind.'

Ezra went first, taking a few tentative steps to test its strength. Once he was satisfied it would hold he took Valiant across. I noticed I'd been holding my breath when I let out a sigh of relief as they reached the other side. Once he'd crossed I followed, trying to ignore how nervous the moss-covered bridge was making me. When I reached the other side I fished out my water canister and took a glug to calm myself down.

Ilyssa went next. She took the bridge two planks at a time in her eagerness to get across it as quickly as possible, muttering, 'Don't look down, don't look down,' the whole way. Once she reached the other side she gave me a relieved smile. Now it was Alaric's turn to cross. It swung ominously from side to side as though one wrong move would bring the whole thing down.

I raised the canister to my lips, but before I drank I noticed something swimming in the water. I recoiled and held the canister away from my face.

'What's wrong?' asked Ilyssa, putting her hand on my shoulder.

'I think something's crawled into my water canister,' I grumbled, peering inside.

'Well that's because you never close the lid,' she said. She put her face close to mine to look.

I saw a spider floating weightlessly in the water, clearly having fallen in and drowned. Before I could reach inside to fish it out, however, I heard a terrible scream. I whipped around just in time to see Mera falling through a broken plank in the old bridge. The canister slipped from my hand as I raced back to the edge of the cliff.

'Mera!' I shouted, staring wildly into the gaping ravine.

Ignoring the shouts of protest from behind me I scrambled back onto the bridge and fell to my knees. I stared down though the broken plank where Mera had fallen into the chasm a hundred feet below. I felt as though my entire body had gone numb. I could see my hands shaking violently as I placed them beside the rotten wood plank that had snapped, uselessly, in two.

To my immense relief I saw that Mera hadn't fallen all the way to the river. She was lying on a piece of earth that jutted out from the side of the cliff. She wasn't moving. With no time to lose, I took a deep breath to collect myself and slow my pounding heart. I shut out the sounds of the others yelling at me to come back. I stretched out my hands towards Mera and mustering every ounce of power within me I growled, '*Hafenian.*'

My eyes snapped open as I felt magic flowing within me. It swirled in my chest and unfurled along my arms. I felt its power filling me, giving me its strength. Every nerve in my body was alive with magic. I imagined it as a glittering, golden light reaching out like a hand from me to Mera. It grabbed her and lifted her off the ground. She was splayed like a rag doll, rising up and up until she was level with me. I walked her back towards where the others where standing. When we reached the end of the bridge I placed her gently on the ground and felt the connection break.

As the link between us severed I felt all the power that had filled me drain away. I pitched forward and landed on my hands and knees. Someone was next to me muttering words and running their hands over my face but there was a roaring in my head and black spots in my eyes that made it was impossible to tell who it was. Someone was speaking. It sounded as though they were shouting through a high wind.

'She needs help. Right now. It's beyond us. Get her to the nearest village as soon as possible. We'll look after him. You get her to safety. Ride as fast as you can. Do not stop. We'll find you.'

The roaring intensified and the swirling darkness enveloped me.

21

Nehriton

I woke feeling sore and exhausted. I blinked rapidly, my eyes unaccustomed to the bright light. As they cleared I saw that I was lying in a room lit by many candles. Thin curtains covered the small window and I guessed by the lack of light from outside that it was night. I heard the sounds of people talking and laughing from another room not far away. Where was I? Had we found an inn? Was Mera...

'Lex?' murmured a weak voice. 'Are you awake?'

I raised my head from the soft pillow and looked to my left. Though my vision was still hazy, I saw another bed in which Mera lay, looking a little worse for wear but very much alive. Relief crashed through me.

'What happened?' I muttered.

'Well, I don't really know,' replied Mera. 'I was unconscious for most it. The last thing I remember was walking across the bridge when the plank broke. When I woke up I was here with Ezra. He told me he that I'd fallen and you'd rescued me, but I'd been pretty badly hurt. He said he'd taken me to the nearest place he could find to get help and he'd come across this village. Nehriton, he said it was called. Ilyssa and Alaric turned up with you the next day. They said you'd been unconscious since the bridge and that they couldn't rouse you. They'll be happy to see you're up. You've been asleep for nearly two days.'

'Two days,' I mumbled. 'Are you all right?'

'I will be. Apparently I was in bad shape when I got here but there was a healer who'd been able to help. She says that I should rest but eventually I'll be fine. But what about you?' She asked, rising in her bed to look at me. 'How are you feeling?'

'I'm fine, I think,' I replied, a little unsure. The buzzing in my head was subsiding and I was able to look at Mera without her image wavering. 'Where are the others?'

'Dinner,' she told me. 'They'll be back soon. They don't like to leave you for long. Normally one of them stays, but I said I'd watch you. They'll be sorry they missed you waking up.'

A feeling of gratitude overwhelmed me. The thought of my friends keeping vigil over me was both strange and oddly touching.

Mera and I had lapsed into silence for a moment and now she spoke. 'I'm so sorry, Lex. I'm sorry about the prophecy, about lying to you, about putting you in danger. You were right. I should have told you straight away. I should have trusted you.'

'It's all right, Mera,' I assured her, feeling only relief that she was safe. 'I forgive you.'

Mera beamed, tears forming in her deep blue eyes She ducked her head and coughed. 'You should get some more sleep. Get your strength back.'

'Fine,' I complied, lying back down. After a moment I added, 'I missed you.'

'I missed you too,' she whispered.

The next time I woke up, my head was completely cleared. I heard people moving about in the room and opened my eyes to see Ilyssa, Alaric and Ezra standing by the door discussing something. At the sound of movement they turned and smiled.

'Lex,' Alaric was grinning. 'Great to see you've come back to us.'

Ilyssa rushed over to me and pulled me into a hug. There was an explosion of butterflies in my stomach and I knew I must have been blushing. When she pulled away she was smiling widely. 'How are you feeling?'

'Fine, fine,' I muttered, sitting up.

'I'm so glad you're awake,' I felt her warm hand on my chest through the covers and was suddenly very conscious of how much of a state I looked. 'We were so worried about you.'

'Sorry I scared you but honestly I'm fine. What's going on?'

I looked across to Mera. She had been propped up with about a hundred pillows. In the light of day her injuries looked much worse. Half her face was covered in bruises and cuts. The skin around one especially angry looking cut on her cheek was swollen and purple. I was sure that it would leave a scar. There was a bandage on her left arm that needed to be changed. Blood from what must have been a very deep cut was already seeping through the pale linen. One of her legs was propped up on yet more pillows. Her ribs were also bandaged in the same off-white cloth as her arm. I winced just imagining the pain she was in.

'We need to go to the apothecary,' explained Ilyssa. 'The healer did all she could but Mera's still in a lot of pain. Also we're trying to figure out what to do about the blacksmiths.'

I furrowed my eyebrows. 'The blacksmiths?'

Ezra answered me. 'We've been trying to find one to help us. You know, to make the sword for Ilyssa. But they've all been too busy. Apparently there's going to be some tournament in the next town over and they're all working to fill out orders for people who want to try their hand at fighting.'

'But there's one more we want to try,' said Ilyssa, looking pointedly at Ezra.

'What?' I asked, confused about Ilyssa's stern expression.

Mera smiled. 'Ezra doesn't think that we should try the last blacksmith because she's a woman.'

181

'That is not what I said,' he objected. 'I have nothing against her being either a woman or a blacksmith. It's just that nobody we spoke to today gave her a particularly glowing recommendation. It doesn't sound like they have a lot of faith in her skills.'

'You've never met her, Ezra,' replied Mera. 'Nor seen her work. She could be better than any of the men you spoke to. They were probably trying to demean her. You really shouldn't make judgments on a person with no basis.'

Ezra held his hands up in defence. 'I'm not trying to judge her. Like you said, I've never seen any of her work. She may be the best blacksmith in the kingdom for all I know. I'm just saying don't get your hopes up. She might not even be able to do it. If she's as busy as the others then we'll just have to wait.'

I expected Mera to argue back but she didn't. I looked between them, waiting for one of them to get angry as they always did, but it seemed that they'd put their squabbling behind them for now. With a sudden and very loud growl of my stomach I noticed just how hungry I was.

'Let me get dressed and eat something and I'll come with you,' I said.

'Oh no, you need to rest,' Ilyssa insisted.

'I don't need to rest. I'm fine,' I assured her.

'Ilyssa's right' Ezra agreed. 'You were unconscious for two whole days. You should stay here and recover.'

'I don't need to spend any more time in bed,' I pointed out. 'As you say, I've been there for two days. I think that's enough, don't you? Trust me, I'll be fine.'

Nobody objected, but I saw Ezra and Alaric exchange concerned looks.

'Look, you don't need to be worried. I just need to get some food into me.' I reached out and took Ilyssa's hand, fixing her with my most determined look. 'I'm fine.'

She nodded, though still didn't look too convinced.

Alaric offered to fetch some food for me. After I was dressed and stuffed with so many rashers of bacon I thought my stomach would burst, Ilyssa, Alaric, and I bid Mera and Ezra, who stayed behind to look after her, goodbye and headed off into Nehriton.

Shops lined the main street that split the town in half. On one side I saw a bakery with a line out the door and stretching down the street. On the other side a woman was having an argument with a shop assistant about the price of some material. We made our way past the butcher, cobbler and barber to the very end of the street where there stood a shop with a dusty sign hanging above the door. The faded letters read *Salus Arts: Apothecary.*

Inside, the shop was dimly lit and musty. Strange objects hung from the ceiling and the air smelled vaguely peppery. Jars lined the walls with dried herbs. The shelves were stocked with hundreds of glass phials. Their multi-coloured contents sparkled in the golden glow of the oil lamps that were dotted around the room. Somewhere a music box played a sweet, tinkling melody. The sound it omitted was like the high clink of metal on glass. Alaric reached out to touch one of the objects that was hanging from the ceiling, only to find that it was a small weighing scales wrapped in silks. It swung back and forth for a moment, clinking slightly, before slowing and becoming still once more.

The tinkle of the bell from the opening door must have carried to the backroom because a man appeared behind the counter. He was small and thin with wispy white hair. His face was lined with wrinkles. He smiled kindly at us as he walked with a slight limp through the doorway behind the counter. He folded his arthritic fingers together and peered over his glasses at us.

183

'Good day. My name is Salus Arts. Welcome. What can I do for you?' he asked in a thin, wavering voice.

'We need sage, arnica and white willow bark please,' responded Ilyssa politely.

His wide eyes glinted as he nodded. 'Someone you know is in pain, my dear?'

'Yes. Our friend fell and is quite badly hurt. The healer told us that she'd need those things,' she explained.

'Ah,' he muttered, rummaging through some glass jars. 'Yes, she's very good that healer. Learned it all from her father, old fool though he may be these days. Here we are, then.' He smiled at us again as he put down a long stemmed plant with small, purple flowers and bumpy green leaves, a strip of pale bark and another flower that looked like a yellow daisy. 'Now, did she explain what to do with them?'

'No but I know,' Ilyssa responded.

'Really?' his eyes widened, looking pleasantly surprised.

'Ilyssa knows all about plants and whatnot,' said Alaric.

'I'm impressed,' he replied as he wrapped our purchases up in brown paper. 'Well if that's the case, that'll be three crowns.'

Ilyssa handed over the money and thanked him.

'You're quite welcome. I hope your friend recovers swiftly,' he said, waving goodbye as we left.

Coming out of the dark shop and into bright sunlight was jarring. For one disorienting moment I blinked rapidly, feeling a little dizzy again, but then the sensation drifted away. I turned to Ilyssa and Alaric who were squinting at the sun.

'Where to now?' I wondered.

'Back to the inn. I want to give this to Mera as soon as possible,' answered Ilyssa, starting off back down the street. 'I know she says she's not in pain but she just doesn't want to draw attention to it. It was good to see the two of you getting on again.'

'I'm just glad she's all right,' I muttered.

'We all are,' said Alaric. 'We're glad you're both feeling better. We were worried you might not wake up for a while but Mera said we just needed to wait.'

'Actually, now that we're on the subject,' Ilyssa rounded on me, her voice sounding rather sharper than usual. 'That was a very stupid thing you did. You could have fallen too and then what would we have done? I want to you promise you won't put yourself in danger like that again. Do you promise?'

'I promise,' I replied quickly, quaking under her intense gaze.

'No more stupid acts of heroism from Lex, then,' Alaric grinned, slinging his arm over my shoulder. 'But seriously, is everything all right between you and Mera now?'

'I think so,' I muttered. 'I mean, it still sort of hurts to know that she'd been lying to me for so long but I think I understand why she did it. Honestly, I don't have the energy to be angry with her anymore. And besides, we have more important things to focus on.'

'Great!' enthused Alaric. 'That means no more awkward silences that we all have to pretend aren't happening.'

Ilyssa and I laughed. We went back to the inn and wound our way up the wonky staircase. I was thankful to be back. However unwilling I was to admit it the short journey to the end of the street had tired me out again. I was out of breath by the time we reached the top of the stairs.

Back in the room Ezra was stretched out on my bed facing Mera. The two of them were chatting happily about what Seion was like during the summer. He appeared to be telling her about a flower that only bloomed for one day a year when our entrance interrupted them and his speech fell away.

'Did you find everything you needed?' he asked, hopping off the bed.

'Yes, it's all here. I'll just put it together for you, Mera,' said Ilyssa, placing the package down on the hope chest at the end of Mera bed.

'This is very kind of you, Ilyssa,' Mera said.

'Don't mention it,' Ilyssa replied, drawing out a knife from her pack and beginning to cut up the yellow flower.

When she had ground down everything into a fine paste she added a small amount of water and passed the murky green mixture over to Mera. I sat down on my bed and tried not to laugh at the face she pulled as she peered into the small bowl. Luckily Ilyssa was now collecting the rest of the herbs and tying them back up in small bundles, so she didn't see.

'Drink up,' smiled Ezra.

Mera shot him a nasty look and in one quick motion she drained the mixture.

'Well done,' commended Ilyssa, glancing at Mera whose face was now contorted into an expression of disgust. 'I know it doesn't taste great but it'll help with the pain, I promise.'

Mera simply nodded.

'Well, now that's all done we should head over to see that blacksmith,' suggested Alaric. 'You should come too, Ezra. You know the most about all things armoury.'

'All right but who's going to stay with Mera?' asked Ezra.

'Excuse me, I don't need to be looked after like a child,' said Mera. 'I'll be just fine on my own, thank you.'

'I didn't mean it like that,' he said apologetically. 'I just thought you might like some company.'

'Always thinking of others,' she said, not unkindly.

'Actually,' cut in Ilyssa. 'Maybe you should stay with her, Lex. You could probably do with some rest.'

'I don't need rest,' I huffed, although I was still feeling slightly sluggish.

'Sitting down for a while won't hurt you,' she insisted.

'You don't want to over extend yourself right now,' added Ezra.

'All right,' I agreed. 'I'll stay.'

'Great,' smiled Alaric. 'Well, we're loosing daylight here people,' and with that he walked out the door.

'Let's catch up with him before he does something we regret,' sighed Ilyssa. 'We'll see you later. The herbs should start working soon. You might need some more when we get back though.'

'Looking forward to it,' Mera responded dryly.

Ilyssa smiled. She picked up her pack and walked out after Alaric. Ezra grabbed his pack too saying only, 'See you later,' before dashing out after the others.

I settled down onto my bed.

'How're you feeling?' I asked.

'Better, actually,' replied Mera. 'What about you?'

'Same. Good thing they're here to tell us to take care of ourselves.'

'Yes, we never would have. I'm glad they're here,' she smiled.

'What!' I gasped in mock surprise. 'Even Ezra?'

Mera looked sheepish. 'There may be a very small chance that I might have misjudged him. He's actually quite nice. He isn't half as smarmy as I thought he was.'

'By all the gods Mera, are you actually admitting you were wrong about something? It's a miracle.'

Mera laughed then her face fell. 'I was wrong about the prophecy as well.'

I lowered my gaze. 'It's all right, Mera. We don't have to talk about it. I understand why you did it.'

'That's because you're an incredibly good person,' she said.

I raised my eyebrows in surprise. 'Praise indeed.'

'Well it's true. And this will be the last time I say it if you want, but I'm really, really sorry that I lied. Because you left everything you had, your mother, your sister, your home, to come with me and I didn't even have the decency to tell you the truth,' she swallowed. 'I love you, Lex. You're my best friend and I promise that I will never lie to you again.'

I felt touched by her words. 'I love you too, Mera. How much will it hurt if I hug you?'

'Not much,' she smiled.

I went over to her and hugged her as tightly as I felt I could without causing her pain.

'Please don't ever scare me like that again, all right?' I muttered into her shoulder, feeling buoyed up with happiness. 'I couldn't do this without you.'

'I won't. You have my word.'

I moved back and pretended not to notice when she wiped a tear from her cheek. I returned to my bed and lay down.

'So what do you think it means?' I asked.

'What's that?' she responded.

'The prophecy,' I continued. 'What do you think it means?'

'Well the first part makes sense I think,' she mused. 'That *magic has dwindled to naught* and there's no hope and all that. That sounds about right. And the *one who can prevail to return what was taken* I always thought meant you.'

'Why, because I'm *small and unimportant?*' I teased.

'No,' replied Mera forcefully. 'Because you have me, the future queen. And your power's definitely growing. You must be the one who can restore magic with help from me. I'm certain. And the Sisterhood certainly seems to agree.'

'Well if I'm going to *fell my adversaries with ease* or whatever it was, it shouldn't be too hard,' I joked.

'The last part has always confused me,' Mera continued. '*He alone is not enough…* I guess that means the others. And it's right, I mean, without them we wouldn't have made it very far. *Only pain and betrayal will come of the queen's bluff…* I suppose that must have meant me lying about the prophecy. It's the last two lines that have me worried. *If this comes to pass, he and more will be lost, beware of your foes, for this is the cost.* What does that mean? Lost is so vague. I mean, it doesn't exactly say death, but it is sort of implied, isn't it? I'm not sure though. You should never make assumptions about these things. They hardly ever turn out the way you think they will. And what about *beware of your foes*? We're always aware. Does that mean that we should be extra aware? Or perhaps there's a foe we aren't aware of yet. But then do we only have to be aware of that foe *if this comes to pass*? And what is *this*? Why does it have to be so ambiguous? If what comes to pass? The prophecy as a whole? The queen's bluff? The appearance of a new foe? I can't make it out. What do you think, Lex?'

I was listening to Mera's words but not really hearing them. There was a mounting sense of fear spreading through my gut, particularly at the mention of my possible death.

'I don't know,' I muttered, stretching my arm across myself and grabbing my shoulder. 'The whole thing kind of makes me feel a little sick.'

'Oh, of course. I'm sorry,' Mera apologised hastily.

Silence fell on the room. It was barely past noon but I could feel my eyes growing heavy.

'I think I might sleep some more,' I muttered.

Mera nodded.

I climbed under the thick woollen cover. 'I'm glad you're all right.'

'You too,' she replied.

I settled down quickly but couldn't stop the feeling of panic rising in my chest. I didn't know why I had brought it up. The image of Aisling swirled in my head repeating parts of the prophecy for me in an eerie, echoing voice. *If this comes to pass, he and more will be lost, beware of your foes, for this is the cost.* I shook my head, unwilling to let my mind obsess any further. I punched my pillow and flipped onto my other side.

It was a while before sleep claimed me. My rest was punctuated with dreams of dark mazes and a deep, booming laugh that echoed off thick stone walls. Every time I thought I had found my way out of the labyrinth I turned a corner just to discover another dead end. With a sinking heart I knew that I was completely lost.

22

The blacksmith

I woke to Ilyssa's gentle hand shaking my shoulder. 'Sorry but if you sleep too much now you won't be able to sleep at all later.'

I scrunched my eyes shut trying to shake the image of an endless hallway from my mind. I pushed myself into a sitting position. Across the room Ezra was hunched on the small chair and Alaric was perched on the hope box at the end of Mera's bed. I moved my feet so that Ilyssa could sit down.

'So,' I started, pushing myself into a sitting position. 'How did it go? Was the blacksmith to your liking, Ezra?'

Ezra gave me a withering look before replying. 'Yes, actually, I was impressed. It's a big forge. She's got quite a lot of journeymen and apprentices running around.'

'So, did she agree? Is she going to make the sword?' inquired Mera.

'Well that depends on us,' Ezra replied.

'What do you mean?' I asked.

'Well there are different types of sword,' Ezra explained. 'The ones I have are Longswords. I would recommend getting one like them because that's what Ilyssa's learned to fight with. Other types of sword require a different technique. But it's your choice, of course,' Ezra smiled at Ilyssa.

'So other than that she can do it? That's fantastic. Ilyssa, you must be so pleased,' beamed Mera.

'I am,' Ilyssa grinned back. 'She said it might have to wait a few days so she could complete the other orders she has now but that she'd be happy to. And as we can't go anywhere until you heal I shouldn't think that will be a problem.

'She ought to make you a very fine sword,' Ezra added. 'We should get you some gloves too. They're not essential but you've probably got enough blisters as it is.'

'There you go, sis,' grinned Alaric, reaching out to pat Ilyssa's knee. 'A sword of your very own.'

Ilyssa was still smiling broadly. It struck me then that this would be the first time that Ilyssa would have something that truly belonged to just her.

'How long do you think it will take?' Mera asked.

'Maybe a fortnight, maybe three weeks,' Ezra guessed. 'It could take much less, but if you want quality then you have to be patient. All we need to do is confirm what we want with her and she should be able start on it within the week.'

'Well we'd better tell her then,' I stated.

'She asked us to come back tomorrow to let her know,' Ezra told us. 'Ilyssa just has to make her decision.'

'Enough about me. What are we going to do for the rest of the day?' Ilyssa asked.

My stomach rumbled. I had missed lunch to sleep. 'How long until dinner?'

'Probably an hour or so,' answered Ilyssa. 'I think I might go and change, actually. Are you all right, Mera? Do you need anything?'

Mera shook her head quickly. 'No, I'm fine. Thank you.'

I shot Mera a look as Ilyssa slipped out the door.

'What?' she asked innocently.

'You shouldn't tell her you're fine if you're not. You wince every time you move. Just because it doesn't taste very nice—'

'You haven't tasted the foul stuff. I'd rather take the pain,' she insisted.

I shook my head.

'Well, I'm going out to the orchard,' said Alaric, grabbing his bow and quiver. 'They've got many a tree that an arrow could be sent flying into. See you later.'

Ezra smiling. 'For someone who's so jolly all the time, he sure is deadly with that thing.'

'Agreed. So what other types of swords could Ilyssa get,' I asked.

'Well there are a few I suppose,' Ezra mused. 'Broadswords are fairly common. They're shorter than a Longsword, as the name would suggest, but probably the most similar. Greatswords are similar too but they're huge and very heavy. You need two hands just to pick it up.'

'A Cutting sword might be good for her,' Mera added. 'They're not too heavy and they're easy to swing. Not very effective against heavy armour though.'

'True,' nodded Ezra. 'Well if she wants something for close fighting then she may as well get a Falchion.'

'Oh no, that wouldn't do. It's only a single edged blade and she's learned with two,' commented Mera.

I listened, entirely nonplussed, as Mera and Ezra continued their discussion about swords. They moved on from that to armour and then on to other types of fighting styles. I was glad they were finally learning to get along. It was much more peaceful that the yelling we'd had to endure before.

'Where did you learn all this?' Ezra asked. 'I didn't think swords and mail was a part of a princess' daily studies.'

'It isn't,' replied Mera, jutting out her chin defiantly. 'But we have an extensive library and a talkative master of arms.'

'Resourceful,' he smiled.

Mera reddened slightly at the compliment. 'What about you?'

'What about me?'

'Where did you learn about armour and weaponry?'

'I knew an armourer,' replied Ezra, scratching his ear.

'Oh, as you do.'

'He was an old family friend,' he clarified

'Ah,' Mera nodded, narrowing her eyes slightly, clearly not satisfied with that explanation.

'He's the one who gave me the swords,' he added.

'I thought a nobleman gave you the swords,' she queried.

'The nobleman asked his armourer to give me the swords,' he explained.

'Right, because you helped him with some thieves. What did you—'

At that moment the door swung open and Ilyssa walked back in. I, who had been beginning to feel like I was intruding on a private conversation, was glad for the interruption.

'Want to go and see how many trees Alaric's maimed in the orchard?' I asked, hopping up.

'Sure,' Ilyssa nodded, taken aback by my eagerness.

I ushered her from the room as quickly as possible and we walked back down the lopsided staircase together. We spent the rest of the afternoon sitting on the soft grass in the orchard watching Alaric perfect his aim in the dimming sunlight.

'Where did he learn to do this?' I asked.

'What, molest innocent flora?' Ilyssa replied as Alaric's arrow swished through the air towards the unsuspecting fig trees. 'I'm not sure, actually. He's always been good at it. He made the bow himself and you've seen him making arrows. Perhaps it's something he picked up from one of his *friends*,' Ilyssa's mouth curled upwards slightly on her last word and I suspected that these friends weren't the platonic kind.

'Has a lot of friends, does he?' I asked.

'He does indeed. Honestly, I don't know how he does it. If he wants to he can make anyone fall in love with him and here I am with no notion of how to talk to strangers. I don't make a very good first impression, I'm afraid. Alaric got all the charisma.'

'That's not true,' I assured her. 'You made a good impression on me.'

'Oh? And what did you think of me when we first met?' she queried, turning towards me so that we sat face to face.

'Well,' I started, hoping I had enough sense not to let the first word out of my mouth be beautiful. 'You were a little overly trusting, maybe.'

'Unquestionably. Mrs Granite was right, I shouldn't have brought perfect strangers into the house.'

'Well I'm glad you did,' I admitted.

'Me too,' Ilyssa smiled warmly.

There was a moment when neither of us spoke. I experienced once more the strange pull towards her and felt myself lean forward.

'Your eyes are very green,' she said suddenly.

'Oh,' I replied, drawing back quickly. 'Yes, I suppose they are.'

'I think green's the most beautiful colour,' she sighed. 'It's calming.'

'Hmm,' I hummed, not sure how to respond.

She nudged me with her elbow. 'What's your favourite colour then?'

'Brown,' I said without hesitation.

She wrinkled her nose. 'Brown? Like mud?'

'More like that earthy brown, you know,' I shrugged.

She raised an eyebrow. 'So in fact... mud.'

'Well, all right yes. Brown's a lovely colour. It reminds me of my favourite things. Like the feeling of roughness from running your hand over tree bark, or the way old wooden furniture creaks slightly when you lean on it, or the softness of furs, or the smell of burning logs on a fire. Even mud has its merits. Don't tell me you don't enjoy the squelching sound it makes when you're walking through it. My favourite has to be the brown of people's eyes, though. That deepness that they hold, that warmth. It's so wonderful. Also, when the sun hits them just right, they look as though they have veins of molten gold running through them. It's beautiful.'

Ilyssa looked at me for a moment. I noticed suddenly that her eyes were similarly sun-struck.

'Well,' she began. 'That's a pretty convincing argument.'

'Yes, I'm quite the wordsmith,' I joked.

'Do you think-'

'Hey, you two!' Alaric's voice interrupted her. I had never wanted to tell him to go away more than in that moment.

I turned to see him walking towards us, twirling an arrow in his fingers. 'It's getting late, isn't it? We should probably head back in.'

'Probably,' agreed Ilyssa, pushing herself off the ground. Seeing that our conversation was over I copied her movements.

'We've left Mera and Ezra alone for quite a while. Think they'll still be getting along?' Alaric wondered, slinging an arm over Ilyssa's shoulders.

'They seemed pretty friendly when we left them,' I commented. 'But we should probably check just in case.

We made our way back to the room where Mera and Ezra were still, thankfully, on speaking terms. We were all hungry so we made our way downstairs. Mera, who was still too weak to leave her bed, remained in the room. Ezra had volunteered to stay with her again, so he took two meals upstairs while Ilyssa, Alaric and I enjoyed our rabbit stew in the loud dining parlour.

We rose late the next day. We wolfed down breakfast and Ilyssa forced Mera to take another dose of pain medication.

'It's good for you,' she chided when Mera made a face. 'It'll help you heal.'

'Does it have to be so bitter?' Mera complained.

The next thing on our to do list was to head over to the blacksmith. Alaric offered to stay with Mera, so Ilyssa, Ezra and I headed off to the forge. We walked along the twisting roads until we came to a building with an open front. Inside it was extremely busy. There were tools lining the walls and benches, and some swinging precariously from the rafters. Hammers, chisels and tongs of all shapes and sizes were scattered about the room, often in the hands of one of the people who were working there. In a corner of the forge a greasy looking boy was pumping a huge bellows into the furnace. Sharp clanging echoed in the room as hammer after hammer was brought down on hot metal. The heat of the furnace billowed over us when we walked in. Sparks flashed and flickered amongst the burning coal. The tang of metal and smoke hung in the air.

Over by an anvil a stout woman was hammering a sheet of metal. Her powerful arms brought the hammer down to bang repeatedly into the worked steel. She noticed us standing by the entrance and paused. She called over a girl who took up the woman's work as she made her way over to us. She had a hard, lined face. I put her in her mid-forties. She brushed her dark brown hair out of her eyes and pulled a cloth from her apron to wipe her hands, which were burned and calloused.

'You've made up your minds then?' she asked briskly.

'Yes we have. We decided on a broadsword,' Ezra handed her the design he and Ilyssa had made that morning.

The blacksmith squinted at the rough drawing. Her eyes flicked for a moment towards me. 'Who's this?'

'Oh, this is Lex,' explained Ilyssa, who was grinning from ear to ear. 'Lex, this is Zaila.'

I smiled and she grunted.

'Well that's all fine,' she said, her eyes still on the paper. 'We've got our last order for the tournament, shouldn't take long, then we'll get started on this right away.'

'How long do you think it will take?' Ilyssa asked.

Zaila pursed her thin lips, thinking. 'Shouldn't take more than three weeks. You'll pay half now and half when it's done.'

'Brilliant,' smiled Ezra.

'I'll need a few more details about the hilt. Eden!' she called over her shoulder.

A young woman came stomping over. She, like Zaila, had a broad, flat nose, thin lips and a stocky build. She looked about twenty. She had stuffed her black hair into a messy bun and it was coming loose. She scowled at Zaila as she approached.

'My daughter. You can pay her. Eden, take this girl to get the hilt details writ down,' Zaila snapped. 'Before the forge burns out, if you please.'

Eden huffed and beckoned for Ilyssa to follow. She led her into a back room and out of view.

Zaila tucked the design into the pocket of her apron. 'She won't take long. You can wait for her here. Don't touch anything.'

She turned back to where she had been hammering on the anvil and shooed the girl away. Ezra and I milled around by the entrance as we waited for Ilyssa to return. After a while she came back out of the small room with Zaila's daughter.

'She doesn't look happy,' I commented as I watched her grab a hammer and start beating the end of a metal rod.

Ilyssa walked up to us. 'She's just upset because her mother says she can't go to the tournament. Apparently she's the best in her family at handling swords and with anyone being allowed to enter she wanted to try her hand at the mêlée.'

'Why won't she let her go?' Ezra queried.

'Apparently there's no one who can go with her and Zaila won't let her go alone. Anyway,' Ilyssa clapped her hands together. 'Where to now?'

'We should find a seamstress to get the gloves made,' suggested Ezra.

After a little help from one of the apprentices in the forge, we found our way to the seamstress. She took Ilyssa's measurements and told us the gloves would be ready in about three days.

'It's strange,' Ilyssa confessed as we walked back to the inn. 'It feels so odd to have people measuring me like that. The clothes I own from Deathgrove are all hand-me-downs that I had to alter to fit,' she smiled shyly. 'I think I'm going to enjoy having something that was made just for me.'

I smiled back, nudging her arm with my elbow. 'Maybe you should get some other new clothes while we're here. Your others must be quite old now.'

'No,' she replied. 'We shouldn't waste any more of our money on me. That sword is going to be costly enough.'

'You deserve it, Ilyssa,' I grinned. 'We wouldn't have lasted two days without you.'

'Oh, that's not true,' she mumbled, turning very red and ducking her head low.

'I'm sure it is,' added Ezra, 'And I know it doesn't look like it with all the faces she makes but Mera really appreciates the medicine you're giving her. Where would we be without you?'

Ilyssa turned, if possible, even redder.

We spent most the week exploring the town and lazing around. Nehriton was much larger than Lilyworth. It was made up of hidden alcoves and winding roads that surrounded the promenade where most of the shops were. The tiny toadstool cottages that clustered around the shops were spread out on either side. Some places, like the mill, stretched as far as the river, which split a few miles up from Nehriton and swaddled the village like a mother's protective arms.

The healer came to check on Mera towards the end of our first week there. Most of her small cuts and bruises were healed, but her skin was still a horrible green and yellow under the bandage on her ribs. The cut on her face was no longer swollen and seemed to be healing nicely. The gash on her arm was now a red-raw scab. The healer told us that her arm should no longer be bandaged but that must be careful not to reopen the wound. She also commended Ilyssa on her knowledge of herbs and medicines.

'The only people I know with superior knowledge are my parents,' she told us.

Healer Asa was a short woman in her late fifties with dark hair shot with grey and heavy lidded eyes. She spoke in a slow, clear voice while her dexterous hands moved over Mera's ankle, unwrapping the bandages there.

'Your father's the apothecary, isn't he?' asked Ilyssa. 'He said he taught you how to be a healer.'

'He did indeed,' she replied, smiling. 'And my mother. They set up that apothecary shop together the year they were married and have worked there ever since. Your ankle's still swollen. It may take at least a month until you can walk on it again. I hope you're not planning on going anywhere soon.'

Mera nodded and breathed in deeply.

'And keep taking those herbs,' she straightened up, slipping her hands into her pockets. 'That bridge should have been removed a long time ago. All the locals know not to use it but travellers like you have no idea how dangerous it is. It was just a matter of time before someone got badly hurt. I still think you're very fortunate not to have done something much worse to yourself.'

'Thank you so much for your help,' Mera grimaced as she tried to sit up properly.

'We were lucky to come across you as well,' added Ezra. 'Most healers I've met wouldn't have known how to act so quickly.'

She smiled. 'You're very kind. Well, I must leave. I have other patients to see before the day ends. You're healing well, Mera. Keep taking the herbs and you'll be back to your normal self in no time. Take care of her, the rest of you.'

We assured her that Mera was in good hands and she packed up her things and left the room.

The next few weeks we spent in Nehriton were some of the most enjoyable during our journey north. With Mera's injuries on the mend, as well as our recently shaken friendship, she began to regain her confidence. She couldn't walk properly yet but after a few weeks she was able to hobble around with some help. Soon she would be able to walk on her own and then, once Ilyssa's sword was finished, we would continue on to Skara Brae. Meanwhile we spent our time in town wandering the streets, popping in and out of the shops and markets and watching the busy locals bustle about their daily lives. Ilyssa, whose interest in herbs had grown considerably since coming to Nehriton, spent a lot of time with the apothecary. She offered to help with the running of the shop in exchange for him and his wife teaching her what they could about botany.

As the weeks went by we began spending more time in the fields just beyond Nehriton. Spring was in full swing now and we wanted to make the most of our down time in sun. Valiant, who was sick of being cooped up in the stables, whinnied with glee when we took him out to the fields by the river. We took turns cantering up and down the riverbank. Mera, who's healing body didn't allow her to ride, laughed joyfully at Alaric who was almost unhorsed when Valiant was suddenly spooked by a falling branch. He rode back to us looking slightly abashed. We had taken a basket of food with us to picnic in the bright sun.

'Maybe we should just stay here,' I joked, biting into a bun filled with jam.

'That would certainly put an end to most of our troubles,' hummed Alaric, stuffing treacle tart into his mouth.

Ilyssa, who was trying not to laugh as jam dripped down my chin, added, 'We could build a little house on the river, live a quiet life.'

'We'd be bored within a week,' commented Ezra. He was lying in the grass with his hands over his eyes to shield them from the sun. 'We've grown used to the excitement.'

'Mmm,' agreed Mera, reclining lazily on the blanket next to me. 'Who wants a quiet life, anyway?'

Eventually Ilyssa's sword was ready. I'd never seen her happier. We took her to the orchard behind the inn so that she and Ezra could try it out. She was as graceful as ever, gripping her sword in her leather clad hands. She stood in position, tensed and ready, waiting for Ezra to make the first move. He lunged and she darted to the side, out of the path of his sword. Ezra pulled back and straightened. They circled each other until Ezra lunged again and Ilyssa parried his blow, the steel of their swords singing. They carried on that way for a while, strike and parry, strike and parry. They were tiring, but neither looked likely to give up. Ezra lunged again. Ilyssa tried to dodge his blow but was too slow and the flat of his sword struck her on the side of her ribs. She staggered sideways and Ezra took her momentary surprise to knock her sword out of her hand.

'Yield!' I heard her call breathlessly.

I rushed forward, worry coursing through me, but neither seemed to be injured, just out of breath. Ilyssa was bending over to pick up her sword when I drew level with them. She was smiling.

'Are you all right?' I asked.

'That was brilliant!' she gushed, wiping the sweat from her forehead.

I smiled at her enthusiasm.

Ezra joined us. 'Well fought, Ilyssa. I thought you almost had me for a minute there.'

'Thanks. You too. Just wait until I get used to this sword. You won't stand a chance,' she grinned.

'I've no doubt,' he replied, pulling his own leather gloves off. 'Let's get cleaned up before dinner,' he moved off to where Alaric and Mera were sitting on a bench closer to the inn.

I looked down at the sword in Ilyssa's hands. It was unassuming as far as swords go. The hilt was simple steel wrapped in black leather for a grip. On one side the words 'Ilyssa Baines' were carved, while on the other was an iris flower. 'It's a symbol of hope,' she had explained when I asked.

Ilyssa turned to me now, still grinning broadly. 'I've really enjoyed being in Nehriton. If it hadn't been because Mera was hurt I'd say we'd been very lucky to find it.'

'I know what you mean,' I agreed. 'I almost don't want to leave. You were really good just now. You've picked it up so quickly. I don't know how you do it.'

'I suppose it's just what I'm good at. Everyone has something they can do well. Just like you have magic and Alaric has the ability to eat a meal meant for four people in one sitting.'

Ilyssa's face was flushed from exertion. Her dark hair was plastered to her face. She was still breathing heavily and her face glistened with sweat, yet she had never been more beautiful to me. I swallowed and ducked my head in the hope that she wouldn't see the longing in my eyes.

'Well I'm going to take a bath,' Ilyssa said. 'And clean my sword. My sword. It still sounds funny to say. Come on then, let's get back to the others.'

I followed her up through the orchard in silence.

We tramped up the stairs and into our respective rooms. It had been a long day and we were all exhausted. Mera was even tired enough to allow Ezra to carry her.

It was just over three weeks since we had arrived in Nehriton and Mera was well on her way to recovery. Healer Asa said that she shouldn't push herself so she was still letting one of us hold her up whenever she walked around but I could tell she didn't like having to lean on someone every time she wanted to go somewhere. All her minor cuts and bruises had vanished and the nasty gash that ran across her arm was now a faded pink scar, as was the one on her cheek. Her shoulder and rib were still causing her a lot of pain and according to Asa would continue to do so for a few more weeks, so Ilyssa stocked up on supplies from the apothecary.

It was time to leave Nehriton.

We packed up our things and with sadness in our hearts we said goodbye to the place that for so short a time had been our home.

23

The dance of truths

We left the sun behind in Nehriton. Not one day after we had set off we were caught in a hailstorm that sent us running for shelter. After cowering under a rocky ledge for a very boring day and half we decided that we couldn't wait for it to pass and headed out into the howling winds. Ezra said that storms in this part of the kingdom could last for days, sometimes weeks on end and that now we were heading into the rainy season we should expect more of them.

'Don't expect it to be too warm either,' he said. 'Meyrom only had two types of weather, hot and cold, and until summer comes it's still going to have winter's chill.'

Mercifully the storm passed the next day and we were able to make good progress again. In the distance I could see the vast mountain ranges of the north. I was glad that we wouldn't have to pass over them. Any day now we would cross the boarder into Meyrom. No one mentioned that Ezra had promised only to take us to the boarder of Seion. We seemed to have come to an unspoken agreement that he would be continuing with us to Skara Brae. I certainly wasn't vying for him to leave. I thought Mera might say something but when I mentioned it to her she didn't seem bothered.

'He's become good company,' she muttered.

Mera still couldn't walk well. She had been riding Valiant since we left Nehriton which meant we were back to holding our packs while she walked. I felt guilty thinking it but I would be glad when she healed. I had become used to walking without it and the past few days had been an adjustment.

That night after settling down in a shallow cave we ended up on the topic of life after Skara Brae. I was struck by the sudden realisation that I had been focusing so much on getting there that I hadn't put any thought into what would happen when and if we succeeded. With the last lines of the prophecy still ringing in my ears I found it hard to contemplate without feeling sick to my stomach.

'What about you, Alaric,' asked Mera after getting very little answer from me. 'Do you still have your heart set on running a tavern?'

Alaric seemed to contemplate this for a moment, stretching out next to the fire. Then he said, 'I don't know. Maybe I'll do something that's a bit more useful. I've got worthwhile knowledge. Perhaps I'll impart it.'

'Are you planning on setting up a school to teach the most effective ways to annoy everyone around you?' Ilyssa asked.

'Actually, little sister,' Alaric replied, leaning forward to playfully ruffle her hair. 'I was thinking more along the lines of the archery skills I have. I don't know if you've noticed but I'm not too bad.'

'Hmm. Well I'm afraid I won't be joining you in that,' she replied, smoothing her hair back down.

'Really? I'm surprised,' said Ezra. 'You could put that sword to good use.'

'I think I'll be wanting a quiet life when all of this is over,' she replied. 'Perhaps I could become an apothecary. Or open a flower shop. I've always liked flowers.'

I had a sudden vision of Ilyssa years from now, laughing and at peace, surrounded by fields of blooming flowers. The thought caused a ripple of warmth to spread through my chest and tugged up the corners of my mouth.

'You could always join him, Ezra,' Mera suggested. 'Put a stop to your endless roaming.'

'And give up the boundless comforts of homeless life?' he grinned. 'I think Valiant and I are happy being free to do and go where we please. But who knows. And you, Mera? Back to the castle for you, I suppose?'

'Well yes, I'll have to,' she replied.

'You don't *have* to,' he insisted. 'You could always choose not to.'

'I didn't mean it like it was some huge burden. I think I'm blessed to have been given the life I had, but that comes with certain responsibilities and I intend to fulfil them. My duty is and always will be to protect my people.'

I smiled at Mera, thinking back to our screaming match in the hut where she had been so adamant that she didn't want the throne.

'I think I'm going to go to bed,' I announced as exhaustion washed over me.

'Yes, good idea,' Mera agreed. 'I'll take the first watch.'

We all settled down into our makeshift beds and tried to ignore the gale raging outside.

The cold had crept into our little cave while we slept and I woke up shivering. The winds must have blown themselves out during the night because when I poked my head outside all was still. We huddled around the fire for breakfast and then quickly packed our things away. We set off, trudging along in the cold, swaddled in cloaks and pulling the thin fabric tighter around us in a futile attempt to stay warm.

In an effort to get us motivated Alaric decided to keep up a steady stream of conversation all through the morning and well into the afternoon. He had just been telling us about all the fur cloaks he was planning on buying when he suddenly asked, 'Do you think it's much further?'

'Alaric,' Ilyssa sighed. 'Do you think that, perhaps, it would be possible for you to stop talking? Just for five minutes. For me. Please.'

I turned to where Alaric and Ilyssa were walking behind me and saw a disgruntled Ilyssa scowling at her brother. I looked forward again and smiled when I caught Mera's eye. She had become more motivated than ever as we moved into Meyrom, forging ahead despite her as yet unhealed injuries. I still noticed her wince every now and then.

'Are you getting bored, Alaric?' I asked. I waited until I was level with them. 'Not regretting your decision to come with us are you?'

'And miss all this walking? Never. I've always wanted blisters the size of my fist,' Alaric joked. 'But seriously is there any chance there's going to be an end to this cold? I'm freezing off important parts here.'

'Thank you so much for that lovely image,' Ilyssa cringed.

'What? Am I wrong?' Alaric asked, looking to me for support.

Not entirely sure how to respond, I settled with a nervous laugh. Ilyssa shook her head and hurried to catch up with the others.

'You know,' mused Alaric, throwing his arm around my shoulder. 'I was worried about my sister when we first left Deathgrove. I hated that place and I know she did too but there was always a part of her that felt safe there, I think. She's the only reason I didn't run off myself. I think it got inside her, you know. There was something poisonous about it. It made her forget that there was good in the world. I thank our lucky stars that you came along. I know that if we'd wanted safety this wasn't the path to have chosen but I'm glad we did.'

He said all this in voice of great calm as though he was talking about nothing more important than the weather. I studied Alaric's stoic face for a moment and wondered what else he was hiding behind his easy going façade.

'You like her, don't you?' he asked suddenly.

'Well, of course I do. She's wonderful. And so are you and Ezra and– '

He cut across me. 'That's not what I meant and you know it. You like her. It's all right. You're allowed to like people. I've liked plenty of people myself. I think it's great. Not that my opinion really matters.'

I felt as though someone had thrown a bucket of icy water over me. I struggled for words but found none.

'She likes you too, you know,' Alaric continued to muse in a voice of complete nonchalance. 'I certainly don't claim to be an expert on love, but I'm pretty good with people. So my advice, not that you asked for it, is don't pretend not to love someone. Don't deny yourself that. It hurts both of you and wastes everybody's time.'

I didn't know what to say. I saw no point in denying it but I felt suddenly very tongue-tied. Before I could think of a response Ilyssa called out to us.

'Stop dawdling, you two!' her clear voice rang out. 'There's a sign that says there's a village not too far from here!'

'Great!' Alaric shouted back and jogged to catch up. I followed quickly after him feeling my face burning in the cold air.

We walked on for the better part of an hour until the sun began to set. Amber light was spilling over the tops of the evergreen trees. It was strangely quiet along the road. I felt my skin prickle uncomfortably.

'Do you hear that?' Mera asked suddenly.

'What?' I asked sharply. 'What is it?'

'I think it's music,' she replied. 'Hey Alaric, I think we're here.'

'Finally,' he muttered, his teeth chattering.

We rounded the bend in the road and found the source of the music. A huge field stretched out before us. It was covered in tents and crawling with people. Banners with words I couldn't quite make out were hung on posts around the edge of the field adorned with huge, red lanterns. Cool blue light was spilling out of a huge tent right in the middle of the field. Rich smells wafted through the air coming, no doubt, from the vendors' carts that lined the bustling, makeshift streets. We approached the field and headed towards a woman who was standing at the entrance.

'Welcome!' she beamed when she saw us approaching and greeted us in the singsong accent of Meyrom. 'Welcome to the Éa Festival. We are honoured to welcome any travellers on this day of joy. Please, come in and celebrate with us. There is a stable for your horse on the other side of the main tent,' she stood back to let us through.

We thanked her as we passed and carried on into the noisy festival. I could see the banners that stretched around the field clearly now. The words read Éa Festival and underneath was the image of a river. Each banner was painted differently from the rest. In some the river flowed gently. In others it swelled and crashed around enormous rocks. In one particularly vivid painting the river was carrying away a fire-breathing dragon.

Ezra helped Mera dismount and led Valiant to the stables. We strolled through the field, enjoying the sights and sounds that issued from nearby tents. We stopped every now and then to admire the displays. One tent was full of carvings. It looked as though the seller, a man so old and stooped that his thin beard fluttered along the table, had spent years carving his vast collection. I was prepared to spend hours admiring the carving of a beautiful waterfall with fish jumping through it but Mera pulled me away before I could get too attached. We stopped for food, which tasted as delicious as it smelled, then moved over to an area that had been cleared for dancing. We sat at the tables that lined the dance floor, pausing to collect hot drinks from a cart manned by a tiny, grey-haired lady, and listened to the silk-soft sounds of violas and the tinkling timbre of bells.

'Right,' Alaric, who had spotted a drinks cart that sold ale, clapped his hands together. 'I'll be over there if you need me,' and he rushed off before Ilyssa could stop him.

'I don't know what I'm going to do with him,' she sighed.

'Oh he's not hurting anyone,' smiled Ezra. 'Let him have his fun.'

'Well as long as fun is all he's having,' she muttered.

Mera was watching the dancing couples with a wistful look. 'It's been so long since I danced.'

Ezra turned to her and jumped up. 'Well then, your Highness,' he began, offering her his hand. 'May I have this dance?'

Mera looked shocked for a moment and then shook her head. 'I can't dance on this ankle.'

'Of course you can,' he insisted. 'I should like to see you dance.'

To my great surprise she said, 'All right.'

She put down her cup and took Ezra's hand. He helped her up and took her into the throng leaving Ilyssa and I alone.

'Am I going mad?' I asked.

'Not unless we just shared a hallucination,' replied Ilyssa, whose eyes were still trained on Mera and Ezra now swaying together on the dance floor. For a moment I felt a slight pinch of jealousy but then it passed. They both looked so happy.

'So,' Ilyssa tilted her head to the side. 'How are you doing?'

'What do you mean?' I asked, confused. 'I'm fine.'

Ilyssa gave me a look. 'Come on, Lex. I know you're not fine. That prophecy has been weighing on you. I can see it in your eyes.'

'You can't see anything in my eyes,' I looked away.

'Yes I can. Don't pretend you haven't been having sleepless nights. You look tired.'

'Oh, thank you.'

'Lex,' she implored.

I knew she was right but I couldn't bring myself to explain the now constant feeling of panic that had settled in my stomach.

'I don't want to talk about it,' I muttered.

'All right, let's talk about Mera.'

'What do you mean?'

'She almost died. You can't just put that aside. You have to deal with things like that,' she insisted.

'But she was fine. And I'm fine, really,' I looked across to where Mera and Ezra were entwined. Mera's head rested on Ezra's shoulder as they swayed together, his arms encircling her waist.

'Honestly, you're worse than my brother. You can talk to me, you know. You're allowed to say when you're not all right. You can ask for help.'

I sighed. An annoyingly reasonable voice told me that I should be happy that Ilyssa cared for me. I took a sip of my drink, nodding.

Ilyssa shook her head. 'Fine, have it your way. Let's talk about when you think Mera and Ezra will get married.'

Her words took me so much by surprise that I almost choked on my drink.

'Get married? You are joking, right?'

'Well yes, I was, but I don't think it's that ridiculous a notion.'

'They'd kill each other an hour after the wedding,' I intoned.

'I don't think so,' she remarked airily. 'They've been getting along quite well recently. Or haven't you noticed all the nights they've spent huddled together? *Planning* or whatever they call it.'

I raised my eyebrows. 'They still argue all the time. They were squabbling over how messy he is just this morning.'

'A lovers' tiff, perhaps,' she grinned.

'Oh Ilyssa, stop,' I covered my ears but I could still hear her laughing.

'Even you have to admit they're getting on quite well at the moment.'

I looked for Mera and Ezra in the crowd again but they had disappeared.

'I dread to think what her father would say if she came back with Ezra in tow,' I commented. 'He'd probably have a heart attack.'

'I think Ezra would do quite well as Mera's husband,' she mused. 'He's already used to her bossing him around and calling her your Highness. The rest shouldn't be much of a stretch.'

I shook my head, half with disbelief at her, half at my own blindness.

The sun had set completely now. Golden lanterns were shinning brightly around every tent. The glittering light was reflected in Ilyssa's eyes and her skin glowed. Her bright smile faded slightly and she tipped her head to the side as her eyes gazed into mine. I took a deep breath.

'Ilyssa would you like to– ' but I never got to finish my sentence because at that moment I heard Ezra's voice calling out above the music.

'Mera wait! It isn't like that.'

I looked across the crowd to see Mera hobbling over to us.

'It's completely like that! I can't believe I trusted you!' she yelled back.

I turned to Ilyssa, alarmed. She looked just as confused as I felt.

'What's going on?' Ilyssa asked as Mera reached us and leant heavily against the table, which squeaked angrily under her weight.

'Oh, nothing important really. Not according to our dear friend here. I just learnt that Ezra, the poor, lonely ranger guiding us through the harsh wilderness, is actually Jezrahiah of house Adalitz, a poor little runaway lordling. He's been lying to us this whole time.' Mera fumed.

'Please,' Ezra implored breathlessly when he caught up to Mera. 'It isn't what you think it is. I– '

'What we think is that you're a lying, deserting sneak! We've been totally honest but you've done nothing but deceive us,' Mera spat.

'Well, that technically isn't true, I mean–' Ezra quaked under Mera glare, silencing himself.

'Oh, I'm sorry. You're quite right. *Technically* he isn't a *poor* little liar. He is, in fact, an extremely *wealthy* little liar. Is that enough technicality for you?' she screeched, attracting the attention of more than a few people.

'Slow down,' I raised my hands, trying to calm her. 'What is going on?'

'He,' she snapped, pointing a shaking finger in Ezra's direction, 'is the eldest son of Lord Adalitz. They're a Seioni noble family. I don't know how I didn't see it before.'

'That'll be how he knew you were a princess,' guessed Ilyssa.

Mera's head snapped towards her. 'Don't defend him.'

'I'm not,' flinched Ilyssa. 'I'm just saying.'

'Don't take your anger out on her,' said Ezra, who seemed to have regained some confidence.

'You don't get to speak,' Mera hissed.

'You can't tell me not to speak,' huffed Ezra. 'Don't talk to me like I'm inferior.'

'You are inferior,' her voice quavered, dangerously low. 'But don't for even a second think that I'm saying that because I was born into royalty. I have never looked down on you because of that. You are inferior because you are a deceiver of good people. You lied to all of us, repeatedly, constantly. I thought I had found a friend in you. I thought I had found someone I could trust. But no, you have simply proven to me that my first suspicious were right.'

'Mera, listen to me,' Ezra pleaded. 'It wasn't like that. I didn't mean to deceive you. I was just trying to live my life in freedom. I couldn't risk my family knowing where I was. I'm not going back there.'

'Oh, please. Do you expect us to pity you, Ezra? Oh I'm sorry, do you prefer Jezrahiah?' she sneered

'Please don't call me that,' he muttered.

'Why not? It's your name, after all,' she spat.

Despite his best efforts I could see Ezra loosing his patience. 'Well then I suppose I ought to call you Princess Mera then. Or would your Highness suit you better?'

'I knew we shouldn't have trusted you. I knew you were bad news right from the start.'

'I have done nothing but help you,' he insisted.

'Liar! Do you really think I'm ever going to believe another word you say ever again?'

'Mera please, just listen to me.'

'No. I am done listening to you.'

She walked off as fast as she could into the thick forest of tents.

Ilyssa and I sat in shocked silence for a moment before I stuttered, 'I... I'll go after her.'

215

I caught up with Mera quickly. She was sitting behind one of the tents, her arms wrapped around her knees. I walked over and sat down beside her.

'Hey,' I said.

'Hey,' she sniffed.

'Tell me what happened.'

'We were dancing. We were dancing and this person comes over. I think he was from Seion. He didn't look like he was from around here. He goes 'my Lord Jezrahiah, is that you?' You should have seen the look on his face. It was as though his whole world had come crashing down. At first he tried to ignore it. Told the man he was mistaken, told me he didn't know what he was talking about. But I knew he was lying. In the end he told me the truth. He said he left because his father was forcing him to marry a girl from another noble family. Apparently this was the last straw for him because the next morning he packed up his things and left. That's when I got angry. I sort of flew off the handle.'

'Yes I noticed that when you were yelling yourself hoarse,' I nodded.

She scowled at me. 'Well he deserved it.'

I tipped my head to the side. 'Did he?'

She sighed. 'I don't know. I just… why didn't he tell us. We're his friends.'

'You know, I felt myself wondering something quite similar not too long ago,' I pointed out.

Mera sighed again, biting her lip to stop it quivering. 'I'm being a hypocrite, I know. It's just that, I thought that I had found someone that… someone that…'

'It's all right,' I slipped my arm around her. 'I understand.'

She laid her head on my shoulder and wept.

24

The woman in the mist

Mera and I stayed tucked away behind the tent until she could cry no more. When she quieted she wiped her eyes and shook herself.

'No more,' she muttered.

We headed back to where we'd left the others. By the time we got there Alaric had returned. He was sitting next to Ezra, his hand on his shoulder, listening carefully as Ilyssa spoke. Ezra had his face in his hands. They looked up as we approached.

'We probably shouldn't stay here,' I said as we drew up to the table. 'It might not be safe. Even if that person who recognised Ezra doesn't say anything we've been talking quite loudly. We shouldn't take the risk of somebody having understood.'

We filed along the path towards the stables to collect Valiant. Ilyssa caught my eye at one point. She pointed at Mera and cocked her head to the side. I shook my head slightly.

I wasn't angry with Ezra. I was shocked at the revelation but I felt that as we had lied to him to keep ourselves safe he was entitled to do the same. Alaric had gone straight to making jokes about the whole situation. Ilyssa too seemed to have forgiven him instantly. Mera was the only one who held a grudge. He tried to speak to her that evening when we made camp but she refused to acknowledge him.

The next day Mera continued to act as though Ezra had ceased to exist. I did think she was being a bit petty now. He looked so sad whenever he looked her way. When he brought his concerns to me I tried to comfort him.

'Give her some time,' I told him as we waded through the thick mist swirling around our ankles. 'She's hurt but she can't stay angry with you forever.'

'I just wish I'd had a chance to tell her–' he broke off, rubbing the back of his neck.

We spoke no more of Mera. Our journey had taken us into a gloomy land. It was as though Meyrom had been drained of colour. There were constant clouds overhead. A thick mist had settled around us. Even the trees seemed to fade to grey as we passed them. I couldn't shake the feeling that someone was watching us. We walked on, no one wanting to stray too far in case they were swallowed by the mist.

We made camp in the tree line while a drizzle of rain fell. We sat around the fire in awkward silence and ate dinner. I now knew what it must have felt like for the others when I had been angry with Mera. I offered to take the first watch that night. When I woke Ilyssa for her turn she brought up Mera and Ezra.

'She's being a bit unfair isn't she?' she whispered.

'She is, and she knows it too, but it won't stop her,' I replied. 'Besides, if you're right about them having feelings for each other then that kind of thing will hurt a lot more. We need to let her get through it in her own time, interfering will just make her angry at us.'

'True. You better get some sleep.'

Part of me wanted to stay up and talk with her but exhaustion stopped me and I was soon asleep.

We walked on the next day in much the same way as we had the one before. Ezra walked ahead of us while Ilyssa, Alaric and I stayed with Mera and Valiant. He seemed sad even from behind and eventually I grew tired of it. I approached him and asked, 'Will you tell me more about your brothers and sisters?'

Ezra came from a huge family. He had five brothers and two sisters, plus a host of uncles, aunts and cousins. I tried to imagine having nine other people living my house and shuddered at the thought. Three was enough for me.

'If you like,' he nodded. 'Enoch's the oldest now that I'm gone. He'll inherit, I suppose. He'll be a much better heir than I ever was. We never got on very well. I think he resented me.'

'You really never wanted that life?' I wondered.

'You must think it's awful for me to turn my back on my family and scorn the privileges I was born with like that. But it's more complicated than it seems. It's suffocating. What Enoch thought were benefits were responsibilities I couldn't handle. I had no freedom. That's all I wanted. Just my freedom and a little bit of peace,' he sighed.

'I think I can understand. So who comes after Enoch?' I prompted.

'Hmm? Oh, Biah. She's actually my half sister. Something you won't find in the pages of the *Historie of Anciente Seioni Familys* is my father's penchant for bringing his illegitimate children into our house. We're not supposed to know about it. I don't think even Biah knows. I overheard my parents arguing about it one night. It never mattered to me. She may be too smart for her own good but she certainly loves me more than Enoch does. Anyway, after her is Neriah. He's forever getting himself into trouble in some way or another. Then there's Micah. Not to play favourites but I'm pretty fond of him. He's another of my father's bastards.'

'Busy man,' I muttered.

'Indeed,' Ezra agreed, a slightly sour look on his face. 'Bless my mother for putting up with him. After him are Ezekiel and Eleazar.'

'Oh you mentioned them earlier. They're the twins, right?' I quizzed.

'They are. If they aren't knights by the time they're my age I'll eat my own sword. And finally there's Hephzibah, or Effie as I call her. She'll have just turned seven but she was five when I left. You know what, forget about not having favourites. She was the best of all of us.'

Ezra's face was downcast. He looked into the distance, lost in a memory.

'You miss her,' I stated.

Ezra shifted and dragged a hand through his shaggy hair. 'I miss all of them. Even Enoch. You understand though. You know what it's like to leave your loved ones behind.'

I nodded. I though of Mum and Elvie and Rab all the way back in Lilyworth and wondered if I would ever see them again.

'Will you ever go home?' I asked.

'I don't know. It's not really home anymore. I never thought that I would go back. I thought that it would get easier but I won't lie, it's been two years and I don't miss them any less than the day I left. But I just know that if I go back I won't be able to leave again and I can't face that.'

All at once the hairs on the back of my neck stood up. I whipped around to try and find the source of whatever was causing the tingling sensations to shoot up and down my spine.

'What's wrong?' asked Ezra, coming to an abrupt halt.

'Shh,' I whispered, holding out my hand to silence him.

The others who had been trudging along behind us slowed down when they saw that we had stopped.

'What's going on?' asked Alaric.

'Shh!' I said again, more forcefully.

For a moment it was quiet and then, appearing as if from nowhere, a woman walked out of the mist. She was small in stature, with pure white hair that fell well below her waist. She wore a plain black dress and a string of silver pearls hung about her neck. Her face was youthful but there was something in her eyes that told me she was not as young as she seemed. She drifted towards us slowly, holding a loaded bow in her hands. Though it was pointed at the ground I still felt a sense of danger. I raised my hands, preparing to use magic to blast her backwards when she spoke.

'Do not fear me, child. I am not here to hurt to you, only to help,' her voice was low and penetrating. Something in the back of my head was telling me that I should listen to her, that she could only be telling the truth, but I didn't lower my hands.

'Who are you?' I asked.

'That doesn't matter. You are going the wrong way. You must follow me,' she commanded.

She turned and something pulled me forwards. Without my consent I found my feet obeying her and I heard the others following behind me too. We walked up a slight incline into mist so thick I could barely see my own hand in front of my face. There was nothing but grey for nearly ten minutes and then all of a sudden my vision cleared.

There were so many flowers I thought for a moment that we had walked into a greenhouse. Colours jumped out at me, shimmering and pulsing. Blue, purple and pink hydrangea bushes lined a stone pathway. Neat grass trimmed a clear, teal-blue pond over which a faded red wooden bridge stretched. Cherry blossom trees surrounded beds of multi-coloured tulips, roses, and irises, sending flurries of tiny pink petals streaming across the garden when the wind rushed through them. On a small hill a willow tree lounged over plump, green bushes, reaching out its long tendrils to brush across the pond's surface. Dragonflies larger than my fist flitted around its edge being chased by fluffy, golden creatures that sprang into the air to catch them. At the top of the path, nestled away behind the wisteria cascades and twisting bamboo, I saw a small wooden house with a neat balcony hugging the edge of the building. As we neared the house the stone path turned into small steps. The woman stopped and turned to us.

'Leave the horse here,' she commanded. 'He will be safe. And your things too.'

We dropped our packs to floor. Alaric helped Mera off Valiant's back and he trotted over to the pond and began to drink thirstily.

The woman continued up the steps and I felt myself mimicking her movements. As we reached the house I noticed another path that lead to a stone shrine sitting under the shade of a maple tree. A small waterfall burbled behind it. A name was carved onto the shrine but I couldn't make it out. The tree's scarlet leaves bristled in the breeze.

'This way,' called the woman.

We climbed the remaining steps and entered the house. The woman pushed open a sliding door and led us through to a small room. As I stepped across the threshold I felt the tranquillity that had clouded me throughout the garden slip away. I looked around the barren room and shivered. The only furniture was a plain, wooden table with a few chairs. The walls were white and bare. In one corner was a large object that was neatly covered by a bleached cloth. The woman removed her quiver and placed it along with the bow down on the table. I sensed great power in her, though the emptiness in her grey eyes unsettled me.

'Who are you?' I asked again.

'You may call me Sami,' she inclined her head slightly.

'My name's Lex, and these are– '

'I know who you are,' she cut me off. 'I have brought you here to help you. If you had continued on your path the mist would have lead you astray and into the path of your enemy. You may rest here tonight and then I will set you on the right path.'

'You mean the Brethren?' Mera piped up.

She nodded. 'I do. They have been close on your heels. You have been lucky not to have been caught.'

'But who are you?' I repeated. 'How do you know who we are or where we're going?'

'As is the intention of your journey magic has begun to awaken. Not long ago the flourishing garden you just walked through was perishing. As magic regains its power, the garden thrives. I am not the only one to have noticed these changes,' she explained.

'Are you a member of the Sisterhood,' Ilyssa asked.

Her mouth formed a thin line. 'I am not. If you wish to stay here and rest I can give you shelter and food. If not I am willing to show you the direction you should take straightaway. Which do you choose?'

I looked around at the others. Their blank faces weren't much help so I turned back to Sami and said, 'We'll stay.'

'As you wish. You may collect your possessions and I will show you to your rooms. Please don't touch that,' her eyes flashed to Alaric, who had walked over to the covered object and was in the process of unveiling it.

'Sorry,' he whispered, looking sheepish and hurriedly putting the sheet back.

Sami nodded her head and then without saying a word she picked up her bow and quiver and left the room.

I let out the breath I didn't know I was holding in. 'Well that was… unusual.'

'I'll say,' said Ilyssa.

'Do you think we can trust her?' asked Mera.

'Yes,' I answered, though I didn't know why I was so confident.

'But who is she? Is she a sorceress?' wondered Ezra.

'I think so. Can't you feel her power?' I asked.

'No,' muttered Mera.

'Come on,' interjected Alaric. 'We can't stand here all day dilly-dallying. Let's go and get our things.'

We stepped back through the sliding door and out into the garden. Retracing our steps we found ourselves at the bottom of a small incline next to a lawn covered in pink moss. I could see Valiant over by the pond nibbling on the grass. We walked over to where we had left our packs. The mossy ground was springy and light beneath my feet. Birdsong echoed in the trees above us. A bright red bird rustled its wings and soared through the low branches of the maple trees. The soft splash of water reached us and I noticed a small stream running from the woods down the side of the hill and into the pond. Everything felt so alive out here. It was a stark contrast to the eerie stillness inside the house.

We collected our things and headed back inside. Sami was waiting for us. She led us up a flight of stairs to a floor that was just as barren as downstairs. There were only two rooms on this floor. The first had three beds, the second had two. Ilyssa, Alaric and Ezra took the three-bedded room and Mera and I were left with the double.

'Please feel free to look around. You may go where you wish though I suggest you don't wander too far. It's easy to get lost in the woods,' Sami informed us before leaving us to our own devices.

We spent the rest of the day outside. Valiant munched happily on some apples as Alaric raced passed him and jumped straight into the pond, sending the water crashing around him. After a minute of paddling amongst the rushes and lily pads he let out a strangled yell and hopped out again as fast as he could.

'What's wrong?' Ilyssa asked.

'Something slimy brushed up against me,' he panted.

Mera knelt down by the pond and peered into it for a moment before letting out a shout of laughter.

'There are fish in the pond,' she said.

She was right. A number of large white and orange fish circled one another. Their mouths wide open to catch the tiny, buzzing insects that landed, unsuspectingly, on the surface of the water.

As evening fell lights began to appear around the garden. I thought that they were lanterns at first but when I passed one I noticed it was a scaly creature with a four spindly legs and six wide, bugging eyes. In the darkness it glowed a fire-bright red and lit the path back to the house.

Once we had returned to our rooms we cleaned ourselves up and headed back downstairs to sit on the balcony. Sami appeared for the first time since she had left us to explore to tell us that dinner was ready. She led us through into another room that had a table laden with food.

'Please sit,' said Sami.

We took our seats and waited for Sami to take hers. She moved towards the empty seat but before she got there she paused by Mera.

'How did you come to be injured?' she asked.

'I… I fell,' faltered Mera.

Sami's hand ghosted over Mera's shoulder. 'You ought to be more careful. *Thurhalath.*'

A bright, green light glowed for a moment around Mera, hummed slightly, then faded away.

'Do you feel better?' Sami asked, taking a seat.

'Much, yes. Thank you,' muttered Mera, a hand tracing ribcage.

'Please, eat,' insisted Sami.

We began to load our plates with food.

'So you have magic?' I asked.

'I do,' replied Sami, taking a bowl of rice from Ezra.

'How do you know who we are if you're not from the Sisterhood?' I pressed.

Sami regarded me with her cold, grey eyes. I felt for a moment that I was falling into their hollowness. My head rang as the sharp pain of grief crashed through me. As suddenly as it had come it was gone again.

Sami spoke. 'The Sisterhood are not the only ones who have knowledge of things beyond that which others cannot see. You have travelled a long way, through many places. The trees have been whispering. News of you has reached me here. You are not far from your goal now but that does not mean the rest will be easy. Your journey so far has been simple compared to what is coming. You must truly support one another if you are to succeed,' Sami's narrow eyes focused on each of us in turn, resting for a moment on Mera before glancing away. 'Skara Brae awaits you.'

'You said the Brethren was close behind us,' said Ilyssa.

'Indeed,' Sami replied. 'They have been following you for some time, though they have not yet caught up to you. I believe they last tracked you to the village of Nehriton where they were asking about your whereabouts.'

'Did anyone tell them about us?' Alaric asked.

'I'm afraid I cannot say. Besides, if they did it may not have been voluntary. The Brethren have their ways.'

Her statement made me shiver. I tried not to think about what could have happened to the people we had met in Nehriton. After we finished eating Sami took away the empty plates and suggested that we get some rest. We traipsed upstairs. An ominous feeling weighed on me as I got ready for bed. Sami's words echoed in my mind.

From the window in our room I could see the small path that led to the shrine. I watched Sami walk along the path. She had a candle with her, which she placed on the stone as well as three flowers. She sat in front of the shrine with her head bowed and didn't move.

I turned away from the window and sat on my bed. 'There's something strange here. Can't you feel it? The whole place just feels... empty.'

'You're the one who said we could trust her. I guess I'm just not as in tune as you are,' Mera responded, hopping into bed. 'Although it does look like somebody has drained the house of colour.'

'Mmm,' I hummed. I reached out and extinguished the lamp, getting into bed myself.

'We're almost there, Lex,' Mera's voice drifted across to me in the darkness.

'I know,' I responded.

'Everything is going to be different,' Mera whispered.

I smiled. 'Wasn't that the point?'

'I know but it's different when it's something you've been talking about for so long compared with the reality of it. You probably regret ever having agreed to come with me.'

'No I don't,' I rolled over so that I was facing her. 'I don't regret any of it. Not for one second.'

Mera smiled. 'I'm really glad you pulled me out of the way of that cart.'

'Me too. Goodnight, Mera.'

'Night, Lex.'

A few hours later I awoke with a very dry throat. I climbed out of bed and padded downstairs looking for water. I saw a full pitcher on the dinning room table. I poured myself a glass and drank thirstily. I poured another glass and almost spilled the whole lot down my front when a voice behind me said, 'It's very late to be awake.'

I whipped around and saw Sami standing behind me.

'I scared you. I apologise,' she said, bowing her head slightly.

'No it's all right,' I replied. 'I was just getting some water. I didn't disturb you, did I?'

'Not at all,' she moved over the window. 'I was watching the stars.'

'Mmm, stars are… very nice,' I muttered, wanting to get back to bed but unsure if it was rude to leave.

'They can be, I suppose,' she mused, still gazing up at the night sky. 'But they are inconsistent. And when the sun comes up they simply fade away.'

A look of intense longing settled on her face. She was silent for a long while, staring avidly into the night, and then she turned to me and said, 'You must be careful. The Sisterhood have a way of manipulating people to their advantage. You can't always trust them. Just make sure you're acting of your own accord and not someone else's. Now you should get to bed. You'll want to be rested.'

She inclined her head again and moved across the room, sliding through a door in the panelling I hadn't seen before. I, slightly unnerved, returned to my room.

Sami's warning about the Sisterhood had my head spinning. Did that mean that the prophecy wasn't to be trusted? Part of me still thought all of this was too grand for a simple boy like me. It all seemed too much, the weight of magic all on my shoulders. Perhaps there was another way. I put it to the back of my mind. Sami was certainly right about one thing, I needed to rest for tomorrow.

The next day saw us rising with the sun. Sami had left out food for us to eat, which we gobbled down hungrily, putting the rest in our packs for later. She appeared with her bow and arrow just as we finished packing and told us to follow her.

'Your horse is waiting for you,' she told us, then headed out through the kitchen onto the back veranda and down some rickety stairs. When we reached the bottom I saw Valiant standing patiently at the start of a path that led into the trees. He nickered softly as we approached.

'I will lead you to the edge of the woods. After that you will have to find the way on your own,' Sami said, starting toward the path.

The light that managed to penetrate the trees was grey and unsettling. The mist was beginning to return. The further from the house we went the thicker it became. I was worried that once the path ran out we wouldn't be able to find our way in the dense, white sea.

A few hours in we stopped to rest. Sami didn't sit with us, but instead stood guard. Her defensive stance was making me uneasy. I would be happy when we left the woods behind us. It felt as though restless eyes were watching us. Yet again I felt that unpleasant tingling in my spine. We carried on. It was a few more hours before we came to the end of the woods.

'It is not far from here. You need to follow this path exactly,' explained Sami. 'Do not let the mist confuse you. You must not deviate from the path or you won't be able to find it again.'

'Thank you,' I said. 'Thank you for everything.'

'You're welcome. I wish you luck. You may need it yet,' Sami walked back into the woods and disappeared into the mist once more.

25

Beneath the stones

'So, I think we're lost. Who agrees?' asked Alaric, dragging his pack behind him so that it scraped along the ground.

'We're not lost, we're taking the scenic route,' replied Ezra.

'Is it still the scenic route if we can't see the scenery?' Alaric asked, gesturing around at the dense mist.

'Would you two both be quiet,' snapped Mera.

'We've been following the same path for hours now,' Alaric continued. 'I don't know about you but I'm getting sick of all this mist. Are you sure we're even going the right way? We could have been going in circles for all we know. It's kind of hard to tell which direction you're going when you can't see more than ten feet in front of you.'

'We're going the right way,' I insisted.

'How do you know?' he probed.

'I don't know. I can just… feel it,' I replied.

'Oh, right. Well you want to know what I can feel?'

'Alaric,' came Ilyssa's voice of warning.

'Never mind,' he muttered, kicking his bag.

I didn't blame him for getting agitated. We knew we were close but with every step we took we found ourselves getting more and more frustrated. It had been a long day punctuated mainly by Mera and Ezra squabbling. She had given up on ignoring him and had now started huffing loudly and saying things like *well if his lordship says so* whenever he spoke. It was getting on everyone's nerves.

Our destination seemed to be just beyond our reach. The mist seemed endless but I knew we were on the right path though. The prickling sensation up and down my spine had intensified. I could feel it reverberating around my whole body. Valiant must have felt it too because he had begun pawing restlessly at the ground. Ezra had to coax him along gently or else he would dig his hooves in and refuse to take another step.

'Maybe we should stop for a while,' Ilyssa suggested.

'Good idea,' I agreed.

Alaric dropped his pack and staggered forward, flopping dramatically down to the ground. 'Do we have any food?' he sighed.

Ilyssa picked up his pack and threw it at him. It flew past his outstretched hands and hit him in the face, knocking him backwards. Once he righted himself he began rummaging through it. I went to sit down next to Mera, who was fishing a scarf out of her pack.

'Is there a particular reason you're in such a foul mood with Ezra today?' I asked.

'Hmm? What's that?' she asked, pretending not to hear me.

'Come on. Why are you making things worse?'

'I'm sorry, Lex,' she responded, wrapping her scarf tightly around her neck. 'I just don't know what you're talking about.'

'All right then, have it your way,' I grumbled, pulling my cloak closer around me.

Ilyssa walked over and sat down opposite us. She gave a smile and said, 'I'll be glad when today is over.'

'Me too,' I agreed.

'Do you think it's much further?' she asked.

'Shouldn't be,' muttered Mera from behind her scarf. 'Looking at the map we're almost there.'

'Well at least we'll finally be out of the cold. I'd be worried it was going to start snowing if it weren't spring,' Ilyssa glanced up at the grey clouds circling overhead. 'The weather's so strange up here.'

'Don't jinx it,' I joked.

She smiled. 'Sorry. What will we find when we get to Skara Brae?'

'Ruins,' Mera said. 'Time will have worn away any buildings that once stood there.'

'I wonder what it used to be like when people lived there,' Ilyssa pondered. 'I wonder if their society worked like ours does. Do you think that-'

For a fraction of a second the image of a building flashed through my mind. It's high, stone arches stretched into the sky, blocking out the dazzling sun. A woman with dark skin and a pile of blonde curls stood alone and out of place at the foot of the building. I heard her voice on the wind, clear as day, *'Hurry.'*

I felt a shiver run through me that had nothing to do with the cold.

'Let's get going,' I suggested. 'We should try and get as far as possible before we lose the light.

I ignored the curious looks on the other's faces and Alaric's whine of, 'But we just sat down.' I hopped up and helped Ezra attach the packs to Valiant's saddle.

I could feel my hands shaking so I stuffed them in my pockets hoping it would go away if I ignored it. It didn't. After a while my arms began to shake too. I kept jumping at noises that always turned out to be someone treading on a stick or Valiant chomping on his bit. Every step caused a rush of noise in my head like the crashing of a wave. It became almost unbearable. I was on the verge of asking to rest when we came over the crest of a hill and it stopped. The shock of being able to hear properly again pulled me up short and it took me a moment to notice that the mist had cleared as well.

Standing at the top of the hill gave me a great vantage point from which to see the entire city of Skara Brae spread out in the basin below. I remembered the picture Mera had shown me in the hut so long ago. It didn't even begin to compare. Vast arrays of tightly packed houses were sunk into the ground. Some were completely covered in grass and heather, nothing more than green and purple bumps. Spread all across the hillside these little houses were springing out of the ground. As they got closer to the hill on the other side of the basin they grew larger, perhaps for housing bigger families, perhaps for more important people. On the other side of the basin at the very top of the hill I could see a ring of standing stones. Though I could not see it I could smell the sea that would be visible from the other side of the basin.

'We're here,' I breathed in the salty sea air.

Mera came to stand next to me. She put her hand on my shoulder, a look of unaffected joy on her face. 'Finally,' she muttered.

'Wow,' puffed Ilyssa. 'That's… wow.'

'Isn't it,' I mumbled, momentarily distracted by Ilyssa's bright eyed enthusiasm.

'Don't get too excited,' came Ezra's voice from behind us. 'We're not done yet.'

'Come on, then,' said Mera.

She scrambled down into the basin below.

'You know it would probably be faster to go around the top,' Alaric pointed out.

'Let her have her fun,' I chided.

We followed Mera into the basin. When I caught up to her she was trying to climb inside a house, the top of which was open to the elements but the side was too steep and she couldn't get a foothold on the soft earth.

'Give me a hand, Lex,' she called to me.

I walked over and gave her a leg up. She pulled herself up onto the top the mound. 'Thanks,' she chimed, before jumping down into the hole and out of sight.

I left her to her own devices for a while and went to join the others who were inspecting the front of a house on the other side of the street. The earth had crumbled away enough to reveal a very small door. Valiant was munching happily on the grass that grew up the wall. As I got closer I saw that it wasn't a small door but only half of one. The lower half was below the ground.

'Has it been covered or did it sink into the earth?' wondered Ilyssa.

'Covered, I guess,' I answered.

'What makes you think that?' asked Alaric.

'Just a feeling,' I mumbled, reaching out to touch the door.

'Well I suppose you're right. If it had sunk then there wouldn't be earth covering the top, would there?' reasoned Ilyssa.

I studied the carvings that were etched into the doorframe. They were strange symbols that I had never seen before but for some reason I felt as though I recognised them. The unpleasant tingling that had abated at the top of the hill returned in full force as I reached out to touch the door.

I heard the same commanding voice whisper again, '*Hurry.*' I squinted and shook my head slightly to clear it.

I turned away from the door. 'Come on then, we don't have all day.'

I looked around for the house that Mera had gone into, but before I could call out her name she hopped over the top of a mound to my left and landed deftly on the ground, crouched like a cat. She was holding something in her hand and as she walked over to us I saw that it was a book.

'A little light reading?' I queried.

'Look at this,' she thrust the book at me.

I took the book and opened its cover, careful not the break the already cracked binding. Inside were the same symbols I had seen on the door. I couldn't shake the nagging feeling that I had seen them before.

'It could be a spell book,' she speculated.

'Or a hundred and one ways to cook fennel,' I retorted.

'Well at least it would improve your cooking,' she scowled. 'We'll take it with us. We might be able to make sense of it later,' She pulled it from my hands and began to walk down the grassy street. I sighed and followed after her.

We walked along the abandoned lanes, stopping every now and then to peer inside uncovered buildings. We made our way up the other side of the hill, panting a little as we reached the top. The ring of standing stones was even more impressive up close. Some stood tall and thin while others had clearly broken in half over time and sat small and dumpy on the ground. They were all covered in a thin layer of moss, the grey stone peaking through in patches. I could feel the power radiating from them.

A woman was standing in the centre of the ring next to a sunken hole in the ground. She was as still as the stones surrounding her, strangely untouched by the wind. She had light brown skin and reddish-brown hair. She was incredibly thin, almost skeletal. I saw the same crown-like ornament adorning her head that Aisling had been wearing, only this one was silver with a sapphire so dark it appeared almost black. A dagger hung at her side. I was the only one who didn't flinch when she spoke.

'You have come so far, young ones, and yet your journey is not yet through,' her voice was as deep and clear as the sea that crashed in waves against the rocks.

'Who are you?' asked Mera, her voice unsure.

'I am Brina of the Sisterhood,' she replied calmly. 'I am here to warn you. For so long I have been bound to another plane but now that the icy grip on magic begins to thaw I have found my way here. You must know the danger that lies ahead.'

She paused, staring at each of us.

'What danger?' I prompted.

'It has stalked you far, across many lands. It has crept into your lives and hidden in plain sight. It will find you, as it always has done. You must be alert and you must be quick. I will leave you now. I cannot stray for too long. Come, enter here and finish what you started.'

'Wait, you didn't tell you us– ' Mera began, but before she could finish her sentence Brina plunged her dagger into the ground. She shimmered for a moment and then disappearing with the wind.

I rushed over to where she had been standing and saw small flowers pushing their way through the grass to sprout in the place the dagger had landed.

'Well that was helpful,' I heard Alaric complain.

'I suppose we ought to go down, then,' said Ilyssa coming to over to the hole next to me. I peered into it and saw stone steps leading down into the darkness below.

'I suppose we had,' I agreed, although Brina's warning had left me a little apprehensive. The last lines of the prophecy came back to me suddenly.

'I can't take Valiant down there,' piped up Ezra. 'I'll stay with him, make sure he doesn't wander off.'

'Are you sure?' I asked. 'I don't know how long this will take.'

He nodded. 'I'm sure. Besides, it might be a good idea to have a lookout. I'll yell if I see anything.'

'All right,' I agreed.

Mera found the things we would need in her pack and one by one we headed down beneath the stones.

I don't know what I had been expecting. More ruins, perhaps. Broken walls and cracked floors, maybe. Certainly not the vast, ornate chamber we stepped into. It was dark at first but somehow I knew what to do. I whispered, '*Ligbryne lícian,*' and the whole room lit up. Torches on every wall blazed with light. On a central plinth was a huge stone carving of a dragon. Real fire was spewing from its angry mouth. The firelight caught on tiny jewels that were set in the walls.

'Wow,' whistled Alaric.

I started towards the end of the room where a throne-like seat was poised just below a carving of the sun. Stone rays branched off it in every direction. In its centre was a glass orb through which orange light danced. I guessed there was fire behind the carving as well. A wide trough filled with water ran around the seat.

'How do you sit on it without getting your feet wet?' asked Ilyssa, who had come to stand behind me.

'Like this,' I said, pressing my palms together in front of me and closing my eyes. '*Forscyrian,*' I whispered, and as I did I moved my hands slowly apart. When I opened my eyes the water had moved so as to leave a deep, dry trench. I walked through it and the water splashed back down behind me. The chair was huge. I felt swamped sitting there but it gave me a good view. From here you could see over the top of the dragon and to the far end of the room where dark corridors must lead to other underground vaults.

'Don't you look noble,' joked Ilyssa from the other side of the trough.

'Ah, King Lex,' drawled Alaric, coming to join us from where he'd been inspecting the stone dragon. He gave a funny sort bow. 'I am your humble servant.'

Ilyssa shook her head. 'You've never been humble a day in your life.'

Alaric gasped. 'You offend me, dear sister.'

'Are we having fun?' admonished Mera, who was crouched down by the dragon placing all the things from her pack on the floor in front of her.

'Sorry,' I apologised. I came back across the water and walked over to where she was setting up. There was a bowl with a shimmering liquid, two phials, and a pouch. I swallowed.

'Now remember,' Mera looked at me earnestly. 'You add the sap of the dogwood tree first. Then you do the first spell. After that you add the crushed carnation roots and peony extract. Then it's the second spell,' she pressed the parchment with the two carefully written spells on it into my hands.

'I know. I remember,' I muttered, unable to suppressed the nerves that were beginning to claw at my insides. What if it didn't work? What if we had come all this way just to fail at the final step?

'You can do this, Lex,' whispered Mera, her hands still on mine.

I nodded woodenly and she backed away saying, 'We'll give you some room.'

The three of them headed over to the water trough. They sat on its edge, watching me. Ignoring my trembling hands I took a deep breath and picked up the first phial.

I emptied the contents into the bowl. It oozed slowly from the tiny glass bottle. I began moving my hands in the pattern that Mera had taught me, chanting all the while.

'*Gesamnian thrymlic magen,*' I said, over and over until the words were just a buzzing in my head. A fierce wind whipped around the room. The fire in some of the torches sputtered out. '*Gesamnian thrymlic magen.*' The contents of the bowl began to smoke. I reached out for the other phial and the pouch. Uncorking the former and untying the latter, I poured the contents of each into the bowl. I closed by eyes and took up the hand movements again, this time chanting, 'Áhreddan thrymlic magen, áhreddan thrymlic magen, áhreddan thrymlic magen.' The wind howled in my ears, buffeting me about it was so strong. I sat as still as I could, moving my hands and chanting.

My head was beginning to spin but I ignored it as best I could, concentrating all my energy on the bowl. The warmth under my hands told me that a fire had sprung up. I could feel its red-hot tongue licking my palms. A sharp blast pushed me backwards and almost toppled me over but I regained my balance, and ignoring the sharp crack of breaking stone from above me I continued chanting.

'Áhreddan thrymlic magen, áhreddan thrymlic magen, *áhreddan thrymlic magen.*'

The heat had become almost unbearable. It snaked its way up my arms and across my chest. It reached my throat and gripped tightly. It was constricting my breathing. I thought I heard someone calling my name but there was too much noise. Whether it was from the screeching wind or searing flames or roaring in my head, I didn't know.

All of a sudden the wind died and the flames retreated. The contents of the bowl sparked, hissed and fizzled into silence.

I opened my eyes.

I felt myself sway precariously to the side, my eyelids drooping. There was an unpleasant ringing in my ears. I shook my head to try and clear it and it realised it was the sound of someone calling my name. I felt hands on shoulders and suddenly I was being dragged backwards. I didn't have the energy to fight so I let myself be taken. I was propped up against something hard and cool. The voices were still calling my name.

'Lex!'

'Lex, can you heard me?'

'Open your eyes, Lex.'

Water splashed across my face. It startled me. My hazy vision began to clear. I became vaguely aware of a throbbing pain across the upper half of my body.

'He's burnt all over. Let's put him in the water.'

I felt myself being lifted and then placed gently into the trough. The cold water enveloped my body. The throbbing pain subsided a little. I looked up into three panicked faces.

'Lex? Are you all right?' came Ilyssa's anxious voice.

'Did it work?' I managed to mutter.

They breathed a collective sigh of relief.

'I hope so after all of the fuss,' breathed Alaric.

'Never mind that, what about you? Are you all right?' worried Mera.

'I'm fine. Really. Just a little lightheaded,' I conceded.

'You had us worried,' huffed Alaric. His hair was in disarray as though he'd been running his fingers through it repeatedly.

'Are you sure you're all right?' asked Ilyssa, whose face had paled.

'Fine. Really,' I insisted. 'I'll just stay here for a bit.'

Mera, who was as white as a sheet, didn't say anything, but I could see her nervously wringing her hands. I tried to smile but it hurt my face so it was probably more like a grimace.

'Those are some pretty nasty burns you've got there,' said Alaric.

I raised one of my arms to see. Raw, red welts were twisted all over my arms like vines. If the pain on my back, chest and the side of my face was anything to go by the marks were probably all over me. The water was soothing the burns for now but as soon as they touched the air they smarted.

'That's going to hurt in the morning,' I muttered, more to myself than anyone else.

'On the plus side you'll have some great scars,' smiled Alaric.

I laughed weakly. 'I suppose. So, did it work?'

'I don't know,' Mera frowned. 'I mean, you did everything right. Everything went in the correct order. But I would have though that…' she trailed off looking pensive.

'Don't worry about that now,' insisted Ilyssa. 'You need to rest. I'll go and see if we have any supplies to treat burns with,' she stood and walked back towards the stairs on the other side of the room. Before she got there, however, she paused.

'Mera,' she called. 'What did you say happened to the people here?'

'They died,' answered Mera, sloshing water back and forth with her hand. It was sending cool waves over my chest and felt wonderful. 'They were all wiped out. Why do you ask?'

'Well, it's just… Where are they?' Ilyssa queried.

'What do you mean?' Mera replied, pausing in her motions to turn to Ilyssa.

'Where are they? Did they evaporate? This is a temple, isn't it? Surely when your world is crumbling you would seek solace in a place like this, but there's nothing,' she gestured around the room.

For a moment Mera looked troubled, then she shrugged. 'Well maybe… over time… I don't know. Is that really important right now?'

'It's just… I have a bad feeling. You heard what that sorceress said. Maybe somebody's been here,' Ilyssa insisted.

'Maybe the people who lived here weren't all wiped out,' Mera reasoned. 'History books can be wrong, especially when it was so long ago. Maybe they took care of their dead and moved on.'

'Or maybe,' came a disembodied voice from the dark tunnels at the end of the room. 'They made the same mistake as you and didn't get out when they had the chance.'

26

The tunnel in the rock

Mera whipped her head around so fast I thought that it would snap off. I raised myself out of the water, ignoring the stinging pain across my chest, and peered over the side of the trough. Ilyssa was scuttling back towards us away from the catacombs.

As I watched a huge figure loomed out of the darkness, followed quickly by a dozen other men. Some wore plain clothes but others wore tunics and cloaks made of rich materials, clearly noblemen. My stomach swooped when I recognised Listoros at the head of the group. I saw Ilyssa and Alaric exchange panicked looks. The Brethren had found us.

I saw that Mera too was staring with fear as the men advanced on us. Her eyes were trained on a tall, thin man with dark, beady eyes and a long, hooked nose. His hair was white and he looked to be approaching sixty. He was swathed in a fur-lined cloak and had a number of chains across his chest. 'Oh gods no,' I heard her say under her breath.

Listoros smiled down nastily at us. His huge arms rested on either side of his body next to twin curved swords. He was covered from head to toe in boiled black leather. In the dull light from the flames the scars that ran across his cheek and down his neck made his face looked mangled. I wondered if my scars would look like that.

When he spoke his voice was low and full of authority. 'I will admit you have been more of a nuisance than I first anticipated. But it was only a matter of time until you were caught. Now, it seems, you have finally failed.'

Mera, who seemed too paralyzed with fear to even speak, gulped.

'Nothing to say? My, my, Princess, that's not like you. I hear you're normally so talkative. At least that's what my good friend Malaigle always says,' he snarled, indicating the tall man that Mera seemed so scared of.

I looked between them, confused. How did this man know Mera? I nudged her and she jolted slightly.

'What's going on?' I asked. 'Who is he?'

'He… he's… ' Mera stuttered. She took a deep breath and steadied herself. 'Lord Malaigle. He's chief advisor to the king. He's been making decisions in the castle for years.'

I shivered to think of the things this man had done, the havoc he had wreaked, the lives he had stolen…

Malaigle laughed. 'Our organisation runs deep into the foundations of your precious kingdom. I'm sure you recognise a few of my other brothers who have joined us today. Lord Mowbray and Sir Frederick, perhaps. You'll have to forgive our lack of formality, your Highness. I'm afraid no one will be bowing for you today. You have things to answer to. And while we have you here, you took some things that belong to my friend here. I think Lord Listoros would like his toys back. He does so like to play.'

His words angered Mera enough that she was able to forget her fear for a moment. She stood, once again defiant. 'Ilyssa and Alaric are not toys. They don't belong to anyone.'

'Oh but that's where you are quite wrong,' Malaigle hissed. 'They have never been free. They were born to traitorous parents. Their blood is tainted. The moment they abandoned their master they became traitors as well. In choosing you they doomed themselves and now they will pay for their foolishness. An apt end to match their parents' sins.'

Alaric rose to stand next to Mera and asked, 'What do you know of our parents?'

'Silence!' Listoros spat. 'When you are returned to me I'll see to it that you won't be asking any more questions. That tongue of yours has always been trouble. Worry not, I will see you rid of it.'

Alaric didn't respond. I could see him shaking slightly but whether that was with fear or anger I couldn't tell. Ilyssa was still crouched down next to me. She slipped her hand into mine and gripped it fiercely. Her other hand rested on the hilt of her sword.

'That's enough reunions for now,' intoned Malaigle, stepping forward into the light. 'We have business to be getting on with. You see you've caused us quite a lot of trouble. I am going to enjoy putting an end to you.'

He motioned for the men behind him to advance.

'No!' I shouted.

'No?' Malaigle asked in a dangerously calm voice.

'You won't be hurting anyone here,' I replied.

'And what right does a simple peasant boy have to give me orders? You are nothing. You will die here, pitiful and screaming,' snarled Malaigle.

'I have every right,' I rose from the trough, shaking slightly from the pain but defiant nonetheless. 'It doesn't matter if you kill us. You're too late. You've lost. The spell has been cast and magic will return.'

'Quiet, insolent boy!' Malaigle roared. 'It matters not what pathetic incantations you think you've performed. You haven't stopped us. Nothing will ever stop us. We squashed your heathenish magic before and we can do it again. We will not rest until every foul, disgusting thing like you has been eradicated from this world. You are not worthy to even grovel at my feet you filthy, revolting thing! You will be the first to die!'

I raised my hand preparing to blast him backwards but as he reached for his swords I changed my mind. I moved my aim to the stone dragon in the centre of the room and yelled, '*Lific alif!*'

A blast of energy shot from me and struck the statue. With a huge groan the stone began to unfurl and come alive. A few members of the Brethren yelled and staggered backwards as the dragon stretched out its long talons. The stone glowed a shimmering orange and gold, its stone turned to scales. Its snout was black and smoking, its deep yellow eyes watching. Suddenly it shot upwards towards the ceiling, which gave a loud crack as deep fissures spread out from the place it has struck. The whole room trembled. I supposed that if the shouting hadn't alerted him, Ezra was definitely aware that something was wrong now.

The dragon was snarling and spitting embers from its snout. Most of the Brethren including Malaigle had moved back towards the catacombs but Listoros and a few others had stayed firmed put. I could see them through the dragon's powerful legs trying to find a way past it.

Ilyssa grabbed my arm. She was shouting, 'Lex, we have to move! Now!'

I nodded and jumped over the side of trough. We started towards the steps in a mad dash. Before we got there an arrow whizzed past, missing us by inches. I looked back towards the Brethren and saw an archer already fitting another arrow into his bow.

'Get down!' I yelled.

We flattened ourselves to the ground just as the man released the arrow but in the end it wouldn't have mattered. His aim was not for us, but for the dragon. The arrow struck the beast on the side and bounced off. The dragon reared, smashing against the ceiling again and breathing streams of fire. Its lithe tail lashed out and knocked the torches off the walls. They were extinguished as they fell. The only light in the room now came from the spurts of fire issuing from the dragon's mouth and the small stream of daylight from the opening at the top of the steps. We needed to get out. In the darkness I couldn't see who was beside me, so I grabbed fistfuls of clothes and dragged them up with me.

'Run!' I cried.

We sprinted for the exit but again we were stopped. As the dragon reared, striking upwards once more, the ceiling began to crumble. A slab of stone came crashing down and struck the person next to me. They crumpled to the floor and dragged me down with them.

I heard Ilyssa call, 'Alaric!' and Mera yell, 'What's going on?'

I reached for Alaric who lay on the ground, unmoving.

'Help me!' I shouted.

Hands were grabbing blindly. Panicked shouts were reverberating around the collapsing chamber. The air seemed to have been knocked out of me. The darkness was pressing in. I could here Listoros screaming, 'Get them! Get them! Don't let them get away!'

Somehow we managed to drag Alaric to the stairs and then we were climbing and finally we reached the top where we tumbled onto the soft grass outside.

It was eerily quiet up here. Panting heavily, I pushed myself up and looked around. The light was fading and I could see looming clouds rushing towards us on the horizon. To my right, Ilyssa was leaning over her brother, weeping softly.

I heard her muttering, 'Alaric. Alaric, look at me. Please.' He was awfully still but I could see his eyes flickering slightly every time she said his name. Dark blood was oozing down the side of his face from where the stone had struck him.

I looked to my left and saw Ezra helping Mera to her feet. He looked stricken as he ran his hands over her face saying, 'Mera, are you all right? I felt the ground shaking. What happened?'

'I'm fine,' muttered Mera, extracting herself from his grasp. 'It was a trap. The Brethren was waiting.'

'The Brethren?' he breathed.

'There's no time to explain,' she moved over to where Ilyssa was bending over Alaric. 'Lex, can you heal him?'

'I can try,' I shivered. I was still wet from the trough and the freezing air was making my teeth chatter.

I shuffled over to Alaric and put my hand on his head. He stiffened slightly, a gasp escaping his lips. I tried to collect my thoughts and remember the spell Sami had performed on Mera to heal her injuries.

'*Thurhalath,*' I whispered.

As the green light enveloped his body Alaric visibly relaxed. Some colour began to return to his face and he tried to sit up.

'No you don't,' I said, resting my hand on his shoulder. 'That spell's new to me. It wouldn't have healed you completely.'

'Well we can't stay here,' muttered Mera as the ground shuddered. 'We'll put him on Valiant but we have to leave now. That was good thinking Lex but I don't know how long that dragon will keep them at bay.'

Ezra looked like he was about to ask what on earth she was talking about but instead moved forward to help us lift Alaric onto Valiant's saddle. He lolled slightly but was able to sit still enough that he wasn't in danger of falling off.

'Here Lex, take this,' Mera was holding out her cloak for me. 'We don't want you to freeze to death.'

I took it without complaint. While the cold had been soothing my burns it was beginning to sting slightly. I wrapped the cloak around myself. We set off, putting as much distance between the Brethren and us as possible.

We went as fast as we were able but it still didn't feel like enough. The fact that we hadn't heard anything from below made me uncomfortable. My skin itched to be away from this place. I kept turning around, flighty as a deer. It felt as though we were being stalked. I envisioned the Brethren springing out at us at any moment. Soon we reached the forest again and plunged into its depths.

Had the spell worked or had our journey been in vain? Surely if it had worked the Sisterhood would have appeared but they were nowhere to be seen. I attempted to take my mind off it by trying the healing spell on my burns. The pain subsided. The welts became pink scars, wrapping around my body like ivy would a tree. I doubted they would ever fade completely.

After Mera had filled Ezra in on what had happened we lapsed into an uncomfortable silence. There was a deep feeling of unease that swathed itself around our throats and leapt out at us from every shadows. Darkness stole through the forest, crouching silently at the roots of trees, staring down at us from the rustling leaves.

Ilyssa was jumping at every noise. She walk next to Alaric, one hand clutching his knee, the other curled into a tight ball. Her face was stricken. She was biting her lip so hard I was surprised it didn't draw blood. I wanted to reach out and ease her pain but I could think of nothing that would bring her comfort. After a while she unclenched her fist and reached out for my hand. We hurried onwards together in the darkness.

The grass became dewy beneath our weary feet as dawn approached. The first rays of sunlight were just tipping the tops of the trees when movement on the path ahead brought us to a halt. Before any of us could panic the amorphous shape moved into view and I saw that Sami was walking towards us. I breathed a short sigh of relief.

'Come with me. We must hurry,' she beckoned us forward with her bow. She didn't wait to see if we followed before walking off the path and into the trees on the right.

'How did you find us?' called Mera, who bounded after her.

'I can find many things,' she replied. 'And you were not difficult to track.'

'What about the Brethren? Did they get out? Are they behind us?' Mera pressed.

'There is no time for this at the present. Everything will be explained to you soon but for now we must hasten ourselves,' she insisted.

'Wait,' called Ilyssa, letting go of my hand and jogging to catch up with Sami. 'My brother's injured. Can you heal him?'

She didn't look back as she answered. 'Have patience, child. We will be there soon and then he will be healed.'

Ilyssa swallowed and slowed down so she was level with us again. I took her hand and smiled at her reassuringly. She could only grimace back.

Sami led us through the woods along no recognisable path, though she seemed to be sure of where she was going. Eventually she stopped in front of a huge grey rock that had a deep split running vertically down it.

'We're here,' she announced. She slung her bow over her shoulder and placed her hands on either side of the divide.

'Do you think this is safe?' Ilyssa whispered in my ear.

'I don't think we have much of a choice,' I murmured. 'She helped us once.'

Ilyssa continued to look worried but before she could say anything else Sami's clear voice cut through the dull morning air.

'*Onscít,*' she commanded as she pushed against the rock.

With a great crack the rock moved apart. The stone swung inwards revealing a torch-lit tunnel that led down into the earth.

'Follow me,' Sami ordered, walking into the stone passage.

The roof was too low for Alaric to continue riding Valiant so Ilyssa and I helped him down. As we entered the tunnel the stone doors closed, sealing us in. Mera was eagerly following after Sami, impatient to see where she was leading us. Ilyssa and I came next, supporting Alaric between us. He was able to walk almost steadily, but every now and then he would stumble. With my arm wrapped around his waist I could feel his rapid breathing. I hoped we'd reach wherever we were being taken soon. Ezra brought up the rear. He tried to sooth Valiant, who was getting more restless the further under ground we went.

The path was sloped steeply downwards. The walls pressed in on us tightly so Ilyssa and I grazed our shoulders on the rough stone. There wasn't a breath of wind. I thought I could hear some kind of humming not far up ahead. As we got closer the noise began to swell to the point that it sounded as though we were nearing a hive of buzzing bees. All of a sudden the tunnel flattened and opened out onto what appeared to be a large balcony. I had to catch my breath as I peered over the edge, stunned by what I saw.

Down below was a vast underground city. Roads spread out like vines, twisting around buildings cut out of yellow stone. Bright lights glittered overhead, illuminating the entire city. From the depths of the streets I heard the sounds of clanging metal and sawing wood. Somewhere close by a woman was singing. The air smelled clean and fresh, as though we were in the open countryside, not deep underground.

People were milling up and down the streets, setting up stalls and opening shops. I saw with a jolt that they weren't the kind of people I had ever seen before. Two of these strange people were walking down a street directly below us. One of them was surrounded by misty vapour that was cracking with flashes of lightening, while his friend, a very small man with a long, white beard, was thumping along next to him with feet three times the usual size. I looked up at the domed ceiling and noticed serpent-like creatures twisting in the air above us, flying between houses that had been carved into the side of the rock.

I turned to Sami, utterly amazed. She gave me what could have been a smile and said, 'Welcome to Callipolis.'

27
Callipolis

While we gazed at the site before us with awe a huge creature soared towards us and landed on the path that led down into the city below. It curled its huge wings behind itself and regarded us with fiery red eyes. It looked like a dragon but unlike the one made of stone in the temple its scales were green and its body lithe. Without flinching Sami turned toward it and said, 'I am waiting for Ryouko.'

The creature, which appeared to understand perfectly, nodded its head and stretched out its wings, taking off again in one fluid motion.

'What was that?' asked Alaric, who was still swaying slightly.

'A Drakaina,' Sami answered, moving over to where we were standing. She placed her hand on Alaric's forehead and muttered, '*Thurhalath,*' in her low voice and backed away again. Alaric brightened immediately, looking slightly shocked at his sudden recovery. 'She and her kin are the guards of Callipolis. The Drakaina and Balaur guard the entrances to the city while the Fenghuang send messages between them.' She pointed up to where flocks of brightly coloured birds were flying back and forth across the domed roof. 'Callipolis is a safe haven for Magic Folk.'

'And you are most welcome here, Children of Man.'

Walking up the path was one of the strangest creatures I had ever seen. He looked like a large cat with tufts of reddish-brown fur covering his body and black stripes running down his sides. He had a thick, fluffy mane and his tail was twisted and knotted in the middle. He padded towards us on long, thin legs, talons clacking on the stone floor. He had black markings around his eyes, which made it look as though he was wearing glasses. He appeared to be smiling. His voice was deep and soothing as he repeated, 'Most welcome.'

'Ryouko,' greeted Sami.

'Thank you for bringing them here safely, Sami. I don't know what we'd do without you,' he inclined his great head towards her.

'It was no trouble. If my work here is done I will return home,' Sami stated.

'Of course. Thank you again,' Ryouko nodded.

She turned back to us. 'This is where I leave you. You will be safe here,' she nodded to each of us in turn and marched back up the tunnel.

I looked at Mera, still amazed at the situation we had found ourselves in.

'Um…' I began, but Alaric beat me to it.

'What are you?' he asked.

'*Alaric*,' scolded Ilyssa. 'I'm sorry, you'll have to excuse him. He's just had a rather nasty bump to the head.'

Rather than being offended Ryouko chuckled lightly. 'I quite understand. It has been a very trying day for you. This must all come as quite a shock. Let me introduce myself and I will explain. My name is Ryouko. I am an Alphyn. And you, if I am not much mistaken, are Alexander Eriksson.'

His large, golden eyes rested on me. 'Yes. Call me Lex.'

'Lex, then,' he smiled. 'And you must be Princess Mera,' he turned his kindly gaze to Mera. 'And who are your friends?'

'This is Ilyssa,' I said, placing my hand on her shoulder. 'And her brother Alaric. And this is Ezra.'

Ezra, who finally seemed to notice that he was staring open mouthed, shook himself.

Mera stepped forward and said, 'I don't mean to be rude, but what are we doing here? What are you doing here? What is this place?'

'Three very good questions. And I shall answer them presently but first I will call Panalin to take your horse to the stables,' Ryouko moved over to a firebird that had been sitting on the railing listening to our conversation. He whispered something and it took off.

'Who's Panalin?' Ezra asked warily.

'A very competent stable master. As an Abada he is in the perfect position to take care of your horse. They have an affinity with nature and Panalin is especially protective of our equine friends,' Ryouko explained.

Ezra nodded though he continued to look unsure.

'I promise he'll be in very good hands. You may wish to remove your packs before he arrives,' he suggested.

We had just begun unloading our things when a small pop announced the arrival of Panalin. I turned and saw a strange man standing next to Ryouko. He was tall with sky blue skin and two great horns atop his head. Both his hair and beard were long and green with tiny, violet flowers growing in them. His large eyes were also green, with small flecks of gold. The firebird that Ryouko had sent to find him was sitting on his shoulder, its red and orange plumage clashing with him horribly. In his hand Panalin carried a long, twisted stick covered in carvings of animals and plants.

'Ryouko,' he said in a gruff voice. 'I was trying to help the tree sprites settle an argument with the water nymphs. What is so important?'

Ryouko smiled gently. 'I have another guest for your stables, Panalin.'

Panalin turned, seeming only now to notice us. 'Oh, they're here, are they? Well, all right. But next time wait 'til I'm finished, would you. There's no telling what those awful sprites will do next.'

Panalin marched over to where Alaric was hoisting off the last of the packs. Ezra still looked a little uneasy as he gripped Valiant's reins.

'Maybe I should go with you,' he suggested.

'Don't be silly, boy,' huffed Panalin, who was now gently stroking the horse's neck. Valiant, who had been whinnying nervously all the way down the tunnel, immediately relaxed. 'Your horse will be safe with me.'

Ezra relented and watched unhappily as Valiant was lead away from him. Alaric clapped him on the shoulder and gave him a comforting smile.

'Well then,' Ryouko said jovially. 'Let me show you Callipolis.'

I noticed Mera hopping slightly with excitement. I smiled at her enthusiasm. After all this time believing that magic had been reduced to nothing I was still wrapping my head around the idea that there was an entire city of Magic Folk living right under our feet. We followed Ryouko down the path as he began to explain how Callipolis came to be.

'We were loosing the war, you see,' he explained. 'And badly too. Most of us knew that if we carried on that way our people would be completely eradicated. That's when the rumours started. I heard it from the Amphiptere. They're those creatures you see flying above us. They prefer air dwellings but this was the best we could do given the circumstances. They told me that there was a place we Magic Folk could go, a place that would be safe from those who hunted us. The elves were the first to find it, I think. They were here when we arrived, anyway. It was smaller then, of course. That's when the Sisterhood appeared. Well, what was left of them, anyway. The Sisterhood used to be a vast group. Hundreds of sorceresses. Very impressive. But the war thinned their numbers down to seven. That's what happened to Sami's wife, you know. Sami and Akemi had lived together for hundreds of years. Akemi was a member of the Sisterhood, though Sami never was. She lived peacefully, out of war, but when the Brethren killed Akemi something in her broke. I'm afraid she blamed the Sisterhood for what happened.'

I thought back to Sami's warning about the Sisterhood. Perhaps she only mistrusted them because of the blame she put on them.

'That's so sad,' mummed Mera.

'It is indeed,' Ryouko nodded his shaggy head. 'So those of us who had survived the Brethren's wrath made our way as far from Culrain as possible. They were mainly situated there, you see, but you could never really be sure where was safe. Eventually we found Skara Brae and from there we found the entrance of Callipolis. The Sisterhood told us that we would be safe here until the time came for us to rally. Then, of course, they told us the prophecy. We've been waiting for quite some time.'

I felt the familiar unpleasant lurch in my stomach that accompanied any thought of the prophecy.

'Wait, you were alive a hundred years ago? How is that possible?' Ezra asked.

'We Magic Folk tend to live long than Children of Men,' Ryouko clarified. 'It's quite interesting actually. A quirk of nature, you might say.'

'So you've been here the whole time? Just waiting?' Mera marvelled.

'That's right,' he confirmed. 'We've grown in size since then, of course. As more Magic Folk found us the city had to be expanded. That's when Bugul Noz came in very handy. He's responsible for most of the tunnels you see around here. Very good at digging, he is. Got the hands for it.' Ryouko chuckled at a joke that only he seemed to be in on.

We were walking up a street lined with houses painted in an array of different colours. It was still early so they were mostly in darkness but every now and then I would see people moving around inside. At the window of a rose coloured building I saw a small, furry face with big black eyes peering out at us inquisitively. I smiled as we passed and the small creature giggled and disappeared from view.

We turned a corner and came across a pen filled with fluffy brown and blue goats dozing quietly. Ryouko paused his commentary and stopped in front of the fence. He stared into the pen for a moment before saying, 'Hu, if you don't come out of there I'm going to get Jidovi to come and make you.'

There was a small rustling sound followed by a tinny laugh, then suddenly something propelled itself from amongst the goats and landed on the fence in front of Ryouko. For a moment I thought it was a bat with its furry, pinched face and fangs, but then I saw it had the wings of a bird and a long tail that swished back and forth.

'Morning, Rykie,' the creature squeaked.

'Honestly, Hu, how many times have I told you to stop stealing the Fomorians' goat's milk?' sighed Ryouko.

Hu leaned in towards Ryouko and whispered, 'Don't know what you're saying Rykie. Just out for a morning walk, I am. But I'm off now.' And with another shrill laugh Hu launched into the air and flew off.

Ryouko sighed again and shook his head. 'That was Hu, a Broxa. They're shape shifters, so watch out for them. If Hu bothers you just threaten to fetch Jidovi. He's one of the giants. He's the only one Hu appears to listen to. Now where was I?'

He started walking again, telling us about the city and how it was built. Though he told us that everyone was equal here something about the way people stopped to say good morning to him as they passed told me that he was well respected.

'The lack of water was a problem initially, but after the water nymphs arrived we were never short of it. Oh hello Buggane, Bugaboo. What are you doing up so early?' Ryouko had stopped to say hello to two people at the side of the road. A huge man, who would have been nearly ten feet tall when standing, was sitting with his back resting against a faded yellow building. He had long, black hair and an expression of great joy on his slightly lumpy face. The woman, who was barely three feet tall and distinctly dishevelled, was perched on her friend's broad shoulder.

'We're waiting for Yuli,' answered the woman.

'She's going to let us help move the oxen out into the field,' added the man in a slow voice, grinning broadly.

'Ah, I see. Oh, now that I have you here Buggane, Bugul Noz was looking for you,' said Ryouko.

'For me?' asked the man, scrunching up his face. 'What for?'

'Something about the southern tunnels. I believe he wants your help reinforcing the walls,' he told him.

'All right,' Buggane nodded slowly. 'I will look for him. Thank you.'

'You'll be by later won't you, Ryouko?' asked Bugaboo, looking down from Buggane's huge shoulder. 'To look at the new furniture we made. It's all finished now.'

'Of course,' nodded Ryouko.

Bugaboo looked curiously the five of us.

Ryouko saw her gaze and said, 'Oh, how rude of me. Let me introduce our new friends. Buggane, Bugaboo, this is Lex, Mera, Ilyssa, Alaric and Ezra.'

'Hello Children of Men,' grinned Buggane.

'Welcome, welcome,' squeaked Bugaboo.

We all mumbled hellos.

'Well, we shall you bid you goodbye for now. Good luck with the oxen,' said Ryouko

'Bye Ryouko. Bye, humans,' Buggane and Bugaboo said in unison.

'Goblins and ogres don't usually get along,' whispered Ryouko as we walked away. 'But those two were raised together. Such a sweet pair they make. I believe their friendship is impossible to break.'

We carried on our journey, listening to Ryouko explain how they survived under the ground with limited resources. I found myself tuning out when he started talking about crop rotations. I turned to Mera, expecting to see her rolling her eyes but instead found her listening intently to everything Ryouko was saying. I suppressed a laugh and looked up at the vaulted ceiling.

The city was a completely different place from down here. Up on the balcony it had looked like a sparkling orb alive with activity. It was darker down here, away from the bright lights that circled the roof. It was taking us a while to walk across it. It had been almost an hour since we had started but we hadn't yet reached the other side. My body ached for food and sleep.

We passed through a row of houses that were cut from something different than the yellow stone of the city. It was pure white and gave off an ethereal glow. There were twisted knots carved into it and the soft sound of music drifted through the gossamer-curtained windows.

Ryouko rushed us over a bridge and past a small lake where there was a great commotion. I heard him muttering, 'Perhaps I should have let Panalin deal with that first.' From the banks of the lake a number of green-skinned people were hurling clumps of earth into the water. Every now and then blue-skinned people would rise from the lake to launch huge balls of water back at them. Alaric chuckled as one of the water spheres landed on the head of a green man, soaking him completely.

I noticed after a while that we were being followed. A short way behind us a group of small, fluffy creatures were bounding along in our wake. Their fuzzy grey tails waggled happily as they scuttled down the road after us. I could hear their squeaky voices chattering excitably but every time I turned to look at them they scampered off to hide. A few minutes later I'd look back and they'd be there again, giggling into their soft paws.

A soft-spoken, willowy woman with hair of fire, whom Ryouko introduced as Iele, interrupted us a short while later. She reminded me of Sami, with her young face and old eyes. I heard a jingling sound and glanced down to see bells around her ankles. Scorch marks appeared on the ground where she walked.

'Iele is in charge of peacekeeping,' Ryouko told us. 'She settles disputes when people can't agree on a solution themselves.'

'It's a honour to meet you,' she chimed. 'Ryouko, I must tell you, Ragana has been causing trouble with the nymphs and sprites again. And you know how riled up they can get. If she carries on like this even I won't be able to calm them down.'

'Yes, I saw the fruits of her labour earlier,' Ryouko muttered darkly. 'I'm sure between you and Panalin you'll be able to help them work it out. For now why don't you accompany us to the Aula.'

We set off again. Ryouko and Mera had entered into a discussion about efficient peacekeeping and Ilyssa, Alaric and Ezra were seeing how close they could get to the creatures following us without scaring them off, so I was left to make conversation with Iele.

'I honestly didn't fully believe in the prophecy,' she began bluntly. 'We've been stuck down here for so long I didn't think we'd ever be getting out. I can't remember the last time I saw the sun.'

'You haven't been outside since you came here? Not once?' I asked.

'No,' she sighed. 'It wouldn't be safe for us to keep popping in and out of the ground. If I were to go then everyone would want to and the whole point of this place is to keep us safe. Someone might see and if the Brethren were to get wind of it then we'd be in trouble. Some people do leave every now and then. Some of the nymphs go out to scout. And Sami is always flitting in and out of here. I should very much like to go with her, just once.'

'So if you didn't believe in the prophecy what made you stay?' I wondered.

'Fear,' she confessed. 'Self-preservation is a very strong thing. Or perhaps, on a less cynical note, there was a part of me that believed we would be saved. I am eternally grateful for what you and your friends have done. My powers have been dulled for so long but I can feel them returning to me already. I had forgotten what it felt like.'

I nodded.

'You have been touched by fire,' she commented, looking at the burn on my neck.

'Hmm? Oh, yes. During the spell,' I muttered, tracing one on my arm with my finger.

'They are a mark of your bravery. You should wear them with pride.'

I felt touched by her words. I had no time to reply, however, because at that moment Ryouko called, 'Ah, here we are.'

We had arrived at the Aula. It was a large, round building with an archway through which I saw a circular table with a few chairs placed around it. Torches in brackets lit the room. I noticed something moving in the flame and as I looked closer I saw a salamander stretching out happily in the heat. I smiled

261

to watch it paddling in the fire as though it were swimming in water.

Standing at the head of the table were two deer. One had a deep brown coat and bronze hooves, while the other was pure white. They were both very large, and their great heads were adorned with enormous golden antlers. As we filed in they ceased their conversation and turned to look at us.

Ryouko stepped into the room and upon seeing the deer smiled and said, 'Ah good, you're both here. Why don't you lot sit down.'

I sunk gratefully into one of the chairs and suppressed a yawn. The others followed suit. Ryouko padded over to the deer and they inclined their heads in greeting.

'Let me introduce to you to Cerynitis and her son Goldenhorn, Callipolis' fastest runners,' beamed Ryouko. 'Cerynitis was just a calf when she first came to us. And we're very lucky she did. Anyway, Cerynitis, Goldenhorn, I'm sure you know who our guests are. Will you be able to take word of their arrival to the camps in the other kingdoms?'

Cerynitis and Goldenhorn both nodded and without a word they dashed from the room.

'There are other places like this?' asked Mera eagerly.

'Not quite,' answered Ryouko. 'I use the word camp for a reason. Most Magic Folk wanted to be as far away from the Brethren as possible without passing through the Endless Desert. Some did try that, of course, but we never heard from them again. Anyway, some people didn't feel right leaving the land they had been born to, so they stayed. There's no more than a hundred in each, though. There's less than twenty in Culrain,' he sat down on the raised stone platform at the front of the room. 'Now, I must ask, if you are able to tell me that is, what happened in Skara Brae?'

Mera set about explaining the events of the previous day. Every now and then one of us would jump in with something she had left out. Ryouko listened in silence, perched on his hind legs. I tried to concentrate on what Mera was saying but my body wasn't cooperating. My head was muffled, my feet ached and my burns were starting to throb nastily again. I wanted nothing more than to lie down and sleep. Just some time to rest… I felt someone shaking my arm and looked up to see Ilyssa at my side.

'You fell asleep, Lex,' she smiled. The dark circles around her eyes and her sympathetic expression suggested that she wanted to be doing the same.

'Sorry,' I muttered. 'It's been a long day.'

'Of course it has, how rude of me. I'm very sorry to have kept you so long,' apologised Ryouko, rising. 'I'm sure you want nothing more than to rest after everything you've been through. I must think on this, anyway. Iele, would you be so kind as to show them to their rooms? And perhaps some poppy julep before bed. It will make you feel better, I assure you.'

Ryouko bid us goodnight and we filed out of the room. Iele guided us down a small path that led away from the centre of Callipolis, bells jingling at her ankles. We didn't come across anybody else on this path but I could hear the sound of the city waking up behind us. She stopped in front of a cluster of small square buildings that was next to one of the tunnels that headed out of the city. She opened the heavy wooden door of the house at the very end of the row and took us inside.

The house was open and spacious. The walls were painted a cool cream colour. Twinkling lights hung from the ceiling.

Iele pointed to the room on the right and said, 'That's the bedroom. The washroom is at the back. You can get to it from the bedroom. It's not much at such short notice but I'm sure it will do for now. I'll leave you.'

'Thank you,' I smiled at her as she walked past us back towards the door.

'Of course,' she nodded and left.

'I'm dead on my feet,' sighed Ilyssa.

'Come on, let's just sleep. We can marvel over the strangeness of it all later,' suggested Mera.

'Good idea,' agreed Alaric, dragging his pack over to a long reclining chair in the corner of the room and flopping down onto it with a sigh.

'There are beds in the other room,' tutted Ilyssa.

'I'm here now,' he muttered, waving a nonchalant hand in her direction and snuggling down onto the velvet covers. He closed his eyes and moaned in relief. 'I have never been this comfortable in my life.'

Ilyssa shook her head. 'Fine. I'm too tired to argue,' she picked up her pack and followed the rest of us into the other room.

Ezra dropped his pack onto the floor next to the bed at the far end of the room besides another door, which must have led through to the washroom. He collapsed onto the bed and groaned. 'I'm so sore.'

'That's because you hunch over when you walk,' commented Mera without looking at him.

'I do not,' he grumbled.

'You do a bit,' I cut in before an argument could spring up between them.

Ezra made a face and kicked off his shoes before stretching out on top of the covers. Mera was watching him with a shrewd expression. I thought for a moment she was going to say something cutting, but all she said was, 'I'll take Alaric his blanket,' and picking up one from a bed she marched out of the room.

Ilyssa placed her bag on the floor by the bed opposite mine. She sat down and rubbed her tired eyes. My eyes traced her hand as it pushed her hair out of her face, tucking it neatly behind her ear. She smiled sleepily at me and asked, 'How are you?'

'I'm fine,' I muttered. 'What about you?'

'Stunned,' she sighed. 'Who would have thought that there would be this kind of life down here all this time? It's amazing.'

'Hmm,' I hummed in agreement. 'We should get some sleep. I have a feeling we're going to be pretty busy soon.'

'What do you think is going happen now that magic is free?' she wondered.

'I don't know,' I answered honestly. 'I can feel it though. I can feel it getting stronger.'

'What's it like?'

'It's like… it's like everything is humming very quietly. It's soft but it's there. Everything has its own sound and the more I listen the better I can hear it. There's a slight vibration to it. I can feel it buzzing at my feet and up through my body. Does that make any sense?'

'I think so. I wish I could do magic,' she sighed and leaned forward. 'Being able to wave around a pointy stick seems fairly benign compared to what you can do.'

'No, it isn't,' I insisted. 'It's seriously impressive. Without magic I can barely defend myself. I wish you could see yourself with that sword in your hand.'

'It's not been much use so far,' she shrugged.

'It might be a good thing if you never have to use it,' I pointed out.

'Still, it seems like a waste.'

'You could practise here.'

'You're right,' she nodded.

'I could help if you wanted,' I offered.

'Really?' she looked up and smiled, biting her lip. 'You'd do that?'

'Of course, I'd love to,' I replied, delighted that she seemed so pleased with my suggestion.

A faint blush rose in her cheeks. 'That's what I love about you. You're so kind.'

'Oh I don't know. It's really you that-'

Before I could finish there was a sharp knock at the door. I jumped at the sudden noise.

'I'll get that, shall I?'

Mera, who had been unpacking some of her things in the other room, reached the door before I did. She opened it to find Iele standing outside holding a leather pouch and a neatly wrapped package tucked under her arm.

'I thought you might be hungry so I brought you some food along with the julep,' she said holding the packages.

'Oh, thank you. That's very kind,' said Mera reaching forward and taking them.

Iele smiled and turned away.

Mera closed the door and went to put the food down on the table.

'There are probably some cups over here,' I said, opening the dusty cupboard and pulling out crockery. I found some mugs and set them down on the table. 'Theses will do.'

Mera poured the orange liquid into four of the cups.

'There's no point waking Alaric just for a drink,' she explained, nodding at his snoring figure.

'Good point,' I picked up two of the mugs and took them into the bedroom.

Ilyssa must have been in the washroom because Ezra was the only one in there when I got back. I could tell by his deep breaths that he had fallen asleep on top of the covers. I set one of the cups down by Ilyssa's bed and sat down on my own.

Mera walked over to the sleeping Ezra and put his mug gently down on the floor.

'That's very restrained of you not to pour it on him,' I joked, taking a sip of my drink. The tangy liquid tickled my tongue. It was sweet and refreshing.

'No, that would be mean. With any luck he'll step on it when he wakes up,' she replied, cradling her cup as she sat down.

'Don't you think it's time to forgive him?' I asked.

Mera sighed. 'I'm trying.'

'Maybe you could start by not arguing with everything he says,' said Ilyssa as she emerged from the washroom.

'Oh, don't you start,' grumbled Mera.

'Who was at the door?' Ilyssa asked, sitting back down on her bed.

'Iele. She brought us some food if you're hungry. It's in the other room. And there's a drink by your bed. It's quite good actually,' I said.

Ilyssa leant over the side of her bed and picked up the cup. She took a sip and smiled. 'Oh, that is good.'

'Well, I'm going to sleep,' yawned Mera, setting down her cup and crawling under the covers. 'Night all.'

'Night,' Ilyssa and I chimed together.

'I can't stay awake for one more minute,' said Ilyssa, putting down her cup and stretching widely.

'No, me neither,' I drained the last of my drink and lay down on the soft bed.

'Goodnight, Lex,' I heard Ilyssa say through a haze of sleepiness.

'Night,' I muttered.

It was strange to think that just a few hours ago we had been running for our lives. I fleetingly wondered whether the Brethren had gotten away from Skara Brae but the soft hands of sleep were pulling me under and I was too warm and comfortable to resist.

28

The council convenes

The next thing I was conscious of was the sound of fluty music drifting through the room. I wondered what time it was. I felt very well rested. I sat up and saw that the others were still fast asleep. I got out of bed and went through to the other room. Mera had laid out some of the food that Iele had brought us the night before. Just seeing it made my stomach rumble and I realised how hungry I was. I reached for the first thing I saw, which turned out to be some kind of pastry that tasted of lemons. I gobbled it down hungrily along with a spiky fruit that tasted like cheese. I could still hear the music but it wasn't coming from in the house so I opened the front door and stepped outside.

It was brighter than it had been before. The great orbs that lit up the city had swollen in size so that it was as bright as day. There was still no one on our little street but I could see people walking past the end of the lane that led into the centre of the city. I looked around for the source of the music. I followed the sound into the entrance of the tunnel. I didn't have to go far to find what I was looking for.

A ring of small, goblin-like creatures with tufty black hair and squashed noses were standing in a circle playing a song on wooden pipes. Some were dancing, kicking their tiny feet high into the air and yipping with joy. When I approached they quieted and turned as one to stare at me with large, black eyes. Then, with a chorus of giggles, they scampered off down the tunnel leaving nothing but dust in their wake.

'Trows are shy,' said a slow voice from behind me.

I whirled around and saw a creature sitting against the wall of the tunnel. I must have walked right past him without noticing but I wasn't sure how. For a moment I thought it was a huge mole. His leathery skin was covered in dust and mud. He had a long, wrinkled snout with bristly whiskers. Tusks the size of my arm stuck out from his snout and curled back on themselves. His eyes were huge and slightly cloudy. They kept darting around the tunnel as though he was expecting something to jump out at him. He wore dirty brown trousers that were worn at the knees and a jacket that had several holes in it. His hands were the strangest part of him. They were black and calloused and each finger was fused together to look like a shovel. Though he was one of the ugliest creatures I had ever seen there was something gentle in his expression.

'Err, excuse me?' I asked.

'The Trows. That's what those creatures are,' he explained. 'They make beautiful music but they don't like people listening to them. That's why I was hiding.'

'Oh, right,' I said. 'Sorry, who are you?'

'Bugul Noz,' he replied. 'Who are you?'

'Lex. My name's Lex. I think Ryouko mentioned you earlier. He said you helped dig out these tunnels.'

'I did,' Bugul Noz smiled shyly. 'You're human, aren't you? You're the one from the prophecy.'

I crossed my arms. 'I suppose I am.'

At that moment I heard Mera's voice calling my name. I looked back towards the tunnel entrance but couldn't see her.

'Well, it was nice-' I began, but when I turned back Bugul Noz had vanished.

I walked back to the house. When I rounded the corner I saw Mera, Ilyssa, Alaric and Ezra standing outside. They turned when I called out to them.

'Where were you?' called Mera.

'Sorry,' I apologised. 'I heard music when I woke up and went to investigate.'

'You shouldn't disappear like that,' she chided.

'Sorry,' I repeated.

'Come on, let's go back in,' said Ilyssa.

We filed inside and sat down at the small table. As the assortment of cheese puffs and oatcakes and something that I still wasn't sure whether or not it was fruit were shared out, we discussed what we were going to do that day.

'We could just walk around and explore,' suggested Alaric.

'I want to try and find the stables,' said Ezra.

I bit into an apple and found that it was bright purple inside.

'Ryouko might want to talk to us again,' Mera pointed out. 'I doubt that was all he had to say on the prophecy. We were brought here for a reason.'

'He'll find us if he wants to talk,' Alaric reasoned.

After we finished eating we headed out into the city. I noticed people staring at us as we passed by. News of our arrival must have spread by now.

We walked through a market that was selling foods I had never seen before. One stall had on display something that might have been bread except that it was blue and smelled strongly of sawdust. At one point we passed a group of giants who were lumbering along in the opposite direction carrying heavy planks of wood across their shoulders. They must have been about fifteen feet in size.

I heard one call in a booming voice, 'Hurry up Jidovi. I'd like to get these to Bugul Noz before we all die of old age.'

Another scowled and yelled back, 'Shut up, Emim. I'll get there when I want to get there.'

Eventually we found the stables. They were at the edge of the city, a short walk to the east of our house. At least I guessed it was to the east. It was hard to tell what direction you were going without the sun to guide you. Behind the wooden stalls there was a short tunnel through which I noticed a large paddock. Winged horses were galloping back and forth across the grass at a great speed. There were a few sprites buzzing around the yard, one of which showed Ezra to Valiant's stall.

We left Ezra to his own devices and walked around the stables ourselves. They smelled of dust and sweat and something sweet I couldn't place. The stalls were mostly empty. There was one that was so huge I couldn't even see over the door but I could hear a deep snuffling from inside. Another housed a couple of tiny bleating creatures that appeared to be half horse half sheep. From a stall on the other side of the yard a beautiful golden horse was sticking its head over the door. It nickered when I went over to stroke it.

I turned when I heard the clacking of talons and saw two griffins walking into the stables. With a jolt I recognised one of them as the griffin that had approached us in Seion and told us that our plans were fruitless. He didn't look surprised to see us.

'What are you doing here?' Mera asked, a hint of accusation in her voice.

'Looking for Panalin,' he replied.

'I meant here in Callipolis,' she insisted.

'I live here,' he answered, looking slightly sheepish. 'Please allow me to apologise for our last meeting.'

'You must forgive him,' the griffin by his side added. 'He was not himself.'

'Who were you, then?' Mera asked.

'Let me explain. My name is Tanto and this is Kama, my wife,' he indicated the griffin standing to his right. She bowed her head low in greeting. 'When I met you I believed her to be dead. I thought she had been killed at the hands of the Brethren. It did not affect me well. As it happens, she too thought I had been killed. She made her way here to seek refuge, thinking I

272

was gone forever. I happened upon a group of Goblins who were making their way here. Something told me it was the right thing to do. I followed my heart and found her again,' Tanto and Kama smiled at each other.

'Well isn't that just-'

'I hope I'm not interrupting,' Iele cut across Mera before she could finish.

'Not at all,' I insisted.

'Ryouko was hoping he would be able to talk to you. Would you come to the Aula with me?' she requested.

'Of course. I'm glad you found each other again,' I said to Tanto and Kama before taking Mera's arm and steering her away, Ilyssa and Alaric following suit.

Iele led the way out of the stables scorching the ground with every step. I noticed that there were small flames licking the soles of her feet. I approached her and asked, 'How are the tree sprites and water nymphs getting on?'

'Worse, I think,' she answered. 'And I don't think Panalin's being particularly helpful either. He keeps loosing his temper with them and threatening to have them removed.'

'Why are they arguing?' asked Mera.

'Well it started as an offhand comment from Ragana about how the nymphs have more respect than the sprites. Well I say offhand. I'm not all that convinced she's free of blame here. Honestly the amount of times that witch has stirred up trouble,' Iele huffed. 'Anyway, the nymphs started complaining that the sprites have been encroaching on their space and it's just escalated from there.'

'My father always told me that getting each side to see from the others point of view was important in mediation,' suggested Mera.

'I can't get them to stop fighting long enough to even have a civilized conversation,' she sighed. 'I'm sure I'll figure something out. Here we are.'

We had arrived back at the Aula. I heard voices inside and for a moment I thought that maybe the Sisterhood had shown up but when I stepped across the threshold it was to see Ryouko speaking with a group of people with giant ears that stuck out from under woolly hats. The oldest of them was a man who had a heavily lined face and fuzzy black hair. He stood at the back of the group leaning on a gnarled walking stick. A man and a woman, both middle-aged and grey-haired, were standing in front of the man. They were gripping the hands of a small, white haired boy. The four of them were watching a girl who must have been a year or so younger me, whose red lips were moving very fast as she spoke.

'-what's right, Ryouko. You know it is.'

'I understand and appreciate your enthusiasm Popis, but there really isn't any call for that right now,' Ryouko sighed when the girl finished speaking. Upon seeing us he brightened. 'Good, you're here. Let me introduce the Pandi family. That's Papya at the back. That's Pinta and Perio there with Pippin in the middle. And this here is Popis. Everyone, this is Lex, Mera, Ilyssa and Alaric.'

'So it's true.' grunted the old man. 'You're really here.'

'All the more reason for us to take action,' said Popis, turning back to Ryouko. 'If we stall for too long the Brethren will regain all the ground they have lost.'

'Popis, please,' begged Pinta. 'Enough of this war talk. You weren't there the first time. Let those who were use that knowledge to decide what to do.'

'Mother, I am done letting other people fight my battles,' she insisted, pushing her white hair out of her face. 'I may not have been there when we were forced into hiding, but neither were you. I plan on fighting for the rights I deserve.'

'Popis, listen to your mother. She's right,' added Perio. 'You know what the prophecy said. We just have to wait.'

'Damn the prophecy!' she shouted. 'I've waited long enough. I want my freedom and I want it now. It's stifling in here. There's no room to breath. I want to feel the wind on my face. I want to smell the summer air. Our people used to dance in the sun and I've never even seen it.'

'You don't know how lucky you are,' Pinta insisted. 'You're fourteen, you've barely begun to live. Pa you were there, tell her,' she turned to the wizened old man.

'I think,' croaked Papya, who had been watching his family argue silently, 'that we ought to clear the room. We are in the way.'

Popis huffed and stormed out and Pinta and Perio followed her. Papya was the last to leave. Before he left he looked to Ryouko and said, 'That won't be the last of it, you know,' and hobbled out.

'That was heated,' commented Iele.

'Yes,' agreed Ryouko. 'Popis has become quite the firecracker. Please, won't you sit?'

Still feeling a little awkward from watching the family argument, we took our seats.

'Now that you're slightly more rested I was hoping we could talk,' Ryouko padded over to us.

'Of course,' Mera answered.

'We have been waiting for you for a very long time and now that magic has been awakened luck is finally on our side,' he smiled. 'The Sisterhood told us that once the prophecy had been fulfilled our path would be clear. Alas, the path is still looking a little blurred. I was thinking, well I was hoping really, that you would have some idea of our next step.'

275

He looked around at us hopefully. When none of us answered his enthusiasm faded.

'Sorry,' I muttered, feeling I had let him down.

I had been wondering a lot about the Sisterhood. None of it made sense. If they had been waiting so long for magic to be released then where were they? They had promised to help and yet they were nowhere to be seen. And what about the prophecy? It hadn't come to pass the way they said it would. It didn't seem right to leave us without answers. Now I thought about it they had only caused trouble for us, showing up and talking in riddles and making things more complicated than they needed to be. I was beginning to be angry with them. Sami was right, they weren't to be trusted.

'No need to apologise,' Ryouko sighed. 'I'm sure we'll think of something.'

'What have you been doing?' asked Mera. 'You know, to combat the Brethren.'

'Gathering intelligence, mainly. Knowledge is power, after all. Though to tell you the truth that in and of itself has proved rather difficult,' he admitted.

'What about some kind of a battle plan?' asked Alaric. 'Or infiltration. The Brethren are good at it.'

'Infiltration we've tried,' he told us. 'Unfortunately there are so few here who can successfully blend in with humans. Even those who can are often discovered. As for a battle plan, whom are we battling? We don't even know who our enemies are.'

'What if there was a way you could find out?' asked Ilyssa.

Ryouko perked up at that. 'How?' he asked eagerly.

Before she could answer, four women entered the room, followed by Ezra. The first was Sami. She walked silently over to an empty chair and flung herself into it in an uncharacteristically angry fashion. She gave me a sharp nod in greeting when I caught her eye. The other three women did not sit. They were tall and lithe with pale blue skin. They were practically identical save for their hair. The first had straight hair that fell to her navel. The second had short hair that had been styled into fierce spikes. The third's hair was curly and had been scooped up and pinned onto her head. They looked like they were in their late twenties but I was beginning to learn that nothing in Callipolis was what it seemed. Ezra walked over to us looking grumpy.

'I didn't know where you went,' he muttered. 'Luckily Sami spotted me or I would never have found you.'

'Sorry,' I apologised. 'We got a little distracted.'

'Ah, you're back,' Ryouko smiled at the three women. 'I sent Kyna, Sanvi and Abira to find Sami and scout for any sign of the Brethren. So, anything?'

'Nothing,' answered Kyna in a deep voice.

'We found the temple. It was entirely collapsed,' Sanvi continued.

'We searched through it. We found no one,' finished Abira.

'That can't be good,' Ryouko muttered.

'I took a twenty mile radius,' added Sami. 'They're nowhere to be found. If I had to guess I'd say they were making their way back to Culrain. Now that they know that magic has been released they won't waste any time in making a counter-attack.'

'You're quite right, of course, but we need a plan of action,' Ryouko said. 'They still don't know where we are but once they've collected themselves they'll be back to hunting us with more fervour than ever. They won't want to risk Mera going back to the king and telling him everything. If only we were more prepared. Sadly most of the information we have on the Brethren comes from when the Fellowship was still formed.'

'Perhaps I should go back,' Mera suggested. 'If I can talk to my father maybe I can make him understand. That was always our plan.'

'Your father thinks you dead, child,' replied Kyna. 'You've been gone too long. What makes you sure he hasn't given up the thought of you?'

'My father may be many things but he would never forget his only child,' Mera replied, scowling.

'Are you sure?' asked Sanvi. 'How well do you really know your father?'

'Are we sure we can trust her?' asked Abira. 'She has grown up under the influence of the very people who hunt us.'

'Excuse me-' began Mera venomously, but Sami cut her off.

'Mera can be trusted,' her voice was full of authority.

'How can you be so sure?' snapped Kyna.

'She could have another agenda,' agreed Sanvi.

'Though you may not have the same powers as me even your dull senses must be able to recognise that she has done everything she could to help us,' Sami drawled.

The three women glared at Sami, though she seemed completely unfazed by it.

'If you insist,' growled Abira.

'Ladies, if we could behave,' Iele's clear voice rang out. I could sense amusement behind her command.

'Excuse me,' Ilyssa turned slightly red as the whole room turned to look at her. I slipped my hand into hers and gave it a quick squeeze. 'I think I might have an idea.'

'Oh, of course, you were going to say. Do go on,' Ryouko nodded at her.

'Um, it's just that, I don't think I mentioned this last night, but Alaric and I used to work for a member of the Brethren,' she mumbled.

'Oh this just keeps getting better,' Kyna said dryly.

'Half of these children could be spies.' added Sanvi.

'How can we trust any of them?' asked Abira.

'You're just going to have to, aren't you,' Sami intoned. 'Because they're the only chance we have of ever being free again.'

'Quite,' Ryouko added. 'Ladies, Mera has been an advocate for Magic Folk for some years now. As we all know she brought Lex into her plan because she trusted him. As for Ilyssa and Alaric, well I'm hesitant to believe that the treatment they no doubt received by their master's hand left them with any amicable feeling towards the Brethren.'

'What about him?' Kyna asked, pointing at Ezra.

'I just brought the horse,' he said, holding up his hands in defence.

'Now Ilyssa, you were saying,' Ryouko prompted.

'Oh, yes,' she said, squirming slightly as everyone in the room turned to look at her. 'It's just that there was a chest in his room with lots of papers and things that I think were about the Brethren. It might tell us who the current members are. That would be something, wouldn't it?'

I remembered Ilyssa telling us about the chest. I mentally slapped myself for having forgotten.

'Well it's not much good sitting in his bedroom,' huffed Sanvi.

'No, but if we were to retrieve it…' Iele trailed off, sharing a look with Ryouko.

'That would be very risky,' he said.

'But it could be done,' she maintained.

'I suppose,' Ryouko muttered pensively.

'I'll go,' Ilyssa said, standing. 'I'll have to. I'm the only one who knows where it is.'

'Then I'm going too,' Alaric got up to join his sister.

'Me too,' I said.

Mera and Ezra both jumped up at the same time, neither willing to be left behind.

Ryouko regarded us inquisitively. Eventually he mused, 'I don't think it's a good idea for you all to go.'

We argued for a while but finally he was able to convince Mera, Ezra and I to stay behind on the promise that Kyna, Sanvi, Abira and Sami would go with them and keep them safe. For a moment it looked as though Sami would object to going with the sisters she appeared to dislike so much, but she changed her mind when Abira implied that she was too much of a coward to go in the first place.

A plan was soon devised to take Ilyssa and Alaric through the tunnels on Callipolis' fasted horses to Culrain and then get them into Deathgrove as quickly as possible. They were to send messages via Cerynitis and Goldenhorn when they got to Culrain and then again when they reached Deathgrove. The rest was up to them not to get caught.

Alaric knew the grounds the best and had spent a good hour drawing a detailed map that showed the path that would get them inside. It would then be Ilyssa's turn to take them through the house and into Listoros' room undetected. The whole thing made me feel sick.

Mera picked up on my worry quickly but she was busy with her own problems. Most of the initial shock of discovering an entire city of Magic Folk was alive and well living beneath her feet had worn off. She was now focused on a member of the Brethren being her father's personal advisor.

When Ilyssa and Alaric went to pack their bags I tried to broach the subject.

'There's no point thinking about that now,' she told me. 'It's something to worry about at another time.'

'If you're sure. But let me know if-'

'Not now,' she cut me off. 'I can't think about it now.'

I gave her arm a squeeze and dropped the subject. I was beginning to feel jittery. All we could was sit and wait and then sit and wait some more. What if something happened to them while they were gone? What if I never had the chance to tell Ilyssa how I felt about her? I had wasted time waiting for her to give me a sign that she felt the same. I should have just asked her. I felt like an idiot but maybe there was still time.

When Ilyssa and Alaric came back the others were already waiting for them. Sami was by the table loading arrows into a quiver while Kyna, Sanvi and Abira stood in a circle whispering to each other. Alaric went over to say goodbye to Ezra and I intercepted Ilyssa by the door. She turned to me as I approached and gave me a tight smile.

'How're you doing?' I asked.

'Good. I'm good, I think,' she answered in a voice slightly higher than usual.

'It's all right to be nervous,' I tried to be reassuring.

'What's to be nervous about?' Ilyssa muttered. 'I'm just going back to a place I spent the majority of my life loathing. It's not like this is going be dangerous, or terrifying, or-'

'Hey,' I interrupted her before she could start panicking. I took her hand and looked her directly in the eyes. 'You don't have to do this.'

'I do,' she insisted. 'No wait, I don't have to. I want to.'

I smiled. 'You are the bravest, most courageous person I know. More so than anyone I've ever met.'

'Oh,' she blushed, lowing her gaze.

'It's true,' I insisted, ducking low so that I was in her eye line as I spoke. 'And do you know why? Because you know what right thing to do and you always see it through. No matter what.'

'I wish that I wasn't so brave right now,' she whispered.

We were standing so close that her breath tickled my cheek as she spoke. I found myself staring at her lips. There was a feeling like that of a fist tightening in my chest. It made my breath grow short.

'Impossible,' I breathed.

Ilyssa gave me a weak smile and squeezed my hand. Our eyes met and I felt once again that pulsing thread connecting us, vibrating on a level that only the two of us could feel.

'All right,' called Kyna. 'Let's not waste any more time.'

Ilyssa held my gaze for a moment longer and then she leaned forward and kissed me on the cheek. I felt my heart jump in my chest.

'Thank you for making me feel better,' she smiled. 'I'll see you when I get back.' She let go of my hand and made her way over to the small crowd of people who had gathered around the table.

Mera caught my eye and winked. I felt myself blushing as I followed her over to the group.

'Yes, right, good,' blustered Ryouko as he got his thoughts in order. 'Let's just go over the plan one more time, shall we?'

'We know the plan, Ryouko,' Sanvi insisted. 'Get to the house, get the chest, get out.'

'It's time to go,' insisted Abira.

'For once I agree. The sooner we leave, the sooner we'll return,' Sami pointed out.

'Well, all right then. Good luck everyone. Panalin is waiting for you with the horses. And Bugul Noz will meet you at the southern tunnel. He'll show you the way,' Ryouko explained, more for his own benefit than the others.

He stood aside to let them pass.

'Bye everyone, see you when we get back,' said Alaric, hugging us all as we passed.

Just as she was leaving Sami paused and took me aside. 'She'll be safe, I promise. I know you want her to be safe.'

'Him too,' I muttered.

'Yes, him too,' she agreed. 'But most of all her.'

'Does that make a bad person?' I wondered.

'Probably,' and with a smile, the first I had ever seen her give, she walked out of the room.

29

The long wait

Ilyssa and Alaric had been gone for four days and we'd yet to receive any news. Not that I was expecting it. Even on Callipolis' fastest horses it would take at least another day for them to reach Culrain. The wait felt eternal. Waiting seemed to be the only thing we could at the moment. Wait for news, wait for something we could use against the Brethren, wait for the Sisterhood.

Magic was returning to the world. I could feel it with every fibre of my being. It drummed through me in time with my heartbeat. It hummed in my mind as I slept. I felt its power surging in the burns that had become faded pink scars across my body. As the bonds that had tied magic down for so long began to fall away it returned to its people in full force. Personally I was glad of the distraction. Magic took my mind off the worry.

One good thing that had happened was that Mera had forgiven Ezra. On the evening that Ilyssa and Alaric had left, Mera asked Ezra to go for a walk and they talked things through. They returned in high spirits. When I asked Mera what happened she just smiled and said, 'Things are right again.'

Mera had also started asking around to see if anyone was able to make sense of the book she had found in Skara Brae but nobody she asked could even identify the language. When I pointed out for the fifth time that the only people alive who could read text that old hadn't yet made an appearance she got angry.

'Well maybe if you spent less time doubting and more time helping me I might be able to get somewhere with it!' she had shouted, flinging the book down onto the table with a huff.

'What's the point?' I had yelled back. 'No one but a member of the Sisterhood will know what it says. Besides, we don't even know if it says anything useful.'

'Well we'll just have to wait until they show up, won't we,' she'd retorted.

'Oh wake up, Mera! They aren't coming!' I'd yelled.

'What on earth brings you to that conclusion?' she'd gasped.

'They were using us. They just wanted to be set free. If they really wanted to help they'd be here but all we've had from them is silence. Accept that we're on our own with this and we'll all be better off for it.'

'How can you say that? After everything! After the prophecy-'

'Forget the bloody prophecy! It was just another way to manipulate us. We've brought back magic and nobody's lost. I don't know about you but I for one am happy about that. Unless you wanted me dead in the end! I'm sure that would make things much easier for you!'

That was when Ezra had intervened. He'd taken Mera to the market to give us space to calm down. My anger had faded immediately and I regretted what I'd said. When they got back I was resolved to apologise.

I sat on my bed waiting for them to return. From inside the washroom I could hear the steady drip, drip, drip of a leaking tap. It was always quiet in this part of Callipolis. The leak was amplified in the silence.

Drip, drip, drip.

I thrust my hand towards the door and muttered, *'Sálnes.'*

The noise was silenced immediately. With relief I heard the door swing open and Mera and Ezra walked inside. I got up and went into the other room to join them.

285

'Hey,' I said, leaning against the doorframe and fiddling with my sleeve.

'Hey,' repeated Mera, looking anywhere but at me.

'Well I'm going to go for a walk,' announced Ezra, giving Mera a look that clearly said *talk to him* as he walked back out the front door.

Mera dropped a parcel on the table and slipped into one of the chairs. I took the one opposite her. We were quiet for a moment and then Mera mumbled, 'Sorry I yelled at you.'

'Sorry I said your book was useless,' I muttered. 'And that you wanted me dead.'

We looked up at each other and smiled. The tension between us disappeared.

'What did you get at the market?' I asked.

Mera reached forward and pulled open the parcel. 'I got more bread. And Ani managed to convince me to get some of that stuff he says is cheese but looks like meat. I hope it's all right. I also got some more hazelnut soup from Gwin. She mentioned that she needs some help cleaning out her attic so I said we would go over tomorrow. Oh and Bugaboo and Buggane gave me this to give to you. They said it was a thank you for all your help yesterday.'

She pulled out a small chisel and handed it to me. One thing I liked about Callipolis was the absence of money. Sometimes people bartered with supplies but as we barely had any possessions we used our skills instead.

Ezra had thought to help with manual labour but after running into Popis and striking up a conversation about fighting she had persuaded him teach defence to anyone who wanted to learn. Her parents weren't particularly pleased but there was no stopping her. Word had spread fast. On the first day it had just been a couple of people but yesterday afternoon had seen a rather large group gathered in the space outside our house, grasping an assortment of broken brooms, riding crops and wooden spoons.

Mera spent some of her time watching him teach but she had begun to spend time with Iele whom she was teaching to read and write. She had managed to find an ancient blackboard, which she had dragged into the Aula for their lessons. They had begun with recognising the alphabet and Iele could now recite the whole thing without any help. In return Iele had been bringing us daily supplies of poppy julep, which appeared to be the most sought after drink in Callipolis.

I had put my carpentry skills to good use. I had mainly been doing odd jobs but yesterday I had helped Bugaboo and Buggane with the furniture they made. They'd promised me the chisel in return.

I smiled, twirling it in my hands. It took me back to the workshop in Lilyworth, the smell of warm dust, the sound of sawing, the rows of the tools lined neatly along the shelves.

'No problem. Listen,' Mera paused for a moment. 'I think you're right about the Sisterhood, you know. I was thinking about everything they've done, how difficult they made things for us. No wonder Sami didn't want to join them.'

I was relieved to hear that she agreed with me but there was something daunting about accepting we were on our own.

'What do you think is going to happen now?' I asked. 'When Ilyssa and Alaric get back do you think they'll have something that will help us?'

'I hope so,' Mera trailed off, looking pensive. 'Do you ever regret coming with me?'

'Why do you ask that?' I wondered.

'So much had changed. I dreamed of this. I dreamed of finding a lost world, of having the chance to save it. But they seem to have made a life for themselves here. Do you think it was worth it?'

'Sometimes I wonder. I could have stayed with my family. We could have carried on as we were but it wouldn't have been right. We wouldn't have found out that the Brethren had infiltrated the castle. We wouldn't have been able to restore magic. And as much as the people here seem to have made a life that doesn't mean they're not still trapped. They deserve the chance to be free. I do think about what would have happened if we hadn't left but I don't for one second regret going.'

'Do you really miss your family?'

'I do. I miss my mum and Elvie and Rab. I even miss Samson.'

'I wish I knew what it was like to love and be loved by a family so unconditionally. Mine was never like that.'

'You do have a family that loves you unconditionally,' I insisted. 'I may not be related to you but I've always loved you. And I know that the others feel the same. Well, maybe not all of them love you like family.'

Mera smiled and shook her head. 'I think that ship has sailed.'

'Don't be so sure.'

At that moment the door banged open and Ezra walked in.

'Have you made up yet?' he asked bluntly.

'Yes, Ezra, we have,' smiled Mera.

'Good. I'd had enough of the awkwardness. We should do something fun to get our minds off all the stress,' he suggested.

'Did you have something specific in mind?' I asked.

'Well actually I was thinking you could show me some of that magic I hear so much about. I've only seen little bits and I was hoping I could see something a little more interesting,' he grinned.

'Was me lifting Mera out of a ravine not interesting enough for you?' I joked.

'Not really,' he teased, sitting in one of the empty chairs and staring at me with challenge in his eyes. 'Surprise me.'

We spent the rest of the day playing with magic. We fetched the spell book from my pack and found to our delight that we were able to pick up new spells with much fewer tries than when we first started. Mera sent most of Ezra's possessions bouncing off the walls. I enchanted a shirt and trousers to look like they were a real person. It stumbled around the room crashing into things and knocking crockery off the table. By the time evening rolled around the house was a mess. There were flowers sprouting from cracks in the floors and lightning flashed from clouds on the walls. I had somehow managed to change Ezra's hair from black to orange but I couldn't figure out how to change it back. Ezra had been forced to wrap a scarf around his head to stop Mera dissolving into giggles whenever she looked at him. I went to bed with my spirits far higher than they had been in quite some time.

We woke the next morning to find that Iele had brought us more poppy julep. She noticed the mess that we had left the room in but didn't comment. She put the container on the cabinet rather than the table, which was still hanging from the ceiling. I noticed that her feet were now completely engulfed by fire. I asked her how the feud between the nymphs and the sprites was going.

'They seem to have calmed down for now,' she sighed. 'I only hope it lasts. Panalin has threatened Ragana that if she doesn't stop stirring up trouble he's going to set the Drakaina and the Balaur on her. That'll stall her for a while, anyway.'

'Why does she like to cause so much trouble?' asked Mera.

'Oh I'm sure she thinks she's very amusing. It keeps her occupied. There's not really much you can do down here and when you've been trapped as long as we have you find ways to amuse yourself,' she explained.

'What do you do for fun?' I wondered.

'I dance,' Iele smiled.

'Really?' I asked.

'Is that so hard to believe?' she smiled.

'No, I just… I've never seen you dance before,' I shrugged.

'Well I don't do it in public very often,' she explained. 'Anyway, I have to help settle a dispute between the giants and Hu. Apparently Hu has been sneaking up to them while they're working in the fields and scaring them into dropping whatever they're holding. It's been the cause of quite a few bruised apples. Honestly, I don't see why people can't just behave. I'll see you later, Mera.'

'Yes, at the Aula. Don't be late,' Mera called as Iele walked towards the door.

'I won't. Goodbye,' she waved.

'What prompted Iele to want to learn how to read and write?' I asked as I poured out the julep.

'Well she says it's just because it's a useful skill but I have an inkling she's got a special friend that she wants to write to,' Mera responded, taking the cup I offered her.

'What makes you think that?' wondered Ezra.

'Well, I asked if she'd be sending messages to people and she said yes, but when I asked who she started blushing and wouldn't tell me,' Mera explained.

'I wonder who it is,' Ezra mused.

'I don't know. I thought it would be rude to ask,' Mera told us.

After finishing our drinks we put the room back to normal and I figured out how to return Ezra's hair back to its usual colour. Then we made our way over to Gwin's house to help her clean out her attic as Mera had promised. Gwin was a Broxa like Hu except she spent most of her time in her female form. She was a small, middle-aged woman with thick black hair and a pointed face. She welcomed us into her home, smiling widely.

'Thank you so much for helping,' she croaked. 'This would have taken me ages to do by myself. '

The morning was spent sorting through boxes and throwing out old furniture. There were plenty of strange things in the attic. We stopped to inspect a funny little music box that sneezed loudly whenever you touched it. There was a bucket and mop that sprung into life when you whistled to it and an innocent looking pen that squirted black ink all over Ezra when he picked it up. Even with all the interruptions we were finished by lunchtime. Gwin fed us more of her delicious soup before we headed off.

Ezra went to his fighting class, Mera headed to the Aula to meet up with Iele and I found my way to Bugaboo and Buggane's house. When I arrived they rushed out to greet me, always eager for company. They chatted happily about how they had helped the giants move the cattle in from pasture. They took great pride in their work. At the end of the afternoon I left with a beautiful, hand-carved spoon and a smile on my face.

By the time I got back to the house Ezra was just finishing his class. Mera was sitting on the steps watching him talk to the group of people gathered in front of him. I went to sit next to her.

'How were Buggane and Bugaboo?' she asked.

'They're good. They said to say hello. How was your reading lesson?'

'Also good. Iele's a fast learner, I'm very impressed.'

'Have you been here long?

'Long enough. He does like to talk.'

'Something you can relate to.'

Mera gasped, pretending to be offended. 'Well thanks very much.'

'Just teasing,' I nudged her gently.

Ezra dismissed his class and came over to us. 'Hello. How are we doing?' he asked, sitting down next to Mera and leaning back against the door.

'Good,' answered Mera. 'Is your class going well, then?'

'It is actually,' he smiled. 'Some of them are picking it up faster than others but I think everyone's enjoying themselves. Popis certainly is.'

I looked over to the girl who was now chatting with some friends. She held a small sword, which surprised me. I knew they had a forge here but I didn't think it made weapons.

'Where did she get the sword?' I asked.

'It was her grandfather's,' replied Ezra. 'Apparently he's the only one who supports her wish to fight.'

'Good for her,' said Mera. 'She should be allowed to learn to fight if she wants to.'

At that moment something went whizzing past us so fast that the wind it left in its wake pushed me backwards slightly.

'What was that?' I wondered.

'I don't know but it must have been going very fast,' marvelled Ezra.

'Wait, what if it was Cerynitis or Goldenhorn?' Mera asked, looking between us.

We all hopped up at once and sprinted towards the Aula. I felt slightly panicked. What if it was bad news? What if something bad had happened to our friends while we had been enjoying ourselves?

We arrived and dashed inside. I saw Goldenhorn standing next to Ryouko on the raised platform next to the table. I looked up at them expectantly.

'They have arrived at Deathgrove,' Goldenhorn announced in his deep, smooth voice. 'They are currently making their way into the house. Should they return, my mother will come to us with news of their success. We can do nothing now but wait.'

And wait we did. We sat in the Aula late into the night waiting for news. I started pacing but Mera dragged me into a chair, whispering, 'Sit down. You're making us all more nervous.'

My hand traced the spot where Ilyssa had kissed my cheek before she left. I began to worry that I would never see her again, that I would never be able to hold her hand, to tell her how I feel. I should have told her before she left. Alaric was right, it was stupid not to. I must have fallen asleep because the sound of hooves clip clopping on the stone floor jolted me into consciousness. I opened my eyes to see Cerynitis standing opposite her son. I stood, the panic rising.

She inclined her huge golden horns and said, 'They have retrieved the chest. They are now returning.'

30
The plan

With the knowledge that Ilyssa and Alaric were safe, time spent waiting for their return slipped through my fingers like sand. The day after Goldenhorn's report, Mera, Ezra and I found ourselves lounging on the edge of the crop fields watching the Nymphs water the wheat.

It was a spectacular sight. The Nymphs would spring through the air, sending sparkling showers of water in dazzling arches over the crops. The droplets caught in the bright lights from above and threw rainbows in every direction. The Nymphs sung a cheery ballad about the sun bringing life to the earth. Ryouko hummed along with them. I sat between him and Panalin, who had come along to oversee the Nymphs' work and ensure that they didn't get into any more mischief.

'The best part is that we don't have to rely on the seasons down here,' Panalin explained. 'We have crops growing all year 'round.'

'Did you dig this cave out when you got here or did it form naturally?' Mera asked from where she was leaning lazily against Ezra.

'Like most of the structures you see in Callipolis we have Bugul Noz to thank,' answered Ryouko.

I thought back to the shy creature that I had met hiding in the tunnels. 'Where does he live? I haven't seen him around.'

'Oh he doesn't live in the city,' Ryouko replied. 'He lives… well I'm not entirely sure where he lives, actually. Somewhere in the tunnels, I think. I have tried many times to persuade him to take a house here but he says that he's fine where he is. He's dreadfully shy. It's awful what happened to him.'

'What do you mean?' probed Ezra.

'Well he's the last of his kind, you see. Plenty of people living here have lost countless loved ones but poor Bugul Noz saw the last of his race die out a long time ago. Fairy Spirits thrived in these lands once but the Brethren tracked them all down. They had them locked away in cages that were strung up in high trees. Now Fairy Spirits can survive almost anything so long as there's earth around but up in those trees there was nothing to replenish their energy. Bugul Noz watched his friends and family waste away. He and one of his sisters managed to escape, I believe, but the Brethren caught up with them. His sister, Buttabee her name was, told Bugul to go on without her. She sacrificed herself so that he could live,' Ryouko shook his head.

'It's outrageous,' Panalin boomed, making all of us jump. 'Bugul Noz arrived here alone and terrified and do you know what people did? They ostracised him because they believed him to be dangerous. He may look beastly but you'll never meet a kinder, gentler creature. People should be ashamed of the way they treat him. I mean they're all perfectly happy to benefit from the fruits of his labours, aren't they? I asked him once why he hides himself away. He told me he didn't want to scare the children. It's disgusting,' he growled, banging his stick violently into the ground. The flowers in his beard turned a violent shade of red.

'I quite agree,' nodded Ryouko. 'It shames me to know that even those who understand what it's like to face oppression can discriminate in turn.'

Panalin opened his mouth to reply but before he could utter a sound the ground beneath us rippled.

'Oh no, it's the Sprites,' he moaned, standing in a hurry. 'Ryouko, fetch Iele. You three better clear off. This isn't going to be pretty.'

I looked over at the Nymphs. They had stopped their dancing. Mounds of earth were sprouting out of the ground like giants molehills. Mera, Ezra and I scurried away as fast as possible, the sound of Panalin yelling behind us.

We spent the next few days much as we had before, working and exploring the city in our free time. I noticed Mera and Ezra spending a lot of time together. I felt a fool for not having seen the connection between them before. They sat so close at meal times they were almost touching. His hand often found its way into hers. She would brush his hair behind his ear when it fell in front of his face. When they spoke it was as though they were the only two in the room. I felt the need to get out of their way when this happened. I didn't mind too much. It was one of these times that I found myself at Bugaboo and Buggane's house. I listened to them recount stories from their youth while we worked.

'We were born here fifty-six years ago on exactly the same day. We've been friends forever,' explained Bugaboo from her perch on Buggane's shoulder.

'Always friends,' Buggane added in his deep, slow voice.

I smiled up at the two of them. They certainly were an odd pair at first glance but you only had to spend a minute in their company to see the bond they shared.

'So you've never been outside of the city?' I asked as I sanded down the edge of the table leg I was working on.

'No, we haven't,' replied Bugaboo.

'Too dangerous,' nodded Buggane.

'But once we're allowed outside we're going to set up a carpentry shop, aren't we, Bug,' she patted the side of her friend's large face.

'Yes Boo,' he grinned.

'Maybe I'll join you,' I smiled at the thought.

'Do you do carpentry because of your father?' she asked.

I shrugged. 'Partly, but mainly because I enjoy it. Apart from magic it's the only thing I'm good at.'

'Play to your strengths,' Buggane agreed.

It was then that Gwin in her Broxa form fluttered in through the open window. She shifted before our eyes into a woman and squeaked, 'They're here! They've returned! My brother saw them arrive not five minutes ago.'

I leapt up. 'I've got to go.'

I muttered a hasty goodbye as I raced out the door. Swelling with happiness, I headed off as quickly as possible for the Aula. I was making my way through the winding streets when something dropped down in front of me, forcing me to halt so that I didn't trip over it. I recognised the small, bat-like creature smirking up at me.

'In a bit of a hurry, are we?' Hu squeaked.

'Err, yes actually,' I said, remembering what Ryouko had said about Broxa being cheeky and wondering what Hu wanted with me.

'No need to rush, my dear. Can't you spare a moment for little me?' Hu made a shrill noise that might have been a laugh.

'Sorry, but I have somewhere to be,' I said, walking past the tiny creature. To my surprise I felt a hand on my arm holding me back. I turned and saw a small man standing before me. His face was sallow and pinched, with a mop of dark, greasy hair that fell into his eyes. His clothes were too big for him. They hung off his skinny body making him look like a child who had found his father's jacket.

'I just want a little talk. Won't you stay for a moment?' he asked in the same high, scratchy voice.

'Sorry,' I repeated, reaching down to removed the bony hand from my arm. 'But I have to go.'

'I don't want much. Why won't you talk to me?'

'Look,' I sighed, impatience getting the better of me. 'Any other time I wouldn't mind but not right now.'

I turned again meaning to leave but Hu's next words caught me off guard.

'Off to see your girl?'

'What do you-' I began, turning back expecting to see a smug look upon his face but instead I saw a woman in his place. She looked much the same as the man who had previously been where she now stood. She had the same messy hair, the same thin face and small frame.

'Oh the things a girl can do to a man,' she rasped.

'I don't have time for this.'

Hu stepped towards me and reached out to caress my face. I shivered at her touch.

'Why do men always think themselves infallible?' she tilted her head and stared into my eyes.

'I don't think-' I started but she cut me off.

'Oh, I'm sure you don't. Who does? Who knows anything?'

'What does that have to do with-'

'Oh, nothing at all. But you know, don't you, that it will mean nothing in the end. Everything you think you know. That when all is said and done it will break you.'

'You aren't making any sense,' I muttered.

'What makes you think I mean to? Does she have your support?'

'Who?'

'The girl.'

'Are you trying to be confusing? Because it's working.'

She paused, studying my face. I felt her breath hot upon my cheek. I tried not to recoil.

'You have just a touch of fate to you. Not enough, though,' she whispered. 'I want nothing. Nothing that you can give. What are words, anyway? Go on then, boy. Run away.'

I took a tentative step backwards, then another. I spun around and walked hurriedly away, painfully aware of Hu's wide eyes on my back. I broke into a run and sooner than I expected I found myself entering the Aula. Before I could register what was happening I was engulfed in warm arms.

'It's good to see you too,' I pulled back from Ilyssa and Alaric to look at their smiling faces.

'We missed you,' Ilyssa grinned.

'We're all very glad you're back safe,' said Ryouko.

I looked around the room. Mera and Ezra were a little way off, smiling happily. Kyna, Sanvi and Abira stood together with Ryouko and Iele around the table on which was placed a carved chest. It was open and there were a number of papers scattered across the table. Sami sat in a chair as far away from the three sisters as possible looking irritated. She grimaced at me when I caught her eye.

'Well, now that we're all here, shall we...' Ryouko gestured at the chest.

'What have you found?' I asked as we gathered around the table. One of my arms was slung over Alaric's shoulder, the other around Ilyssa's waist.

'Names, mostly,' replied Kyna.

'There's a list of the members of the Brethren,' said Sanvi.

'The number of them that have infiltrated the Castle is extremely troubling,' added Abira.

'Indeed,' agreed Ryouko. 'But what's most troubling is this.'

He nodded towards a scroll that lay in the centre of the table. On the parchment was the image of a woman. Her eyes were deep blue and piercing. She had a long face with arching brows and plump lips. Her face was painted into an expression of intense disapproval. Her silvery hair was twisted into a golden crown. I recognised Mera's mother immediately. The queen's beautiful face stared out at me from under the word *preservation.*'

'What is this?' I asked, letting of Ilyssa and Alaric to pick up the parchment.

'We're not entirely sure,' answered Ryouko. 'There's nothing else here that explains it but I believe that the Brethren are moving in on the royal family of Culrain. With the princess missing and the king being fed lies by Malaigle the queen must be the last weak link in their plans to eradicate magic forever from within the castle. If there is one person a king should listen to above all else it's his queen. We must ensure that their plan, whatever it may be, does not come to pass.'

'But we don't even know what their plan is,' Ilyssa pointed out.

'Which is why we should make our way there immediately,' came Mera's voice from across the room.

I turned to where she was standing. Her face was pale and set. The bond between Mera and the queen had been strained for as long as I could remember but I could see that she was afraid for her mother now.

'You want to go back to Culrain?' I asked.

Mera fixed her eyes on me. 'We knew we'd be going back eventually. This seems like a good enough reason.'

'What do you plan on telling your parents you've been doing all this time?' asked Iele.

'The truth,' Mera intoned. 'I think it's time they finally heard it.'

'But what about the prophecy?' Kyna asked.

'We thought you were meant to help us leave this underground prison,' Sanvi reminded us.

'Do you plan on abandoning us after we risked our lives to help you retrieve this information?' Abira probed.

'Perhaps if you were willing to open your eyes just a fraction you would be able to see that this is clearly the path that you have been seeking,' cut in Sami.

'We see no such thing,' snipped Kyna.

'We see another reckless mission,' sniffed Sanvi.

'The Sisterhood would not be this vague in their instructions,' added Abira.

'Your density never fails to astound me,' replied Sami. 'You forget that of everyone here I am the only one who had known the Sisterhood and I can assure you that they enjoy nothing more than being aggravatingly vague.'

'I have to agree with Sami,' Iele said. 'The Sisterhood doesn't give orders. I think Mera's right. She and the others must return to Culrain and we must go with them.'

'You're going to come with us?' Mera asked, surprised.

Iele nodded. 'It is my opinion that we have squandered enough time hiding under the feet of our enemies. This is our fight. We must stop leaving it to others. As much as I am thankful for everything that the Fellowship did for us during the war they were more allies than anything. We were always strongest when we stood together. We are fragmented now. We have spread ourselves too thin. We must be united again.'

'You make a valid point,' conceded Kyna.

'Though it is still a ludicrous thought,' added Sanvi.

'We cannot merely traipse into the Castle and demand an audience with the king. We'd be executed the moment we set food inside Drammear,' pointed out Abira.

'No, but with their daughter returned to them the king and queen may be in a lenient mood,' Iele said. 'Enough to listen to what she has to say. Enough, perhaps, to agree to meet one or two of us. Their current hatred is unfounded. It was not born to them, but taught. Once they have been given the opportunity to form their own opinions they will come to see how wrong they have been.'

'That would be quite an undertaking,' Kyna spoke slowly, as though her mind was running through every possibility.

'And one that would require a great amount of persuasion,' Sanvi's eyes flicked to Mera. 'Would you be prepared for that?'

'I would,' Mera nodded stiffly, her lips forming a thin line.

'It will take more than just your word. Your father has been taught from birth that our kind is evil and untrustworthy. It is a deep-seated hatred spanning generations,' warned Abira.

'So was I and yet here I am. My father is not a cruel man. He may have been taught to hate but he was born kind. The right words will catch his attention and he will see reason,' Mera promised.

'He'll have proof, too,' I cut in, glancing between the three sisters, slightly intimidated by the intensity of their gaze. 'We'll give him proof.'

'I'm sure the word of a nobleman's son will be of some help,' added Ezra.

'And if anyone needs a homeless orphan I'm more than willing to offer my services,' said Alaric.

'Make that two,' nodded Ilyssa.

Mera smiled at us. She had slipped her hand into Ezra's and was squeezing it tightly.

'What do you think, Ryouko?' asked Iele.

'Well,' he said, looking around the table. 'It appears that we're all in agreement. I think it is clear that this is the route we must take even if you do not believe it is the one that the Sisterhood wishes for us to travel. We must, as they say, forge our own path. And now I believe we have come to my favourite part of any plan. The details.'

The next few hours were spent arguing over exactly how we were going to infiltrate the castle. Kyna wanted to have only a small number of Magic Folk coming with us. Sami thought that since this was in the interest of all the beings in Callipolis that anyone who wished to join us should be allowed. Sanvi was worried about the number of people who may be lost should something go wrong, so Abira suggested that anybody who went should have some training in battle. After Ezra pointed out that we didn't have enough time to train an army, Ryouko decided that in the interested of fairness all those who were healthy enough should be permitted to go.

It was decided that once the company had reached Culrain they would set up camp in the Great Forest as close to the castle as possible. Mera dug out her old map and plotted the position on it. The camp would remain safely inside the forest where non-magic folk hardly ever dared to venture. Then Mera, Ilyssa, Alaric, Ezra and I would make our way into the city and using a hidden entrance Mera had found as a child, we would steal into the castle. If we had our timing right we would be able to find the king alone in his chambers.

The most difficult part would be getting out if it went wrong. For a while Mera tried to persuade us to let her go alone but after we made it clear that most definitely wouldn't be happening, she conceded. Instead the escape would fall to me. I would be in charge of putting any guards that we came across safely and silently to sleep. Sami showed me how to seal a room so that no one would be able to hear what was going on inside. That way, should the king not react the way we hoped he wouldn't be able to sound the alarm until we were on our way out. We would be able to exit the same way we entered, through the secret passages that lead through the walls of the castle. All we would be able to do then is pray to the stars that all went well.

Ryouko promised that he would put out the word in the morning, but for now the day had grown late and we should head home. We left the Aula too anxious about the plan and too excited to be back in each other's company to feel tired. Ilyssa and Alaric had returned safe and sound. The only thing I could focus on was Alaric's buoyant smile and Ilyssa's warm hand tucked in mine.

31

The last night

As soon as we returned home we pounced on Ilyssa and Alaric, eager to hear everything about their journey to Deathgrove. We sat around the table, all except for Alaric, who splayed out on the reclining chair having, as he told us, missed the luxury.

'Most of it was pretty uneventful, really,' Ilyssa explained through a mouthful of bread. 'We didn't stop off at any of the camps in the other kingdoms apart from the one in Culrain. Ryouko was right, there were only about twenty of them living there. There was this old family of Goblins who I'm pretty sure they were only there because they were too stubborn to move anywhere else. The rest were sorcerers who were better able to fit in with non-magic folk. We stayed there for one night and then we continued on to Deathgrove. It wasn't far from there. It only took us a few hours. We set out after darkness fell and got in through the servants entrance. Sami did something funny with her hands and the lock just melted away.'

'It was great,' Alaric mumbled, stuffing his face with sugar drops.

'It was,' Ilyssa agreed. 'Anyway we managed to sneak up to Listoros' room without being seen but then it got a bit tricky. We had to get in, find the chest and remove it, all with him asleep in his bed. Kyna, Sanvi and Abira went in first while Sami, Alaric and I guarded the door. I don't know what they did in there but eventually Sanvi told us it was safe to come in. Sami stayed outside while Alaric and I went to fetch the chest. Listoros didn't move a muscle the whole time.'

'I've got to say,' came Alaric's muffled voice from behind a mouth full of sweets. 'Being in that room wasn't half tense, was it?'

'Being anywhere near that house was awful,' admitted Ilyssa. 'I won't be going back there in a hurry.'

'You won't need to,' I assured her.

'He's right,' nodded Mera. 'We have all the information we need.'

I thought for a moment about our freshly laid plan. 'Do you think many people will want to come with us?'

'I expect not,' answered Mera. 'I think they've gotten too used to the idea of the safety Callipolis provides. Going with us would expose them. Not that I blame them. They just want to live in peace.'

'I'm not so sure,' Ezra intoned. 'I have an inkling that more of them will want to fight than you think. Look at Popis. That girl is full of fire. I'm certain she'll come.'

'If her parents let her,' Mera muttered.

'I doubt that would stop her,' Ezra smiled. 'She's almost as stubborn as you are.'

'An impressive feat, I'm sure,' Mera replied dryly. 'Well, perhaps that's for the better. The people who come won't be fighting anybody. They'll just be sitting and waiting. If we manage to get back to them it will mean peace, not war.'

'That's the hope,' Ezra mumbled.

Ilyssa yawned suddenly. 'I think I'll go to bed,' she announced. 'It's been a long day.'

'Oh Ilyssa, it's barely evening,' Alaric complained, sliding into the chair next to her. 'Don't go to bed yet. Why don't we talk about the beautiful awkwardness that was Sami and the sisters?'

Ilyssa stood up. 'Yes that was a little awkward. And yet somehow I find that I'm able to go on without discussing it. Goodnight all,' she waved, acknowledging our chorus of 'Night!' before slipping into the bedroom.

'Was it really that awkward?' I asked.

'Oh, it really was. It was the tension when they weren't hurling insults at each other that was the worst of it. They stopped speaking to each other completely after a while. It got to the point where Ilyssa and I were taking messages back and forth like carrier pigeons. Ilyssa got annoyed after a while. She told them that if they weren't able to talk to each other respectfully then they clearly weren't responsible enough to come with us. I think she was really on the verge of sending them all back. Luckily they decided that the mission was more important. Anyway, as great as it has been seeing you all again, I'm in need of a walk. I tell you, sitting down all day really takes it out of you.'

'I'll go with you,' I offered.

Alaric, who had missed out on exploring the city, was excited to see all the sites. I took him to the night market where he enjoyed sampling food, getting on particularly well with the boy who manned a stall of caramelised walnuts. He insisted we walk back past the stall at least three times before we moved on.

There was exactly one tavern in Callipolis and Alaric found it within the hour. I'd been showing him the lake carven, which served as Callipolis' water supply. It was a large cave filled with water and a thin pathway that circled its edge. Green, glowing vines climbed the walls, tangled up in one another and crisscrossing along the ceiling with shining yellow and purple flowers sprouting from their tips. The light from the plants was reflected in the water below. It was a quiet place with the only noise being the small gurgle of water as it entered the cave from an underground river and the occasional giggle of a Water Nymph who came to the surface to watch you. We had just walked out of the cave when Alaric perked up at the sound of singing.

'What's that?' he asked.

'It's probably people in the tavern,' I said, knowing exactly where this conversation was going to go.

'Do you think we could-'

'Go on, then. I'm getting tired anyway. You go and have your fun,' I said, smiling at how Alaric almost bounced with joy at my answer.

'Thanks Lex, you're a great friend. I see what my sister sees in you,' he called as he ran off towards the bright lights of the tavern.

I walked slowly back to the house, wondering all the way what exactly Ilyssa had told him she saw in me.

By the time I got back the candles had burned low. Over on the reclining chair Mera and Ezra were lying next to one another, their hands entwined, their eyes closed, breathing softly. I smiled before blowing out the last candle.

'I didn't want to wake them. They looked so peaceful,' Ilyssa's voice floated towards me in the darkness.

From the light streaming in through the window I saw that she was holding a blanket. I watched as she walked over to Mera and Ezra and draped it across them.

'Where's Alaric?' she asked in a low voice so as not to wake our sleeping friends.

'He found the tavern.'

'Of course he did.'

Ilyssa walked over to where I was standing and made as if to sit down in one of the chairs but then changed her mind. I caught the familiar scent of honeysuckle that I always smelled when she was close. I found that my breathing was becoming rather difficult.

'I thought you went to bed,' I muttered.

'I did. I was coming to get some water,' she replied, her deep brown eyes almost black in the darkness of the room.

'Oh. Right.'

'I'm glad to be back here. With you,' she whispered, gazing into my eyes.

'I'm gad you're back. I was worried about you.'

I felt her hand ever so gently graze across my arm. It was as though an explosion had gone off inside me. Electricity crackled through me from where her fingers had brushed my skin. Some force was pulling me towards her and I was unable, or simply unwilling, to resist.

'Yes, Sami said-' she began, but then trailed off. Her warm breath caressed my neck.

'What did Sami say?'

'It doesn't matter.'

And then she was kissing me. And I was kissing her back. My arms reached around her and pulled her to me. Her lips were soft and warm. The feel of her lit a fire within me. For a moment she was all I could sense in the world, the caress of her silk-soft skin, the sound of her laboured breathing, the taste of honey rich on her tongue.

A sudden crash had us flying apart. I looked down and saw that we had bumped into the table and knocked a glass jar onto the floor. I cursed under my breath and reached down to pick up the broken shards.

'What's going on?' Ezra's voice sounded bleary and thick with sleep.

I looked over to see Mera and Ezra stirring, completely oblivious to what had just happened.

'Err, nothing,' I panted, my voice slightly higher than usual. 'Broke a jar.'

'Don't worry, we'll clean it up,' Ilyssa breathed.

'Is everyone all right? Nobody stepped on any, did they?' Mera asked.

'No, no, it's fine,' I babbled. 'We'll just get it off the floor. You stay there.'

I wished they would go to bed so I could talk to Ilyssa alone.

'Well we're up now. We should probably go to bed, anyway,' Mera reasoned, pushing herself off the chair and walking over to us. 'Lex, why don't you just fix it?'

'Oh yeah,' I replied, slightly flustered. I put the pieces of glass down on the table and muttered, *Remian.*

The broken shards jumped back together to reform the glass jar. Luckily it had been empty so there was no spill to clean up.

'There. No harm done,' Mera smiled.

Ezra stood behind her, their hands still joined, looking around the room. 'Where's Alaric?'

'Tavern,' I answered.

'Of course,' he smiled. 'I reckon we should get to bed. That chair isn't as comfortable as it looks,' he let go of Mera's hand, kissed the top of her head and walked towards the bedroom.

'Well, goodnight. Again,' Ilyssa muttered, staring at the ground and following after Ezra.

'Night,' Mera called after them. She turned back to me with a look of concern. 'Are you all right, Lex? You look flustered.'

'What? Oh no, I'm fine. Just... loud crash, you know.'

Mera nodded slowly.

'Are you all right?' I asked.

Mera smiled a wide, genuine smile before answering. 'Yes, I'm definitely all right.'

'Are you happy?' I asked.

'I'm very happy,' she grinned.

'Good,' I nodded.

'Come on, it's getting late. Let's not just stand here in the dark,' Mera tutted before turning on her heel and walking into the bedroom with me trailing behind.

Ilyssa had already slipped into bed so I had no chance to talk to her that night. Maybe it was best to wait until morning. I went to bed still feeling her lips on mine. But the next day I couldn't talk to her either. She was gone by the time I awoke and when I saw her later I couldn't get her alone. She wouldn't look me in the eye. With a pang I wondered if she regretted our kiss. The thought made my chest ache. Every time I looked at her I thought about the way her lips had felt on mine. I remembered the fire in my fingertips burning as my hands traced her skin. I remembered her breathless, flushed, and I wanted nothing more than to do it again.

I wanted to talk to Mera about it but there was no time. Ryouko had begun to tell people about our plan and a lot of people seemed interested. There was preparation to do. Iele had roped me into helping gather supplies. She, Sami and I were sat in the Aula going through what we had and making a list of the things we still needed. My mind wasn't with them. I couldn't stop thinking about Ilyssa. It was as though a something in my brain had clicked into place. I could only hope that she felt the same but the way she had been has acting I wasn't sure. If I could just see her...

'That should be enough water,' Iele was saying. 'Though if the numbers keep growing we'll need another barrel.'

'People are very eager to go,' Sami commented.

'I'm not sure why,' I muttered. 'They won't get to do anything but wait.'

'But it's a chance to leave Callipolis, isn't it,' Iele reminded. 'Most of us have never done that before.'

'You're right, I forgot,' I replied, feeling sheepish. 'Well we won't starve. Now that the giants have decided to come they've brought enough food to feed a small army.'

'Yes I think I've got that written down. Could you check I've got right?' Iele passed the list to Sami who took it from her and began to scrutinise it.

'How are your reading and writing lessons going?' I asked.

'Things have been better,' Iele admitted. 'I'm just not improving.'

'You're too hard on yourself,' Sami insisted. 'The letter you sent me was very impressive for someone who has only been learning for as long as you.'

'Well Mera helped me with that,' she admitted.

I smiled, remembering Mera's belief that Iele was learning to write for someone she was harbouring affection for. 'She's right. Just keep practicing and you'll get it eventually,' I promised.

The fire around Iele's feet crackled. 'Thank you, Lex. I think we've done all we can for now. We'll have our final numbers later this evening but I can't imagine it'll be that much more. Why don't you go home.'

'All right,' I jumped up, eager to find Ilyssa. 'I'll see you tomorrow then.'

When I got back to the house everyone was there. They were sitting around the table waiting for me.

'Lex, good, you're here,' Ezra called as I came through the door. 'We're having a last hurrah.'

He indicated the food that had been laid out on the table. There was an assortment of things, bread and soup, cheeses and meats and pastry. There was a bowl of fruit too and a jug of poppy julep.

'We thought we'd have a sort of picnic as it's our last night here,' Mera explained, handing me a plate and showing me to a seat between her and Alaric. 'Just help yourself.'

It was quite the feast. I loaded my plate with all of my favourite things and dug in. I tried to catch Ilyssa's eye while we ate but she was looking anywhere but at me. My heart sank. Could she really have changed her mind that quickly? How could she go from kissing me one minute to ignoring me the next? I tried not to let it show how much it affected me but it felt as though someone had punched me in the stomach. I lost my appetite and feigning tiredness I went to bed early. I heard the others talking happily for a little while longer until sleep pulled me under.

The next day we rose early. We packed up our things and headed to the southern tunnel. There was to be a group of about fifty of us travelling to Culrain included Ryouko, Iele, Sami and the three sisters. Cerynitis and Goldenhorn had also agreed to accompany us but would only stay for as long as it took us to reach the castle. After that they would return to Callipolis.

Due to our large number we were unable to ride the winged horses that had taken Ilyssa and Alaric back to Culrain in such short a time. Instead they were to pull our supplies and us along in huge carts.

'I think that's everything,' Ryouko said as Sami lifted the last of the crates into a cart. 'And everyone seems ready to go.'

'No point in delaying then,' Sami agreed. 'Let's get going.'

She and Ryouko went to join Iele while Mera, Ilyssa, Alaric, Ezra and I hopped into a cart of our own. Way ahead at the front of the company I could see the hulking form of Bugul Noz. He was to lead us through the tunnels. At Ryouko's signal he took off and the winged horses followed suit. We were on our way back to Culrain.

That night when we stopped for dinner Bugaboo and Buggane joined us after the giants shook them off.

'They're friendly enough, the giants,' Bugaboo explained. 'But you have to be careful not to upset them. Jidovi's the worst of them but the others aren't so bad.'

'He's angry just 'cause,' Buggane told us.

'Novaci and Chelua let us go to their wedding,' grinned Bugaboo. 'Chelua likes the water so they had the ceremony by the lake. Novaci did look funny with all the lights bouncing off her shiny head, but she didn't mind because Chelua said she looked beautiful.'

'That's lovely,' smiled Ilyssa.

'It was,' she replied. 'And then Emim and Urias, who're so old they can't even remember how long they've been married, sang a song for them, which sounded so sweet with their nice voices. They almost sang me to sleep.'

'They did, Boo,' added Buggane. 'You snored.'

'Oh yes, Yuli had to stop his speech to wake me up,' Bugaboo remembered, ignoring our stifled titters. 'It was a nice day.'

The next day when we stopped for lunch we were interrupted by the sound of raised voices close by. I, along with Ilyssa and Alaric who had just finished eating, stood and went to investigate.

We headed towards one of the huge carts from behind which the voices came. As we rounded the cart I was surprised to see Popis having a heated conversation with Iele.

'Popis,' Iele sighed. 'What are we supposed to tell your parents?'

'Don't tell them anything,' Popis replied, folding her arms angrily across her chest. 'They don't need to know. It's not any of their business.'

'I think they'll have noticed when they woke up and you weren't there,' Iele responded, her mouth set in an uncharacteristically hard line.

'What's going on?' Ilyssa asked.

They both turned towards us.

'Popis here has decided to join us. Without her parents permission,' Iele explained.

'I don't need their permission. I don't belong to them,' Popis huffed, the red beads in her long, pale hair clinking together as she jutted out her chin.

'But they do deserve to know where you've gone' insisted Iele. 'And certainly when you've left to go somewhere that could be very dangerous.'

'Oh please, there's nothing dangerous about it. We're barely going to stick our noses out of the ground,' the determined look in her eye faded slightly. 'Look I just want to see the sun. Just once.'

Iele's face softened and she sighed, raising a hand to pinch the bridge of her nose.

'It's too late to send her back now,' reasoned Ilyssa.

'Guess she'll just have to stay,' added Alaric.

Popis grinned and turned back to Iele, who sighed again.

'I suppose you're right,' she conceded. 'I better go and tell Ryouko we've got a stowaway. Popis will you,' she paused, searching for the right words, 'stay here and behave?'

'We'll look after her,' I offered.

Iele gave us a small smile before walking off.

'I don't need looking after,' Popis insisted as we walked back to where Mera and Ezra sat.

'I know,' I smiled. 'But I though I'd say it for Iele's sake. She's likely to worry otherwise.'

'All right. Just so you know,' Popis nodded.

If the others were surprised by Popis' presence they hid it well. They welcomed her openly and offered her some of the remaining food. Ezra patted the ground next to him and she settled herself down to munch on the spiced meats.

Popis was livelier than I'd ever seen her. She spoke animatedly about what she was going to do once Magic Folk were safe to go out in the open once more. She listened intently to our description of the world above. I found it strange to be talking to someone who had never seen the sky and stranger still when she became excited about the prospect of rain. Ezra warned her that she would probably learn to hate it but she just grinned and said, 'If you had been dreaming of something like this all your life you wouldn't let the threat of getting a bit of damp put you off.'

It took us a few more days to reach the camp in Culrain. It was as small as Ilyssa had described. I couldn't shake a feeling of unease. It certainly wasn't the sort of place I would choose to live. It seemed that others in our party also felt this way. We stayed just long enough to eat dinner before we moved on again.

I had only seen Bugul Noz once or twice since the beginning of our journey. He lingered just long enough to tell us where to go, then dashed off again into a side tunnel. Now though, he appeared to be staying as close as he dared. I often spied him out of the corner of my eye peering around a corner or burrowing with surprising speed and dexterity with his shovel-like hands into the side of the tunnel. When I asked Ryouko about it he told me that Bugul Noz was getting anxious about how close they were to the castle.

'I'm sure he feels more secure being closer to the group,' he said. 'There is safety in numbers, after all.'

Ryouko was certainly right about that. For now we were safe underground with a small army of Magic Folk but very soon we would be going into the castle with barely more than our wits to protect us. The thought of it made my stomach turn.

Mera didn't appear to be faring much better. She often sat, pale-faced, surrounded by parchment, going over the plan again and again. Only Ezra was able to pry her away.

Ezra himself was remaining remarkably calm. Occasionally I could see worry in his face, as well as the faces of Ilyssa and Alaric, both of whom had masks of confidence so cracked I wondered how they didn't shatter. There was nothing I could say to any of them that would help. I tried suggesting that they stay behind when we got to the forest but they wouldn't hear of it.

We didn't have long to worry though. We soon arrived in a hollowed out cave at the edge of the Great Forest and settled down to wait until dusk arrived. Our hiding place was some hundred yards from the walls of Drammear. There was a short walk through a narrow path that led to the surface, the entrance of which was hidden at the bottom of a great oak, and then a stretch of grass we would need to cross to reach the city.

Popis kicked up a fuss when her offer of a scouting mission was shot down.

'Now listen here, Popis, you promised you would behave,' Ryouko reminded her.

'I am behaving,' she huffed. 'I was just suggesting-'

'We all know what you were suggesting, child,' Kyna interrupted. 'And we all know it would be a terrible idea that we would be remiss to consider.'

'As you have been told before you are not sufficiently well prepared to face that danger. And you stand out too much,' Sanvi added.

'Quite right,' Abira nodded. 'You would lose us our position and then where would we be? This place isn't well defended.'

'That isn't true,' Popis scowled. 'I'd draw no more attention to us than Cerynitis and Goldenhorn would and they're going right out to see when that lot get the castle.'

317

'That was a little harsh, I think,' Iele stated.

Kyna's nostrils flared. 'Just because you wish to find fault with everything we say doesn't mean you should needlessly-'

'Popis,' Sami called from where she sat with her bow slung over her crossed legs. 'You are eager to be free, I understand, but you must remain here while there is still danger. Then you shall have your freedom.'

Sami's words put an end to the argument. The three sisters turned away to talk to Ryouko while Popis stomped unhappily over to us, plopping herself down with a resounding sigh. Iele went over to Sami. She pulled out a knife and began cleaning it aggressively with an old piece of cloth. Sami looked up, watching her silently for a moment before reaching out and putting her hand on Iele's arm. Iele ceased her violent movements and closed her eyes for a moment before turning to look at Sami with a look of great softness. I turned away quickly as a pang of jealously sprung through my chest.

Time sped up just as I wished there were more of it. Before long the sun had set and it was time to leave. We made our way around the friends we had made in the short time we had been in Callipolis. Ryouko wished us the best of luck and success in our endeavour. Kyna, Sanvi and Abira blessed us with a fruitful trip and a speedy return. Bugaboo and Buggane hugged us all multiple times and told us that they would be up the whole night so that they would be the first to see us come back. Sami and Iele stood together, a complementary pair. They wished us well, hoping only that we would return safely. Others simply nodded to us, a silent sign of solidarity.

Popis stood by the exit waiting for us to depart.

'I wish I could go with you,' she grumbled.

'Don't worry,' Ezra replied, his smile unusually tight. 'You'll be the first to see the sun rise.'

Popis beamed at him and as we walked along the tunnel she raised her arm, sending us off with a salute.

We hurried along the passageway, eager to catch up with Cerynitis and Goldenhorn who awaited us by the oak tree. We emerged in darkness at the edge of the forest. From here you could see every tinkling light in the city. It was so vast, even from afar, with all its twisting roads and hidden alcoves and trundling, runaway carts.

We paused here to catch our breath. Mera and Ezra had moved forward, hand in hand, towards the castle with set faces, bracing themselves for what was about to come. Alaric moved off to talk to Cerynitis and Goldenhorn leaving Ilyssa and me alone. We stood slightly awkwardly without speaking. She fiddled with the scabbard of her sword, which she'd strapped to her waist. I knew now was the best chance I'd have to say something. With my heart pounding I turned to face her.

'Ilyssa, there's something I have to say.'

'Lex I-'

'Please, let me say it. I know it may not be what you want to hear but I have to say it. The other night when you kissed me… it was the happiest I've ever been. I know you might regret it but I don't for one second because you're kind and you're beautiful and you're all I've ever wanted. I'll never say it again if you don't want me to but you're perfect to me and I'm so glad for the time we've had. And I'm telling you this now because there's a very good chance that we'll be thrown into a dungeon and condemned to death before the sun rises but it doesn't mean any less because of that. I love you. I think I've loved you since the moment I first saw you wield that sword. I've loved you completely and unabashedly and with everything that I am and ever will be. I know I don't have a lot to offer, but I'm offering everything I have.'

Ilyssa stood before me open mouthed, the moonlight washing over her face. Her eyes were wide and she seemed lost for words. After a second that felt like an eternity she spoke.

'I don't regret it.'

'What?'

'I don't regret it, Lex. I just… I didn't know how you felt and I was scared and when you didn't say anything I thought you hadn't wanted it.'

'Of course I did. Of course I wanted it.'

I pulled her into my arms and held her as tightly as I dared. I felt as though my heart had swollen to three times its usual size.

'We were fools not to say something sooner,' she said into my shoulder. 'Look at all the time we've wasted.'

'Let's not waste any more. If we get out of this-'

She pulled back and looked me straight in the eye. 'When. When we get out of this. Let's not worry about that now. Let's just focus on getting through today. And just so you know, I love you too.'

I took her hand in mine and squeezed it. No one could be as happy as I was in that moment. Before either of us could say anything else Ezra called to us, 'Come along you two, that can wait.'

We moved over to where the others stood, our hands still entwined. The five of us stood in a circle facing one another. Mera was the first to speak.

'This is it then. Last chance to turn back.'

'No way,' replied Alaric.

Mera nodded sharply. 'Good. Then stick to the plan and we'll be fine. Let's go.'

We set off, leaving the safety of the forest behind, unaware of the eyes that followed us in the dark.

32

The secret passageway

The journey through Drammear's shadowy streets passed in a haze of numb fingers, turned up hoods and hushed whispers. Soon enough we arrived outside the entrance to the castle's gardens. We huddled together. No one dared to speak lest the guards patrolling the grounds hear us, and everything was ended before it even began. We crouched low, waiting for Mera's signal to tell us that the coast was clear. On her command we scurried through the black, iron gate and up the wide path lined with bushes towards a large fountain, which gurgled quietly in the dark. Behind the fountain I saw the rise of the castle. A hundred glass windows reflected the pale light of the moon.

We squatted behind the fountain as Mera fiddled with a large stone at its base. Eventually it came loose and she slid it out of the way to reveal a low, narrow passageway. Without a word we slipped inside. Alaric, the last in, brought the stone back over to cover the hole. As he slipped the stone back into place we were plunged into darkness.

'Is everyone all right?' Mera asked, her voice echoing loudly in the dark tunnel. There was a general murmur of assent and she continued, 'We just need to follow this path. It'll take us to the dungeons and then we can get some light.'

We followed her, a silent procession marching onwards. We were stooped low to avoid scraping our heads on the roof of the tunnel. The air inside was musty, the walls coated in something slimy. I wondered how long it had been since something living had passed through here. Nothing human, at any rate. As if to confirm my thought I felt something brush over my foot. Startled, I yelled and leapt back, landing directly on Ezra's toes.

'Ouch!' he yelped. 'Watch it, Lex.'

'Sorry, sorry,' I panted, trying to calm my franticly beating heart. 'Something ran over my foot. There aren't rats down here, are there Mera?'

Rather than answering me directly she said, 'Let's keep going.'

We walked on for a while longer and eventually the tunnel became wider and high enough to stand in. Then Mera stopped so abruptly I nearly walked into her.

'Are we here?' Alaric called.

'Wait,' Mera muttered in reply.

I could hear her hands on the wall, fumbling with the stones to our right. After a minute of frenzied patting and scrambling she let out a frustrated huff and cursed loudly.

'What's wrong?' Ilyssa asked from somewhere behind me.

'There's supposed to be a gap that you can reach through and open a latch from the other side, but it's been blocked off. Well, I suppose it's a comfort to know that the Royal Guard is actually earning their wage. We're going to have to go up another way,' she explained.

'Is there another way?' asked Ezra. 'I don't think we're going to be able to get into the castle from the grounds. Not without being seen.'

'No, I don't mean going back outside. From here this tunnel goes up into the castle walls. It's just that I've never done it without a light before and it can get a little complicated if you don't know where you're going.'

'Can't we get some light?' Alaric suggested. 'Lex, can't you conjure up some fire?'

'And set light to what? We didn't bring any torches,' I pointed out.

Mera cursed under her breath again. 'Well we'll just have to go up this way. We've no other choice. Come on, don't get left behind. Careful now, there are stairs just up ahead.'

We followed Mera up the tunnel into the bowels of the castle. All we could hear as we climbed were our own halting steps. Whoever had made these tunnels had done a good job. The walls on either side were so thick that no sound could penetrate them. An eerie, tingling sensation was prickling its way along my spine. I began to feel as though my chest were tightening, my breaths lagging. Every sound inside the tunnel was magnified. There wasn't one speck of light to guide us.

Every now and then Mera would call out that there was a corner ahead. I was surprised by the number of turns we took and I began to wonder how many rooms we could possibly pass. Once we came upon a dead end and had to backtrack. We had climbed three sets of steep, narrow stairs before Mera brought us to a halt again. Her hands made a strange slithering sound as they ghosted over the wall. Eventually she found the place where stone became wood. She pushed hard and a small door opened.

We stumbled into the room. It appeared to be one of the many guestrooms, though thankfully it was unoccupied. Even in darkness the castle's extravagance screamed at you. There were lush, cream carpets rolled across the floors. Silk covered chairs with plush, embroidered cushions were placed around the room. A four-poster bed stood at the end of the room opposite a fireplace.

We didn't linger. Mera led us to the door on the other side of the room and silently we slipped out into the hall.

'This is it,' Mera whispered, pointing to the end of the hallway. 'Those are the king's chambers.'

Outside a set of gilded doors stood two heavily armoured guards. They hadn't seen us yet, hidden in the shadows, but it was only a matter of time.

'All right Lex, it's your time to shine,' whispered Ezra.

I nodded and slipped into the corridor. Before the guards could unsheathe their swords I had stretched out my hand and whispered, '*Sweofot.*' They were still for a moment and then with an ominous creak they fell to the floor.

The others came scurrying forward. We headed towards the guards, eager to get inside before the noise attracted any unwanted attention.

'Are they going to be all right?' Ilyssa asked, pausing to check on the two men now snoring softly at our feet.

'They'll be fine,' I assured her. 'They're just sleeping.'

'Come on,' Mera said, leading us towards the now unguarded doors. She paused for a moment, her hand on the cold brass handle, before turning it slowly and pushing open the door.

The room was bathed in a warm yellow light that sprung from lamps and a crackling fire. The walls were a rich cream colour with a border of gold. They were adorned with large paintings but over them was a fine layer of dust. There were closed doors on the other side of the room that must have led to the rest of the king's apartments. The carpet had been worn down from years of use. In the corner of the room was a large, mahogany desk covered in parchment, some of which had fallen, unnoticed, to the floor. Sitting in a high-backed, velvet covered chair and poring over the documents was King Cynric. At the sound of the door clicking closed he turned to face us.

He was not what I had expected him to be. His greying hair fell into his eyes. The skin around his neck was loose, as though he had lost a lot of weight in short period of time. His face was prematurely lined and there were deep bags under his eyes. He looked to be on the wrong side of fifty.

Despite his dishevelled appearance he sprung to his feet when he saw us. He stood for a moment, a look of utter shock on his face, before hurrying across the room and pulling Mera into his arms. I heard his deep voice muttering into her hair.

'You're alive,' he whispered. 'Thank the gods you're alive.'

I saw surprise on the part of Mera's face poking out from behind her father's shoulder. I looked away, not wanting to intrude on their private moment. The rest of us stood awkwardly by the door. I took the opportunity to whisper the spell Iele had taught me to keep people outside from hearing what was happening in the room. Eventually the king released his daughter, the ghost of tears shimmering in his eyes. He spoke in broken, unfinished questions.

'How is this…? Where have you…? Who are…?'

Mera swallowed. Then she straightened, bringing herself up to her full height.

'Father,' she breathed, taking his arm gently and leading him back towards his seat. 'Please sit down. I have a lot to tell you. No, don't call for the guard yet. You need to hear this alone. Sit down and I will tell you everything.'

The king looked as though he were about to object, his eyes flicked briefly towards Ilyssa, Alaric, Ezra and myself, but a second later he changed his mind and took his seat.

Mera stood in front of him and began to speak. She told him everything that had happened. He sat in silence and listened. By the time Mera finished he had his hand pressed over his mouth, utterly amazed.

'I don't believe it,' he muttered. 'I can't believe it.'

'Father,' Mera implored, kneeling down in front of him so that she could look directly into his eyes. 'I know that this is difficult to understand but I'm begging you to think. What if what you've always been told is wrong? You're a compassionate man. Somewhere inside you've got to see that what's being done to these people is wrong. Magic isn't inherently evil, Father, nor are those who practise it. What point is there in attempting to eradicate a people whose only wish is to live peacefully? Hatred only leads to more hatred and this bitter anger that has been festering within our kingdom for generations is infecting us. We must clean it out. Please, Father, the Brethren are inside the castle. We have to stop them before it's too late.'

The king's hand dropped. He stared at his daughter, the low light flickering across their faces. Slowly, he inclined his head.

Mera let out the breath she had been holding in and looked back at us, smiling. I stepped forwards, ready to tell him about the city of Magic Folk waiting for freedom just as we'd planned but before I could begin the doors opened and seven people walked in.

I recognised Listoros immediately as he marched into the room along with five other heavily weaponed Brethren members who had been at Skara Brae. Malaigle walked with him, venom in his eyes. A blonde woman of extraordinary beauty led the men into the room

Unlike her husband, Queen Sarai looked every part royalty. She flowed into the room, tall and commanding, encased in an ice blue silk dress, which rippled with her very step. She could not have been a day over thirty-five. Her sharp eyes surveyed the room, drinking everything in. When they fell on Mera her fine eyebrows arched but she didn't move, nor did she speak.

'Sarai,' the king stood quickly, almost knocking over his chair in his haste. 'Our daughter has come back to us.'

'Yes,' the queen's stony voice rang through the room. 'She has a habit of doing that.'

'Mother,' Mera's voice was slightly higher than usual. 'Come away from those men. They're dangerous.'

The queen's only response was a slow, cold laugh. I turned to Mera, both willing her to understand and hoping she would never have to. I saw her eyes darting between her mother and the members of the Brethren who had been trying so hard to kill her. Her face crumpled as realisation swept through her.

'No. You can't...' her voice trembled. 'You can't be with them.'

'With them?' King Cynric spoke up. 'Sarai, what is going on? Malaigle what are you doing here? I thought you were treating with the representatives from Beagbach this evening. Will somebody please –'

'Oh would you shut your mouth, old man,' the queen snarled.

The king opened his eyes so wide they were in danger of falling out of his head.

She fixed the king with her icy gaze. Though her eyes were the same blue as her daughter's they held none of Mera's warmth. 'You have been nothing more than a puppet for quite some time. Though I must say you have played the part well. I suppose the sense of entitlement instilled in you since birth counts for something.'

'Mother please,' Mera's voice was strong despite her shaking hands. 'Whatever they have told you, whatever they have offered you, it isn't-'

'Isn't what?' spat the queen. 'Worth it? You garrulous little girl. This is what I have been working for my entire life. I have been trained since birth in how to lead, how to rule. Like my mother before me my whole life has been dedicated to the cause. The Brethren of Peace has been within the walls of this castle since the beginning and I have led them to this victory. It's passed through bloodlines, you know, mother to daughter, so I'm sure you'll understand why you've been such a disappointment to me,' she was staring down at Mera with a look of intense disgust. Mera glared back, matching her mother's anger, though I could see sorrow softening the hard lines around her mouth. 'My mother always stressed the importance of blood, of purity. I quake to think what sin I committed to end up with such vermin for a child. Such high hopes... but alas, I birthed a rat, a pitiful, disgusting sickness that has done nothing but infect my plans and dash my hopes and dreams. You are no better than the filth with which you associate yourself. Worry not. Once I rid myself of you they will be next to go. They will watch you die and then fall like flies as easily as the ones you left so sure of their safety in their hole in the ground.'

My head snapped up at her words. Out of the corner of my eye I noticed the others' panic-stricken faces but I kept my eyes trained on the queen. She couldn't mean... she couldn't...

When the king spoke it was with a voice that quaked and hands that trembled. 'So it was all a lie?'

The queen fixed her gaze on him and with a cruel smile said. 'You were nothing more than a means to an end.'

The king nodded slowly, sorrow clear on his face. He sat down heavily in his chair, pressing his hands firmly into his eyes as though if he blinked hard enough this could all have been a bad dream. The tears that Mera had been so forcefully keeping at bay spilled over and rolled silently down her cheeks.

The queen sighed as though bored with the proceedings. She turned her elegant neck to the side to glance at Listoros who stood grinning hungrily down at us, his hands resting on the handles of his twin swords.

'Enough of this. Put an end to this disappointment,' the queen commanded, stepping back as the Brethren advanced.

On instinct I moved towards Mera, feeling the others do the same behind us. I was still reeling from the shock but I felt white-hot anger beginning to unfurl inside me. Ezra was the first to speak, his voice as strong as steel.

'Do you really think we'll let you hurt her?' he barked, unsheathing his blades.

The queen laughed again from behind her barricade of brothers. 'What are five children and an old man who has never even tasted battle going to do to stop me?'

'Why don't you ask your pet?' replied Alaric, indicating Listoros, who was glaring at us, eager to sink his swords into our flesh.

'We've beaten you before, we can do it again,' added Ilyssa.

'We'll never stop fighting,' I insisted. 'You can kick us down and kill our loved ones and violate our culture but you will never stop us fighting. You cannot take that away from us. Your fear, your hate, your anger, none of it will matter because we will always have something worth fighting for. When you tear down the lives of the innocent you only make us stronger.'

'Your words are meaningless,' the queen sneered. 'You are meaningless. Your petty fighting is nothing more than a child's feeble fists smacking against their mother's back. You will be eradicated along with the rest of your disgusting kind.'

'You have always underestimated magic,' Mera whispered through her tears. 'It will be your undoing.'

'Enough!' The queen screeched, finally loosing her temper. 'Listoros, end this now!'

We sprung into action at once.

'Protect the king!' Mera yelled as I caught her arm and dragged her to the side of the room, narrowly avoiding Listoros' sword.

Alaric responded to her words, running to the king and muttering a hasty, 'Your Majesty,' before grabbing hold of him and pulling him to the back of the room.

Ezra had intercepted Listoros. Next to them Ilyssa was battling fiercely with Malaigle, who was having problems keeping up with her lightning fast footwork. The sound of singing steel just barely masked the sound of voices from behind me where Alaric appeared to be arguing with the king. He was attempting to persuade him to run into the next room but the king didn't seem to be cooperating.

'Please, your Grace,' begged Alaric. 'It's for your own saf-' but before he could finish his sentence the dark haired archer standing in front of the queen shot a well-aimed arrow in their direction and Alaric had to swing his own bow violently to prevent the arrow burying itself into the king's head.

I didn't have time to see whether Alaric persuaded the king to run to safety because the remaining three men were now advancing on Mera and me. While her magic was enough to keep them at bay it was doing nothing more than pushing them back a few feet at a time.

I took a deep breath and yelled, '*Hafenian,*' just as one of the men threw a dagger.

Instead of speeding towards us the dagger and the swords in the hands of the two other men facing us lifted into the air. The men stood, watching with horrified expressions as their weapons hovered above them. I took advantage of their momentary panic to shout, '*Edcierras.*'

The weapons spun in the air and shot back towards their owners, all of who yelled and ran. I watched as they sped from the room, their daggers and swords following them all the way.

'Well done,' Mera smiled, watching the men run through the open door and down the deserted corridor. The queen's screams of 'Cowards! Deserters! Traitors!' echoed after them.

We didn't have time to celebrate, however. The queen was now yelling at Listoros to finish us off. I turned with dread to see Ezra sprawled out on the floor, a crimson stain blossoming through his shirt. His swords had been knocked from his hands and his eyes flickered weakly. Next to me I heard Mera gasp.

Ilyssa had taken up the fight with Listoros but she wasn't doing well. Malaigle was on the floor, apparently unconscious, but she was winded, her face shining with sweat. The way she was trying to keep weight off her right leg suggested that it was injured. With sudden clarity I could see exactly what was about to happen. Ilyssa stumbled, letting the tip of her sword drop and lowing her guard. Listoros took her lack of defence as his opportunity. He raised his sword, preparing to bring it down on Ilyssa's head and cleave her in two.

With all the power that I could muster I raised my own arm, feeling the familiar static flow of energy coursing through me and I yelled, '*Farblad!*'

There was a crack like thunder and a fierce blast of air whipped about the room, pushing everything back with its immense force. There were bangs and yells as objects and people were thrown around the room and the sickening crunch of a body slamming into the wall.

As the wind died down I saw that everybody had been knocked to the floor and all the furniture had been thrown backwards against the walls. The archer who had been protecting the queen scrambled to his feet and fled through the door. It slammed closed behind him.

The queen sat slumped and dazed on the worn carpet. Realising that she now greatly outnumbered she gathered her skirts and rose but before she could get through the door Alaric fitted an arrow to his bow and shot it towards the queen. It caught in her long sleeves and burrowed into the wood. She tried desperately to pull it free but the arrow was wedged in too deep. Shaking, hair wild, she sank back to the floor, defeated.

My eyes turned back to Listoros. The strong wind had forced him off his feet and smashed him against the far wall where he had slithered to the ground. His body now lay splayed and broken, a twisted expression of rage on his face half obscured by the blood that trickled down from his crown and into his mouth, a vile red that dripped onto the cream carpet, permanently staining it.

The king's voice came from far off. 'Is it over?'

Nobody answered him. I knew that if I spoke my voice would tremble. My mind raced and whirred, trying to understand, trying to make sense. When it couldn't I closed my eyes and tried to forget the image now burned into my brain forever.

33

Aftermath

Listoros was dead.

For many years I could not truly recall what had happened after the events that occurred that night. I remembered Mera rushing forward and falling in front of Ezra, sobbing and pleading for him to wake. I remembered a scared voice calling for guards and a warm hand steering me to a seat. What I remembered most of all was the image of the broken body, the tangy, metallic stench of blood and the feeling of rising bile in my throat. I could not remember leaving the castle but the next thing I knew I was standing in the cavern where we left the company of Magic Folk, staring at the bodies of my friends, unable to move for the grief that tore through me.

Someone had put them into rows. Lengths of ripped red fabric obscured them. I stood over the body of what had once been Bugul Noz. The piece of fabric that lay over his body left his face exposed. His shovel-like hands lay limply by his sides. The thick wads of fur that covered his skin were clumped together with blood. His kindness, it seemed, hadn't been enough to save him.

To his left lay the bodies of Ryouko and Goldenhorn, their wise features now grotesquely sagged. Cerynitis was not present. I saw her only once more for the funeral where we said goodbye to our dead. She was not heard from again.

I lifted my eyes to see Ilyssa and Alaric attempting to comfort Bugaboo, whose whole body shook with violent sobs for her dead friend. Ilyssa was seated with her hand softly clutched in Bugaboo's trembling one. Alaric was speaking, slowly and quietly, an unsure hand resting on the small woman's shoulder.

At the far end of the hall four giants clustered around their three dead companions. Novaci, the huge, white-haired giantess, had thrown herself over Chelua, who lay forever unmoving on the ground. Her powerful fists pummelled into Chelua's great chest as she shouted his name, as though this would wake him from some deep slumber. Emin and Urias clutched each other, howling in pain. They looked beyond consolation. Yuli, normally the quietest of all the giants, was hurling rocks across the room. They collided with the wall on the other side, smashing into a fine powder and raining down to the floor.

My heart lurched worst of all when I saw Popis lying near the entrance. She must have been the first to see their attackers, the first to see that something was wrong, the first to be cut down. She hadn't even had a chance to see the sun. Now she never would. Ezra sat by her side, his eyes glazed, looking more ghost-like than the bodies surrounding him. His head and shoulder were bandaged, the linen stained with blood. As I watched, he removed one of his swords from its sheath and laid it down gently over Popis' small body. Mera approached him. Before she could say a word Ezra turned, collapsing into her, hiding his face against her neck and dissolving into tears. Mera closed her eyes, holding onto him as though scared he would slip away from her.

I felt my heart shatter. It struck me that I didn't know half the people lying dead in the cavern yet they had given their lives for us. They had died believing that we would be able to bring them into a better world but all we had brought them was death. The weight of guilt from all these stolen lives was crushing.

The Brethren had known we were coming. They had seen us from a distance, walking towards the castle thinking we had been so clever to avoid detection. All they had to do was retrace our steps. We had given away our friends and left them to be massacred. That was all we had found out from the queen before she silenced herself, cutting out her own tongue and nearly drowning in the blood. She had been saved, however, and now resided in a dungeon cell, awaiting the decision regarding her fate.

'It's always harder to condemn someone you love,' said Ilyssa when Alaric asked why the king hadn't yet sentenced the queen to death. 'No matter how much they have wronged you. '

Perhaps her purgatory will be a worse punishment, alone in her cell with only her failure and bitter thoughts for company.

We put our dead to rest in the ways that our ancestors had for thousands of years but it didn't help to ease my grief. I watched as the flames licked the wooden pyre and thought how ironic it was that this would always have been their fate. If the Brethren had succeeded then Magic Folk would have been burned just the same. I felt the accusing eyes of those who had died watching me. It didn't feel right being at their funerals when it was my fault that they were dead. What right did I have to mourn them? I left early, walking the seven miles back to the castle in the pouring rain.

I began to lose myself. I was angry with the Brethren. I was angry at the Sisterhood's lack of interest in the souls that had been ripped from this earth for their stupid prophecy. I was even angry with those who had died for needlessly risking their lives. Mostly I was angry with myself. Sleep became a thing of the past. I lost all sense of time. I was withdrawing into myself and despite my friends' concern there was nothing I could do to stop it. Poison had invaded my mind. It was as though I was drowning, struggling through a thick, molten tar. While others swam by me with ease, my skin burned and my lungs couldn't draw in air. Every time I tried to breathe my mouth filled with the thick, black stuff, choking me, gagging me.

The dreams were the worst part. On the nights that I was able to sleep I was plagued with visions of dripping blood, of cracked skulls, of wronged friends who screamed and grabbed at me as I tried to run. I was never able to escape them though. They always caught me in the end.

I stopped eating. I stopped speaking. I even felt my magic leaving me. It was as though I was ceasing to exist. My body became a skeleton, too weak to even lift myself out of bed, too small, too fragile, too pathetic. I was close to becoming nothing more than a whisper bound in bones and blood.

I think it was Mera's idea to take me home. She had become angry with me fairly quickly, snapping when I wouldn't eat, yelling when I wouldn't answer. I felt like I was failing her. I have so much regret from that part of my life but the pain I caused my friends was the worse if it. Without them I would never have been able to pull myself back into the light. To this day I cannot adequately explain what had happened to me, just that I wouldn't wish it on my worst enemy.

I began to change again. I don't know what triggered it. Perhaps there comes a point where there is no farther for you to fall. Either the darkness can consume you or you can begin to climb again. Or perhaps this torture had been my punishment and I had simply done my time. Either way, when I was next brought food I picked up a spoonful of soup and swallowed it. The next day I had two.

I was still in a state of listlessness when I returned to Lilyworth. I sat silently in the back of the cart, squished next to a sack of potatoes. Ezra sat at the front leading the horses while Mera, Ilyssa and Alaric sat with me in the back talking about the changes to come to Culrain. I wasn't listening. From where

I was seated I could see the familiar rolling hills that marked the road into Lilyworth. I noticed I was biting my dirty nails. Ilyssa took my hand in hers. As we turned onto the path that led to my home my heart began to pound.

The cottage was so different from my memory of it. Yellow and pink flowers bobbed their heads in the light breeze. The roof had been re-thatched and shone gold in the sunlight. I could hear the slight whistle that the wind made as it passed through the straw. The cracked grey walls had been given new life by fresh, white paint. The smell of lavender floated towards me from the bushes under the windowsills. It looked once more like the cottage of my childhood.

The door banged open as our cart rumbled to a stop and my sister came running out. I nearly collapsed when she crashed into me, burrowing her face in my shoulder and crying freely.

'You're back,' she sobbed. 'You're back. Why did you ever leave?'

It took me a moment before I was able to raise my own arms and wrap them around her, stroking her hair. *I'm sorry,* I thought, unable to speak for the tar that glued my mouth shut. *I should never have left you.* Elvie was already dragging me back towards the cottage, speaking so quickly that I could barely keep up. I felt such a rush of panic as we neared it that I almost missed her saying, 'Oh you'll just love the baby!'

I opened my mouth in shock but Elvie didn't have time to elaborate because we had walked through the front door and there sitting at the dining room table, holding a baby, was Mum.

When she saw me she jumped up and hurried forward just as Elvie had. She held me tightly, muttering, 'Oh Alex, you've come home. You're safe. Thank the gods you're safe.'

Mum had cut her hair short. I felt its soft ends brush against my knuckles. When she eventually pulled away from me she was smiling brightly.

Mum reached up with her free hand and caressed the side of my face. That was when she noticed the scars that poked out from under my shirt. She opened her mouth in shock and then abruptly closed it again. She shifted the baby on her hip. The child cooed softly. Elvie was still holding my hand. I felt her squeeze it gently.

'You must be wondering who this is,' Mum smiled, trying and failing to keep back the tears in her eyes. She brushed them away quickly.

The baby had a tuft of curly, dark hair, a broad nose and a wide, joyful smile.

'This is Dawn,' Mum told me. 'Samson's cousin passed away about a month ago leaving her all alone, so we took her in.'

Dawn giggled happily, oblivious to the horrors of the world. She reached out with her tiny hands, grabbing enthusiastically. She caught hold of my matted hair, tugging on it with surprising strength. I ignored Mum's chastisement of, 'No Dawn, we don't do that,' and uncurled her hand from the strand of straw-dry hair, replacing it with my finger. She screamed with delight.

'Hello Dawn,' I rasped, my voice rusty from disuse.

She giggled again and I felt something flutter inside my chest.

That night, when Samson returned home, I was filled with worry. We hadn't been close when I left but now I was the one on the outside and I wasn't sure he'd be willing to let me back in. My panic was short lived, however.

Samson walked thought the door closely followed by Rab who came straight over to me. Before I knew what was happening I was in his arms. When he pulled back he was smiling widely.

'It's been boring here without you, kid.'

That was when Samson walked over. He put his hand on my shoulder and smiled.

'It's good to have you back, son,' he nodded.

The cottage was far too small for all nine of us. The baby had a small cot in Mum and Samson's room. My old bed was free but it certainly wouldn't fit five people. Samson was most distressed by the idea of a princess and a nobleman sleeping on the floor but Mera wouldn't hear of putting him and Mum to any trouble. As she insisted on telling them, she had been sleeping on the ground for many a month now. She could do it a little longer. In the end she and Ilyssa went in the spare bed and I went in with Elvie. Alaric and Ezra made a makeshift camp in the space between the dining room table and the fireplace.

I tried to act as normally as I could but it seemed as though I had forgotten how. I found almost everything too taxing. My emaciated body wouldn't let me stand for more than a few minutes without feeling winded. Eating was still a difficulty. Anything more than something the size of my palm and I'd throw it back up again. Most days I sat silently with Elvie and Dawn as they played. I watched Dawn crawl across the floor while Elvie and Alaric egged her on.

On the days that the cottage became too crowded for my overloaded mind to bear I would shuffle outside and sit in the spring sunshine listening to the birds chatter until my heart stopped thumping.

Elvie had certainly noticed the difference in me. I knew that Mera had explained everything in the letter she had written to Mum but what Elvie knew of it I had no idea. I heard her ask Mera and Ilyssa early one morning while I was pretending to be asleep. There was a pause and I imagined Mera and Ilyssa exchanging looks.

'You're brother isn't quite himself at the moment,' Mera explained.

'But why? Why isn't he eating anything? And why isn't he speaking? He's barely said one word since he's been back,' Elvie insisted.

'Your brother's not well, Elvie,' Ilyssa clarified. 'It's difficult to explain because it's not the kind of sickness you get when you have a cold. Sometimes things happen to us that are bad and our minds don't like to think about it so they stop working properly. It's like when you break your arm and you can't use it until it's healed. Something like that happened to Lex and he's quite sad right now.'

'So he's sick?' Elvie sniffed. 'Will he get better?'

'We certainly hope so,' Mera sighed.

Soon enough I found that I was able to stand long enough to pick the apples from the apple trees in the garden. Once Ezra and I had filled the basket to the brim we sat down to rest. He had been telling me stories of his family when he paused.

'I've never lost anyone before,' he said, looking up at the sky. 'I didn't know Popis for long but she… she deserved more than that. She was so young.'

I didn't know what to do with this strangely solemn Ezra, so I put my hand on his shoulder and whispered, 'I would do anything to bring them all back.'

'But they're gone,' he muttered.

'I know,' I nodded. 'But I'd still do anything. They were our friends and they died for us. It's this guilt, Ezra. It's choking me.'

'They died for their own freedom, Lex,' Ezra insisted. 'They died so that others could live.'

'They didn't know that they would be dying, though, did they? They had no idea what they were getting themselves into.

340

And we led the Brethren right to them. Our actions were the direct cause of their deaths,' I spat out bitterly.

'You can't blame yourself for that. The only people to blame are the Brethren. Blame the queen. They are the ones with blood on their hands, not us,' Ezra insisted.

'Perhaps not you, but I do,' I reminded him.

'Lex,' Ezra's face fell. 'Killing Listoros was your only choice. If you hadn't done something, Ilyssa, and probably everyone else too, would be dead.'

'I'm still a murderer,' I muttered.

Ezra turned to look at me with a sudden fierceness. 'You are not a murderer, Lex. Do you hear me? That man was corrupt and he was evil and if you hadn't killed him he would have killed us all and enjoyed it too. You are a hero. I know it doesn't feel like that now, but I promise you will get through this.'

'How can you know that? How can you know that anything gets better after this?' I wondered.

'Because I've been where you are now,' he confessed. 'It was some years ago, just after I had left home. I was in a city looking for a place to stay when a man cornered me. He tried to rob and kill me. I hadn't wanted to hurt him but he had a knife at my throat and there was only one option left. I still think about it sometimes. I can remember trying to wash the blood out of my clothes for days.'

I stared at him, completely lost for words.

'It was hard,' Ezra continued. 'I won't pretend that it wasn't. For a long time I wondered who he had been. I wondered if he'd been running from something like I was, if he'd had a family who would never see him again. But I couldn't let myself wallow in those thoughts or I'd have been lost in them.' Ezra brought his hands up to rub his face and sighed. He hugged his knees to his chest. His warm brown eyes were squinting slightly in the sun. 'You can get through this. I know you will because you're stronger than it. And don't forget that we'll be there to help pull you out.'

I nodded slowly. Ezra shook himself, his usual infectious smile returning to him.

'Let's get these apples inside, shall we,' he suggested.

We lifted the basket and walked together back to the house.

34
Mending

With the peace and tranquillity that home provided I began to find myself again. It was difficult and on days that I felt myself slipping back into old habits I'd become so panicked that I couldn't draw in breath. I was forced to sit for hours on the hill that overlooked my cottage until the tightness in my chest loosened and I could breath again.

Mera had duties to return to at the castle. She and her father worked tirelessly to round up the remaining members of the Brethren. The list found in Listoros' house was instrumental in leaving the kingdom short a few lords. I wasn't surprised to hear how many had infiltrated the castle. With them removed Mera was also able to fulfil her promise to reintroduce magic to the kingdom. There was resistance at first but with the king proclaiming it an offense to harm Magic Folk it became safe enough for them to come out of hiding. After that it would only be a matter of time before they proved their worth. Despite how busy she was Mera always made time to visit. She was back and forth from the castle so often it was like she never left.

Ezra too returned home to his family in Seion. He decided it had been long enough. He sent us a letter when he arrived saying that he had talked with his father and that he was to take on the role of heir while his younger brother, Enoch, was away with his new wife.

'Is he expected to give back the role once his brother returns?' Mum had asked with concern.

'Knowing Ezra he'll be more than happy to give it back,' Alaric had told her. 'That was never the life he wanted.'

From what he wrote he was mostly content to be back with his family. Apparently he had been able to convince his father that he should be allowed to choose his own bride. It seemed that Ezra's disappearance had forced his father to reconsider his perspective on some things.

Even though we missed our friends terribly we had to admit it was much easier to fit everybody into the cottage without them. Alaric was able to move out of the dining room and into the bedroom where he slept on a bedroll between the two palettes. It certainly wouldn't do forever but it worked for the moment.

'Perhaps another room could be added. There's no shortage of land here. We'll certainly need the space once Dawn gets older,' Samson had suggested from the dining room table where he sat fixing his lute. 'They're not going to be able to fit in that one room forever.'

The next evening I overheard Alaric and Ilyssa arguing about the issue. They were sitting on the back doorstep taking shelter from a smattering of rain that had descended while they were picking apples.

'We can't stay here forever,' Alaric had reasoned. 'We've trespassed on their kindness for long enough. There's plenty of space for us at the castle and we'd be back amongst it all. You read Mera's letter. Iele and Sami had come down to negotiate for peace. Don't you want to see our friends again?'

'I know,' Ilyssa had sighed. 'I do feel guilty. Kate and Samson have been so kind but I can't leave Lex. You can't ask me to.'

'I don't want to leave him either but this can't go on forever. If we went up to the castle we could still visit. There's work up there. We could start to actually build lives for ourselves. I know how you feel for him but he's not ready for that yet. He needs to heal first.'

'Do you really think I'm that selfish?'

'Don't be angry with me. I'm just saying what you know to be true,' Alaric had placated.

'I won't leave him,' Ilyssa had insisted. 'Not until I know he can stand on his own two feet.'

Their discussion had me thinking. Ilyssa's words had warmed me but Alaric was right. I couldn't be the one to hold her back. I was struck by an idea that would prove to her that I was healing. Though I was still not ready to go back to work I was determined to put my neglected carpentry skills to good use. It would be nice to be doing something productive again. When I mentioned this to Ilyssa she was delighted.

'That's a brilliant idea,' she grinned at me over the pan of peas she was shelling. 'What were you thinking of making?'

'I'm not sure. Something for Dawn, maybe? She doesn't have anything of her own, all of it used to be Elvie's or mine. Some of it's even older.'

'What about a cot?' she suggested.

I mulled it over for a moment.

'It would be lovely,' Ilyssa went on. 'The one she's in at the moment was made for your grandfather, your mother told me. It would be nice to have a new one for her.'

Spending time with Ilyssa was the best part of any day. She never tried to force me to speak about what was plaguing me and wasn't afraid to let silence fall between us.

'Walk before you run,' she told me when I mentioned this to her.

When the time came that I was beginning to find the words she was there to hear them. I felt her compassion as though it were a tangible thing, reaching out and holding me when I tried to explain. I don't know if she ever fully understood but she was a comfort nonetheless. We hadn't talked about what had been said before we entered Drammear but I could still feel her love. She had my heart and I had hers. If we could last through this then we could last through anything.

Now that I was getting stronger I was able to walk with others into the fields to pick the wild berries that grew there. The sun shone through the trees, leading Ilyssa, Alaric, Elvie and I down the dappled pathway towards the succulent blueberry bushes, baskets in hand and eager for the day to begin.

Alaric and Elvie raced ahead playing a game of chase. Every time one of them caught up to the other they would fall dramatically to the ground, howling in mock pain as though their life was leaving them. After a few minutes of the game they were both covered in mud and grass stains that would be a chore to wash out. Alaric was much faster than Elvie but he put on a good show of going slowly enough for her to catch him, sighing dramatically as he fell and standing up again quickly to tickle her. Out of the corner of my eye I saw Ilyssa shake her head, astonished that her brother was able to act so much like a carefree child after all that had happened.

I smiled. 'She took to Alaric pretty quickly, didn't she?'

'He always gets on well with children,' Ilyssa replied, swinging her empty basket back and forth. 'I think he'd be a great father but I don't know if he'll ever get the chance.'

'Why not?' I asked, surprised.

'Well I don't know about you but I don't really see Alaric as the settling down type,' she intoned.

'Hurry up, you two,' Alaric called from where he and Elvie stood on the path ahead. 'Or the blueberries will have all been picked before we get there.'

We hurried after them, reaching the blueberries at last and filling our baskets to the brim. We returned home sun-kissed and laden down with fruit.

It was around this time that I began to start work on Dawn's cot. She was a strong child and completely unwilling to sit still

346

for more than a minute. Trying to hold her was a nightmare. She would wriggle and squirm and flap her tiny arms and feet about, giggling all the while until you had to put her down for fear of dropping her. The only time she would agree to be still was when I laid her down on my stomach and dangled my father's pendant, which Mum had returned to me, in front of her. She would lie there for hours watching the small wooden carving swing back and forth.

Soon enough her cot was complete. I refused to let anyone see it before it was finished, nervous about its outcome, but in the end I was proud of what I made. The base sat on two curved slats, which allowed the cot to be rolled from side to side. There was a covering at the top from which hung a new pendant on which I carved the image of a butterfly flying across the sun.

Mum was delighted. She hugged me tightly when I brought it in. 'Alex, it's wonderful. Your father would've been very proud.'

'This is great, Lex. Who knew you had it in you,' Alaric grinned.

'We'll put the sheets in now, shall we? Then she can sleep in it right away,' suggested Samson.

So in they went along with Dawn, who gurgled and cooed, confused by her new surroundings. When she noticed the pendant she giggled happily, reaching for it with grabbing hands.

'I think she likes it,' Ilyssa smiled.

'Of course she does, Lex made it,' added Elvie.

I put my arm around her shoulders. She grinned up at me, her little smiling face giving me such warmth.

Mera visited us the next day in the pouring rain. She ran towards the door, scarf held over her head to keep off the downpour. She looked slightly worn but ecstatic to see us nonetheless. She hugged us all in turn and when she reached me she gave me a kiss on the cheek and said, 'It's good to see you, Lex.'

I smiled, always feeling just how much I'd missed her when she returned.

She brought with her gifts and news from Drammear. For Ilyssa she gifted a rare plant species that been brought by a visitor from Foraise. Alaric received a bottle of the finest oak mead that the royal cellars could provide. He beamed, giving Mera a hug and admiring his gift with glee. A box of chocolate covered bonbons was given to Elvie, who was delighted to have something to sate her sweet tooth. For Mum and Samson, Mera had brought a set of fine cotton sheets and thick woollen blankets. They were thrilled by the gift, Samson making awkward jerking movements with his body as though he were disagreeing with himself about whether or not to bow. Finally for Dawn she brought a silver rattle engraved with her name. We sat around the table as she handed each of the gifts over, marvelling at their beauty.

'Thank you Mera, these are wonderful,' Mum inclined her head. 'We're lucky to have a friend in you.'

'You're welcome Mrs Tubal-Cain. And thank you for letting me stay with you again. Your hospitality is endless,' replied Mera, ever the diplomat.

As for news, the trials of the remaining Brethren members were about to begin. Later, when Mera and I were sitting outside scrubbing the potatoes in a large bucket she told me about them. I didn't ask whether that included her mother and she didn't say. Most of the members had been caught by now, though not all had made it to trial, and there were still a handful that had managed to evade capture. These included the Viscount Doran of Mayfield, who had spent most of his sixty years making his way through every brothel in the kingdom, Sadon of the Sewer, also know as The Rat and generally known as a sneak-thief who did the Brethren's bidding in the lower town of Drammear, and a man named Hanthaw, who had been Malaigle's serving boy.

'And we would desperately like him captured alive, you know, but unfortunately some of the Royal Guard have been taking the term *possible lethal force* a bit too much to heart,' Mera informed me. 'I always said they were useless. Well, you know how they are. Anyway, this Hanthaw could be very valuable. Given that Malaigle's not speaking he might be able to tell us a lot more about the members who died before we could talk to them.'

I shivered slightly at her words.

Mera's face scrunched up at my reaction. 'I'm sorry, Lex. Gods, I'm always putting my foot in it, aren't I?'

'It's all right,' I shrugged.

'No, it's not all right,' she insisted. 'I've been such a terrible friend. You were in trouble and I didn't know what to do, so I blamed you. I'm really sorry, Lex. I'll be a better friend to you from now on. I promise.'

She looked so sad and misty eyed all I could think to do what lean forward and pull her into my arms.

'Mera, I never blamed you,' I muttered into her shoulder. 'You're my best friend and I love you. So no more tears.'

She snuffled quietly for a moment, before releasing me and wiping her eyes. I changed the subject quickly before she started apologizing again.

'So have you heard from Ezra recently?

Mera blushed slightly. 'Um, yes I have actually. He tells me he's planning on coming back to Drammear soon.'

'Really?' I asked, surprised. 'I thought he was going to stay with his family for a little while. He's only been there a couple of weeks.'

'Well I don't think he's planning on staying here for long. It's just a short visit. His brother's about to come home and I imagine he'll be shunted to the side a bit. Not that he minds, but he's really quite bored having nothing to do. Actually I had an idea about that. Given that he's spent so much time with the people I think he'd do really well as a diplomat for Magic Folk. You know, he could help mediate when things get a bit sticky, which I'm sure they're bound to do. Besides, the way things are progressing it'll be necessary to have good relations with other kingdoms to be able to help Magic Folk there too. I'll suggest it to him when he comes. I promised I'd take him down here to see you lot too while he visits. He's really missing you all. Oh and while I remember, Iele sends her regards.'

'Oh, how is she?' I asked, slightly ashamed that I had made no effort to reach out to my friends that had survived along with me.

'She's simply flaming. Literally. You know how she used to leave scorch marks on the ground? Well she's progressed to actual fire now. You don't want to be walking behind her, I assure you. And the number of bed sheets she's accidentally singed. Honestly, I'm thinking of equipping the guard with buckets of water just in case. But she's well, I believe. Not that I've seen much of her, admittedly. She went back up to Callipolis with Sami to tell them what had happened after everything and they decided to stay there together. She and Sami get along so well together. They're quite sweet actually. Sami was wearing colour when I last saw her.'

I smiled. 'Good. I'm glad they're happy.'

'Actually there was something else I wanted to ask you. There's been some talk amongst the Magic Folk. You haven't heard anything from the Sisterhood have you?'

I shook my head. 'I haven't had anything to do with magic in months.'

'You still can't perform magic?'

'No. I've tried but there's nothing.'

'I'm sorry. I suppose you were right about the Sisterhood. I was just so sure…'

I wished I could tell her something different but I honestly didn't believe in the power the Sisterhood claimed to have. I hadn't felt so much as a nudge to indicate that my magic had any inclination of returning to me. It was well and truly lost. Strangely, I found myself not minding. I had discovered other things that were just as worthy of my time.

At that moment Ilyssa and Alaric came with food and a message from Mum telling us to take a break. Our lunch was cut short by a sudden and torrential downpour. We hurried inside, laughing about our ruined clothes.

The storm lasted all evening and well into the night, lashing against the house and rattling the windowpanes. Thunder rolled through the hills, making Elvie shiver in fear and wriggle under the blankets to hide. She stuck her cold feet against me, trying to keep warm. It was a restless night. I woke at every clap of thunder and once or twice when Elvie kicked me in her sleep. I rose early, feeling a sudden and immediate need to walk. I slid out of bed, slipped on my shoes and cloak and made my way outside.

The grass was wet and springy beneath my feet. Though the storm had passed on the scent of rain still clung to the air. The sun was yet to rise so it was the moon that lit the path I travelled. I had never been into this part of the forest before but my feet seemed to know which direction to go. They took me into a quiet glade. The ground was covered in bluebells, an indigo haze hovering atop the green grass. Something told me to stop here so I did, staring around, perfectly at ease.

Through the haze stepped seven women. They formed a triangle that pointed directly towards me. Four of them made up the back row, two in the middle and one at the front. Though they wore clothes so vastly varied they could only have heralded from across the Five Kingdoms, they each had a circlet inlaid with precious gems. They hummed with power. I felt it vibrating towards me across the forest floor, pulsing through the earth and tickling my feet through my well-worn shoes. I had no trouble guessing who they were. The Sisterhood had arrived.

35

The glade

I recognised Aisling with her dangerous smile and dark eyes walking at the back of the group. Standing next to her was Brina. I recalled also the face of the woman at the front, who led the Sisterhood into the clearing. She was the same woman who had sent me the vision of Skara Brae as it had once been, calling me onwards. She stood tall, her dark skin glowing in the first rays of sunlight that had begun to penetrate the forest canopy. The edges of her circlet were lost behind her curly yellow hair. Her dress shimmered and danced as though it were liquid gold and in her hand she grasped a slim, hollowed piece of wood through which one would shoot darts. I had no doubt that the batch she carried would be tainted with poison. The High Sorceress of the Sisterhood stood before me, her eyes crackling with intensity as they bore into mine.

The two women who stood behind her were warriors. The one on the left was tall and muscled, her body riddled with scars. Her bronze skin was leathery, as though she had spent all her life without water. In her almond eyes I saw sandstorms raging. The skin of some great beast was wrapped around her shoulders. She held a golden bow tightly in her thick hands, an arrow poised and ready to fire.

The woman on her right was tiny in comparison. She had deep, grey eyes, a lupine face and short, raven coloured hair. She wore animal skins too, and what looked like moss crawled over her wrists, ankles and stomach and clutched at her neck. Her sword, a strange curved thing, was fastened at her waist. The wooden handle was carved into the snarling face of a wolf.

Behind them Aisling nodded to me, her gown still flowing in the non-existent breeze. Brina next to her was as skeletal as I remembered. As close as I was to her now I could see that her skin was stretched taught across her skull. Her hair was pulled into a long braid that she'd swept over her shoulder and brushed against her long, stick-like fingers. On her left was a large, thick-lipped woman with an expression as stern as the crack of a whip. Her circlet was placed on her domed, shaved head. She moved in the shadows, her dark face unreadable. Her large black eyes were unfocused and I saw that she was blind. The image of a lion was painted onto her skin, but it wasn't still. It prowled over the undulations of her flesh, opening its mouth wide in a silent roar. The last of them was small, plump girl with pale skin and hair of fire. Her ocean blue dress flowed over her as she moved, like the currents in a river.

'Alexander Eriksson,' the High Sorceress' voice was sweeter than honey. 'My name is Fallyn. Please, let me introduce my sisters. This is Cahira and Fianna,' the two warriors inclined their heads briefly when their names were called. 'You know Aisling and Brina of course, and here are Moya and Ena.'

The women at the back nodded their heads in greeting. When Ena was introduced she gave an excited giggle and hopped slightly.

'You are probably wondering,' my eyes snapped back to Fallyn. 'Why we are here before you after such a long absence.'

'Something like that,' I muttered, finding my voice a little shaky.

'Yes, we have much to answer for in your mind,' she nodded solemnly. 'Though we have always acted how we aught. The prophecy was of the upmost importance. It needed to come to pass no matter the consequences.'

'So you knew the what the consequences would be?' I asked, feeling anger prickling over my skin. 'You knew what would happen to my friends, to me, and you let it happen anyway?'

Fallyn looked down at me as though she were patiently explaining a simple concept to a slow child. 'You must understand, that in the grand scheme of things-'

'No, hang on,' I interrupted her, ignoring the tightening of Cahira's bow. 'The grand scheme of things isn't an acceptable reason for the deaths of so many people. They died, needlessly, for your prophecy and yet here you stand untouched by any of this. I suppose it's easy when none of it really affects you.'

'Oh, but we have felt it, Alexander. We have felt the suffering of our people all this time. All their pain, their agony, their screams for release, we have heard and felt it all. We trembled with it, we-'

'It's not the same!' I shouted, rage coursing through my veins. 'Echoes! That's all you felt. All you could have ever have felt, otherwise you would never have allowed this to happen. I was so lost,' my voice cracked. I closed my eyes, unable to stop the tears that leaked down my cheeks. 'Where were you when we needed you most?'

Fallyn's voice darted through the glade towards me. Her words scratched me, breaking the skin and burrowing beneath, settling in my bones. 'We could not. We could not interfere. Our fate was tied to the prophecy as much as the Brethren's was. A nudge or two was all we could afford you or everything would have been forfeit. But it has now been fulfilled and so has our purpose here. This will be the last you see of us. We have always known this. It was our sacrifice.'

'Wait, what do you mean?' I looked up, angrily pushing the hot tears from my face. 'You can't leave again. We still need your help.'

'We have no more help to give. We have done our share, as you have yours. We thank you for your part in this,' as Fallyn said her final word the Sisterhood turned as one.

I rushed forward, yelling, 'Stop!' my hand outstretched, but it was to no avail. They were already gone. It was then that the tears really came, thick and fast, an unstoppable wave crashing against the shore. Every bad memory, every poisonous thought, every gut-wrenching feeling I'd had in the past few months flooded my mind. They crawled inside my skull, into my eyes, down my throat. Tar was spewing from my mouth. It choked me, pinned me down, constricted my chest. I couldn't hear my breath for the storm raging in my ears but I could feel them, haggard and pained, weak and desperate. I slumped to the ground, knees pulled tight into my chest, hands clamped over my ears. The pain was excruciating. I bit my lip to keep from screaming and tasted blood, hot and bitter in my mouth.

Then, without warning, everything was still. My head cleared, my chest loosened, my tears ceased. I lay there for what might have been hours as my breathing returned to normal. I pressed my hand to my chest and waited for my heartbeats to slow. My body felt wrecked but I sat up nonetheless, bringing half the forest floor with me.

'Enough,' I muttered to myself. 'This has to end.'

I rose, limbs still shaking, and began the long walk back to my cottage in the light of a new day.

I was halfway home when it began to rain again. There was nothing I could do about it. My body still felt too weak to run so I plodded on, getting drenched. I was half drowned by the time I got back. I walked through the door, peeling off my sodden cloak as I went, but before I was able to get it off completely, Ilyssa pounced on me.

'Where on earth have you been?' she gasped, her arms wrapping tight around me.

'I went for a walk,' I muttered.

I looked over her shoulder to see Mum standing with an arm around Elvie next to Mera who looked very pale.

Ilyssa pulled back from me, keeping her hands firmly on my arms. 'We were so worried. We had no idea where you were. Alaric and Samson are out looking for you. Why are you so muddy?'

I felt instantly guilty, realising only now what they must have felt upon waking and finding me missing. I brought my hand up to Ilyssa's.

'I slipped but I'm fine. I'm sorry, I didn't think I'd be so long,' I apologised.

'You gave us quite a fright,' added Mum looking thoroughly relieved.

Elvie sighed loudly and shook her head. 'See, I told you he was fine. Lex is always doing stupid things. I don't know what you're all so worried about.'

'That he is,' agreed Mera.

'Oh thanks,' I intoned.

'Really stupid,' Ilyssa muttered, staring at me intently.

'I'm fine, I promise,' I insisted, circling the back of her hand with my thumb.

'Well why don't we get you into some clean clothes,' Mum suggested.

'Good idea,' I agreed.

Once I was dry Mum sat me down with a bowl of soup. She slipped into the seat beside me and took my hand, looking pained.

'Alex-' she started.

'Mum, I'm sorry for making you worry. I'm sorry for leaving you, for not letting you know I was safe. I've been a terrible son,' I lowered my eyes.

'Alex,' she repeated. 'I am so proud of you.'

My eyes snapped up. Her face was sincere, the lines around her eyes crinkling slightly as she smiled. Her smile gave me warmth. It buoyed me. I felt my lips tugging up of their own accord. Mum sighed, patting me on the cheek and rising from the table to leave me to my soup.

I had just finished my last spoonful when the door banged open and Alaric, Rab and Samson came stomping in, flicking water and mud all over the floor.

'We couldn't find him,' Alaric started. 'We looked-'

The sight of me sitting at the table brought him up short. I grinned up at him sheepishly.

'Thank the gods,' he muttered, before stumbling towards me and throwing his arms around my neck.

Slightly winded, I clapped him on the back

'Are you all right?' Alaric asked as he moved back, an expression of tenderness he normally reserved for his sister alone etched across his face.

'I'm fine,' I smiled, finally believing my own words.

'Good. Don't do it again,' he chastised, pointing a warning finger at me before sitting down heavily in the chair beside me and scraping his wet hair out of his face. 'Any chance of a bowl of soup for a man who's spent his morning getting drenched for no good reason?'

'Of course,' Mum replied, supressing a laugh.

'I'll get changed,' Samson said, looking even wilder than usual with his tangle of hair completely soaked through.

He clapped me on the shoulder as he walked past. 'Good to see you safe, Lex.'

Rab walked over to me and sat in the chair on my other side. He slipped off his boots and said, 'You had us concerned there, kid.'

'I'm sorry, I didn't mean to be such a bother,' I replied.

'Well no one's hurt so there's nothing to worry about,' he ruffled my hair the way he used to do when I was a child. Warmth spread through my chest and I felt glad to be home.

I wasn't able to speak to the others about what had happened in the forest until the next morning when Mera planned to return to Drammear.

'So they're just… gone?' Alaric asked.

'I don't know,' I answered.

'But what does that mean?' Alaric wondered. 'They're not, you know, dead? Can they die?'

'I don't know,' I repeated. 'I didn't really get a chance to ask.'

'I don't think they can die,' Ilyssa proffered.

'But that is so inconvenient,' huffed Mera. 'This whole thing was their idea. Surely they planned for what would happen afterwards.'

'I think they wanted to leave that for us to decide,' I said.

Alaric wrinkled his nose. 'Bit weird, though, isn't it? I mean, if I were an immortal sorceress who spouted prophecies I'd certainly want to stick around for the glory.'

'You always want to stick around for the glory,' Ilyssa muttered.

'That, my dearest sister, is because glory is a wonderful thing,' he insisted. 'Tell me who wouldn't want it?'

'Well the Sisterhood don't seem very keen on it,' she pointed out. 'Look, I don't think we should be worrying about it. What's done is done and there's no point stressing over something you can't change.'

A few months later I found myself sitting on the hill above my cottage awaiting the arrival of Mera and Ezra the following morning. Ilyssa sat beside me clutching a letter we had received from the two of them a week prior. Alaric and Elvie had been entertaining Dawn with a very noisy song and dance that they had taken much pride in creating. Ilyssa and I had escaped after the third rendition leaving Mum and Samson to nod politely, indulging the two performers. Most of the letter was filled with the usual stories of court life but jammed in at the bottom was single line devoted to the news that Mera and Ezra were to be married.

'Read it again,' I grinned, watching the sun make its slow descent in the sky.

Ilyssa shook out the letter and cleared her throat, 'Ahem. *As the three of you are our closest friends I feel it only right to be the first to tell you that Ezra and I are betrothed.* Trust her to make such a happy thing so formal. She makes it sound as though they haven't been half in love with each other since the day they met.'

I nodded. 'It'll be good to see them though. I'm glad Ezra's coming too. It's been so long. You'll be glad to have someone to spar with again, I'm sure.'

'Well my sword's been gathering dust here. You've been no help with your two left feet,' she joked, poking me in the ribs.

'Hey,' I scowled, rubbing the spot where her finger had prodded me.

I cast my eyes over the low hills beyond the cottage. The sky was stained silk, all red and orange and yellow seeping together. Fluffy pink clouds rolled over the hills, clearing the way for the sun to bathe the land in a golden hue. I looked towards Ilyssa, who smiled serenely back at me. As the sun kissed the horizon I took her hand in mine.

'Do you think they'll be happy?' she pondered.

'If these past weeks have taught me anything,' I said quietly, 'it's that you can't predict the future, but they've also shown me what can be achieved when you have faith. If there are any two people who can be happy together, it's them.'

THE END

Acknowledgements

First and foremost I would like to thank my agent and editor James Essinger for having faith in a young writer and for his continued advice and honesty.

Secondly, I would like to thank my parents for their love and support and for pointing out all of my (many) spelling mistakes. I could not have done this without you.

Thirdly, my gratitude to Jessica Coleman, who read the first draft many years ago, and whose wit and humour were a big part of making this book what it is today.

Fourthly, a big thank you to Eden and Ethan, who kept me smiling and writing when I could have easily given up. Here's to many more years of your weird and wonderful ways.

And finally, thanks to all my friends who have given me the encouragement I needed to get up and do what I needed to do. So thank you to Charlotte, Kate, Lois, Yasmin, Rhiannon, Anneli, Tianyuan, Laetitia, Luc, Jemima, Tom, Grévin, Caitlin and Katy. I'm so lucky to know you all.